BOOKS BY TIM MCBAIN & L.T. VARGUS

Casting Shadows Everywhere

The Awake in the Dark series

The Scattered and the Dead series

The Clowns

The Violet Darger series

The Victor Loshak series

FIVE DAYS
POST MORTEM

FIVE DAYS
POST MORTEM

a Violet Darger novel

LT VARGUS & TIM MCBAIN

FIVE DAYS
POST MORTEM

PROLOGUE

Soon.

A voice in your head.

Your voice.

It sounds small just now. Tight and skittish.

Soon they will know. They will all know.

You walk now in the dark. Only the moon above to guide you.

You pick your way through the woods. Creep away from the dump site. From the surging water of the river, the rapids that tumble over each other endlessly.

You're excited and scared and thrumming with a current of cold energy. Dark energy. Cruel impulses that you don't understand. An appetite for violence and destruction.

An appetite for death.

Some wickedness pushed you here, and now it will push you somewhere else. Anywhere else.

The faint glow of the deed still burns in the hollow of your chest. A throb of pleasure that you can never hold on to, that never lasts.

And sweat leaks from your palms. From your brow. Sops the hair along your hairline. You are greased with it. Glistening with it.

Soon.

You tell yourself your own story in your head — a rushing stream of words not unlike the river. That disembodied voice in your skull cataloguing and commenting on the things

1

happening to you. Recording snippets of words and playing them back. Little whispers narrating for you.

And you watch yourself watch yourself. Consciousness of consciousness of consciousness. Shadows of shadows. Infinite levels. Echoes that overlap and drown everything out.

Soon. Soon. Soon.

They will know what you did.

The branches pop and crunch as you bend them out of your way. Crashing through. Too loud. You need to get out of here.

Sometimes you wish you could turn it off. That voice in your head. That self in your head.

But no. It doesn't work that way. Once it's off, it can't come back.

The big sleep. The dirt nap. Like the girl in the river back there.

Gone for good.

You can still see the water pull her away from you. Sucking and ripping. The current a thrashing, violent thing. Wild. Aggressive.

The memory flares in your head. A searing flash of images. Burning so bright that it pulls you away from the here and now. Incinerates reality for a bit. Melts it right out of the way.

Stops your chest mid-inhale.

And she is there. In your head. The movie of her projected into your skull just as she was minutes ago.

Floating. Sinking.

Pale skin glowing purple in the moonlight. The dark of the water lapping at every side of her. A flutter of black wetness that seems excited to touch her, to take her away.

Tendrils of hair dance in the current like snakes, whipping around her face. Wet coils of darkness. Undulating.

She disappears under the surface like it was a magic trick. And you hold your breath. Wait. This overwhelming empty feeling pulsating inside of you like it could burst out of your ribcage in a bloody spray.

And then she pops up in the rapids a few beats later. Reappearing. Completing the magician's illusion.

Ta-da.

And she is already rushing away from you. Fast. Shrinking and fading. Bobbing along the water's surface, the rapids flinging her limpness about like a toy boat. Rough with her.

She disappears around a bend. The white of her skin is the last pop of brightness you see in the half-light.

Reality coagulates before you. Overtakes the memory.

And your truck appears there. Parked in the dirt along the edge of the woods.

You climb in. Jerk the key in the ignition. The steering wheel cold against your hands.

You tear out of the parking lot. Dirt and stone flinging every which way. Tinkling against the undercarriage.

And your heart hammers in your chest. Jaw clenching and unclenching.

And little splotches spatter the edge of your vision. A pink and black quiver in the periphery.

The world will know.

Soon.

((

The fishing lines flicked in and out of the water with little snaps and swishes. Hooked flies fluttered on the surface and retreated with each pluck of the appropriate string.

Dan and Jim didn't talk for long stretches when they were out on the water like this. They just stood on the muddy banks of the river and fished and slurped down cans of Deschutes, listened to the sound of the river rushing past.

That was the point, though, Dan thought. To relax. Get away from life's troubles. It was all either of them wanted. If they handled it right, they didn't need to talk.

The sun crept over the horizon and kept climbing, dawn giving way to full daylight. Still, neither fisherman saw any returns on his line-flicking efforts. Not so much as a nibble.

"They ain't bitin' hardly at all today. Tell you what," Jim said just above a whisper, breaking a long silence. He said "what" as though the word started with an h — "Tell you h-what."

And there it was — what Dan thought of as Jim's redneck accent making one of its cameo appearances. The twang didn't dominate his friend's speech patterns. It just poked its head out once in a while to say *thang* or *purty* or something about the *po-lice*.

These little linguistic flourishes never failed to amuse Dan. He didn't look down on them. Didn't judge. More than anything, he found himself at a loss as to where this way of speaking had come from in his friend's case.

They'd been friends from third grade on, had experienced all the same things in life — more or less — for the next 26 years, and they were from Oregon for Christ's sake, not Alabama. Even so, touches of this vernacular had crept into Jim's speech somewhere along the way, laid down roots that seemed unlikely to be ripped out easily.

Life was full of mysteries, great and small.

Dan knew that this accent existed in varying degrees in any rural area in the country. It was just weird that it'd happened to Jim and not him.

"Ain't too hungry, I guess," Dan said, not sure why he felt the need to fall into an *ain't* call and response. Maybe the dialect was infectious, like yawning.

Both men paused the casting of their lines and stared into the muddy water as though some explanation lay there, just beneath the surface. If the river knew why the fish were laying off, though, it offered them nothing. The water swirled and churned and moved along. Babbled out its endless wet sound.

Jim broke the motionless spell to get back to it, flicking his line out over the ripples and jerking it back, falling into an easy rhythm.

Dan took a break from casting to try to adjust his poncho. The seams along the shoulders had shifted forward and the fabric now restricted his throwing motion some, made him feel awkward.

Once he had that fixed, he fished a hand into the cooler for another can of beer, cracked it, brought it to his lips and slurped. Tasted good. Hoppy and bright. At least they had that to fall back on. Fish or no fish, they had good beer. He'd savor this one before he went back to his rod, he thought and let his gaze drift out over the water.

He watched the bobbing object a while before he really noticed it. A bloated looking thing upstream, slowly drifting their way. As it drew closer, the size of it started to become clear to him.

It was big. Puffy. Looked naked. Even before the notion of it being a body truly occurred to him, he thought it looked naked. Like a blowup doll bleached white.

Dan shifted his feet, the mud sucking at the rubber soles of his boots. The beer can remained frozen mid-lift, halted just shy of his lips and held there.

And now Jim saw it as well. He stopped casting his line, the faintest little sigh coming out of him as he did a double-take and locked onto the mass in the water.

"Goddamn but she's all tore up," he whispered, his words whistling a little between his teeth. He repeated the last three words but slower, dragging them out. "*All* tore up."

They both stood very still, the sound of the river seeming to swell to fill the silence.

Dan remembered to breathe, the air making a ragged sound as it entered his nostrils and throat. He could feel his pulse squishing in his ears.

The dead body seemed to make sense to his eyes in stages.

A female, he thought. Pretty far gone to bloat and rot. The lifeless white of the thing going pale purple in places. Skin sloughing away in others. Soft and wrong and pulpy somehow. Like pulled apart wads of wet paper.

The body hit a surging spot in the current, and its bulk twirled in the water, the head now turning to face them. The river seemed hell-bent on sliding the dead thing toward them, and Jim took a step back instinctively.

The mouth was open. Gaping.

No. Not open exactly.

The jaw was gone. And the teeth on the top were missing too. Pulled away as the flesh went mushy. Swollen and colorless and as soft as the Friskies pâté he fed his cat this morning. Spongy.

The face sheared off at the gummy palate. The once-pink flesh draining to something pale and wrong. Pearly. The shade of a maggot with the faintest pink hue.

A floater, Dan thought, not sure where the words came from. *A floater.*

CHAPTER 1

Darger sat in one of the hard-backed chairs at her dining room table. Her laptop rested on the table in front of her, its screen casting a diffuse glow over her face.

Her eyes flitted down to the corner of the screen, checking the time yet again. Any minute now.

She shifted in her seat, feeling fidgety. The chair was probably the least comfortable in her apartment, but in a way, that was good. It would keep her alert. She'd tried the sofa, but the soft cushions and throw pillows made her feel like she was slouching. Next she'd moved to one of the stools in the nook off the kitchen. Not bad, but the height was all wrong, causing her to hunch over the keyboard.

She adjusted the angle of her computer screen and suddenly noticed the layer of dust, lint, and dried splatters of God-knows-what on the surface. Pulling her sleeve over her hand, she wiped at the filth, resorting to scraping at some of the spots with a fingernail.

Why had she agreed to do this?

She already knew the answer: Because Loshak had asked her to.

He said he was worried about her. Felt responsible. And the guilt trip snapped onto her like a bear trap wrapping its jaws around an unsuspecting animal's foot.

Well, she thought as she waited for the call to come in, *at least I have nothing to lose*. She didn't need the job, after all. She was only technically "on leave" from the FBI. She could go back whenever she wanted.

Maybe.

But did she even want to go back? She still hadn't decided.

She wondered if what Loshak told her was true. That consulting was different. Different rules, less bureaucracy. She was a student of psychology, after all. Any institution — whether a lumbering dinosaur like the FBI or a small private consulting firm — was a beast of bureaucracy. Humans were creatures of social order, which was just a more scientific name for bureaucracy. All of society was ruled by the arbitrary dictates determined by the top of the pecking order. So the question was not whether there was bureaucracy at Prescott Consulting, but what kind.

And if she didn't want to return to the FBI, then she did need this job. Or *a* job. Her mother might have married into being independently wealthy, but Darger had not, and she would rather chew off her own foot than be financially dependent on someone else.

Yeah, she thought. She might need this job after all.

Maybe that was why she was so nervous.

An electronic jingle from the computer's tinny speaker announced the incoming Skype call.

Darger took a deep breath and used the reflection on the screen to make sure she didn't have anything in her teeth. Smoothing her hair with one hand, she reached out with the other and answered the call.

Dr. Margaret Prescott looked like she was in her late forties, but Darger thought she was probably older than that given the mandatory retirement age in the FBI and the fact that Dr. Prescott been one of Loshak's mentors.

She wore a cream-colored silk blouse with a matching jacket over it, and her blonde hair was sheared into a stylish pixie cut.

"Violet," the woman said with a charming smile. "It's a pleasure to finally be speaking with you."

Darger nodded at the projection on the screen.

"Dr. Prescott. Thank you for the opportunity."

The older woman waved a dismissive hand. Her fingernails were manicured, but unpainted and cut short. A gold watch encircling her wrist glittered in the light from a desktop lamp. It looked expensive.

"Call me Margaret, for Christ's sake. Or just Prescott if you're more comfortable with that. I reserve my academic title for when I'm on the stand as an expert witness or for my byline in the psych journals."

"Very well… Prescott," Darger said.

She wondered if it was a test. A real kiss-ass would try to ingratiate themselves by insisting on referring to her as "doctor." And calling her Margaret given the circumstances would smack of over-familiarity. The simple surname acknowledged that they were peers but also maintained an air of professionalism.

It was possible Darger was over-analyzing, but Loshak had cautioned her that Margaret Prescott was shrewd and calculating. She'd hardly needed the warning. Dr. Prescott was a pioneer in the field of Criminal Psychology, and though Darger attended Quantico years after her departure as an instructor there, her reputation lingered on the campus.

Above all, she'd been known for her elaborate psychological cunning. Playing mind games with students and faculty alike.

Constantly testing people.

Prescott rested her chin on a closed fist and leaned a little closer to her computer's camera.

"I'd love to say Victor has told me so much about you, but that simply wouldn't be the truth. He's very tight-lipped about his protégé."

"Yeah, well, I think Loshak might have been absent the day his preschool class learned about sharing."

With her head thrown back and her mouth open wide enough that Darger could see a silver amalgam filling in one of her molars, Dr. Prescott laughed.

She had the laugh of a jackal. It made her sound slightly unhinged, like maybe she was such an expert when it came to criminal psychology because she was a little insane herself. In an odd way, Darger kind of liked her more for it.

Amusement lingered in her eyes when Dr. Prescott spoke again.

"What our dear Victor *did* tell me is that you're frustrated with the red tape that hinders the Bureau all too often. If that's the case, it might be that our operation is more to your liking. Of course, I don't want to give the impression that I employ a bunch of trigger-happy cowboys. We always strive to be thorough and professional. We dot our *i*'s and cross our *t*'s, we just do it more efficiently than most law enforcement agencies."

The muscles in Darger's gut tensed. This topic was a potential minefield, one of Prescott's famous traps. Answer too enthusiastically about being free from the limitations of the FBI, and she might come across as not only undisciplined but disloyal.

"I can appreciate that. And I don't have a problem with the

11

rules and regs. It's the politics I'm not interested in. Not when it prevents me from doing my job."

"I'm glad to hear you say that," Dr. Prescott said with a frank nod, and Darger felt herself relax a little.

Settling back in her seat, the doctor blinked thoughtfully.

"I have a feeling this is going to work out beautifully for both of us. Are you married?"

The sharp left turn into personal territory threw Darger for a moment, and she didn't answer right away.

A conspiratorial smirk spread over Prescott's face.

"To be clear, I'm not asking as your employer. That would be illegal."

The bark of her hyena laugh roared over the line.

"Um, no. I'm not married."

"Boyfriend?"

"Not presently."

"Girlfriend?" There was a slight arch of an eyebrow there, as if Dr. Prescott thought she was being salacious with this one.

Darger felt her jaw clench, the muscles tighten at her temples. Why was any of this Prescott's business?

"Nope," she said, and she almost left it at that. Almost. "I mean, I experimented some in college, but I've never been in a serious relationship with a woman. Are you terribly worried that might affect my ability to work for Prescott Consulting?"

Darger immediately regretted these words, and even more the taunting tone in which she spoke them. She'd meant to be on her best behavior, all smiles and non-threatening, and now she was challenging her potential boss in their first conversation.

For her part, however, Margaret Prescott seemed unfazed.

Her smirk widened into a manic shark's grin for a beat, and this time her head fully tipped back when she laughed.

"That's great. I love that. You're a firecracker, aren't you? Victor told me, but goodness. You're the real deal."

Her voice sounded guttural with laughter now — like a giddy grandma, Darger thought. But within the time it took to clear her throat, Prescott had composed herself and returned to firing questions.

"And where are you from originally?"

"Colorado. Outside Denver."

"Of course! The Leonard Stump connection. I'd forgotten all about that," Prescott said.

The smile faded from Dr. Prescott's perfectly made-up lips. Even transmitted over the screen from a thousand miles away, her crystal blue gaze was penetrating.

"Tell me, how are you holding up after that? From the little Victor told me, it sounded like it was a rather dramatic experience for you."

"I passed all of the FBI fitness tests, if that's what you're worried about."

Lowering her chin, Prescott's stare intensified.

"Violet, dear, I'm not talking about the Bureau's silly physical fitness exams. I'm talking about *you*."

The sudden concern threw Darger, and she felt off-balance.

"Oh. I'm… fine." She steeled herself, regained her composure. "The physical therapy sucked, if I'm being completely honest. I don't recommend getting shot in the head if you can avoid it."

Prescott threw her head back again and cackled.

"Jesus! He said you were tough, but I think that was an

understatement."

The tassels of gold chain hanging from her ears dangled as she shook her head back and forth.

"I don't know how much he's told you about our operation here, but Prescott Consulting is one of the top forensic psychology consultancies in the country."

"You have quite the reputation. I followed the Mozes trial in the news. I understand it was your work that got him convicted?"

"A fascinating case," Prescott said, running a hand through her short hair. "We'll have to find a moment one of these days to discuss it. His mother is a classic narcissist. She'd make a fabulous case study for one of Victor's classes at Quantico. But that's for another time. We have a case out in Oregon — a very rural community with limited resources when it comes to this type of investigation."

"And what type of investigation is that?" Darger asked.

"A suspected serial murderer. We've had three bodies turn up — all in bodies of water, the latest found in the Clackamas River by a couple of fishermen. The first body they chalked up to an accidental drowning. The girl went missing after some sort of school sports event, and no one could explain why she would have been anywhere near the river. Then again, these things do happen."

Prescott picked up a shiny gold pen and toyed with it as she spoke.

"When the second body was found, people started to talk. Two women, gone missing miles from the river, only to end up being fished out five days later? It didn't add up. By the time Shannon Mead — the third victim — went missing, the phrase 'serial killer' had started to pop up in the media, on the lips of the victims' families. The locals couldn't ignore the pattern anymore. And that's where we come in."

Darger was jotting down notes on a pad of paper.

"Where exactly in Oregon is this?"

"Sandy is the name. A small town outside of Portland. They've only got two detectives on staff, so this is a bit out of their league. All the deceased have been pretty far gone to decay by the time they've been found, which makes the forensics tricky, as you can imagine, so we've been assisting with that. But what they really need is a profiler, so I'd like to send you out there on a trial basis. It will give both of us a chance to see if this is a good fit," Prescott said, and then her eyes narrowed slightly. "You'd be working as an independent contractor, just to be clear. And I have to remind you that you're not technically working in the capacity as a law enforcement agent. I assume you're licensed to carry a concealed weapon, but I wanted to be clear on that. I'm sure you know as well as I do that law enforcement personnel are creatures of habit. It can be a difficult transition for some to enter the private workforce."

Darger gave a single nod.

"I doubt it'll be a problem. How soon do you need me there?"

"Tomorrow, if you can be ready that quickly."

"I can do that."

The doctor clapped her hands together.

"Excellent. I'll have my personal assistant coordinate with you to send over the case files and make the necessary arrangements. I do hope we'll have an opportunity to meet in person soon, Violet."

"Likewise," Darger said.

Even after they'd said their goodbyes and disconnected the call, Darger swore she felt those piercing blue irises staring at her through the screen. The gaze was alight with the hunger of a keen predator, like a hawk or a lioness.

Something in those eyes told Darger to tread lightly with Margaret Prescott.

CHAPTER 2

The rented Ford Fusion zipped through the twists and turns of the rural Oregon road. Darger followed the winding path of the Clackamas River, surrounded on all sides by green. There were the trees themselves - Grand Firs and Lodgepole Pines — but also the vines and moss clinging to nearly every surface. The foliage of the undergrowth almost seemed to explode from the ground.

She passed a lone farmhouse on a hill, bordered on each side by two massive Ponderosa pines. The house wasn't small, but the trees were easily three times as tall, towering over the structure, dwarfing it.

It struck her that there was something wild about the trees here, the way they encroached on the road, reaching limbs toward the vehicles speeding by. It felt like a place that belonged to the forest. Like at any moment she might be swallowed up by a cluster of the conifers.

An uneasy feeling wormed in her gut. She wasn't sure if it was the environment making her feel claustrophobic or her current assignment.

Was she nervous about the job? She was truly on her own this time. She'd always had Loshak there before. Always had a partner to lean on. But maybe it would be good to fly solo for once. Not that she blamed Loshak for any of her ill will toward the FBI. But sometimes change was good.

Then there was Margaret Prescott. Darger couldn't help but feel like she was under the microscope for this case. It was a

17

test, after all. And Dr. Prescott wasn't known for grading on a curve.

She mulled over the details of the case as she drove. A floater — such an endearing term — discovered by two men out fishing on the river. The woman's body was so badly decomposed, her entire bottom jaw had disintegrated while she lay submerged in her watery grave.

The body belonged to Shannon Mead, an elementary school teacher who'd gone missing five days earlier. She was the third dead woman to be pulled from the river in as many months.

A shiver ran up Darger's spine at the thought.

Bodies found in water had always creeped Darger out more than others. She thought it could have something to do with a particular memory burned into her mind from childhood.

She and her mother had been visiting family in Minnesota. Their home was on a small lake, and one of Darger's second cousins — once or twice removed, she could never remember — had taken her on a tour of the waterside.

They spent the afternoon plucking at lily pads and chasing frogs. And then they found the turtle.

It was a massive specimen, just the very top hump of its shell protruding from the water.

"Let's see if we can catch him," Darger's cousin said.

The older girl crept to the water's edge, plunged her hands into the water on either side of the shell, and grabbed hold.

"I got him!"

She lifted then, but as the shell cleared the water, they saw that something was wrong.

The turtle had no legs. Nor a head. In fact, it was just an

empty shell.

Or almost empty.

Thick white clumps of tissue poured from the orifices, the liquefied remains of the dead turtle. This chunky matter was accompanied by a terrible odor. Death, decay, and rot.

Darger's cousin shrieked and dropped the shell back into the water, and both girls ran back to the house where they fell into hysterics when trying to explain to their parents the horror they'd uncovered. Her cousin's mother eventually calmed them down with Froot Loops, of all things. Darger could still remember clutching that paper Dixie cup filled with dry cereal, crunching away while tears congealed on her cheeks. Her mother had always refused to buy "sugar cereal," so the little neon circles had been a rare treat for the young Violet. She was pretty sure that was why she remembered it so well.

Well, that and the smell of the dead turtle. It was fishy and foul, and her recollection of it was worse than the smell of any dead body she'd witnessed to this day.

Another reason for her to be feeling some amount of anxiety, she supposed.

She wondered if the locals would be more accepting of a consultant outside of law enforcement. The cooperation between the FBI and local jurisdictions was usually tenuous at best. Perhaps being on the case as a privately-employed consultant would be less threatening to the local cops. Not that she'd be doing her job any differently. Technically she and Loshak had always been acting as consultants. That was how the BAU operated. The cases they worked were still under the purview of the city, county, or state police force. But that didn't matter to the local guys, who always treated them like double-crossing interlopers swooping in to steal their thunder.

There was also a possibility that lacking the shiny FBI credentials would mean they wouldn't take her seriously at all. The thought caused her to glance down at the empty space formerly occupied by her badge.

"I'm a civilian now," she muttered out loud.

Civilian. The word felt oddly-shaped on her tongue.

She could still picture her badge and ID tumbling toward the Detroit River. Flapping like moth wings all the way down from the MacArthur Bridge to the water.

She'd left that out when she'd talked to Loshak afterward. She wasn't in the mood to explain that in the mindset she'd been in at that particular moment, tossing her badge away like an old candy bar wrapper had seemed like a perfectly reasonable thing to do. Loshak only would have chided her for being impulsive, which was true. She just didn't want to hear it.

Working at the FBI had been her singular goal for most of her life. To be in a place where she was considering leaving that dream behind had her questioning her sanity some days.

The wooden sign for the small park appeared on the roadside to her left, sinuous vines winding around the lower halves of the posts. This was her destination. Darger turned onto the narrow lane and followed the path to a parking lot set only a stone's throw from the river. The water sparkled in the early afternoon sunlight.

Darger parked and got out, glad to be able to stretch her legs after the long flight and then the drive out into the boonies.

A few other vehicles were scattered about the lot, but none of them seemed to be law enforcement. Good. She wanted a fresh, quiet look at the scene. By herself. It was how she worked best. Well, that wasn't entirely true. But she was on her own now, and that was fine.

She walked closer to the water's edge where a lichen-covered picnic table stood watch over the day use area. She recognized it from some of the crime scene photographs.

Flipping the file open, she paged through the photos, stopping when she reached those focused on the small park. The local police had been thorough, collecting what bits of possible evidence they could from the spot, in case it had served as the scene of the murder, though Darger was sure the killer would have opted for somewhere with more privacy. Under the cover of the nearby forest, for example.

Darger inhaled. It smelled like cedar and cool, clean water. Her eyes flitted from the glittering surface of the river to the green boughs that swayed gently in the breeze. It was the kind of setting she'd expect to see featured on a motivational poster, with a cheesy, clichéd phrase about nature and relaxation written beneath.

Relax. That was what the two fishermen had been trying to do a couple days ago when they discovered the body of Shannon Mead. The bloated, waterlogged corpse was a pale pinkish-gray, the color leeched from her flesh like a dead fish.

The file indicated the men had found the floater about a quarter mile upstream from the park. By the time law enforcement arrived, the body was mostly submerged, tangled up in the aquatic weeds and deadfall at the river's edge.

Knowing of the many uncertainties an investigation faced when a body spent any amount of time in water, Darger figured they'd probably never know exactly where Shannon Mead was killed and dumped. Still, she wanted to see the place where they'd fished her body out of the river.

Fixing her gaze on the looming fir trees that bordered the parking lot, Darger tucked the folder under her arm, zipped up her parka, and stepped into the woods.

CHAPTER 3

Darger threaded her way through the dense Oregon wilderness, a tunnel of greenery arching overhead. The towering trees cast a permanent shadow that caused an artificial twilight beneath their canopy.

The air was thick with a damp, mulchy smell. Fresh earth, still wet.

It felt like a jungle. Sounded like one, too, with all the birds calling and insects chirping. She thought of the farm she'd passed on the drive and the small field planted with a cover crop of alfalfa. She suspected that the farmers around here were constantly at battle with the encroaching forest.

Her footsteps barely made a sound on the soft carpet of moss and pine needles covering the forest floor. Though the parking lot was only a short distance behind her, she felt far away from the rest of the world. She looked over her shoulder, but the trees completely blocked the view of the small park. It was a little creepy the way the forest seemed to close in around her, cutting her off from her car, from civilization.

It felt different than most crime scenes she'd been to before. More claustrophobic. More secluded.

The file rested in her hand, a manila folder packed with gore. Darger glanced down at a photo of Shannon Mead's bloated, fish-white corpse. Mottled. Skin sloughing off in places. There were wounds all over, too numerous to count — whether they occurred before death or were the result of being in the water so long would be almost impossible to determine at this point.

The photographs were grisly enough; she could only imagine how gruesome it would have been to see it floating down the river unexpectedly. A bulbous gray-white thing bobbing and flitting along with the whims of the water. Creeping ever closer.

She shuddered a little and glanced away from the folder, checking her location.

Just ahead she spied something flapping in the breeze. A stripe of yellow bisecting the natural greenery. Plastic tape emblazoned with big black letters: *CRIME SCENE - DO NOT CROSS*. It cordoned off the little area where they'd pulled the body out. Probably not much point in it, since she doubted there'd been many gawkers way back here in the woods. Just procedure, but….

A twig snapped, and Darger caught movement near one of the huge hemlock trees.

There was someone crouching in the northwest corner of the crime scene area, just at the water's edge.

A man.

And her first thought was that serial killers often returned to their scenes. It was a way to relive the crimes, revisit the dark fantasies. To feel those violent impulses wash over themselves again and again.

Adrenaline spiked in her bloodstream. Made her pupils dilate. She sucked in a gasping breath.

Her hand moved to her hip, reaching for her Glock. Instead she found air.

Right. No FBI-issued Glock today, of course. She was carrying her personal weapon — an M&P Shield.

Different holster. Inside her jacket.

Her fingers found the grip of the weapon, latched onto it. She didn't like the unfamiliar feel of it, but at least she was armed with something.

All of this confusion threw her enough that she reconsidered her actions. Her palm rested against the butt of the pistol but did not draw it.

She blinked a few times. Really studied the man squatted there near the river.

He wasn't in uniform, but he was wearing semi-professional clothes: khaki pants, a shirt, and tie. And latex gloves on his hands.

And it clicked finally. Not the killer. A local detective, maybe.

Sensing her presence, he turned, looking surprised for a moment and then popping upright.

"Oh. Hello," he said, raising a gloved hand.

Darger noted that he held a pair of tweezers and a small glass vial — the type often used to collect evidence — in the other hand.

A crime scene tech, she thought, relaxing another degree. But a new annoyance took the place of her earlier alarm. She'd wanted to be alone with the scene. Wanted to stand in the middle of this wooded area and hear only the sounds of the wind whispering through trees and the burble of the water. Wanted to know what the killer heard and felt when he trudged out here with Shannon Mead.

No small talk. No distractions.

But now? Now she'd be expected to shake hands and make polite chit-chat.

She couldn't help but sigh as the man removed one of his gloves and extended his hand.

"Ted Fowles. Entomologist."

He was tall and almost painfully thin, the most prominent features of his face being his prominent nose and hollowed cheeks. His Adam's apple protruded from his neck like Mt. Hood in miniature.

Darger stepped forward and introduced herself in turn.

"Violet Darger. Criminal profiler," she said, missing the Special Agent title. It carried a certain ring of authority. "Wait. Entomologist? So you're one of those bug guys?"

"Yep. Bug Guy. That's the preferred nomenclature, actually."

Fowles seemed to find the exchange amusing, his mouth spreading into a lopsided grin. His blue eyes peered at her through a pair of eyeglasses, the kind with a rim of tortoiseshell on top and thin wire underneath. They made her think of a nerdy professor from the 1950s.

His good humor did nothing to rub off on Darger. She was still frustrated to be sharing the crime scene.

"Sandy PD didn't tell me anyone would be out here," she said, not able to keep a bit of the irritation from creeping into her voice. And maybe a little part of her was still coming down from being startled.

"Oh, I suppose they didn't know," Fowles said, running a hand through the thatch of dark, wiry hair on top of his head.

She raised an eyebrow, feeling a little suspicious now.

"They didn't send you out here to collect evidence? So what is this? Extra credit?"

His head quirked to one side, an oddly bird-like movement.

"Sorry, I thought… well, Margaret didn't tell you?"

It was a moment before Darger was able to process that question, feeling more perplexed than ever. What the hell did Margaret Prescott have to do with this?

"Tell me what?"

"I'm with Prescott Consulting."

And the first thing Darger thought but didn't say out loud, thankfully, was, *No, I'm with Prescott Consulting.*

He filled in the rest for her, in case she was too slow, which at the moment it seemed like she most definitely was.

"We're going to be working together."

(

To Fowles' credit, he seemed to take a hint and left Darger alone with the scene soon after dropping his Prescott bomb, but not before Darger had a chance to ask when he'd been assigned the case.

"Two weeks ago," he said.

Meaning that Dr. Prescott would have known Fowles was here already and certainly could have told Darger she'd be working with someone. Had she sent Darger in blind intentionally or had it simply been a detail she'd overlooked?

The more Darger considered it, the more she was certain that Margaret Prescott was not the type of woman that overlooked much of anything.

"More mind games courtesy of Professor Prescott," Darger grumbled to herself.

It occurred to her that perhaps her prospective boss had heard rumors that Violet Darger wasn't always the best at playing well with others.

Shooing a bug away from her face, she tried to refocus her attention on the scene. Annoying as this little plot twist may be, she couldn't let her emotions distract her.

Time to get to work.

She studied the terrain, trying to imagine the killer dragging a victim out here. If she were still alive — and drowning as the cause of death would seem to suggest that — she must have been incapacitated somehow. Bound, certainly, if not unconscious. It would be hell either way. Carrying that dead weight through this dense forest would be no small feat. The killer would almost have to be a large man, strong. Even if the girl had walked back here on her own two feet, the killer would need to be able to overpower her during a struggle, if she tried to run or fight. And then there was the part where he had to hold her down as the water filled her lungs.

Strong. And brutal.

Darger suddenly flashed to her own nightmare memory — the feeling of water invading her body, sucked into the places where it didn't belong. For a moment, she swore she could feel Clegg's knees grinding into her back as he tried to drown her.

Goose bumps spread over her arms, and she put a hand out to steady herself against a tree.

Years had passed since that first case with the BAU, when a serial killer named James Joseph Clegg had almost added Darger to his list of victims. But he hadn't. She'd won in the end. It had been pure, dumb luck, but Darger was alive, and Clegg was dead.

She closed her eyes and took a long, deep breath in.

Focus on the task at hand. Not the past. The here and now.

The smell of rotting leaves and a vaguely fishy odor from

the river seemed to envelop her. Maybe it was her imagination, but the scent had been cleaner back at the park.

She exhaled and opened her eyes, feeling a little more grounded in the present.

OK. Back to work.

Dead leaves crinkled and crunched as she stepped closer to the edge of the riverbank and peered across the water. Nothing but more trees. It was a very isolated space, which made perfect sense for a dumping ground. Less sense for a kill site, if only because it took so much damn effort to get out here. It was planned, then. At least somewhat. The killer knew this place. Knew that parking in one of the small lots along the river during the off-hours — at night, most likely — would carry little risk of being seen. Knew he could walk into this stretch of woods and commit his dark deed.

A local then. Not surprising considering the three victims had all been from the area. That suggested a certain comfort with the place. It also meant it was more likely that he had some kind of personal connection to the victims. The three women themselves had little in common apart from their gender — a school teacher, an accountant, and a high school sophomore, ranging in age from 15 to 43.

So where to start? The killer's connection to any of these women could be the smallest thing. He might have walked his dog in front of Shannon Mead's house for all they knew, crossed paths with Maribeth Holtz at a grocery store, gone to the same church as Holly Green. It could be anything, or so it seemed.

The shimmering of the mirror-like surface of the water caught Darger's eye, drew her gaze straight down. She stared at her wavering reflection and wondered if Shannon Mead had glimpsed the fear in her own eyes before her head was shoved under the current.

Again Darger flashed back to her own near-drowning experience, felt the cold, dark waters shroud her face, blocking out the light and sound of the world.

Her heart started beating harder and faster. A frightened thing trying to crawl up into her throat.

She remembered the burning in her lungs. The sound of her pulse booming in her head like a bass drum. The panic of knowing she was about to die, the animal urge to fight with all she had to try to prevent it.

She gasped and pulled herself out of the memory. The light of day returned, as did the chirping of the birds and the soothing babble of the water.

Gazing around at the lopsided rectangle outlined by the yellow tape, she decided she'd seen enough.

Ferns swished against her thighs as she picked her way back through the dense foliage. Her boot came down on a twig, breaking it in two. It sounded like a bone snapping.

A break in the trees ahead signaled to Darger that the parking lot lay just beyond. Pushing through the fronds of a fat fir tree, she found herself back on solid, paved ground.

The sky was overcast, but the light here in the open was so much brighter than under the canopy, Darger couldn't help squinting. Through the slits of her eyes, she noticed she wasn't alone. Dr. Fowles was sitting on the rotting picnic table. She hoped he wasn't waiting around for her.

But as she approached her rental, his long legs unfolded, and he got to his feet.

"You're still here," Darger said.

It wasn't exactly a question. More of a challenge. Just because Prescott had sent them both out here, Darger didn't see why that meant they had to play tag-along with one another.

"See anything interesting back there?" he asked.

She glanced back at the wall of dense foliage before answering.

"A shit load of trees."

He laughed, Adam's apple bobbing.

Where Margaret Prescott's laugh had been the harsh bark of a jackal, Fowles' was an unrestrained, loose sound from deep in his chest. Relaxed. Pleasant.

At last Darger found herself warming up to him a little. It wasn't really his fault if Dr. Prescott was playing mind games with them, after all.

"What'd you get?" Darger asked.

"Hm?"

She pointed at the top of the vial that barely protruded from his shirt pocket.

"Oh! Calliphoridae." Dr. Fowles pulled the glass tube out and held it out so Darger might get a closer look. "*Lucilia sericata*, to be specific. Third instar."

He rotated the vial between his thumb and index finger as he spoke. Something small and white wriggled within its transparent prison.

It was a maggot.

A shudder ran through Darger, and she recoiled instinctively, letting out a quiet grunt of disgust.

Fowles grinned.

"Not a fan of insects, I take it?"

"Not the creepy, crawly, squirming types. No," Darger said, with perhaps too much conviction considering this was his bread and butter. "Sorry. Butterflies are OK."

The corners of his mouth quirked into a smile, one side a little more than the other. It made him seem rakish, a little mischievous.

"Well now that we're on the topic of maggots, I don't suppose you're hungry?"

CHAPTER 4

The inside of Fowles' car was a hodgepodge of clutter. Not necessarily dirty — there were no fast food wrappers or stray French fries that Darger could see. But there were vials and baggies and kits for collecting specimens. At least five bottles of water in various states of emptiness. An unopened box of disposable plastic food containers with lids. Three-ring binders. A flashlight. Two rolls of paper towels. A sweatshirt and a clean pair of socks rolled into a ball. Scissors. A package of batteries. And books — textbooks and paperback novels and spiral-bound sketchbooks.

Darger picked up one of the sketchpads and opened it. She was stunned at what she found inside: pages and pages of perfectly rendered insects. Some were done in full ink and watercolor, others just quick pencil sketches.

"Wow. These are great."

"Oh. Just a little hobby."

"Just?"

He shrugged.

"It was what got me interested in bugs, actually. I had one of the old Audubon field guides for insects when I was a boy, and I would spend hours paging through it. Copying the drawings. Or trying to. When I got older, I thought I might go to school for art, but my practical side won out. I don't think I would have fared well in modern art schools, only drawing bugs all the time."

Darger smiled, admiring the work on the pages as she

flipped past them.

"Why bugs?"

"What do you mean?"

"What makes a guy decide to devote his life to—" she pointed at a black and white beetle rendered in pencil "—that?"

"Are you kidding? They're fascinating! Such diversity. Did you know there are 1200 species of blow fly in the world? Eighty in America. Then there's Drosophilae, fruit flies. To witness the evolution of a species in a matter of days... I mean, if that doesn't excite you, what does?"

Chuckling at his enthusiasm, Darger let the sketchbook fall closed.

"You don't have to share if you don't want to," Fowles said, "but I would be interested in hearing what you got from the crime scene."

"Got?" Darger repeated and set the sketchbook back where she'd found it.

"You know. Observations. Feelings. Insights."

Darger shrugged, a little surprised. The science geeks tended to look down on their profiling associates. Profilers relied heavily on intuition — something that was not easily taught in the classroom or replicated in a lab. And thus, the scientific circles of law enforcement often treated profilers as professional guessers, at best. At worst, they considered them snake-oil salesmen.

But sharing her thoughts with Fowles couldn't hurt. Sometimes talking things out led to a surprise revelation.

"Well the water angle is probably the most obvious," she started.

"What about it?"

"From a symbolic standpoint, I mean. Carl Jung considered water to be the most common representation for the subconscious."

The trees outside her window whizzed by in a blur of green as she spoke.

"Jung? Isn't he a little outdated at this point?"

She tried not to smirk at that. She'd been expecting it, really. It was a classic Science Geek response.

"All human behavior has a subtext, a second meaning beneath the surface of the action — that's pretty much the heart of human psychology, past and present. Jung's central concept was individuation — essentially each individual's development of their sense of self, and I'm certainly mindful of that as I examine criminal behavior. If there's one thing all serial killers have in common, it's a crisis of identity. Anyway, you're a biologist. What's the one thing every known organism requires for survival?"

Fowles nodded. "Water."

"So it's something of a paradox, the fact that we can drown in one of the things we need most to live."

"You think the killer is trying to be ironic?"

"Not on purpose. I doubt he's even aware of it. But I do think there are always reasons behind behavior. Sometimes those reasons are based on instinct. Old animal urges. Subconscious connections being made without our knowing it. Water has an elemental power. It's just as capable of dealing death as it is of giving life. A flash flood or tsunami is equally as destructive as any volcano or earthquake."

The tires hummed and bumped over the asphalt.

"Water also represents change. It has an almost limitless

ability to shift, flow, or alter its shape to fit whatever holds it. I think many ritual murders are an ill-fated attempt at transformation, one way or another."

A line formed between the doctor's eyebrows.

"What kind of transformation?"

Darger shook her head.

"Hard to say at this point. It usually has to do with gaining control. Powerless to powerful. Weak to strong. Submissive to dominating."

She let her thoughts snowball, talking through them out loud.

"Think of the commitment it takes to drown someone. A bullet kills instantly, and you can do it from a distance. Just move a single finger, pull the trigger. Easy. Mechanical. The killer is detached from the physical act. Drowning, though, would prolong the violent act, and the killer has to be physically close to the victim. It's very personal."

A huge semi hauling a load of raw lumber whooshed past, jostling the car with a burst of wind turbulence. Darger barely noticed.

"I mean, just imagine what it would feel like. You drag a living person to the water. And you push her down, face-first over the edge of the riverbank. She's struggling now, trying to fight. You climb onto her back to hold her under, and all the while, she's writhing and jerking, fighting desperately to pull her head above the water. Every muscle of her body hell-bent on survival. You'd have to hold her there for three or four minutes… it would require an almost loving embrace. You would possess not only ultimate power over the life of another being, but an intimate closeness in that same moment. The frenzied movements of the victim probably arouse you, the death struggle becoming something like a sex act."

She realized the car had come to a stop somewhere in there. They were in the city, parked on the street in front of a yoga studio. A couple strolled past on the sidewalk, walking a pair of enormous Great Danes.

This happened often when she got in the zone with a profile. She lost herself in it, and the outside world ceased to exist.

Her eyelids fluttered rapidly as she crawled out of her daze. She turned, found Fowles staring at her.

His forehead was riddled with a series of creases.

"You've got obscenities like that taking up space in your head, and you find bugs off-putting?"

Darger laughed. "To each his or her own, I guess."

CHAPTER 5

Darger climbed out of the car and followed Fowles down the
sidewalk, trying to figure out where they were headed. There
was a restaurant beside the yoga studio they'd parked in front
of, and judging by the decor Darger spied through the
windows, it was a higher-end place. The tables in the outdoor
courtyard were packed with diners, and they all looked to be
upper middle class professionals to Darger: doctors, lawyers,
academics. Most were probably in their late 20s or early 30s
and stylish, but not in an ostentatious way. Darger wasn't sure
she'd fit in, but Fowles and his retro horn-rimmed specs would
be right at home.

When they came to the door of the place, though, Fowles
kept walking. Darger's focus flitted ahead. Just beyond the next
intersection, a rustic wooden sign for a diner caught her eye.
Maybe Fowles was thinking of something a little more folksy.
Food to fit the thick swaths of forest they'd just returned from.
Bacon and eggs. Pancakes hot off the griddle. Rib-sticking,
lumberjack fare.

But instead of proceeding through the crosswalk, Fowles
took a hard right turn. Another hundred yards down the
sidewalk, he finally came to a stop. Darger didn't understand, at
first. There was nothing here. Just a big parking lot.

Then she noticed the line of people queuing in front of a
white truck. Darger studied the red lettering on the side of the
vehicle and finally understood. It was a food truck.

"I hope you like Korean tacos," Fowles said.

38

"Never had 'em. But I like Korean food, and I like tacos, so I don't see how we could possibly go wrong here."

The half-smile seemed to constantly play at the corners of the entomologist's mouth, but now the crinkles at the corners of his eyes deepened. Darger decided she might as well take the opportunity to do a little digging about her potential employer.

"So how long have you been with Prescott Consulting, Dr. Fowles?"

"It's not *doctor*, actually. Not yet, anyway. I won't defend my dissertation until next spring."

"What's your thesis?"

"Well, I won't give you the full official thesis title, because it's nearly a paragraph all by itself, but the subject is the effect of environmental factors on arthropod succession in human remains. I've just completed the largest forensic entomological decomposition study with real human cadavers. It's more common to use pigs, but thanks to Dr. Prescott, I received a special grant that allowed me to conduct the study at a body farm. And to answer your initial question, I've been with the firm for three years."

She'd noted that he'd now referred to their boss by both her Christian name and her official title. Interesting. Familiar on the one hand, professional on the other.

"And you like the work?"

"Absolutely. I probably don't have to tell you that there's not an incredibly high demand for full-time forensic entomologists in most bodies of law enforcement. It's much more common to have a faculty position at a university and only be called upon from time-to-time to aid in an investigation. Working for Dr. Prescott is a unique opportunity for someone like me."

Darger nodded, secretly disappointed that it didn't seem that she'd be getting any dirt on Margaret Prescott. She should have known. Fowles struck her as too professional — and perhaps too kind — to badmouth their boss.

"Are you the only Bug Guy, then? Or does Prescott Consulting have a whole slew of your kind?"

The roguish half-smile returned in full force.

"So you're really going to keep going with the 'Bug Guy' thing?" He shook his head. "I knew you were an entomophobe."

"I'm not afraid of bugs," Darger said. When Fowles raised an eyebrow, she added, "Not any more than your average *normal* person."

"I am the sole entomologist on staff, though there are other analysts with different specialties. Antonio Miles runs all the polygraphs. Felicia Barrett is our handwriting expert. Dr. Granholm spent 40 years as a top forensic pathologist before joining Prescott Consulting. There are others, but we tend to work solo."

The line for the food truck had moved at a steady pace since they'd arrived. Fowles and Darger were at bat.

Darger couldn't decide between the chicken, shrimp, or beef bulgogi tacos, so she got the three-way combo that came with one of each. They came in a paper food boat, topped with kimchi slaw, sesame mayo, and cilantro.

She and Fowles stood side-by-side on the sidewalk while they ate, feet spread apart to save their shoes from being splattered with the juice that sluiced down through their fingers. It was sloppy eating, and an errant droplet of sauce found its way onto Darger's sleeve. She glanced over at Fowles, noting that his clothing remained immaculate. Of course.

She dabbed at the splotch with a napkin and refocused on her remaining tacos. They were savory and sweet, creamy and tangy, crunchy and chewy all at the same time. And then a little pungency from the kimchi. In short, delicious.

Fowles paused in between tacos, watching to see how she was enjoying the food.

"I almost took you to the bougie Peruvian place down the street. And the food there is excellent — don't get me wrong — but something told me this was more your style."

Darger licked a piece of cilantro off her knuckle and shook her head with satisfaction.

"You weren't wrong."

Yeah, maybe he wasn't so bad after all. Darger liked that he'd opted for the food truck over trying to impress her with something extravagant or expensive.

Fowles wiped his hands with a brown paper napkin, then wadded it up with his food tray and threw the whole mess in a nearby garbage can. Darger finished her last bite and did the same.

"So what will you do next?"

"I was thinking I'd go talk to Shannon Mead's family. Maybe look over her house, try to get a feel for who she was. Right now it doesn't look like the three victims have much in common, aside from being female. If I dig deeper, though, maybe I'll find some connection."

When she looked at him again, the pervasive smile had faded.

"I noticed that. From the files, I mean. How different they

seemed from one another."

Darger thought he was probably flicking through the crime scene photos in his mind, recalling each grisly tableau.

She did the same, calling them up in order.

Holly Green was the first. A student at Sandy High, fifteen years old. She was on the volleyball team. Popular. Outgoing. A loud and friendly personality by all accounts. She'd gone missing after a volleyball tournament. Five days later, her body was found in a creek on the rural northern edge of Sandy. A Boy Scout troop spotted her lodged under a concrete bridge. A dark thing bobbing in the water. Swollen to a blimp-like shape.

A 43-year-old accountant named Maribeth Holtz was the next victim, found washed up near a local reservoir. Married with two college-aged sons, both out of state. She and her husband, a mechanical engineer, lived a quiet life. Almost hermit-like, without many social contacts in the community. Initially, this led the police to suspect Maribeth's husband for both murders. But Mr. Holtz had a solid alibi for both disappearances — he was on a business trip, at an engineering conference at Georgia Tech where he even appeared on a panel that was streamed live on the internet within the window of time the medical examiner's report suggested the murder took place.

And finally Shannon Mead. 28. Single. Only in her second year at Litchfield Elementary School, but already popular among students and parents. Still very close with her own parents who lived a few miles away on the outskirts of Portland. She and her mother were both prominent figures in the Presbyterian church, active participants in a variety of charitable causes.

There had to be something linking the women in a place as small as Sandy. Some way the killer knew all three or a connection to the town at the very least. Had the murders occurred in the city, she could have accepted that the victims were random. But a dot on the map like Sandy had to be chosen.

When his Subaru came into view, Fowles pulled a set of keys from his pocket and aimed the fob at the vehicle, unlocking the doors. Darger climbed into the passenger seat.

He started the car and then turned to look at her.

"Would it be OK if I came along?"

"When I talk to the family?"

He nodded.

"Are you sure you want to? It can be pretty… intense."

"If you think my tagging along would be inappropriate, I understand. But I'm a proponent of cooperative learning and reciprocal teaching. The better you understand the entomology, the better for the investigation. And vice versa."

Again, Darger was surprised by Fowles. Most of the science geeks she'd known over the years wanted nothing to do with the walking, talking human evidence left behind after a homicide: the grieving family members, the jittery witnesses, the shifty-eyed suspects. The geeks preferred their specimens to stay safely contained in Petri dishes and under glass slides.

She considered the fact that he might regret his decision once they were knee-deep in the emotional quagmire of bereavement. But if he wanted the experience….

"I have no objections to your coming along. But I need to grab some things from my car. We'll have to drive back to the park first."

"Not a problem."

She watched Portland shrink in the rearview mirror as they headed out of the city and back into the countryside, and she wondered what other peculiarities Fowles might reveal.

CHAPTER 6

"It's your turn, by the way," Darger said.

"My turn?" He regarded her quizzically, still watching the road out of the corner of his eye. "For what?"

"I thought we were swapping information. All that cooperative learning stuff."

He turned back to face the windshield as he spoke, hands fidgeting on the steering wheel.

"I've made the mistake of delving into the more graphic forensic details around mealtimes in mixed company before. I just wanted to give you ample time to digest your lunch."

"Very thoughtful. But I think I can handle it."

"OK. Do you remember the *L. sericata* I showed you?"

It was a moment before Darger figured out what he was referring to.

"You mean the maggot?"

His persistent smile widened.

"Yes. The maggot," he said. "*Lucilia sericata* is one of the first—"

Darger stopped him.

"Biology was never my strongest subject. All that Latin jargon. Do me a favor and pretend you're talking to an idiot for a minute."

"I don't think you're being fair to your intellect, but as you wish. The common green bottle fly — also known as the sheep blow fly — is one of the most typical species we find on carrion. It is also often one of the first. In my own study, we consistently

45

observed *L.* — sorry, blow flies — on the cadavers within fifteen to twenty minutes."

"Wow. But you were outside, right? What if the corpse is indoors?"

"That would be a study I'd love to take on sometime in the future, but as far as I know, no one has tested that specific environmental variable. There are certainly examples in the literature that suggest both blow flies and flesh flies are present within hours, even in a closed room. I'd guess that certain factors — whether or not there was a window left open, for example — would affect just how quickly the insects arrive. But these are remarkable scavengers. Perhaps the most efficient in the world."

Darger suppressed a shudder. She didn't want Fowles thinking she was some kind of wuss.

"Flesh flies?"

"Sarcophagidae. Another major player. You see, the particular conditions of the body, the environment, the time of year, ambient temperature and humidity, etc... all of these variables have an effect on what forensically-relevant arthropods are in abundance as well as what life stage they're in."

"Forensically-relevant arthropods. Thanks for dumbing it down," Darger said.

Fowles rolled his eyes but smiled along with her.

"The important bugs."

"Right."

Fowles reached behind him, into the detritus of papers and books in the back seat and drew forth a 3-ring binder.

"Perhaps pictures would help make things more concrete

for you," he said, handing her the folder.

Darger set it in her lap and opened the cover. Keeping his eyes on the road, Fowles pointed at the first set of photographs. One showed a cadaver in a field, surrounded by parched brown grass. Underneath that was a close-up of a fly.

"Allow me to use our friend the green bottle fly as an example."

Its eyes were blood red, and the lack of pupils made them seem directionless, almost sightless. But the fly's thorax was a lovely shade of iridescent green, bright and metallic.

"Huh. It's kind of pretty," Darger muttered.

This statement excited Fowles enough that he slapped his hand against the steering wheel.

"Now you're starting to see! Even the non-butterflies of the world can be beautiful in their own way."

Darger flipped the page, past more images of various insects — flies mostly — on the corpse. A few pages in, she was greeted by a macro shot of four flies and what looked like a pile of rice.

"The life cycle begins here. After mating, the female flies find their host. Usually some form of carrion—"

Closing her eyes, Darger held up a hand and interrupted.

"Sorry. *Usually* carrion?"

"Yes, well… myiasis with *L. sericata* is not uncommon, especially with sheep in the UK and Australia. But there are isolated human cases now and again."

"Do I want to know what *myiasis* is?"

"It's an infection of fly larvae in living tissue."

"And back to bugs being totally disgusting."

"They're not all death and decay, though. Have you ever

heard of maggot therapy?"

"Now you're just making things up."

"I'm not! When traditional methods fail, and under the guidance of a trained physician, sterile maggots can be applied to an infected wound. Not only do they consume the necrotic tissue and the infectious bacteria and thus clean the wound, they also release antimicrobial enzymes. It's supposed to be quite painless."

Darger raised an eyebrow.

"Just out of curiosity, where does one obtain sterile maggots?"

"You raise them, of course."

"Oh, of course."

Fowles redirected her attention to the folder with a jerk of his head.

"Anyway, we were discussing the life cycle of the green bottle fly. The female extends her ovipositor—"

Darger fixed him with a dubious look.

"Sorry. Her… egg tube. The eggs are deposited, as many as two or three hundred at a time, on the host."

"So those little clumps of rice are eggs?"

"Precisely. At 70 degrees, the eggs will hatch in approximately 21 hours."

He indicated Darger should turn the page. She did.

It was a full-color spread of maggots. They were small, yellowish, and plump, feeding off the red-pink flesh in masses.

"Here we have *L. sericata* in the first instar stage. Which is really just a fancy way of saying larval stage. This species will progress through three instar stages, each with a specific duration. Sticking with our example of 70 degrees, over the course of four to five days, they will grow from 2 mm to 20 mm. The larvae are essentially feeding machines, eating non-stop for those five days. The spiracles on the rear end allow it to breathe while it eats."

"Handy," Darger commented before Fowles continued his lecture.

"So the first instars migrate into the body, excreting special digestive enzymes that speed up the putrefaction process. They like both their temporary home and their meals to be wet and soupy, you see. But don't let that fool you. Their mouths are equipped with a set of teeth-like hooks which they use to scrape and shred the decaying flesh."

Darger's vision blurred. She'd always felt she had a strong stomach, but this was beginning to make her queasy.

She snapped the folder shut.

"I did warn you," he said. "About my sharing directly after a meal."

"It's not the pictures. I mean, it *is*, but it's because we're in a moving car. I get motion sickness from reading in the car and…"

"Looking at pictures of maggots eating human flesh?"

She laughed and rubbed at her brow.

"Yeah."

"Then here's the abridged version. Earlier I gave you a time frame for the life cycle at 70 degrees. But when the ambient temperature rises, things really start to get exciting. The life cycle is accelerated. At 80 degrees, for example, the time it takes for the eggs to hatch goes from 21 hours to 18."

"And the same goes for the larval… I mean, instar stages?"

"Yes! Exactly. At 80 degrees, they would cycle through the

first, second, and third instar stages and on into the prepupal stage in only three days. That's why knowing the ambient temperature and other environmental factors is so crucial for estimating the postmortem interval."

Pushing the stomach-churning images from her mind, Darger tried to focus on what Fowles was telling her.

"So you take samples from the body, figure out what stage they're at and then count backward to figure out when the person died. Is that right?"

"Correct."

"What kind of effect does being in water have on the life cycle of the flies?"

His eyes practically lit up with what Darger could only describe as childlike delight.

"Now that's the kind of question that leaves no doubt in my mind that you would have made an excellent biologist. Forget your trouble with Latin. You have the innate curiosity and stubborn tenacity of a born scientist."

Cocking her head to one side, Darger raised an eyebrow.

"Are you flirting with me?"

Fowles chuckled.

"It's just that you've gotten right to the heart of the problem. Now keep in mind that the only studies I know of were conducted with pig carcasses. There's anecdotal literature on arthropod succession on submerged human remains but no official studies. I'd love to get another grant and use the body farm to do one myself, but I'm getting off-track again."

He put a hand to his head, and the gesture reminded Darger of an absent-minded old man.

"Being submerged in water drastically changed the blow fly

colonization on the pig carcasses."

"How so?"

"The entire life cycle was delayed five days."

"Huh. That matches up with the time of death for our victims. Does that mean you didn't find any blow fly activity on them?"

"Not exactly."

He swallowed, his face growing more serious.

"The larvae I found in Maribeth Holtz were second instar."

Even as a newbie to the world of forensic entomology, Darger knew that didn't make sense. She tapped a finger against her cheek, pondering it.

"OK. Maribeth was found in shallower water. Maybe she'd washed up on shore for a while. And the temperature could have expedited things. Was there a heat wave that week?"

"That's what I initially considered, but it wasn't nearly warm enough to explain that kind of acceleration to the life cycle. And then they found Shannon Mead."

"And she was the same?"

"I found first instar on Shannon. Not as far along as Maribeth Holtz, but still much further advanced than if she'd been in the water for five days."

"Based on the insect evidence alone, how long would you have guessed she was out there?"

"Six or seven days, at least."

"That's impossible. She was only missing for five. That's how we know he's killing them soon after he abducts them."

He shrugged.

"I'm just telling you what the bugs are telling me."

"Are you saying the bugs talk to you?"

He smiled. "In a manner of speaking."

Darger sighed, trying to take it all in. But it didn't make sense.

The medical examiner's time of death matched up with when the women had been abducted. There wasn't room for the women to be dead *longer* than they'd been missing.

"So what you're saying is, something's rotten in the state of Denmark?"

"Denmark?"

"Not a big Shakespeare buff, eh, Bug Guy?"

"I guess not."

Fowles cleared his throat.

"There is another thing."

"What?"

"I'll show you."

((

The trees loomed overhead as the car wove through the isolated Oregon wilderness. The sky had gone overcast, and the gloom beneath the canopy was even heavier now. The scenery Darger could discern on either side of the road was an endless sea of deep green boxing her in.

After some time, they broke through into open terrain again. They passed a large man-made dam, an incongruous thing of metal and concrete amongst the wildness of the trees. And then the sparkling, crystal clear water of a reservoir beyond.

Fowles pulled to the shoulder and parked the car near a rocky little beach. Darger recognized the place from the file.

"This is where they found Maribeth Holtz," she said, so

quietly she seemed to be talking to herself.

Nodding, Fowles climbed out of the car. Darger followed. He continued some distance from the stretch of beach where Maribeth was found.

A large piece of driftwood blocked the path, and Darger scrambled over it. She wondered, as she did with Shannon Mead, what Maribeth saw when the killer dragged her out here. What she felt. Did she know she was going to die? Did she scream for help? Beg for mercy?

They pushed through a patch of wild huckleberry, and then Fowles stopped.

Something odd sat on the shoreline — what looked like a plastic laundry basket with a cement block on top. It seemed wrong here in this pristine wilderness. Too ugly, too artificial.

"Is that a laundry basket?"

"Yes."

She noticed something else. There was an object inside the basket, and whatever it was, the surface of it was swarming with flies.

"Ted?"

"Yeah?"

"What's in the basket?"

"A hog leg."

Fowles removed the brick, explaining as he did, "To keep the carrion animals from running off with my experiment. We usually use heavy iron cages in a more scientific setting, but I was improvising."

He lifted the basket, revealing the rotting piece of meat covered with a mass of flies, buzzing and twitching and rubbing their disgusting little legs together.

"Aha!" he said, jubilantly. "I knew you'd be here!"

"Are you talking to the pig leg or…?"

"I'm talking to him," he said, pointing at a large beetle among the smaller bugs.

Darger bent closer to get a better look, holding her breath against the smell of rotting pork. It was a little under an inch long, with a shiny black head. Its elongated lower body was covered in tiny hairs that looked almost like velvet in an elaborate black-and-grey pattern.

"He's kind of fancy-looking," she said.

"*Creophilus maxillosus.* The hairy rove beetle."

Pulling another plastic vial from his pocket, he collected the insect.

"And he eats dead things, too?"

"Actually, no. *She's* a predator. Her favorite food is the larvae and eggs of the various flies."

"Yum."

"We don't typically use the adults for estimated PMI, but they'll generally start to show up around the bloat stage, 2-3 days after death."

"OK. How long has Porky been out here?"

"One and a half days," he said, obviously excited to reveal this nugget of information. "That was one of the startling things I found in my study. In moist, wooded areas — near swamps, rivers, lakes — the adult hairy rove beetles showed up to the cadavers earlier than in open fields. As early as 24-36 hours sometimes. So that was what I expected to find with Maribeth. In fact, I expected to find some potential larval activity. It's the perfect environment. Damp. Food source nearby. This is their jam."

"Their jam?"

Fowles nodded.

"So? Did you find any hairy beetle larvae on Maribeth?"

"None."

Darger crossed her arms over her chest.

"So now you're telling me that the beetle evidence suggests Maribeth Holtz was dead *less* than we originally thought?"

"Not exactly. I think it means that perhaps Maribeth Holtz's body was… somewhere else for part of the time she was missing."

"Where?"

"That I can't say. Just not here. And not in the water."

"It doesn't make sense. Why would he drown her here, drag her somewhere else for a few days or whatever, and then bring her back to dump the body?"

Fowles' eyebrows drifted up in slow motion.

"I'm afraid that's more your wheelhouse than mine, Violet."

CHAPTER 7

The ride to the home of Shannon Mead's parents was relatively quiet.

Darger mulled over what Fowles had explained about the entomological evidence, but couldn't make sense of it.

"What about weird weather patterns? A microclimate or something. Or some other variable that might have screwed up the life cycle of the bugs?" she'd asked.

"If something had been off with just one of the bodies, I could accept that," he conceded. "But for all of them to be so incongruent with my expectations, not to mention the literature... no. We're missing something."

Something was rotten, for certain, and it wasn't just the leg of pork Fowles had left out for his experiment.

All the entomology jargon swirled around in her head: instars and spiracles and ovipositing. That and trying to straighten out the conflicting timelines was giving her a headache.

They stopped off at Darger's rental car so she could collect her files and then headed onward to meet with Shannon's family.

Right. That was Darger's true mission. She needed to put the entomology questions out of her mind for now. The bug stuff was Fowles' responsibility. His wheelhouse, as he put it.

It was her job to focus on the victims. On their lives, their families, their day-to-day activities. The bugs weren't going to tell her who the killer was. But the rest of it just might.

Darger unfolded Shannon's file, hoping another look would shake something loose. She formulated a list of questions in her head for Shannon's family. Were there any ex-boyfriends in the area? Had she mentioned anything strange happening in her life recently? Breathy crank phone calls or being followed?

She flipped idly through the files for Maribeth Holtz and Holly Green trying to connect the dots. Different ages, different looks.

When they reached Shannon's parents' house, Fowles parked on the street and pulled the key from the ignition. He glanced over at the photograph of Shannon smiling out from the manila folder in Darger's lap.

"The file said she volunteered at the soup kitchen in Portland most weekends," he said, a faraway look coming over his features. "It's a shame, really. She sounded like a kind person. A giver."

Darger had called ahead to make sure their visit wouldn't be an inconvenience for the Meads. Mrs. Mead met them at the door, shaking each of their hands in turn and then inviting them inside.

"You'll have to excuse my husband. He hasn't been… he's just not up for all the questions, today." She fiddled with the necklace that hung around her neck, a small gold cross on a simple chain. "He and Shannon were very close."

"I understand," Darger said.

She started with the easy questions first, asking about the basics of Shannon's day-to-day activities.

Mrs. Mead described her daughter as intelligent, outgoing, compassionate.

"She loved reading and learning and art, but she wasn't shy.

I always used to say she was a bookish extrovert."

Fall through Spring, her time was mainly filled with teaching, though two or three times a week Shannon took a dance fitness class with a couple of her girlfriends. She taught an after-school French class in the spring.

"Just rudimentary, of course. The kids would learn how to introduce themselves in French. A few basic phrases. The lyrics to *Head, Shoulders, Knees, and Toes*. Shannon called it 'Baby French.'"

Mrs. Mead pinched the crucifix pendant between her fingers and ran it back and forth over the chain.

"She usually took some kind of class in summer, when her school year was over. Last year she did pottery, the year before that was Greek and Roman mythology."

Darger moved into deeper waters, asking about Shannon's romantic life.

She'd been engaged a few years back, but they'd decided to call it off. It had been an amicable break-up, according to Mrs. Mead.

"He lives outside Eugene now, a couple hours south on I-5. I know the police have spoken to him. Nothing would shock me more than to find out that Michael had anything to do with this."

Finally, Darger pulled out the photographs of Maribeth and Holly, set them in front of Mrs. Mead.

"I know what you're going to ask."

Darger raised an eyebrow.

"You're going to ask if I know either one of them," she said, shaking her head. "I'm sorry. But the answer is no."

"Neither one looks familiar?"

A sad smile played at Mrs. Mead's mouth.

"Now they do. They're two perfect strangers to me, but because of their connection to Shannon's case, they somehow feel like… part of the family. And I've wracked my brain, trying to think of something they might have had in common."

She patted the picture of Holly with her hand.

"Like the Green girl. I know she went to Sandy High. Played volleyball. I tried to think of a time Shannon might have mentioned attending a game or maybe some other function there. But I just can't see it. Shannon was never really into sports. She did student government when she was in school. And Quiz Bowl."

"Do you know who did Shannon's taxes, by any chance?" Darger asked, looking for a connection to Maribeth Holtz.

Mrs. Mead's head bobbed up and down.

"Shannon has been preparing her own taxes since she got her first job in high school. We taught all of our children how to do them. Should be something they teach in school, if you ask me, but…."

"Are your other children nearby?"

"If only," she said with a patient sigh. "My daughter lives in Hawaii, and my son in London. Can't imagine they'd be able to provide the connection, but the police have their phone numbers if you want to speak with them."

She placed her palm over the gold cross and held it to her chest, as if to make sure it was still there.

"I wish I could tell you more. I'm sorry."

Mrs. Mead reached out a hand and brushed her fingertips over the photographs of Maribeth and Holly. She opened her mouth as if to speak, but the silence stretched out for some time. Just as Darger was about to ask if everything was all right, Mrs. Mead found her voice.

"I got a call earlier... from the police. They said... they told me they were releasing her house?"

Her voice went up at the end, like it was a question.

Darger nodded.

"It means they've finished processing it. That they've gone through and have taken whatever evidence they needed."

The wisps of hair on either side of Mrs. Mead's head bounced as she shook her head from side to side.

"I understand all that. I just don't know what we're supposed to do now."

Fresh tears sprang to the woman's eyes and rolled down her cheeks.

Fowles plucked a box of tissues from a side table and passed it to Mrs. Mead. She took one and dabbed at her face, murmuring her thanks.

"I mean, what do I do with everything? All of her things? Sell them? Give them to charity?" She sniffed. "I'm trying to imagine having a yard sale, surrounded by what's left of my daughter's life. Putting those little round colored stickers and marking the price. A dollar for this. Ten dollars for that. What's the point?"

Darger frowned.

"I'm sure there are some things you might like to keep. Items that have sentimental value. And then maybe it would be easiest to donate the rest."

"But that's just it! All that's left of my daughter are a bunch of useless... *things*. Clothes and books and furniture. It seems like there should be more." Her voice cracked on the last word, and the rest came out small and pinched, as if something inside the woman had been damaged by her anguish. "It's not enough. It's not… fair."

Darger found herself at a loss for words. Mrs. Mead's grief filled the room, threatened to envelop her.

"You have her memory," Fowles said. His tone was quiet, calm, almost detached. "Of all the billions of years the universe has existed, she was here only a short time, and you were lucky enough to know her, to be with her. You'll always have that in here."

When Darger glanced over at him, his eyes gazed out the living room window, a faraway look on his face, his index finger still tapping at his temple.

"Truly the universe is full of ghosts, not sheeted churchyard specters, but the inextinguishable elements of individual life, which having once been, can never die, though they blend and change, and change again forever."

A hush came over the room when he'd finished. Mrs. Mead stirred.

"What was that? A poem?"

The entomologist's eyelids opened and closed a few times in rapid succession, as if he suddenly remembered where he was.

"It's from one of the Allan Quatermain novels by H. Rider Haggard. *King Solomon's Mines*, I believe," he said with a sheepish shrug. "My grandmother was into poetry. When we were kids, she used to give us a dollar if we could memorize a poem or quotation."

Mrs. Mead rose to her feet and padded over to a desk against one wall.

"Could you write it down for me? I'm supposed to read something at Shannon's service, but I haven't been able to find anything that seems… right. But that — what you just said — I liked that."

She held out a pad of paper and a pen, which Fowles accepted.

"Of course. I'd be happy to."

While he scribbled away Darger sat forward and looked the woman in the eye.

"With your permission, Mrs. Mead, I'd like to take a look around Shannon's house."

"But the police said they already took anything they thought was relevant."

"It's not so much about finding evidence. Seeing where she lived, how she lived, will give me a better sense of the person your daughter was."

Darger saw how the past tense caught at Mrs. Mead's grief and instantly regretted it. The woman placed a hand over the necklace and nodded.

"Whatever I can do to help."

CHAPTER 8

The interaction with Shannon Mead's mother played over in Darger's head as they drove on.

She was beginning to think she'd unfairly pigeon-holed Fowles as a run-of-the-mill science geek. The type that preferred their work and their subjects to be isolated in a sterile laboratory environment, separate from the messy real world.

But that was dead wrong. Not only had Fowles requested to come along on her visit to the Mead family home, but he'd participated. Gotten his hands dirty.

Fowles braked for a red light, and while his attention was focused on traffic, Darger took the opportunity to study him.

There was a sprinkle of freckles over his cheekbones, just below his eyes. They were very faint, and Darger figured them for the type that only came out after getting a lot of sun.

Two of his long, bony fingers tapped out a little rhythm against the steering wheel as he waited for the light to turn green.

What a strange man, she thought. Bugs, art, and a head full of random quotations. She wondered what idiosyncrasy he'd reveal next.

She played a game in her head, trying to guess what it might be. Maybe he built ships in bottles. Or played the harpsichord. She was still coming up with scenarios as they rolled through a suburban street shaded by mature trees. The car slowed to a crawl.

"Do you see a house number on that one?" Fowles asked,

pointing at a small Tudor style cottage.

"No," Darger said. "I don't see numbers on the next one either."

They rolled past a third house, and Fowles pointed at a set of shiny brass numbers over the door.

"3216. Shannon Mead's house must be one of those two back there."

Darger looked for other signs that one of the homes belonged to Shannon — mainly, did one look unoccupied? There were no vehicles in either driveway, no lights on visible through the windows.

Fowles pulled to the curb and parked the car. On the opposite side of the street, a group of kids huddled together under a giant elm tree. They stood in a tight circle, each one presenting a fist in the middle.

It was clear to Darger that they were playing some variation of eenie-meenie-miney-moe. When the cluster dispersed, one of the boys ran over to the elm tree, covered his eyes, and practically pressed his face into the bark. They climbed out of the car just as the other children scattered out of sight. She could hear the boy counting down from thirty.

"We could ask one of these kids," Fowles suggested. "Though I hate to interrupt a game of hide-and-seek."

"I'm almost surprised kids still play games like that these days."

The boy whirled around and called out, "Ready or not! Here I come!"

Fowles lifted a hand and waved.

"Excuse me. Do you know where Shannon Mead lived?"

The boy looked startled for a moment, caught off-guard by

a stranger talking to him. His eyes went from Fowles to Darger, and he seemed to relax a little.

"Are you more police?"

"Sort of. We're working with the police."

"It's sad about Miss Mead," the boy said, scratching his elbow. "On Halloween, she always gave out the King Size candy bars. Not those little mini ones."

Finally, he pointed at a blue bungalow with white trim.

"It's that one."

They thanked him and then watched him run off in search of his friends.

As they crossed the neat square of lawn in front of Shannon's house, Darger couldn't hold back her latent curiosity any further.

"Do you play any instruments?"

His eyebrows furrowed.

"No. Why?"

Suppressing a smile, Darger shook her head.

"No reason."

Fowles put his hands in his pockets and turned to her.

"Do you?"

"What?"

"Play an instrument?"

"Not unless you count a very brief stint with the clarinet in sixth grade," Darger said, cringing internally at the memory. "Jazz band."

They climbed the front steps, and Fowles held the screen door aside while Darger inserted the key Mrs. Mead had given her into the lock.

"I had grand visions of becoming some kind of clarinet

prodigy, I guess. That was before I realized how much practice was involved. Turns out you actually have to play the thing to get any good. And you start out sounding really, *really* bad."

The hinges on the door squeaked as Darger pushed it open and entered the house. She took a few steps into what appeared to be a living room and then stood still for a moment, taking it in.

It was nearly silent but for the *tick-tock* of an antique clock on the wall. A row of plants stood along a windowsill with a watering can shaped like an elephant. There was a bookshelf in the corner loaded with books, the spines arranged by color. A cross made of reclaimed wood hung over the sofa. In the center of the cross, there was a hammered metal heart with the word "LOVE" stenciled across it. Shannon's life seemed to have been filled with it. Her love of family, love of teaching, love of God.

Darger moved further inside, past a small dining area and into the kitchen. Despite the light let in by a sliding glass door, it felt dark inside now that the sun had slipped behind the trees. She flipped on the kitchen light and studied the items on the counter: spice rack, bread machine, stainless steel canisters labeled *Flour* and *Sugar*. Shannon must have liked to bake.

From behind her, Fowles spoke. "That surprises me."

Darger turned to face him.

"What does?"

"That you gave up on the clarinet. You seem like a very… determined woman."

She'd been joking earlier when she asked if he was flirting with her, after his comment about her possessing the stubborn tenacity of a scientist. But here it was again.

Then again, he was essentially saying she was thick-headed,

wasn't he? He was just tactful about it, unlike, say, her partner.

Or was Loshak now her *former* partner?

She sighed.

"That might be true about some things. But I also don't have a lot of patience for failure. And playing the clarinet for that semester felt like an ongoing failure."

"Are you this hard on everyone or just yourself?"

Darger stared at him, not sure how to answer.

Finally she said, "Yes."

He laughed.

"I take it that means you're not going to answer the question."

They explored a hallway with a bathroom and a bedroom that had been converted to an office/exercise room. One side of the room housed a desk with a computer and a printer. On the other end, a recumbent exercise bike was shoved in the corner.

The last door Darger pushed through led into Shannon's bedroom. The room featured a matching Craftsman-style bedroom set with photographs of family and friends clustered on top of the dresser. Scented candles on the nightstand. A handmade quilt on the bed.

Darger was still taking it all in when the telltale buzz of a phone set to vibrate interrupted the silence.

She spun around, patting her pocket even though she knew it wasn't hers.

Fowles was peering down at his phone with a look of... Darger wasn't sure what. Alarm? Excitement?

"I have to take this," he said, not looking up. "Please excuse me."

Naturally, this aroused her so-called *innate curiosity*. She watched Fowles move off toward the kitchen where he'd have some privacy for his call, chewing her lip and wondering what was so important.

Darger's gaze fell from the photographs on top of Shannon Mead's dresser to the drawers beneath. She slid one open, rifled through a tangle of tank tops and camisoles. The police had already been through here, would have taken anything they deemed "of interest." But Darger couldn't help poking around, searching for something they might have missed.

Like a diary. That seemed like the kind of thing a bookish extrovert might be into. She closed the first drawer and tugged the next one open, revealing stacks of neatly folded jeans and leggings. No diary.

After checking the last drawer, she took a brief inventory of the closet. It was clear that Shannon had been a fan of prints — florals and stripes and polka dots and plaids. Darger looked down at her blue Oxford shirt and navy pants. Maybe now that she wasn't a Fed, she could incorporate some more festive items into her wardrobe. She picked at the hem of a green paisley number on one of the hangers, tried to imagine herself in it. It could pass for business casual. But then she'd have to get shoes to go with it. Boots wouldn't cut it. And once you were accessorizing your footwear, there was everything else to consider — jewelry, hair, bag, etc.

Darger took a step back from the closet and pushed the door closed. There was a reason she'd never been into fashion. It was just too much damn work. If she bought everything in navy, black, and gray, then she barely had to think when it came to dressing herself.

Besides, she still hadn't decided she was through with the

Bureau. Her little stint with Prescott Consulting might be just that — a stint.

The echo of Fowles' voice rattled around the hard surfaces of the kitchen. Still on the phone.

Finished with her search of the bedroom, Darger's eyes strayed to the window. If she was going to take a look around the outside of the house, she'd better get to it. It would be dark soon.

CHAPTER 9

You wait for her. You don't know why. It has become a habit. One of the stops you make during the day. Walking by her place. Checking on her.

Watching her.

Watching her as much as you can. Every day. Sometimes for hours at a time.

Watching from across the street during the daylight hours. Creeping closer as night falls. Peering through her windows. Your face pressing right up to the glass. The glow of life just on the other side of that sheet of brittle clear. The shadow of her moving through the light, a darkness bending toward your face as though to touch you.

But now she is gone. Away. Off at work or some such thing.

You sit on a bench across the street from her building. Resist the urge to kick at the pigeons pecking around near your feet. It's not an impulse toward some vicious bird attack. You just want to push them a little with the sole of your shoe. Nudge them. Feel them. You don't know why.

Cars rush past on the street. Kick up gusts of wind that feel crisp now that fall is here. And leaves scrape along the sidewalk when the pedestrians pass you by. No one really looking your way.

Often you hide. You're good at it. Sometimes in the bushes. Sometimes up a tree. You peer out from the shadowed places.

But other times you hide in the open. Like here on the bench.

You're not invisible. The people passing by may see you. Let their eyes fall over you. But they do not notice you. They do not think about you. They just keep moving.

You are no one. Nowhere. Nothing. You know this. You can see it yourself when you look in the mirror.

The face drawn long. Narrow. Weak. Cheeks all sucked in and gaunt. And even so the little lumps along your jaw. Adipose tissue. Soft and rounded. The sag of someone older, someone fatter. Eyes that turn down at the corners. Dim. Empty.

You are not worth remembering. Not worth really seeing at all. And you like that just fine.

No. That's not true. You don't like it. But you accept it. You understand it. Understand that it is the way of things in this place, in this world. It exists the way gravity exists, the way the wind and rain exist, the way the moon waxes and wanes.

Your eyes dart back to her place, to the walk leading up to her building.

Empty. Nothing occupying the concrete steps, the sidewalk trailing off into the distance.

She should be here by now, shouldn't she? You think about this. Maybe not.

You can never quite keep track of her schedule. Time won't hold still in a way that will allow it. The minutes speed up and slow down. Never really make sense to you.

But you've sat here long enough in any case. You rise. Tip forward into a walk. Feet pattering over the concrete.

You wander.

You wander through time and space. Not really understanding much of any of it. Not able to grab hold of it, fully grasp it. It all flits around about you, life. An angry, thrashing world. Nonsense, most of it. Meaningless sound and fury.

So you walk. You keep moving whenever you're not watching her, whenever you're not watching her place.

You walk. Especially in the dark. When the city sleeps.

You walk.

You walk the night. Sometimes all night long.

You walk down railroad tracks and alleyways, and when you hit the outskirts of town, you cut across unkempt fields wet with dew. Feel your socks grow damp up to the ankles. Cotton soaking up the moisture like a sponge until your feet are sopping and clammy.

And then you turn around and walk back.

The world looks wholly different at night, in the dark, in the stillness. Unrecognizable. A little scary.

And you stare into the dirty places, the ripped open places, the shadowy places.

The secret places.

All of it painted in shades of black, smudged in gloom.

It's not dark now, though. Not still. Not at all. The day still burns bright around you.

The cars whoosh past in all directions, sheets of wind whipping off of them. The air moves. Alive. Picks up the slack of your shirt and mashes the wrinkles into your chest. The smell of exhaust hangs everywhere here.

And the pedestrians trickle along the cement. All the little ants busy as ever, looking to get back to their hill.

You walk among them, but you remain apart. Something separate. An other.

You like to watch the people. All their energy, all their passion, expressed in facial twitches and hand gestures. Arms windmilling and legs churning for no reason you can figure.

But it's not the same, walking during the day. Not like at night. Not when it's black and lonesome, and you're the only one alive for miles.

So you circle back toward her place. Back toward your bench. Sit.

Your hands are sticky, you realize. You rub them on the thighs of your pants, but it doesn't help. You ball your fingers into the palms and listen to the tacky sound as they peel apart, almost like cellophane. Jelly. That's what it feels like. A thin layer of grape jelly over everything from the wrist down. Did you forget to wash them at some point? Have you showered? Changed your clothes? Been home in the last few days?

You try to think, try to remember, but you can't. The days and nights blur together when you get like this.

It seems, sometimes, like time should stop once in a while. Wait for you. Let you catch up and find your place. But it never does. It rushes on and on and on.

And she appears just then. Her figure taking shape on the sidewalk like a mirage on the horizon, a shimmering thing turning real, turning solid before your eyes. A dark spot in the ether gelling into human flesh.

And she looks good. She's a little bigger now. Not quite the scrawny thing she was back in school. Filling out in the hips and thighs. A little belly. But good nonetheless.

Always that pleasant look on her face, just like when you were kids. The tiniest smile perpetually curls her lip as though she might be thinking about candy and puppies and sheets with absurdly high thread counts at all times.

And it occurs to you that she is not the one you were thinking of. Close. But she is someone else. You get them confused sometimes, these girls you watch. You start to think of all of them as one — a specific one.

One that's a long time gone.

But this one is here, you suppose. Here and now. It's just as well.

And you are moving. Going to her. Not by choice, or at least it doesn't feel that way. You are drawn to her. Pulled to her. Energy grabbing you by the scruff of the neck and carrying you along. Something that is meant to be. Some hand of fate intervening. Impulses firing in your head like cannons.

When you get within an arm's length, she looks at you. Blinks. Blinks again. Three times.

The smile wilts, shriveling like a time-lapse video of a rotting animal, but then it blooms again.

She says your name. You tell her you were just passing by. All smiles.

She invites you in.

It would be rude not to accept, wouldn't it?

She unlocks the door into the hallway of her building and disappears into the opening there.

You hesitate just shy of the doorway. Look back over your shoulder at the pedestrians streaming past on the sidewalk, and something about it makes you smile.

You like to watch the people. There are so many. So, so many. You will never run out.

CHAPTER 10

The kids were still playing hide-and-seek when Darger stepped out from the hushed interior of Shannon Mead's house. She could hear their shrieks and giggles from the doorstep and then caught sight of a streak of red as a girl scampered by in search of a fresh hiding spot.

Darger moved away from the door, the smile fading from her lips as she remembered her task.

Something in her gut told her that the killer, an obsessive type, would have stalked his victims. It went back to the manner of killing. The drowning. Close. Personal. Hands-on. It wasn't the kind of death you'd dole out to a stranger.

No, the killer would have felt like he'd known these women, even if the relationships were only figments in his imagination.

And if she was right, if he'd been here, he might have left something behind.

She strode out to the street first and studied the windows, wanting to know how much of the Mead house one could see from the sidewalk. He might have started out small — driving past or strolling down the sidewalk to get a quick peek at Shannon's life.

The living room featured the largest window on the front of the house. And right now, with the drapes only partially closed, it gave quite a clear view inside.

Turning in a circle, Darger looked for likely hiding spots. Places the killer might have used to watch the house for longer periods of time. Once a quick peek wasn't enough to satisfy his

75

fantasies. But the front was too open, too visible to the neighbors. There were no alleys or empty lots to hunker down in. He might have parked his car on the street and spied from there, but Darger got the sense this was the kind of neighborhood that would have kept an eye out for that sort of thing.

She crept closer to the house now, checking the windows and doors for marks. If the killer had tried to jimmy a lock or use a pry bar to get in somewhere, he might have scratched the paint, dented a screen, broken a lock. But everything looked intact out front. Again, this wasn't a surprise. If he'd tried to get in, the sides or back of the house would have given him more cover from the prying eyes of nosy neighbors.

Darger ducked under the low-hanging branches of a Japanese maple as she rounded the side of the house. The leaves tickled against the back of her neck, and she paused to rub the resulting goose bumps from her forearms. A privacy fence ran around the perimeter of the small yard, separating Shannon Mead's rectangle of lawn from the houses on either side.

The back was the same as the front. Windows locked, screens unmolested.

She started back the way she'd come, eyes on the ground now. Looking for footprints, cigarette butts. Anything that might suggest someone had been here, waiting. Watching.

The yard was grass, a little patchy in spots with a smattering of weeds reaching their spindly arms toward the sky. A row of barberry bushes grew along the foundation of the house. In between the round masses of foliage, the dirt lay mostly bare with the scraggly remnants of spring tulips.

It was something in one of the stretches of sandy ground

that finally caught Darger's eye. She stepped closer to the house. Frowned at the impression in the dirt. It was a perfect circle, maybe a foot in diameter. She traveled the length of the house again, looking for similar marks, but only found the one.

She went back to it. Crossed her arms, thinking. There was nothing in sight that she could see that would make that kind of mark. Something the crime scene techs had done? But what? It had to be something else.

Her eyes roamed higher, up the clapboard siding. There was a window above her. In fact, the circular indentation in the soil was perfectly centered in front of the window. She was near the back corner of the house, which would make this Shannon's bedroom.

Darger backed up across the yard, trying to get a better view inside the window. When she reached the fence, she noticed that one of the boards was broken off at the top. She peered through the gap at the bamboo hedge growing on the other side of the fence.

Among the green, something bright blue grabbed at her. It was a bucket. One of the run-of-the-mill, five-gallon variety.

Darger turned from the fence, took a step away, then whirled back around.

She didn't have a ruler handy, but the opening of the bucket sure looked to be about twelve inches in diameter, a perfect match for the impression she'd found in the dirt.

Excited now, she jogged around to the back side of the fence, eager to get a better look at the bucket. She glanced up at the house. It was getting dark now, and they'd left a light on inside. Darger could see clear into Shannon's house from back here. Through the sliding glass door, she watched Fowles pacing back and forth in the kitchen, phone pressed to his ear.

He had no idea, no sense that he was being watched. A little prickle ran through Darger — half-thrill, half-guilt.

Yes, this would have been a perfect spot for the killer to stalk Shannon Mead. And when he got comfortable, wanted more, he crept a little closer, used a bucket he'd found — or maybe brought along — as a makeshift stool.

How many nights had he watched her? How long before watching in the dark wasn't enough and the urge to kill overcame him?

The bamboo leaves shivered and whispered in the breeze.

Except there was no breeze.

Darger froze.

"Hello?"

And then the bamboo hedge rattled violently, and she could tell the way the movement shifted along the fence line that the person concealed by the foliage was running away from her, trying to escape.

"Stop!"

She pursued, fumbling for her Glock and cursing again that it was not the trusty sidearm she was familiar with. She pulled the 9mm free, and reaching the edge of the fence before her quarry, she held the firearm out.

"Come out with your hands in the air. I'm a federal agent."

Shit. She wasn't really, though. She only had a moment to worry about the implications of not having any official authority to arrest a suspect when the person she'd been chasing stepped out from the hedge, arms raised high.

CHAPTER 11

Glasses sweat on the coffee table. Vodka and orange juice within.

Her place is cozy. Modest. Small rooms with rounded doorways and soft, warm colors on every wall.

Tangerine.

Moon yellow.

Pink seashell.

It's like some place an elf would live, which seems right to you. It seems just right.

She talks, and you talk. The conversation bounces back and forth between you like a tennis ball. A thing to be tended, to be stoked, to be kept alive with constant attention, constant care.

But you know the talk won't last. It never can.

The lulls in between speaking grow longer. Grow thicker in the air around you. Substantial.

And you can feel it. The awkwardness. It's not here. Not yet. But it's close. Threatening. Encroaching.

You lift your glass to your lips. Drink. The orange juice seems sour. Unpleasant. No match for the boozy warmth of the 100-proof Popov that makes your mouth pucker ever so faintly with each sip.

And you look at her. The red flushing her cheeks. A strange look in her eyes.

You study this last detail. Try to read the meaning held there. The eyes open wide and wet. Little flurries of blinks spasming over them but their expression unchanging.

Fear.

She is frightened. She is frightened of you.

You sit back in the little loveseat. The soft cushion bearing the weight of your torso. Propping you up.

You can't.

You're doing it again. Scaring her. Creeping her out.

You always do this. Always scare her. All of them. All of the *hers*.

And your thoughts spiral again. Sucked up into your head. A vortex.

You look down into that well of yourself. The bottomless black hole of self-observation, self-obsession.

Watching yourself watch yourself watch yourself. Endless layers.

Apart from her. Apart from all of them.

An other.

And the sweat brings you back to the moment. That little trickle at your hairline. You dab at it with your sleeve. Try to look nonchalant.

But it's too late. You can see it on her face. It's already over.

After all the time you've waited. The hours and days you've spent watching her, and it's already over. Already past.

You know what she sees when she looks at you, and you can't.

You stand. Lightheaded. Excuse yourself.

Setting your drink on the table. Moving.

You can't.

You glide away from this room. Walls morphing from tangerine to cranberry. The floor seeming to slide by beneath you. No sense at all that your legs are the ones moving you along. Whole body numb.

You stand in the bathroom mirror. Looking yourself in the face. That pouchy awful face.

You can't.

Your eyes retreat. Fall back from that confrontation in the glass. Full of tears now.

And the water spirals into the sink. Thundering out of the faucet. Slapping against the porcelain. Covering the breathy sounds coming out with your tears.

You watch it twirl down the drain for a long while before you head to the kitchen for a knife.

CHAPTER 12

Darger's gun arm lowered immediately.

The person she'd been pursuing, the one she'd chased from the bamboo hedge, was only a little girl.

Still, her heart pounded in her chest. She tucked her pistol in the holster and got down on one knee, in part so she could be eye level with the girl, but also because her bloodstream was so choked with adrenaline, she was feeling a little wobbly.

"Geez, kid. You scared the crap out of me."

It was the same girl she'd seen when she was first coming out of the house. One of the kids playing hide-and-seek. She had on a red t-shirt and denim shorts, and she looked terrified.

"I didn't mean to. It was my turn to hide."

The kid's eyes were wide and wet with soon-to-be tears.

"Hey, it's OK. You're not in any trouble. I just… thought you were someone else."

Surprisingly, the girl's face turned serious.

"The litterbug."

"The who?"

"The man I saw hiding here before. He left a bunch of wrappers. Did you know it takes 20 to 30 years for candy wrappers to decompose?"

"Uhh, no. I didn't. What's your name?"

"Nora."

"I'm Violet," Darger said, aiming a thumb at her own chest. "Can you show me the wrappers?"

Nora led Darger into the natural little pathway between the

bamboo hedge and the fence. It was the perfect place for a kid's secret lair… and also for a stalker to lie in wait. They reached the bucket, and the girl pointed at the crumpled bits of cellophane and foil littering the ground.

Pulling on a glove, Darger plucked up one of the wrappers. It was for a Quaker Chewy Granola Bar. Chocolate Chip.

Nora gestured to a dented Red Bull can near the bucket.

"That'll take over two hundred years to biodegrade."

"Really?" Darger said, eyes scanning all the trash left behind in the little area.

How long had he been watching Shannon? Weeks? Months? However long it had been, she prayed this was his trash. Prayed he'd left a print or two behind.

"And that water bottle," the girl said, "that'll take 450 years."

Darger crossed her arms.

"So you're some kind of environmental expert?"

Nora blushed and shrugged.

"I want to be a marine biologist, and my teacher, Mrs. Potts, showed us a video of a mama sea turtle trying to lay her eggs on a beach covered in a bunch of trash. And one time, I watched a documentary on TV with my parents, where a dead whale washed up on shore and when they cut it open, it was filled with garbage."

"Yeah, we're not always the best at taking care of our planet, are we?"

The girl's hair whipped at the sides of her face as she shook her head.

"Can you tell me about when you saw the man hiding back here?"

Nora scratched her belly, thinking.

"It was a while ago. Right in the middle of summer, when it's still light out at bedtime."

"What time is bedtime?" Darger asked.

"Nine o'clock."

"OK, and you saw the man then?"

Nora didn't answer right away, and Darger saw some emotion flit across her face. Fear? Uneasiness?

She crouched down so they were eye-to-eye again and let her mouth spread into a disarming smile.

"It's alright. You can tell me."

Nora's tiny lips pressed together in a tight line, like she was trying to force the words to stay locked inside. But finally she relented, sagging a little like a deflated balloon.

"I like looking at the stars before I go to sleep. So I can say my wishes. But it was too light out. So I waited until everyone else went to bed. And then I got up and went to the window. And that's when I saw him."

"Was it someone you recognized? Someone you've seen before?"

Nora's brow furrowed into an exaggerated frown.

"I couldn't really see his face. It was too dark. I think he was wearing a hat. Like a winter ski hat. But other than that, it was really just a shadow blob."

"A shadow blob. OK. Could you tell if he was young or old? Anything like that?"

"Not really."

"Is there anything else you remember about him?"

"What about his height? Would you say he seemed taller or shorter than me?"

The girl studied her.

"About the same, I think. Maybe a little taller."

"And how big was he? Skinny? Fat? Muscular?"

"Skinny-ish."

Darger pondered this.

It was the opposite of the conclusion she'd come to at the Shannon Mead crime scene, when she'd determined the killer would have had to be fairly powerful. Could the kid be mistaken? Or was Darger missing something?

"Well, if you ever change your mind about the marine biologist thing, you'd make a great detective."

The kid pursed her lips, all seriousness.

"I'll think about it."

Darger chuckled and waved a hand at her.

"I bet you won this round of hide-and-seek. You should go find your friends, and let them know you didn't turn invisible."

Nora bid her farewell and scampered out of the hedge, leaving Darger alone in the hideout. She got out her phone and put in a call to the local police department, telling them what she'd found and asking that a crew of crime scene techs come out to collect the evidence she'd found.

After she hung up, she glanced up at the Mead house. Fowles wasn't visible in the window any longer, and he'd turned the lights out. He was probably out front, wondering where she'd disappeared to. She turned away from the fence, ready to leave the confines of the bamboo sanctum when something caught her eye.

Right next to the broken slat in the fence Darger had peered through earlier, something was scrawled onto the wood in what looked like black ballpoint pen.

The symbol seemed to be an upside-down heart with a cross through it. Had the killer made this mark? Or had it been one of the dozens of kids that had probably used this place as a hiding spot for games or a retreat from annoying siblings over the years?

Whatever it was, Darger pulled her phone from her pocket and snapped a photo of it. She'd make sure to mention it to the crime scene techs once they arrived.

She found Fowles seated on the front steps. She could tell by the way he perked up when she appeared from around the side of the house that he had something.

"I have something, too," she said, amused at his eagerness. "But you first."

He stood, brushing the back of his pants as he did.

"I just spoke with the lab down in Berkeley. I have some colleagues there that have been developing a system for determining the age of blow fly larvae using gene expression. It allows for a much more precise timeline. They can estimate an age within two hours of the actual."

"That's pretty impressive."

He nodded.

"It seemed the sensible thing to do, given the paradoxical nature of my own findings. And the lab guys were thrilled with the opportunity to aid in an official investigation. They rarely get out in the field."

"What'd they find?"

"They confirmed it. The larvae on Shannon Mead were 34 hours old. Around a day a half. Factoring in the five-day delay introduced by the water, that would put the time of death around 6.5 days before discovery."

Darger rubbed at her brow, suddenly frustrated. It didn't make sense with the timeline of Shannon's disappearance. And yet, there it was.

She glanced up at Fowles. The constant wonky smile he usually wore had been replaced by a grim line.

"Why do you look so down? I would think you'd be glad to be proven right."

He sighed.

"I have to admit to being relieved to know that my original estimation wasn't far off. But it seems a little selfish to feel good about it," he said, glancing back at Shannon Mead's door. "Considering."

"We can't control all of the craziness in the world," Darger said. "We can only do our jobs. Nothing wrong with feeling good about a job well done."

"I guess I'll feel better when it leads to something tangible for the sake of the case."

"True. We're still missing something," she said, clenching her jaw. "The timelines don't quite match up. I hate that."

They didn't speak for a moment, both lost in their thoughts. Eventually, Fowles broke the silence.

"You said you found something?"

"I'll show you," she said.

She led him to the fence behind the house and pointed out the bucket, the food wrappers, the scribbled symbol.

"How long do you think he watched her for?"

Shaking her head, Darger crossed her arms over her chest.

"The kid I talked to said she saw him back in the middle of summer, when the days were longest. That would make it around 3 months before her death, so… at least that long.

Probably longer than that."

Her eyes drifted up to the house again, the dark windows looking like vacant eyes.

She imagined Shannon Mead going about her daily routines. Grading homework and watching Netflix. Baking bread. Never having an inkling that a pair of predatory eyes was watching all the while.

Waiting.

CHAPTER 13

You move. Flee. Leave her behind.

Brisk air surrounds you. Touches you with crooked fingers. Cold and dry.

And the world outside smears together. Bright and strange and bustling. An endless sprawl of concrete and asphalt, of cars and pedestrians.

All of those moving pieces seem to come together now. To writhe as one being.

Society. The world. A wretched thing that spasms there before you. Shudders. Pulses. Like a fly with its wings ripped off.

Squares of sidewalk roll past underfoot. Looks like that broken TV you had as a kid. Like you need to adjust the vertical hold knob to steady the picture somehow.

And your head thrums. Buzzes. White noise like radio static.

Confusion bangs about in your skull. Confusion tinged with the last thrill of the hunt, the last twinge of gratification if that's even what a kill brings you.

The final image of her still burns in your skull. Seared there for always.

Face down in the bathtub. Hair all flat and soggy. Fresh holes perforating her left side where you pressed the steak knife as though to ventilate her torso.

It felt hot in your hand, the knife. And it wanted to hurt her. Wanted to bite and rip and penetrate.

You peeled her sweater off halfway, the waistband pulled up over her left shoulder, the fabric all bunched against that side of her neck. Skin and bra strap exposed. You don't remember doing this, don't remember touching her shirt at all, but you must have. You must have.

And you still feel the struggle in your skin, in the muscles of your arms and shoulders and neck. Hot and jittery. The violence still twitches inside of you. It wants only to lurch forward again and again. To take control and express itself with your limbs, with your fists, with your blade.

And you need to move her. Need to dispose of her. The spent shell that's left of her must be concealed. Destroyed.

But you can't bring her out. Not here. Not like this.

The daylight still shines down from the heavens. Glints off the mud puddles. Brilliant light glittering everywhere. Lighting up this shithole of a city, of a world.

No. You'll have to come back after dark. Move the body when the shadows will aid you. Protect you.

You walk. Try to focus on the concrete cells still rolling along below. Try to block the ugliness of the city out.

It makes you sick sometimes to walk around in this place. To smell the mud smell, the acrid smoke of the industrial areas, the animal musk of all of these people stacked up on top of each other like crabs climbing over one another to get out of the bucket.

Sometimes you can't take it. Can't stand to breathe it in. To let even the vapor of this world touch your nostrils, crawl inside of you, waft its stench in the vacancy of your chest. It assails you whenever you're on the street like this.

You.

You.

You.

It is always "you" in your head. Never "I." You don't know why.

And it's there. Your building. Another brick heap stacked high into the heavens indistinguishable from any of the rest, all those apartment windows like portals into a hundred separate lives, a hundred separate worlds. People living in the same structure yet forever segregated. Strange to each other.

The bricks must have been red once, but the sun has bleached them to a pale pink over the decades. The color of Pepto-Bismol. The lines of mortar look strange etched into that shade. All pink and gray like an aging human body stripped naked.

You see your hand reach for the doorknob, alarmed for a second at the sight of it, as though this flesh somehow wasn't your own. Foreign. Disembodied.

The inside of the building smells like bean soup, just a little, but you're away from the cold. Away from the city. One step removed, anyway.

It occurs to you that the hallway of your building sits between two worlds. A quiet place resting between home and the revolting world. The awkwardness of being in neither always gives you goose bumps. Striking and strange to walk betwixt the worlds. Almost religious.

And now wooden stairs creak as you climb them, your world tilted into an ascent. Three flights of moaning risers and cracking treads, the grains of lumber lifting their voices to squawk at you like birds.

It's an old building. Built just after the turn of the century.

Still standing for no good reason.

You move down the hallway like a camera zooming in. Going slow to build the tension maybe. Almost there.

And the door stands between you and yet another world. A barrier of thin wood just taller and wider than a casket. Painted pale yellow.

You hesitate at this final threshold. Needing, somehow, to muster some fresh willpower to push through and be done with it, to find your way home after another of your excursions.

At last you bring the key to the deadbolt. Push it in. Twist. And the door moves aside.

You shuffle through the doorway. The air feels different than that in the hallway. Warmer.

And the faint bean soup odor fades out. Replaced by the waft of some kind of potpourri in a little decorative ceramic pot on the table just inside your place. You're not sure what exactly the wood chip looking crap is. Its presence here wasn't of your doing.

The door to your cell clicks shut behind you, and you slide off your shoes.

Home. Home is where the heart is. At least for tonight.

You stride down the hall, and there she is. Callie.

Your body feels different when you see her. Some frequency changing in your head like an unseen hand shifting the radio dial.

She stands in the kitchen. Plucking little styrofoam KFC containers out of a plastic bag. Arranging chicken and green beans and mashed potatoes and gravy on two plates.

Strands of dark hair hang down in front of her face. Revealing only the chin, the jaw, the full bottom lip.

She senses your presence in the kitchen doorway. Looks up at you. Smiles.

And that tension leaves your upper back. That twitchy violence vacates your body. Some strange lightness fluttering in your head like dragonfly wings instead. The wind flows in and out of you with ease. No more tightness in your chest to hold it back.

You move to her. Kiss her on the cheek and then on the smiling teeth.

You feel like someone else when you touch her, express affection for her physically. And maybe you are someone else in these moments. Maybe you are.

"I made KFC for dinner," she says, and you laugh a little.

It's one of her recurring jokes. Claiming she made whatever fast food she just bought.

"My favorite," you say. This is what you say no matter what, the completion of the ritual.

You take the plate, and the two of you move to the couch. Watch the news while you eat. Channel 7. They always lead with the blood and guts when they can, so they trounce all the other local channels in the ratings.

The anchors talk about a fatal car crash, a daycare worker charged with child molestation, a local election the polls say will be too close to call. Nothing about the killings tonight, though, which is a surprise.

Still, seeing the graphics flash on the screen, hearing the strange cadence of the anchors, it brings back a twinge of that fear, that loathing feeling you get when you watch them talk about what you've done. Even with Callie next to you, you feel it.

And the picture of the body opens in your head. Slumped in the bathtub. Waiting there even now for you to take care of things before someone finds out.

Other pictures open, too. Flashing in your head like a strobe light.

There was another body you couldn't move. Before this one. And the daylight wasn't a factor in that one. Too big. Too heavy and awkward. A slick sack of flesh that slid out of your grip over and over. Plopped back into the bathwater. Splishy-splashy.

You had to leave it. Had to. Certain it would be the one that got you caught. The nerves made you sick for the next week. Flu-like symptoms that wouldn't go away. Your whole body going hot and cold at the same time, sweating and shivering.

But the days and weeks went by, and somehow, nothing happened. No headlines. No Channel 7 news van camped outside the place to get their shots of the grisly details. Nothing at all.

Could it be there still? The corpse submerged in bathwater. It'd be broken down by now. Something closer to a skeleton face down in a puddle of goo, a pool of liquefied human remains. Something that would smell a whole lot worse than bean soup.

Callie clears the plates.

"Are you staying tonight?" you say, your voice smaller than you want, weaker than you want.

Her smile looks sad.

"Not tonight," she says. "But soon."

You try to smile back, try not to sulk too openly, try to conceal the wound peeling open your ribcage, laying bare your heart.

Even if she has redecorated your place, she has to hide this thing between you. So she says. You don't know why.

Sometimes you think that if she just stayed with you, moved into your place, you wouldn't go do the things you do. Wouldn't need to.

But maybe not. Maybe that's not true at all.

She comes to you. Sits on the couch next to you. Touches you. Her frail body leaned up against yours.

"Tomorrow. I'll stay tomorrow night. I promise."

She is a wispy thing. All made of sticks with a soft layer stretched over them. Feminine. As light as one of those desserts that's mostly made of air. As light as a soufflé.

And her arms circle around you. Squeeze.

CHAPTER 14

Darger's foot tapped impatiently in the hotel elevator. She couldn't wait to get to her room, to take a bath and wash away the sticky feeling she always got from traveling.

Her stomach lurched a little as the elevator came to a stop with a ding. The brushed steel doors parted, and Darger exited into a hushed hallway that smelled like lemon cleaner. The wheels of her suitcase bumped over the seams in the carpet.

She paused in front of her room, swiped her keycard in the electronic lock, and waited for the light to turn green. When it did, she wrenched the door open and entered.

It was a dumpy little room with striped carpet and ugly, boxy furniture that might have been considered contemporary twenty years ago. The sink was placed in the sleeping area, with only the toilet and the tub/shower combo in the bathroom proper. A true sign, in Darger's opinion, of a high-class joint.

Margaret Prescott's assistant had asked Darger what kind of hotel she preferred, if there were any particular amenities she requested. The girl seemed surprised when Darger told her to book whatever was cheapest. Had it been another one of Prescott's tricks? Or maybe that was supposed to be one of the perks of being a private consultant.

Whatever the case, Darger didn't fool herself into thinking that a higher-priced place was any less grim and disgusting as a cheap one. The fact was, she was still resting her head on a pillow a thousand other people had slept on and showering in a stall a thousand other people had been naked in.

Hotels were hotels. They never felt like home. And she wasn't here to soak in the hot tub or to laze around in a robe ordering room service. There was work to do.

She switched on the TV. It was one of those house shows. The woman — Darger assumed she was the prospective buyer — was whining about the lack of a walk-in closet in the master suite and the color of the granite countertops in the kitchen.

"And where are my all-stainless appliances?" the woman demanded.

First world problems, Darger thought, snorting derisively as she slid out of her jacket and kicked off her boots. She considered changing the channel, then changed her mind. She only really wanted some background noise.

The bathroom light flickered twice before coming on all the way. Darger swept the shower curtain out of the tub and turned on the taps.

Water gushed from the chrome fixture, sounding like a thousand drums playing at once as it struck the bottom of the basin. She wiggled her fingers under the stream to get the temperature right, then stood back and watched the burbling flow. Her mind churned along with the water.

Finding the stalker's lair behind Shannon Mead's house could be big. Very big. They might be able to get fingerprints or even trace DNA from the wrappers and bottles. And then there was the symbol scribbled on the fence. Was it a clue? A calling card left by the killer?

She bounced on her feet, feeling giddy. The way she always felt when a new piece of evidence was discovered.

And then she thought of Shannon Mead's mother. The anguish on her face as she wept for her daughter. Darger's glee vanished as quickly as it had appeared.

She peeled off her socks and left them in rolled up balls on the floor. As she unbuttoned her shirt, she considered the puzzling evidence Fowles had found. Why did the blow fly larvae on Shannon Mead suggest she'd been dead for almost seven days when she'd only been missing for five?

Darger picked up one of the complimentary bottles of bath and shower goop on the counter, squinting to read the miniature print on the label. Honey Lavender Conditioner. She set the bottle down and picked up the other two. They were the same flavor as the conditioner, but one was labeled Shampoo and the other Body Wash.

"That'll do," Darger said to herself.

Twisting off the lid, she gave it a sniff and then squirted a blob of the body wash into the tub. It frothed and foamed for a few seconds, and then most of the suds dissipated. Not exactly a bubble bath, but at least it smelled a little nicer than the straight tap water, which reeked of chlorine.

She stood by and watched the waterline rise millimeter by millimeter. As it crept closer to the overflow drain, Darger leaned over the edge of the tub and turned off the water. The rumble cut out, and the sing-songy voices of a TV commercial filtered in through the open bathroom door.

The water rippled beneath her, and she caught sight of her reflection in the undulating surface, remembering the sensation that had overwhelmed her when she'd gazed into the water at the spot where they'd pulled Shannon Mead from the river.

Darger froze, a prickle of precognitive awareness running through her before the revelation hit her fully.

The autopsy confirmed that Shannon Mead's cause of death

was drowning. There was water in her lungs.

The only way she could reconcile the insect evidence with everything else they'd found was to imagine the killer drowning her in the river, taking her somewhere else, and then returning her to the river. And that made no sense.

But what if he hadn't drowned her in the river after all?

What if the water in her lungs had come from another source?

Darger stared down into the bathwater.

Like a bathtub.

She closed her eyes, and a revised version of the kill scene played out in her head. He stooped, not next to a river this time, but a bathtub, pressing his victim's face down near the drain, water cascading from the faucet to obscure her features.

Darger bolted for the door, bare feet slapping over the tile, then remembered her phone was in her pocket. She wrestled it out, found the phone number for the local medical examiner's office, and dialed.

The phone gurgled in Darger's ear as she paced the room. Her bath was forgotten. Everything but the mystery of Shannon Mead was forgotten.

CHAPTER 15

Time changes when you're alone. Especially in the dark. It elongates. Stretches out like a soft piece of taffy. Loses what little meaning it ever has for you.

You can't help but check your phone over and over. Lighting up that blinding screen in the gloom like some kind of beacon. The minutes slow until they stop, until you're certain they'll reverse soon, that time will go backward. That the fabric of this plane will unravel or cave in or implode. That nothingness will conquer everything at last. Put humanity out of its misery.

You hunker down in your bed. Wrap yourself in scratchy blankets like some shroud. Offer yourself to the gods of slumber. But you know they won't oblige, know that sleep won't take you. Not for a while, anyway.

So you blink and fidget. You stare into the black, stare up into the wall of shadow where the ceiling should be. It looks hollow now. Empty.

The whole world is empty. Whenever you're alone, the world is empty.

But you're not uncomfortable, even if you're feeling weird. You're used to it.

The restless part of you wants to head out. To walk the night. To see all there is to see in the dark, when the rules of the day no longer exist.

But you can't. You can't. You need to rest for now. You'll go out in your truck tonight. Move her in the deepest dead of the night while the rest of the world sleeps. Much later than this.

So you sleep off and on. Shake yourself awake every fifteen minutes or so.

In fractured dreams, you ride a gondola through the canals of some foreign city. Pushing it along with your oar.

The boat drifts atop the water. Cuts through its surface like one of your knives. Picking up speed.

The sensation of movement dredges up half-formed memories of riding in a canoe as a kid, feeling exhilarated by the way you both moved on and through the water. The way the pointed tip of the vessel seemed to part the lake and push some of it to each side. Excited by that. And yet scared to death the aluminum thing would tip and dump you into the black depths. Tumble you down into nothingness. A kind of wet abyss that could steal your breath.

This canal, too, seems deep. Treacherous. Unknowable.

The water churns everywhere around you. Dark water that lurches and spits along the side of the boat. Murky. Almost looks like it's boiling in places. Disturbing somehow to look at.

And strange concrete structures rise up from the water's edge. Towers. Tall cylinders that reach for the heavens, these strange tubes set against the horizon. Silos, you think. And you know, somehow, that these buildings house people. Stack them right on top of each other like freshly split firewood. Pile them up into the sky.

You can imagine the smell of it. All of that humanity confined in tight quarters like that. Something akin to a barn smell, an industrial livestock smell, a factory farm nightmare, but a version that would retain some particularly human note to it. A bodily stench like Swiss cheese and dirty socks entwined with the normal manure odor.

You adjust your grip on the oar. Fingers tightening around the wood so hard that it almost hurts.

And you plunge the thing toward the bottom of the canal. Thrust it as hard as you can. Dig around a bit.

But you feel nothing solid. Nothing beyond the resistance of the water itself. If the bottom is down there, you can't reach it. Can't find it.

And still you pick up speed. Accelerate even without rowing. The water froths now where your iron prow slices into it. A violence to the act that you find exciting.

The concrete changes on the horizon ahead. The walls of the canal closing in. Forming a tunnel. A hole in the wall that the water flows into.

You stare into the mouth of the thing. The darkness. And you resist the urge to steer the boat off to the side. You know you must enter this cave for good or ill.

You swallow hard as the threshold nears. Brace yourself for whatever comes next.

The concrete hole swallows the little gondola. Seems to suck it right up.

And the darkness is total. Endless. Stifling.

You can feel it somehow on your skin. A cold prickle that worms into your pores.

You know that it means you harm, the darkness. That it holds you in contempt.

You drift for what feels like a long time. The little boat rocking beneath you. The water rockier now than it was before.

Somewhere ahead a glow takes shape. Yellow light

flickering on the concrete, on the water. A lantern hanging from the rounded wall.

And getting closer, that glittering light shimmers off the walls. Shiny. Wet walls. Wet and red.

Bloody.

The concrete arch above you seems to morph as you go deeper. Flesh now coating the cement. Seeming to thicken over it like some kind of fungal growth advancing the length of the tube.

Skin. Human skin.

Some of it has the texture and shade of a pale inner arm. Hairless and milky white.

Other parts consist of red flesh like the inside of a lip, glistening as though lubricated with saliva.

And your heart thrums now. Rapid fire beats. Your chest heaves.

Somehow you know that all of life's mysteries await at the end of this length of tunnel. All will be revealed.

You want to know where this goes more than you've ever wanted anything, and yet you remain deathly afraid of actually arriving there.

But whatever you want or don't, this journey ends soon. You can feel it.

Terrifying and exhilarating.

The lantern light fades. The dark returning. But you can see the end ahead. A semi-circle of light.

The boat slams atop the water now. Popping up and crashing down, the wood of the hull cracking with each thrust. The waves hateful and violent around you. You huddle and hold on.

And as you near the light at the end of the tunnel, you snap awake. In your room. In your bed.

It's time to move the body.

CHAPTER 16

Darger climbed into bed and felt the sheets slowly go from cool to warm to match her body heat. She tried closing her eyes, but they kept snapping back open to stare at the popcorn ceiling, that ugly texture emerging from the shadows.

Alert. Wired. The opposite of sleepy. She may as well have just chugged three coffees and washed them down with a Red Bull.

Her mind raced around the same loop over and over. She couldn't stop thinking about her new bathwater theory, tumbling the potential ramifications in her thoughts, even if she wouldn't know anything for certain until tomorrow morning. Her gut believed the hunch, though, and during those fleeting moments when she could keep her eyes closed, she could see it happening that way in her mind's eye. Her instincts told her that it fit, that it was right.

She'd had to call two different after-hours phone numbers at the medical examiner's office before she finally got through to an actual human being. The woman's voice was flat and atonal, but a bored-sounding secretary was still better than an answering machine.

"Dr. Kole won't be in until morning," the woman had said.

"I understand that, but I just have one quick question, and it's very important."

Something in Darger's tone must have been convincing, because eventually the woman agreed to call Dr. Kole at home. It was another twenty minutes before he returned Darger's call.

With the man himself on the line, she explained who she was and what case she was interested in.

"OK, sure. Shannon Mead. What about her?"

"The water in her lungs. Did you take a sample?"

"That's standard procedure."

"Was it tested?"

"I'm sure you know that we take dozens of samples that are only tested if it's deemed significant to the investigation."

"Is that a *no*, then?"

An irritated sigh rustled over the line.

"It's just that I think in this case, testing the water might be significant."

Darger went over her theory, and the silence that greeted her when she'd finished had her worried Dr. Kole had hung up on her.

"Hello?" she said, once the quiet had stretched into several seconds

"I'm here." Dr. Kole grumbled. "It's an interesting hypothesis, that's for sure."

There was another pause before the doctor spoke again, like he was still considering it.

"I'll test the water samples, but it will have to wait until morning. Your call interrupted a family dinner."

Darger punched the air in celebration and felt a sense of victory.

"Right. My apologies. And thank you for taking time to speak with me. Please enjoy the rest of your evening."

But the triumphant feeling had faded. Hours later, lying awake in the dark, Darger only felt antsy. Her mind wanted to explore this new possibility, follow the varying paths of logic, but she knew it was unwise to get ahead of herself. Nothing had been confirmed. She had to wait.

Waiting was not Violet Darger's strong suit.

She'd always been impatient. She walked up escalators and fidgeted in long lines and snuck peeks at Christmas gifts. She purposely arrived at the movies five minutes late so she wouldn't have to sit through the previews. And she repeatedly burned her mouth on pizza even though she knew going in it was still too hot to eat.

Even with her relationships, Darger could see now that she'd hurried several of them to a premature end. First with Luck and then with Owen. It was like she saw the end coming, maybe not soon, but at some point... so wasn't it better to just get it over with already?

Rip off the band-aid. Pull the plug. Get on with it.

Part of her liked moving on, getting away from the drama, running back to her job and tuning the rest of the world out. It felt like here in Oregon, consulting, she could live between the worlds. She could get away from all her big decisions, put them off. Drop the world. And she liked that.

Because all of those big turning points loomed just around the corner, waiting to leap out and shape the rest of her life. Would she go back to the FBI or not? Would she rekindle things with Owen or Luck? Would she find a way to appease her mother and spend more time with her, find a balance between the demands of her family and career?

For now, she could get away from all of those people, relationships, choices. She didn't have to pick, and she liked that. She could live in stasis indefinitely. She could worry about it later.

Maybe the real core of her problem revolved around the notion that relationships always meant giving up some element of control, even the non-romantic ones. Her mother, for example, who was always griping at her about working too hard, like she should half-ass her job or something.

Even Loshak had a tendency to boss her around, to dole out life lessons whether she wanted them or not. He'd been the one to suggest this hiatus from the Bureau in the first place.

"Get some distance and figure out what you want. Because the FBI isn't going to change. If you have the notion in your head that you're the one to try to change it, let me correct your thinking. It's too big and too stupid to change. All bureaucracies are. That's a fact of life."

And she'd listened to him. And now she was here, squirming restlessly in an unfamiliar hotel bed, with her eyes wide open and gazing up at the textured ceiling.

Waiting.

CHAPTER 17

The city is dead.

It's so late. So dark. So quiet.

Your truck rumbles through the night. Engine growling out warnings. Tires swishing over wet blacktop. Headlights piercing the gloom.

There are others out in the downtown area. Nocturnal creatures on the hunt, always looking for something. Hungry animals snuffling around at all hours. All the people who can find no satisfaction in the daytime, in the straight world. The junkies. The drunks. The whores. The thieves. The sick. The loathsome. They all come out after dark.

But you encounter no other vehicles over the last six blocks of the journey. No pedestrians. No sign of movement apart from the shifting shades of the traffic lights.

The city looks strange when it's empty like this. Disturbing and stark. The puddles of red light spread over the vacant concrete, crawl up the brick and glass walls of the buildings. Apocalyptic.

You park in the alley running between her building and a high-rise tower of offices. Tuck your truck in the shadows along a dumpster and still its engine. It coughs a little as the rumble dies out.

And then the quiet is overwhelming. Makes your skin crawl. And you hesitate for a moment with your hands on the steering wheel, electricity thrumming in your palms. Jaw muscles clenching over and over. Rhythmic spasms you feel in your cheeks.

Eventually you will yourself to exit the vehicle. Step out into the night. The hair on the back of your neck tingling all the while. Spittle flushing your mouth and squishing loudly when you swallow it.

The air is thicker here. Dank. Catches in your throat, in your nostrils, cool and wet and heavy.

You walk up a set of cement stairs to the big front door of the place, pulse glugging in your neck hot and fast. The bricks of the building look orange with the streetlights glowing on them, the color of the push-up popsicles you ate as a kid.

And now an arched double-door stands between you and the place you need to be. Dark stained wood. Beveled details. Ornate. About eight feet tall with a big window cut out of each side.

Yellow light spills through the glass to light you up. Makes you feel exposed. Vulnerable.

And you fumble with the keys on the key ring you swiped from her place. Her keys.

Try one in the deadbolt. No love.

Your eyes keep flicking inside the building as you work through keys, part of you sure that someone will appear there next to the mailboxes just inside the door. A witness to your presence. Someone who will see your face.

But no one shows. On the fifth key, the door swings open, and you cross the threshold, arms and legs now trembling from the adrenaline.

The air is dry inside. Warm. A little stuffy. It smells like caramelized onions.

You don't dally in the common area. You climb the steps

two at a time, light on your feet, soundless and quick, gaining confidence now.

On the fourth floor, you make a left, glide down the hall, find her room number, 4H. You wrote it on the palm of your hand earlier with a sharpie to be sure. No confusion.

Now another door stands in your path, but this one is not so tall, not so intimidating as the first. It's painted dark green, the color of the seaweed wound around a sushi roll, and the gold letters mounted above the peephole glitter a little in the hallway light.

You crack it open on the second key. A wedge of darkness pouring into the opening, somehow looking like black smoke to you in this moment.

You step inside, ease the door shut behind you. And you wait now for your eyes to adjust to the dark inside. No lights. No evidence. Nothing that could be seen from outside.

In time, form emerges in the void. Shapes and contours congeal in the darkness. Solidify. Become real.

You move through the living room, round the corner to the bathroom. Slow and steady. Fingertips grazing along the wall beside you.

The bathroom is deep within the unit, far from any window. That makes it darker than the rest — a black hung up around you like a thick loam — but it also means you can turn on the light without consequence.

Your hand reaches for the light switch. And for just a second, you picture the tub vacant. The body gone. Like the dead thing just got up and walked away.

But the light hits. Blinding. Awful. And even through squinted eyes you can see the shape of it.

The body remains where you left it, face down in a powder blue bathtub. Hair all spread out in the couple inches of water you drowned her in.

And then you see the other person in the room. Your double.

The face in the mirror stares back at you. You look upon this nocturnal creature, not unlike all the other hungry animals out there tonight. Ugly. Restless.

And you see the desperation in the eyes. The deflated balloons for cheeks. Fleshy bulges so saggy they look like they'll fall off any day now. Just peel away from the skull and flop to the ground.

You rest your hands on the edge of the sink and lean in close to see every pore in the swollen face. Every little hair in the eyelashes. Those strange whorls in the irises of the eyes.

In ancient times, they thought of mirrors as bewitching pools, as powerful conduits, as strange portals to distant dimensions. They thought mirrors were magic.

And maybe that's true in a way.

Maybe it makes more sense for there to be two of you in this room. Facing each other. Looking at each other. The protagonist and the antagonist of this story. The hero and the villain. Both.

Finally there's someone for you to talk to, right? Someone to spill all of this internal monologue onto, this tidal wave of words perpetually crashing in your head. The only person fit for the job. The one you're always talking to anyway.

You.

You.

You.

You're looking at you. The only person you really know, and the only one who knows you. The perfect match, or so you suppose.

The absurdity of it makes you smile. Both of you flashing those yellow teeth, crinkling your eyes at each other. An inside joke.

You blink a few times. Ease back from the glass. At last your attention turns back to the corpse in the tub. The soggy thing. It doesn't smell yet, at least.

You know from experience that the body will be all stiff now. Rigor mortis tightening the muscles into something hard, something more akin to wood than meat. Knotty lumber stretched over a skeleton.

And you know it will be difficult to move her. That you'll have to wrap her in blankets and try to be discrete.

The stiffness means carrying her would be impossible. You can't sling her dead weight over your shoulder like you would with a limp body. There's no way to help distribute the weight. She's a big awkward statue more or less. Your arms alone couldn't bear her down three flights of stairs.

Could you drag her? Down three flights of stairs?

You close your eyes, and your imagination whirs to life. Playing movies in your head. You picture her blanket-wrapped skull thudding down step after step, bone hammering against wood. Thump. Thump. Thump. How many stairs would it be? 45? Perhaps 60? 90? And you see the peepholes up and down the hallway all going dim, the neighbors rushing to see what's causing all the noise.

Not good.

You lick your lips. Have to think.

There are only so many ways to get out of this place.

There's one thing you could do, you think. Still risky, but not so bad as the steps.

You pry the petrified corpse out of the water, tinted pink from the blood. Hook one hand under a crooked elbow and the other under the hip on the opposite side. Turning her as you lift. Plopping her on the bathmat.

Christ. Heavy. Even this second plan will provide its difficulties.

Her face looks bloated. Maggoty white beneath the strands of sopping hair. The texture grotesque. Marshmallow soft.

Even just a few hours in water can inflict so much change upon flesh. A metamorphosis that's hard to believe when you see it close up.

And you strip her bare. Peel the clothes off those stiff limbs, forcing the joints the best you can. You don't know why. It's just the way it has to be.

She lies before you. Naked. Dead.

And it occurs to you in a flash that you could do anything to her now. Anything.

No one would ever know. No one would ever see.

Anything.

You could get a knife from the kitchen and carve her up. Dismember, decapitate, disembowel her. Stretch her guts around this apartment like rubber bands.

You could touch her wherever you liked. Fuck her. Though, looking at the maggoty flesh, this one does not appeal to you even a little.

You could even cook her and eat her. Slice off something or other and fry it up.

Anything. Anything you wish.

And even though you want none of these things, there is a sublime feeling attached to these observations. An overwhelming feeling that is somehow mystical. A sense of incredible awe — religious awe — tinged with horror.

Because none of the rules are real. None of them. It's all pretend.

Society creates all of these rules, etches its order onto nature, onto chaos. But it's not real.

And what you feel here isn't power. You wield power over her, yes, but that is not the source of this spiritual feeling.

Freedom is.

Your freedom here is utterly absolute. Society cannot touch it. No one can. Not all the king's horses nor all the king's men.

That's the arresting truth in this moment, and something about it is both sacred and terrifying. Awful and beautiful.

You flick the little metal switch beneath the faucet, and the water in the bathtub lurches, begins to spiral down the drain with a slurping sound.

Sucked down that metallic portal in the porcelain. Transferred to some other place far, far away.

You track out of the bathroom's glow. Feel around in the half-light to find blankets in the closet in the hall.

And now you kneel on the linoleum. Swaddle the rigid thing like a baby doll. Cover that bloated face with a green and black striped afghan, the milky flesh tone still visible through the little holes in the knit pattern.

A second blanket blocks her out for good, and there is a relief in that somehow. Just covering the body instantly eases some tension in your shoulders, in the muscles just beneath your sternum, makes it a touch easier to breathe.

And maybe that's why we bury the deceased, you think. Put them someplace out of sight, out of mind.

They're like collapsing stars, the dead. Imploding things that threaten to suck us into their gravity fields. Swallow us up.

The dead body becomes the physical manifestation of the dying of the light. We have to plant them in the dirt as a way of keeping their strange darkness at bay.

You scoop her under the arms and drag her out into the dark of the living room, eventually lifting and propping her up on the couch.

And you rest a moment. The strain of just those few seconds of work beading perspiration on your brow and top lip, constricting your breath enough that now you need a moment to get it back.

When you're ready, you move to the window hung above the couch where the body lies. You feel around for a latch for what feels like a long time, fingers finally finding the hooked metal piece and sliding it aside.

Now the window comes open, and a slice of that thick night air comes whooshing into the apartment, into your face. Cool and damp. Heavy like a wet blanket.

You poke your head out. Look down at the world three floors below.

This side of the building faces the alley where your truck is parked, though you can barely see the vehicle at the moment. It's dark. All swathed in shadows.

Straight down from your vantage point, you find that bushes run just along the building. Boxwoods shaped into a clipped box. A row that traces along the perimeter of the brick structure like a moat. And that's good, you think. That'll work just fine.

You lift the body again. Arms shaking as you elevate it to the window frame and balance the center mass the best you can on the sill.

Again your head dips, eyes descending to that row of bushes below. They'll break the fall, maybe. Prevent the loud thud, at least a little.

Something about all of this reminds you of watching TV as a kid, some curly-haired late night host dropping a watermelon off the roof of his studio, watching it belly flop and explode against the asphalt below.

You don't think the corpse will burst like that. The rigor would seem to work in your favor. The rigid thing might break here and there — crack like concrete — but it will mostly keep together, mostly stay within the confines of the blankets.

Or so you hope.

You take a breath and hold it. Heartbeat picking up speed. Stomach knotting and untying over and over.

It's better to be quick about this, you know. You're reasonably concealed in the darkness, but you should get out of the window as soon as you can.

Still, you need to give this a second. Let your nerves catch up.

When it feels right, you give the body a little shove.

It teeters on the edge for a fraction of a second, and then gravity rips it out into the void.

CHAPTER 18

The clock on the bedside table glowed blue-white. It was a harsh glow, and Darger couldn't help but feel like the numbers were taunting her.

3:42 AM, they sneered. *You are never going to fall asleep.*

She rolled away from the clock, shut her eyes. Focused on breathing slow and deep.

That lasted for three minutes, and then she was looking at the clock again.

The numbers chortled. *3:45.*

Darger turned onto her back, mashing her head into the pillow with annoyance.

She just needed to clear her mind. Think of something relaxing. Tranquil.

A peaceful forest. Wind whispering through the trees. And a waterfall. The steady drum of the water showered down from a cliff above into a wide, shimmering pool. A fine mist hung in the air where the water struck the rocks below. Something bobbed gently in the water. It was pale and fleshy, and as it turned in the swirling current, Darger saw a woman's head. It was Shannon Mead's jawless face.

Darger's eyes snapped open.

Fuck it.

She threw off the covers and crawled over to her bag, sliding her laptop from its case.

If she couldn't fall asleep, she could at least try to get some work done.

She ignored the triumphant laughter coming from the digital clock.

Propping her pillow against the headboard, she leaned back and clicked through the files Prescott had sent. There were a lot. Hundreds of crime scene photos. Pages of autopsy reports. Dozens of witness interviews on video. Multiply it all times three. Darger had been over all of the photographs and skimmed most of the documents, but she hadn't made it through all of the videos yet.

She scanned the list of video files, trying to remember where she'd left off. Opening one, she caught a snippet of the interview with Maribeth Holtz's husband.

"Can you think of anyone that might have wanted to hurt your wife?" the detective asked.

Mr. Holtz's head was shaking from side to side before the question was even finished.

"No. No one. My wife hated conflict. I don't think I ever heard her even raise her voice at someone."

Darger closed the video. She'd watched that one already. The man had seemed numb with grief. Despite the fact that he wasn't crying, he kept wiping his face. Like maybe he could swipe away bereavement the way windshield wipers dispersed rain.

She skipped past the next two videos and tried another. This one featured Holly Green's parents, the mother dabbing at her face with a tissue and rocking herself back and forth from time to time. One claw-like hand gripped her husband's arm as if holding on for dear life.

Darger had watched that one on the plane. At one point, she'd caught herself on the verge of tears and shut it off to avoid the embarrassment of crying in public.

When she opened the next file, she almost gasped.

The witness in the video bore an uncanny resemblance to the photos of Shannon Mead — when she was alive, that was.

The woman sat in the interview room, barely moving. Unblinking and calm. She seemed distant. Detached, almost. And when she spoke, her voice was small. A girl's voice — hesitant and timid.

DETECTIVE: Thank you for coming down here Miss Porter. Do you mind if I record this interview? Makes it easier on us and you. We don't have to come back, asking the same questions over and over.

PORTER: No. I mean… no, I don't mind.

DETECTIVE: Great. Thanks. Could you state your full name and age for me?

PORTER: Kathryn Renee Porter. I'm thirty-seven years old.

DETECTIVE: Now, tell me what you saw the evening of September 19th.

PORTER: I was leaving work, and I saw Shannon -- Miss Mead -- in the faculty parking lot.

DETECTIVE: And you work up there at the school, is that right?

PORTER: Yes. I'm part of the custodial staff.

DETECTIVE: OK. Do you remember what time it was?

PORTER: I think it would have been about seven o'clock. The lights in the parking lot had just come on.

DETECTIVE: And what was Miss Mead doing? How did you come to notice her?

PORTER: It was pretty late. Aside from us and some of the

maintenance workers for the district, people aren't usually around that late. Not unless there's some sort of function after school. So her car was one of the only cars in the lot.

DETECTIVE: How did she seem to you? Scared? Pissed off? Worried?

PORTER: No. She was… I almost want to say relaxed. She was like that. Always smiling and upbeat. She came to me once after one of her kids stuck a Mentos in her Diet Coke. She was soaked head to foot, but she was still smiling.

The detective interrupted.

DETECTIVE: Sorry, say that again? A *what* in her Diet Coke?

PORTER: You know... Mentos. The, uh, freshmaker. It's a candy. Or a mint, maybe? I'm not really sure. It comes in a long roll, like Lifesavers. Apparently they have a very volatile reaction with Diet Coke. It creates kind of a Coke volcano.

DETECTIVE: And the kid did this on purpose?

PORTER: Yes. He said he'd seen it on YouTube and thought it would be a funny prank.

DETECTIVE: Was he trying to... I don't know, get back at her for something?

PORTER: Oh, no! No, everyone loved Shan- Miss Mead. There wasn't anything malicious in his intent, I don't think. The student was quite upset, on the verge of tears, and she was actually comforting him. Which I thought was pretty forgiving considering Miss Mead was the one covered in Diet Coke. She just kept chuckling about it and patting his shoulder. She called it an "impromptu science experiment." I don't know many people that would react that way. I certainly wouldn't have.

Nodding, the detective scribbled something on his pad of

paper.

DETECTIVE: Back to the evening of the 19th. Did you talk to Miss Mead?

PORTER: Yes, I asked if everything was OK. She said her car was acting up. I offered her a ride or to use my phone to call someone. She said, No thank you, that someone was coming to get her.

DETECTIVE: Did she say who it was?

PORTER: No.

DETECTIVE: She didn't mention Uber, or that she'd called her boyfriend or anything like that?

PORTER: I don't think she had a boyfriend.

DETECTIVE: No?

Kathryn Porter tucked a strand of hair behind her ear.

PORTER: I mean... we never talked about it. I just assumed... she didn't seem the type.

DETECTIVE: What type would that be?

PORTER: I don't mean anything by it. I only meant that she was very... 'proper' isn't quite the right word. She just always struck me as very modest. Virtuous. I can't imagine her traipsing around town with some man.

DETECTIVE: Would you say you two were friends?

PORTER: I don't know. 'Friendly' might be a better word for it. We'd say hello when we passed in the halls. And we had our little jokes.

DETECTIVE: Jokes?

PORTER: Oh, well... our hair? I got my hair cut a few months back, and I guess the kids thought we looked alike after that. So she started calling me her twin.

Kathryn's cheeks got a little pink. A nervous smile flickered briefly over her lips and then disappeared.

PORTER: Just one of those silly things, really. We don't actually look like twins, of course.

It was true. Despite her initial reaction, the more Darger watched, the more she realized it was mostly the hair that caused her to see any resemblance. Both women had blunt-cut, shoulder-length hair, dark brown and parted in the center. Kathryn was less dainty than Shannon, who had an almost elfin appearance with her heart-shaped face and small, freckled nose. Shannon's chin came to a point where Kathryn's was more square, with a heavier jaw. And according to Shannon's driver's license, she was 5'3". It was hard to tell in the video, but Kathryn looked taller and more athletically built. Shannon Mead had been soft and feminine. Kathryn Porter was all sharp angles.

Horsey was the word Darger kept thinking, which she knew wasn't all that kind. But it was true. Something about Kathryn's long, hard face reminded her of a horse.

Kathryn continued speaking in the video, twisting her hands in her lap now.

DETECTIVE: And did she say anything else to you?

PORTER: Not really, because her ride came just then.

DETECTIVE: You saw the car?

PORTER: Only from a distance. It was coming down the driveway to the school, and Shannon pointed and said, "That's my ride."

DETECTIVE: Did you see the driver at all?

PORTER: No. Like I said, it was only from a distance that I

saw the car at all. As soon as she pointed it out, I said goodbye and drove away.

DETECTIVE: What did the car look like?

PORTER: It was getting dark, and I don't have the best eyesight. It was definitely a... what do you call a regular old car? Not a truck or station wagon?

DETECTIVE: A sedan?

PORTER: That's it! A sedan. And I think it was maybe brown or red? Something sort of warmish. Not blue or green.

DETECTIVE: OK. And could you tell anything about the driver? Male or female? How they drove?

The woman shook her head.

PORTER: No. I'm sorry. I—

The woman's words seemed to cut off as if she were being choked. Indeed, her whole body seemed to tense, fingers closing into fists. Her chin quivered, and Darger thought she might be on the verge of a panic attack.

But then she collapsed, shoulders slumping forward.

PORTER: I just can't stop thinking about that night. I feel like it's my fault.

DETECTIVE: It's natural to feel that way. A lot of witnesses do. They feel like if they'd done something different, then maybe the person would still be alive.

With a shaky hand, Kathryn wiped at her top lip.

DETECTIVE: But you didn't kill her. You tried to help her. And what you're doing now? That's helping her too. Because everything we learn puts us one step closer to finding this guy. OK?

She nodded, and then the detective took something from his pocket and slid it across the table to her.

DETECTIVE: I want you to take this card. It has my cell number on it. If you think of anything else, please give me a call. Anything at all.

They stood, and the detective opened the interview room door and ushered the woman out.

Darger brought out her own case notes and jotted down a few things. Questions to ask. Leads to follow up on.

Check school surveillance footage.

Uber/local taxi service? Call for ride logs.

She yawned and glanced at the clock. It was almost 4:30. Her meeting with the locals was scheduled for ten o'clock. If she went to sleep now, she could squeeze in close to five hours.

Or she could go over her profile again. Give it one final polish.

She heard her mother's voice in her head. *You're working too hard.*

And then Loshak. *There has to be balance, kiddo. Turn the computer off and get some shut-eye.*

Fuck balance, Darger thought, and picked up her laptop.

CHAPTER 19

In the city, all the lights keep the night at a distance. Hold the real darkness somewhere up above. A perimeter glow that protects civilization like a dome.

Not out here in the woods. The dark surrounds you, envelops you, presses itself into your skin.

The night is right on top of you.

Somewhere ahead, the river sloshes and babbles. Wet sounds that somehow reassure you in the dark. Something to focus on, to work toward.

It's close. The end of all of this is close. Just a few more minutes.

You drag the bundle out toward that sound, moving slowly through the thicket. Elbowing your way through various types of plant life.

The woods seem sinister at night. Thick and dark. Nearly impenetrable. All angular shadows and insect sounds. A tangled mess to pick your way through.

A place empty yet cluttered, vacant yet teeming with life and sound. Strange.

And the blanket keeps getting snagged on branches. Prickers gripping the fabric and holding on. Sticks prodding the corpse and springing off, wobbling for a long time after. Some of these you can muscle through. Rip out of like a running back breaking an arm tackle. Others you have to stop and detach.

Dead leaves hiss where the bodyweight glides over them.

Raspy sounds. And you realize that you're blazing a trail now, mashing everything down, wearing something of a groove into the soil.

You have to remember to kick at this disturbed path on the way back. You won't have time to erase it or even conceal it much, but you can muss it up some. Better than nothing.

And even the night's chill cannot fight off the body heat you work up in this process. You have to stop a second and put your hands on your knees. Breathe. Let the sweat sluice down the back of your neck.

The river is close now. You can see it somewhat in the moonlight. A dark flutter not so far away.

It occurs to you that you don't know why you go about it this way. Disposing of the bodies in the water. Rivers and lakes and ponds. Why?

There are probably forensic advantages to this. Destruction of evidence and the like. The washing away of fingerprints. The water's effect on body temperature and the rate of decay throwing off any ability to surmise an accurate time of death.

But you weren't thinking of these things the first time you lowered a corpse into the wet. Not at all.

It just seems like the way it's supposed to be. You put the dead in the water. Natural, somehow.

There's some feel of a ritual to it. Something religious or spiritual about being submerged in the water.

It feels final. That's all. Putting them in the water feels final.

And the water sounds dislodge strange memories, strange feelings you only experienced as a child. Playing with your toys in the bathtub. Safe and warm. Innocent. Pure. The wet sounds take you back to this place, even if the context is different.

Maybe it takes them back to that place, too. These girls. You put them in the water, and they can be innocent again. Maybe.

You can make them pure again. Can make them clean.

You grab two fistfuls of blanket and pull the body the last few feet to the water's edge. Rest it there on the precipice.

Up close, you can see the moonlight shimmering on ripples along the top of the river. Little shards of light that undulate and shimmy. Painted and erased over and over.

And even in this morbid moment, life is beautiful and dark and strange. So stimulating. It's almost too much to bear.

You lift the bundle the best you can, get it a couple inches off the ground so it's clear of any foliage. And you thrust with all of your strength to launch it out into the coursing stream. Arms flexing. Legs pistoning. Hips torquing.

And then all that weight is gone from your hands. All that tension released.

The bath sounds are everywhere. Splashing and gurgling. But it's not quite right. Not how you remembered it. This water is cold. The pitch of the wet sound is off.

And it smells just a touch like a swamp up close. No scent of baby shampoo to be found here.

The blanketed corpse bobs in the water. Dunks under and pops back up. Flutters along. Half-twirling as the current catches it and starts to pull it along. The white of the blanket almost glowing in the dark.

You squint to watch until the darkness swallows it for good, to watch it for as long as you can.

CHAPTER 20

Darger glanced at her phone, checking the time again. She'd arranged to meet Fowles here and had arrived early. Usually she was only early for appointments when she was nervous. Was she nervous?

Excited, for sure. She hadn't told Fowles what the medical examiner had found in the water sample from Shannon Mead's lungs. In fact, she hadn't told him about the test at all. For some reason, she'd wanted to tell him in person. So the breakthrough would have maximum effect.

A bell clanged over the front door as someone entered the small restaurant. Darger looked up, but instead of Fowles, two women entered, one young, one old. The younger woman held the door for her elder, who stooped over a walker. She had a wild tuft of white hair on her head. Coupled with the curvature of her spine, she looked like a palm tree being blown sideways in hurricane winds.

Darger picked up the cappuccino in front of her, swirled the steaming elixir to redistribute the foam, and took a sip.

It occurred to her for the first time that she was behaving a little like her partner. Withholding information so she could reveal it with a flourish? Straight out of Loshak's playbook. But it was different, wasn't it? She wanted Fowles to know that it was his work that had led to it. The inconsistencies he'd found with the insect activity on the body had been the first loose thread, a thread they'd pulled on until the knot unraveled and the truth became clear.

The doorbell jangled again, and this time a familiar figure stood on the threshold. Fowles paused just inside the door, head swiveling to search the place. The cornflower blue eyes lit up when they spied Darger sitting in the back corner. He gave a small wave and headed over.

The spunky barista with the messy ponytail bounced over to take his order. Fowles ordered a cold brew with milk, no sugar.

"We have two different cold brews — light and medium."

"Light, please," Fowles said.

As the barista skipped off to make the coffee, Darger shook her head.

"What?"

"As well as being born with a natural curiosity, I also have an innate suspicion of anyone who prefers light roast. There are three things in this world that are meant to be dark: coffee, chocolate, and the night."

Fowles chuckled and shrugged.

"To be honest, I don't drink much coffee. Makes me jittery. I usually stick to tea."

"Not a coffee drinker? Now I'm even more dubious."

The waitress dropped the coffee off a moment later before scampering away to another table. Darger let Fowles take a sip before she gave him the news.

"You were right."

"About?"

"Shannon Mead was indoors when she died."

He froze with his cup halfway between the table and his mouth, eyebrows furrowing in confusion. He set the mug back on the table.

"How do you figure that?"

"I was thinking about what you said, about the larvae not being consistent with a body that's been in the water since the time of death. And then I was drawing myself a bath and—"

She saw the realization ripple over his features.

"A bathtub!"

Darger nodded, grinning.

"I called the M.E. and asked him to test the sample they took from Shannon's lungs. The old fart made me wait until morning, but he did it. It was municipal tap water."

Fowles wiped a hand down the side of his face.

"Do you ever feel guilty for getting this giddy about a breakthrough in a case? It seems wrong, in a way."

Darger shrugged and gulped at her cappuccino.

"It's not exactly a barrel of laughs, this kind of work. I figure we have to squeeze a little joy from somewhere. Otherwise we'd probably all just kill ourselves after five years of slogging through the grimness."

A sad smile touched the entomologist's lips.

"I suppose you're right. So what's next on the agenda?"

"I'm supposed to meet with the locals this morning. Present my profile."

His eyes sparkled with sudden interest.

"Would you mind an extra member in the audience?"

Darger sighed.

"I guess not."

He quirked an eyebrow. "You don't sound wild about the idea."

"No, it's fine. I've always hated public speaking is all. Also, this place doesn't have donuts."

"Sorry? Donuts?"

Darger rubbed her forehead.

"Oh, it's this stupid theory my partner has." She shut her eyes and shook her head. "He always brings a metric fuck-ton of donuts to task force meetings. He's got this whole philosophy about it and not just the part about the locals being friendlier after you've bribed them with food. He analyzes the flavor choices — what it means if you choose a jelly-filled over a chocolate sprinkle. How there's an unspoken one-donut-per-person code that almost everyone respects."

"I still don't understand what the precise problem is."

"I can't find donuts. Nowhere in this whole town."

"That seems odd. Every town has a donut shop."

"Oh, they have one. Apparently it's award-winning, too. But it's closed for renovations."

Leaning back in his chair, Fowles seemed to give her predicament serious thought. He tapped a bony finger against his chin.

"What about the grocery store?"

Darger's eyes went wide.

"God, no. Loshak has a very strict policy against grocery store donuts. It would be blasphemous."

She let her shoulders slump and gestured with a tic of the head toward a display case near the door of the cafe.

"I was hoping they'd have some here. But all they have are muffins. I can't bring muffins to a task force meeting."

"Why not?"

"I don't know. They seem so... dainty and pretentious."

Fowles laughed.

"I'm being serious."

"I know. That's why it's funny," he said, then made an attempt to suppress his amusement. "I think you're going to have to decide between the pretentious muffins and the abhorrent grocery store donuts."

Darger looked him dead in the eye.

"Muffins."

Fowles rapped his knuckles against the table.

"An excellent choice. Now, as for your fear of public speaking, I have a trick for that."

Darger squinted at him suspiciously.

"I hope you're not about to suggest I picture you in your underwear."

"As if you weren't already," Fowles said.

Darger couldn't hold back a snort. That settled it. He was definitely flirting with her now.

"In all seriousness, I took a course that required public speaking, and this really helped me. I used to get so nervous before speaking that I made sure to bring along a toothbrush so I could freshen up after my inevitable vomit session."

"Yikes," Darger said. She finished off her cappuccino with one final gulp. "OK, let's hear it."

"It's pretty simple, really. You stop thinking about yourself as a speaker. Stop thinking about it having to do with you at all. You are merely a vessel for delivering information. You are here to present your profile... to move the information from Point A — your brain — to Point B — the brains of your audience. Focus on how to do that best, and you'll forget about everything else."

"That sounds... too easy."

"It takes some practice to shut that voice off. The voice that keeps telling you to worry about whether you're wearing the right shoes or what if you stumble over your words and sound like an idiot. But if you focus on the outcome, focus on explaining the material, everything else has a way of falling to the wayside."

The chair scraped against the floor as Darger pushed away from the table. She tossed her empty cup into a nearby waste bin and then turned to face Fowles.

"I'll try it. But if that fails, I might have to fall back on the picturing you naked thing."

"A minute ago I was in my underwear."

"I move fast, Fowles," she said with a wink. "Try to keep up."

CHAPTER 21

The Sandy Police Department was housed in a small, two-story building across the street from a Lutheran church. Inside, everything had a rustic-but-modern feel. Wood plank floors, a big stone fireplace in the waiting area, and bright natural light streaming in through the windows. It seemed more like a real estate office than a police department.

There was a young woman ensconced behind a front desk made of glass and granite. She took their names and asked them to have a seat. But before Darger and Fowles even reached the little cluster of chairs in the waiting room, an older man with an ample belly strode out of a back office and intercepted them.

"Good to see you again, Mr. Fowles," he said with a nod, then thrust a chunky hand at Darger. "And you must be Ms. Darger. I'm Jeff Furbush, Chief of Police."

The Chief's grip, like pretty much every law enforcement officer Darger had ever encountered, was firm and steady.

"I was dubious about hiring an outside consultant agency. I'll confess to that. But it's already paying off. First with the evidence you found in the bushes at the Mead house. I'm a little embarrassed we missed that."

He released her hand and took the default cop position of standing with his legs shoulder-width apart and his hands on either side of his belt. This not only kept the path to his sidearm open, it made him appear wider. Dominant body language — universal among mammals — probably subconscious in this case.

"Could have been anyone's mistake. I only stumbled on it by accident, really."

"Don't be modest, now. I'm a firm believer in giving credit where it's due. When it comes to testing the water from the Mead girl's lungs… well, that just never would have crossed my mind. What made you think to do that?"

Darger was used to butting heads with the local law enforcement, so this level of praise came as a bit of surprise. She blinked a few times, almost suspicious. When the shock wore off, she angled a thumb at the entomologist.

"Actually, Fowles is the one that deserves all the acclaim. He's the one that discovered the inconsistencies in the bug stuff. If not for that, I never would have considered the bathtub angle."

Fowles shrugged and rubbed the back of his neck.

"It was a joint effort. I think we can share the credit."

The Chief's bushy eyebrows twitched like a pair of restless caterpillars.

"Well, I'll tell you what. Without another lead, this sumbitch probably would have stalled out. The investigation, I mean. I don't mind admitting to that."

Furbush gestured at the bakery box in Darger's hand.

"And who gets credit for these?"

Darger lifted the lid, revealing the twelve muffins.

"There's blueberry and apple cinnamon."

He licked his lips, eyes growing wide.

"I could lie and tell you that I'm watchin' my figure, but…." Chief Furbush said and plucked a muffin from the box.

He took a bite and led the way to a small conference room

located just beyond the front desk. Furbush paused and addressed the secretary through a mouthful of muffin crumbs.

"Marcy, could we get a fresh pot in the conference room?"

"Of course, Chief."

Darger and Fowles found two empty seats in the conference room while Chief Furbush introduced his staff and updated the group on the two new breakthroughs: the trace evidence found outside Shannon Mead's home and the water sample results from the M.E.'s office.

"Of course, we'd be nowhere without the keen eyes and bright minds of our two consultants," Furbush said. "I say we give 'em a round of applause."

A smattering of clapping echoed around the room. Darger let her gaze wander over to Fowles, who winked. The warm welcome they were receiving was almost baffling to her. She wanted to take it at face value. To revel in feeling like an appreciated member of the team.

But the cynical part of her brain started to dissect the dynamic the same way Fowles might pick apart an insect he was studying. She wondered if the fact that she was here as a consultant and not as a Fed was part of it. In theory, Sandy PD was her employer — they'd hired her, through Prescott Consulting. And they could just as easily fire her if they didn't approve of her work. They had control. So maybe it was still a pissing contest, with the balance of things just a little different than usual.

She glanced over at Fowles again, caught the lopsided smile playing on his lips. Or maybe she should forget about the power dynamics for a minute and just appreciate the camaraderie.

The scattered applause petered out, and Furbush suggested that Darger go over the profile.

She turned to Fowles and handed him a stack of printouts.

"Can you hand these out for me?"

She stood, tugging at her sleeves as she approached the head of the long conference table. Facing the group, she flashed on her first case with Loshak. She'd had to present her profile to the task force solo, and she'd done a fine job of trampling all over the toes of the locals. It was strange to be here without him. Left to navigate this case alone.

But that wasn't right. Loshak wasn't the one who'd left now, was he?

She cleared her throat and gestured at the entomologist, who was distributing the copies of her profile like she'd asked.

"Fowles is passing around hard copies of the profile, but if anyone wants a digital copy for your phone or computer, just let me know."

Was it her imagination, or did her voice sound small and weak, with just the slightest waver to it? She had the urge to bring her hand to her mouth so she could chew her nails. Wouldn't that make for a good intro to her profile.

Fowles caught her eye then and gave a little nod. She remembered the advice he'd given her earlier.

Focus on the profile. On delivering my information into their brains.

She'd spent the early hours of the morning refining it. Getting it right in her head. Organizing the pages of scrawled notes into a cohesive narrative. She could do this. She was prepared.

Darger took a deep breath and began.

"The probabilities suggest we're looking for a white male ranging from 25 to 40 years old. Probably average to large in terms of build and in decent shape. Remember he's got to be strong enough to hold the women down and athletic enough to carry or drag them to the dump sites. All of the victims have been petite women, under 5'4" and 120 lbs or less. He doesn't have to be The Incredible Hulk, but he's definitely no 98-pound weakling, either."

Glancing up from her notes, she was glad to find all eyes locked on her, unblinking. Good. She hadn't put anyone to sleep yet.

"Usually we paint these guys as loners. No friends. Probably not much interaction with family. I don't think that's quite right here. I think this might be a wolf-in-sheep's-clothing kind of guy. He has maybe a handful of casual relationships. Probably not genuinely close, mind you. But he'll be the guy that people will say, 'Bob? A murderer? I never would have guessed! Sure, he was a little odd, but…'"

Darger waved her hand dismissively.

"The evidence and nature of these crimes all but scream two words to a profiler like me: obsession and chaos. We're talking about an incredibly focused, driven, manic individual. A stalker. Someone who watches people and wants to incorporate them into his rich fantasy world, which is where he prefers to live and spend as much of his time as possible. And yet the murders themselves probably seem to come out of nowhere. Even the killer, I think, might be surprised at his actions. He doesn't enter the situation with murder in mind. Something — some kind of external stimulus, probably — pushes him to it at some point. Like a switch getting flipped in his head. Something snaps, and he kills."

She snapped her fingers.

"That's not to suggest these crimes are random. Nor are they pure crimes of passion. Parts are planned. We have evidence he was stalking Shannon Mead. It's likely he stalked the others as well, for weeks or even months. He has to be somewhat meticulous to get away with following these women, with watching them in their homes. And even the manner of killing proves forethought. If he's killing them by drowning them in the bathtub, then he's got to incapacitate them somehow. He's got to fill up the tub. After he drowns them, he has to transport them to the dump site. There's a ritual here."

Darger frowned, thinking she was getting ahead of herself. She went back.

"But it starts with the watching. He follows them, fantasizes about them. And that satisfies him for a while. I doubt the fantasies are the violent sort. This is not a sexual sadist we're dealing with. He probably imagines very tranquil, conventional scenes. Snuggling on the couch watching a movie together. Walking through the door when he gets home and her waiting to give him a peck on the cheek, with dinner ready on the table. He doesn't think he wants to hurt them. Doesn't fantasize about the killing in any direct way."

Darger paused and took a sip of water. One of the patrolmen — he was Mantelbaum, if she remembered right — piped up with a question.

"So like… he thinks he's in love with them?"

"Yes. He probably does."

A look of disgust crossed his face. "What happened to asking a girl out for coffee?"

Darger shook her head.

"He's too insecure for that. The rejection would be too painful. So he stalks. Follows. Watches. And he gets these girls enmeshed in the fantasy. Pretends they're lovers. There's a possibility that impotence, or a fear of impotence, or maybe just a fear of sex itself plays a role here. He might not envision them as lovers at all. His fantasies might be purely PG-rated."

"Jesus."

"We haven't encountered piquerism on this case, but it reminds me of the phenomenon. In certain murders of women, the killer will insert objects into the victim's body, primarily the vagina, breasts or anal cavity — the act is known as piquerism, which is French for 'to prick.' In some cases, like Andrei Chikatilo and Albert Fish, it presents as a sort of a fetishization of stabbing, a link between stabbing and sexual gratification."

Her throat was getting dry now, and she stopped for a drink of water.

"But for another subset of these kinds of killers, particularly those who insert random objects into the victim's vagina, their fear of asserting themselves runs so deep that they act it out without grasping the sexual component at all. To them, the expression of violence is more infantile. An urge without meaning. They don't consciously connect the penetration to the concept of rape or any kind of repressed sexual desire, and they achieve no sexual pleasure from the act. It's almost like their brains disassociate from sex and act out these bizarre violent behaviors in place of any kind of normal sexual outlet."

Everyone fell quiet for a beat after that. Finally, Fritz Kwan, the younger of the two detectives in the department, raised a hand. She recognized him from some of the witness interview videos.

"You said before that it's like a light switch getting flipped on when he kills. What flips it?"

"Rejection would be my best guess, be it imagined or real. If the object of his fantasies rejects him, in real life or in his head, it breaks the reality he's been crafting for himself."

"And it pisses him off," Detective Kwan said, his tone somewhere between a question and a statement.

"Yes. He gets angry, and the violence becomes a way to reassure himself of his power over the situation. It's probable that he incapacitates them first. Knocks them out, probably by a blow to the head, considering none of the toxicology reports for the victims showed drugs or alcohol in the system."

Darger crossed one arm under the other and rested her chin on her hand.

"If we ever get a chance to talk to this guy, I wouldn't be surprised if he claims to not remember doing it. He'll say he blacked out during that initial moment of violence. But the actual killing, the drowning of the women, he'll remember that in great detail," she said. "This murder by drowning… it is very personal. Very intimate."

She let her eyelids fall closed for a beat, collecting her thoughts.

"It takes several minutes to drown someone. He could use a gun. Or a knife. There are a dozen different ways you could, for lack of a better phrase, get rid of someone. More quickly. More cleanly. He chooses to hold them down while they fight for their last breaths. And he's chosen that method for a reason. He enjoys it."

Glancing down at her notes, Darger continued.

"The fact that he's chosen the river as a dump site suggests a comfort with water. He might be a fisherman or a boater. Maybe a swimmer. Someone outdoorsy. Probably goes hiking or camping in his spare time. A truck or SUV or maybe a van would make transporting the bodies more convenient."

After another sip of water, she continued.

"In terms of his early home life: overbearing mother, probably violent and emotionally abusive. It wouldn't surprise me if the family was oppressively religious. Drowning the women, depositing them in the river… it's almost like a baptism. And that would have made Shannon Mead an ideal victim. He would have seen her as the picture of purity. The perfect woman. Pious and chaste and devoted to work, family, and God."

She'd saved her best point for last, and she straightened as she got to it.

"We have one ambiguous tie between victims so far. Holly Green attended Sandy High School. Shannon Mead worked at Sandy Elementary and was last seen in the parking lot behind the building. Different schools, same district. It could be that our killer's work relates to the schools. Making deliveries… something that would take him to more than one of the schools in the district."

Darger flipped the page of the profile she'd written up and found she'd reached the end. That was it. She'd done it. And Fowles had been right. If she just focused on the information, she barely thought about the fact that she was addressing a group of people.

She set down her notes and was about to ask if there were any questions when Marcy, the secretary, took a hesitant step into the room.

"Chief Furbush?"

Furbush stood, hitching his belt up.

"What is it, Marcy?"

"I didn't mean to be eavesdropping, honest. It's just... the door was open."

"If you have something to say..."

"I sort of overheard what was being said... about the girls being drowned in the bathtub."

"We don't know that it's a bathtub for sure. But go on."

"It's just that, back in '99, there was a girl in town that was murdered. Christy Whitmore. And this all reminded me of it is all."

With a sigh, Furbush propped his fists on his hips, clearly annoyed that Marcy wouldn't just get it all out at once.

"Why is that?"

"Well because she was found drowned in the bathtub. They never caught the guy that did it."

CHAPTER 22

You drive around after the body is gone. Go out on the back roads south of town. A stretch of rural flatlands pocked with crappy homes and vast expanses of grass. A few trailer parks sprinkled in for good measure.

Muddy driveways seem to dominate this area. Brown gashes leading up to every shithole house. That smooth black kind of mud that never seems to dry all the way, instead ranging from chocolate milk runny to oatmeal thick as the weather permits.

But you barely see these things along the roadside. Too sucked into that dark galaxy spiraling in your head.

You grit your teeth when you remember it. The violent encounter. The water splashing around her. The little twirls of pink drifting out of the wounds in her side.

And then the jettisoning of the spent shell. The blanketed thing thrust out in the water. The current taking her. The river doing away with her for good.

Feels like you were under a spell when it happened. So stimulated as to have moved without thought, without free will. Some unseen force gripping you around the shoulders, directing you.

It's confusing to think back on it, to remember. You don't know what to make of it.

The images in your head are striking, titillating, and vexing all at once. Somehow you can only replay them over and over, relive them again and again. Stare into them like the meaning

145

might pop out of there eventually. Some explanation for any of this.

Day has broken somewhere in the midst of this internal rant, a process you recognize only vaguely from your vantage point deep within your thoughts.

A pink dawn cresting the horizon. Bars of light shooting out of that strange orb to sprawl over the asphalt before you, reaching out to vanquish the night.

You wonder, sometimes, what Callie would think if she knew. Would she disown you? Hate you? Fear you? Turn you in?

Probably. It would make a certain amount of sense.

For other people, the darkness inside themselves stays mostly covered up, maybe. Mostly blocked from their view. They can only see glimpses of it now and then.

Like when Callie saw that Channel 7 news story about a guy who let his dog freeze to death last winter, she got so upset, so disgusted, she said she hoped they put him to death. Send him to the gallows, the electric chair, the firing squad. Cut off his fucking balls first. Or shove a red hot poker up his ass.

Anything. Anything.

Make him hurt. Make him feel pain. Make his suffering last and last and last.

And you could understand that. The story was pretty pitiful. The pup had tried to crawl under its house in the end, tried to dig down into the cold, cold ground. It was the only way it could think to keep warm, to survive.

Anyway, her outburst wasn't so different from the feelings you have sometimes, was it? The dark impulses that come over you without warning, that seem to compel you to act out in ways you don't really understand.

Other people could never see that you are both of these things, though. The one who loves Callie and the one who goes out to kill. You are both at once. Everyone is both at once.

Gentle and violent. Light and dark. Love and hate.

Just as she is a kind and gentle person who periodically has these violent fantasies about people who abuse animals or molest children. Sweet and funny but still with that streak of darkness somewhere in there. She is both.

We all hold that inside of us, you think. That lust for violence, for vengeance. That urge to lash out, to maim, to kill. Sometimes it doesn't quite make sense to us, and sometimes it hides where we can't see it.

But it's always there. Always. The darkness is always there.

You blink now, noticing how bright it's gotten outside. The sun is fully risen, and it beams down from behind a bank of clouds.

You've been driving around for hours without even realizing it.

This always happens after. After a kill. You seem to lose yourself for a time. Like an unanchored boat drifting out to sea. Floating aimlessly.

And you know that you should get home, get cleaned up, but you're not ready. Not ready for your thoughts to slow down, not ready for this to be over.

You want to understand it first. Even if you know you can't, you want to keep moving. Keep going until you understand.

CHAPTER 23

Darger sat forward in her seat, staring at Furbush's secretary with intensity. She wanted to hear more about this cold case.

"When was this?"

Marcy's eyes shifted between Darger and Furbush now, bright with nerves and perhaps a little excitement at finding herself the center of attention.

"1999. May, I think."

Wrinkles of disbelief lined the Chief's forehead.

"You remember it down to the month?"

"It was just before we... before I graduated. Christy and I were in the same class. It was all everyone talked about for the rest of school through commencement. Our class planted a Crape Myrtle in front of the auditorium and dedicated it to her. There's a plaque and everything."

Darger turned to face Furbush, feeling a growing excitement in her gut. Finding a connection to a cold case was just the kind of thing that could break an investigation like this wide open. But they'd need to see the files first.

"Do you have the old case files here?" Darger asked.

"It was before my time, but I'm sure we do. The thing is, 1999 would still have been mostly paper. This department only went fully digital in 2007, but not all the old stuff has been transferred over," Furbush said, then paused and exchanged a glance with Marcy. "We'll have to check the records room."

Picking up on the hesitation, Darger crossed her arms.

"Is that a problem?"

"Well, we just moved into this building about six months ago. The records room is still in need of... a bit of organization."

"It's in total disarray," Marcy interjected. "It'll take me some time to locate the file in that mess."

Fowles had been so quiet for the last several minutes that Darger had nearly forgotten he was there. When he spoke from just behind her right shoulder, she jumped a little, startled.

"I can help look," he offered.

Furbush clapped his hands together.

"Excellent."

As Fowles followed Marcy out of the conference room, the Chief assigned various tasks to the rest of his men until only Darger and the two detectives remained.

"What's the status on the evidence recovered from the Mead place? The candy wrappers and whatnot?"

Portnoy, an older detective with a large, coffee-colored birthmark on his cheek, answered.

"I know they recovered a partial thumbprint from one of the bottles. They're still working through all of it."

"We swabbed everything for DNA," Kwan added. "It'll be a few weeks before we hear back from the lab on whether there's anything to analyze."

"I know I'm playing catch-up here," Darger said, "so forgive me if I'm rehashing work you've already done."

"Go ahead."

"I was wondering if there was anything noteworthy on the school surveillance cameras the night Shannon Mead disappeared."

Detective Kwan was already shaking his head.

"The only outdoor cameras are mounted at the entrances and exits of the school. Neither parking lot is visible in any of the footage, so we can't see the car that picked her up. But we do have Shannon Mead on camera leaving the school at 6:47 PM."

"What about the witness? Kathryn Porter?"

"She's on there, too. She comes out about ten or fifteen minutes after Ms. Mead."

Darger nodded, satisfied that they'd been thorough on this front.

"Any chance she called a cab that night?"

"We checked her credit cards. No record of paying for a ride," Furbush explained.

"What about talking to the cab companies directly? See if any of their drivers remember a pick-up at the school?"

Furbush pawed at his chin with a thick-fingered hand.

"Wouldn't hurt. There are only two local cab services in town, and I can't imagine they routinely get called out to the school."

He waggled a finger at Kwan and Portnoy.

"Why don't you two explore that avenue?" he said, then turned to Darger. "And while we wait for Marcy and Fowles to unearth that old case file, I think there's someone you and I can talk to. Someone who would know the Christy Whitmore case intimately."

((

Chief Furbush's predecessor, Bart Milton, had been on the force at the time of the Whitmore murder. He'd retired six years ago, but he still lived in town. Furbush found Milton's phone number in one of the old department contact sheets and gave him a call. The former Chief of Police said he'd be happy to fill them in on the case, so as Marcy and Fowles headed up to sift through the files in the records room, Darger and Furbush climbed into his Explorer and drove out to Milton's house.

Milton lived in a small cottage in the outskirts of town, with a nice view of the Sandy River out his back door. An elderly golden retriever lounging on the porch got slowly to its feet as they exited Furbush's SUV.

An old man with a pair of hairy caterpillars for eyebrows and a waxed handlebar mustache greeted them at the door.

"Come on inside. I'll make some coffee."

He pointed to a mat near the door where they could leave their muddy boots. Darger slid hers off and set them beside the orderly row of items already there: rubber galoshes, Reeboks, loafers, and a pair of polished black boots of the same type Milton had probably worn with his police uniform when he was still Chief.

In socked feet, Darger and Furbush padded after Milton into the kitchen of the small cottage. Like the rest of what Darger had seen of the place, it was clean and sparse. There was a sort of military efficiency to the way things were organized. There were no dirty dishes to be found on the counter or in the sink. A single bowl, mug, spoon, and saucepan dried on a rack nearby. The remnants of a bachelor's breakfast, which he promptly cleaned up as soon as he was finished.

Milton pressed the button on an electric kettle. Almost instantly, it began to rumble and gurgle. His eyes flicked over to Darger.

"You a Fed?" he asked.

"Uh, sort of. I'm a consultant at the moment," she said. "Is it that obvious?"

"For me, it is. Just something you get a feel for after a few decades in law enforcement. I can walk into a crowded room and the cops stick out at me like a porcupine on a nude beach."

Darger snorted at the colorful analogy.

Milton turned and gestured at the dog, who had followed them inside and now stood watching them from the kitchen doorway, tail swaying back and forth in slow arcs.

"Daisy don't show it much, but she's happy as a clam you're here. We don't get too many visitors."

Darger wondered if he was voicing his own loneliness through the dog. Daisy's muzzle was upturned into a lazy canine smile, sure, but she looked happy the way a lot of dogs always looked happy.

"Anyway. The Whitmore case," he said. "I remember it well. Never sits right when a case goes unsolved, but there are always a handful that really stick with you. Christy Whitmore was one of those, for me. I think about her probably once a week. I'll drive past her mother's house or the tree they planted out at the school. Can't help but feel like I missed something."

The kettle came to a full boil, hissing and spitting. Milton switched it off, opened the cabinet, and plucked three mugs from the shelf.

He filled each cup three-quarters of the way with hot water, then added a generous spoonful of instant coffee from a jar, stirring to dissolve the brown crystals. He handed one of the mugs of murky brown liquid to Darger and another to Furbush.

"Dress it up how you like it," he said, gesturing to a half-gallon of 2% milk and a jar of sugar he'd set out on the table.

Darger added a splash of milk and took a sip.

About the best thing she could say about it was that it was hot. It looked like coffee, and even kind of smelled like coffee, but the texture was all wrong. It was watery, with a strange chemical sweetness and powdery mouth-feel she always noted with instant coffee.

"Why don't we go sit in the sunroom and talk?"

He led them to a room on the back of the house with wall-to-wall windows offering the best view of the river out back. It was furnished with a set of wicker furniture — a sofa and two chairs. Milton took one of the chairs while Darger and Furbush shared the couch.

"I imagine the Whitmore murder was a big shock in a small town like this," Darger said. "The violent crime rate must be pretty low."

Both men nodded. Milton blew over the top of his cup, took a sip, and then spoke.

"I was a detective up in Spokane before I came out here. And you're right. This place was a cakewalk by comparison. The kind of town where no one locks their doors. Where they add stoplights less due to heavy traffic and more as a conversation piece. But the Whitmore murder got people scared. I had a sense that everything changed after that."

Daisy plodded into the room and plopped down by Milton's side, chin resting on her paws.

"Happened at the Whitmore place. Upstairs bathroom off the guest room, one that didn't get much use. They found her face down in one of those big clawfoot tubs that'll probably outlive all of us. Hair all fanned out in the water. Body bruised up pretty good. Best we could tell it'd happened in the afternoon — the water temp made the time of death tricky to pin down to anything more specific than an 18-hour window — but nobody found her until the following evening. Her mother, of course."

Eyes on the ceiling, Milton went on.

"I still remember her 911 call. Hysterical. A shrill sound in my ear, gurgling out syllables that didn't seem to be forming words. Took me more than a full minute to make out what she was saying."

His lips twitched after that, but he said no more.

"Did you like anyone for it? Back then, I mean?"

Milton reached down to pat Daisy's head, stroking the red-blonde fur.

"All dead ends. We looked at the family first, given the nature of the crime. The father was out of the picture from a young age, living in New Zealand. Or maybe it was Fiji. Somewhere out there in the South Pacific. We ruled the mother out right away because she'd been at work at the time of the murder. She was a nurse. Pulled a double-shift at the nursing home she worked at the day Christy died, otherwise she would have been discovered sooner. No siblings or other family in the area."

The former Chief took a long pull from his coffee cup and swallowed with a satisfied sigh.

"There was an ex-boyfriend, some other classmates we gave a once over. Nothing came of it. We gave one other fella a look-see, name of Bradley Wright. He was known around the neighborhood as someone to hire for odd jobs. Cleaning gutters, fixing leaky toilets, and so on. He'd done a little roof repair for Ms. Whitmore the year before the murder. We did a little digging, turns out he was a registered sex offender. Gross Sexual Imposition was the actual charge, from back in Ohio, which was apparently where he hailed from. The prior was twenty years old at that point, but we gave him a good look anyway. Thought we had our guy for a hot minute, too, but he ended up with a pretty solid alibi. And then everything just seemed to dry up."

Darger turned to Chief Furbush.

"Might be worth a shot to see if Bradley Wright is still in the area."

"Oh, he's in the area, alright," Milton said with a decisive nod.

Darger sat up a little straighter. "Yeah?"

"He's got a place out at Fir Hill."

"Shit," Furbush muttered, then glanced at Darger. "Pardon my French."

"I don't understand. What's the problem?"

"Fir Hill is a cemetery," he explained.

"Bradley Wright is dead?"

Darger's glance drifted over to Milton, who nodded.

"Died a little over five years ago, if memory serves. Got drunk and smashed his F150 and himself into smithereens out by Milham Park."

Darger swallowed into an empty stomach. She'd sensed something, a lead, and now it was snatched away.

He must have picked up her disappointment.

"I'm sorry I don't have more for you. I mean it when I say that the Whitmore murder has been stuck in my craw since the day I walked into that bathroom and found her all bruised and battered in the tub. I know how it is to want to find a lead, a suspect, anything and to come up empty-handed."

As they bid Milton and Daisy farewell, Darger clenched her jaw. She felt the unanswered questions spinning in her mind like a cyclone. More confusion. More frustration. This case didn't want to cooperate, that was for sure. She trudged back to the car on Furbush's heels, lost in her own thoughts.

Her door shut with a dull thud. She reached for her seatbelt and drew it over her chest and lap.

The engine rumbled awake, and just as Furbush shifted into reverse, his phone rang. He plucked it from the holder on the dash and answered.

"Chief Furbush," he said, then paused. "Yeah. OK. Great. We're heading back there now."

Ending the call with a swipe of his thumb, he returned his phone to its dock on the dashboard and turned to Darger.

"That was Marcy. They found the file."

"Good. Now we just have to hope there's something worthwhile in it."

CHAPTER 24

Darger, Fowles, and Furbush huddled over the Christy Whitmore file, going over it piece by piece.

First they laid out the dozens of photographs of the crime scene. Christy's body slumped in the tub. A puddle of water on the floor next to a sodden bathmat. A razor and can of shaving foam that had been knocked across the room.

Obvious signs of a struggle.

Then there was Christy's skin, a map of welts and scratches and bruises that stood out against her dead white pallor. The girl had put up a fight.

It was just like Milton had described.

And it was different from the other murders in so many ways. Christy had been found soon after death, so despite the bruises and marks, she mostly looked peaceful. There was still a wrongness to her, if you really looked. The way all corpses looked *off*. But she wasn't rotting and falling apart. There was no bloating. If they hadn't made the leap that the new drownings were likely occurring in a bathtub, Darger never would have assumed this case was related to the others.

"Take a look at this," Fowles said. "It's from an interview with Christy's mother."

Darger took a step closer, and he pointed out the section of interest.

WHITMORE: Dustin is the one you should be looking at. He's the one. I know it.

DETECTIVE BLAKE: What makes you think that?

WHITMORE: It's not rocket science. He's spoiled. Used to getting anything he wants. So when Christy broke up with him, he couldn't just let it go. Not without making her pay the price.

DETECTIVE BLAKE: But do you have any evidence to that effect?

WHITMORE: Isn't that your job, detective? I'm telling you, he's no good. He's the one that took my baby girl from me.

Even though it was only black ink on white paper, Darger could practically hear the fury in the words.

"So who's this Dustin guy the mother keeps bringing up?"

Marcy was in the midst of preparing a fresh pot of coffee across the room. She paused mid-scoop.

"Dustin Reynolds. He was Christy's boyfriend."

"OK. Yeah, Chief Milton mentioned looking at a boyfriend," Furbush said.

"Do we have an interview with Dustin in the file?"

Furbush paged through his stack of papers.

"I've got it here."

He passed Darger a few pages stapled together.

She skimmed through the interview, which had been conducted with an attorney present. Apparently Dustin's parents weren't taking any chances, and Darger probably would've done the same if it were her kid in the hot seat. Especially with Christy's mother gunning for him.

Still, the fact that all questions went through a lawyer made for a sterile interview. Just clean, hard facts. Where Dustin was the day of the murder (skateboarding with friends at a local park and then to Subway). When he'd last spoken to Christy (at school the previous day). If he could think of anyone who would have wanted to hurt Christy (No way).

Darger set the interview aside and paged through the remaining contents of the Whitmore file.

"Marcy?" Darger called, and the woman poked her head into the conference room. "Do you know if Christy's family is still in town?"

The wheels of Marcy's office chair squealed as she rolled herself into the conference room.

"Her mother still lives in the same house. Not sure how. I don't think I'd be able to stay in my home knowing something like that happened there."

But Darger knew that for many people, it was all of the good memories that kept them in the same place. Especially for a parent. The marks on the doorway that showed how their children had grown or the spaghetti-stained handprint on the kitchen wall.

"I think I should go talk to her," Darger said.

Furbush took a long pull from his coffee mug and made to stand up.

"Great idea. I'll come with."

"I think maybe I should go alone," Darger said, chewing her lip.

Frowning, Furbush crossed his arms over his broad chest. "OK. Why?"

"Did you take a look at those?" she asked and pointed to a pile of pink sheets tacked in the back of the Whitmore file.

"Not really. What is it?"

"Complaints. Filed by Mrs. Whitmore against this department."

"Complaints about what?"

"Corruption. Incompetence. It looks like she wasn't happy with how the investigation was being handled. They go on for quite some time after Christy's death. I think she held a bit of a grudge."

Hands on his hips, Furbush frowned and pursed his lips.

"I didn't even work here then."

"I know. It's just that… emotions like grief and anger don't usually bring out logical behavior. If she holds this department accountable, it won't matter to her that you weren't part of the investigation. Just showing up on her doorstep in that uniform might be enough for her to slam the door in our faces."

His mouth worked like he was chewing on something.

Darger prayed he would see reason. This wasn't about egos. She only wanted what was best for the investigation. But she also couldn't force him to sit the interview out. It was still his investigation. His jurisdiction.

Finally, he sighed.

"No. You're right. I'd be pretty pissed off if my daughter was killed, and we never found who did it. Can't be an easy thing to live through." He rapped his knuckles against the table. "If you think my presence might disrupt things, or upset her, then you should go alone."

Relieved, Darger got to her feet. As she pushed in her chair, an idea came to her.

"Actually I'd like to bring Fowles along with me," Darger said. "Assuming she's got an axe to grind with law enforcement types, having a genuine civilian with me might make her less cagey."

Fowles frowned in mock disappointment as he followed

Darger to the door.

"You mean you didn't choose me for my effervescent personality?"

CHAPTER 25

The house Christy Whitmore had died in — and the house her
mother still lived in — stood in a small subdivision next to a
Christmas tree farm. A quiet area, Darger thought. Quaint.

Beside the little beige ranch-style home was an expanse of
green lawn with a large brush pile at one end. Toward the back
of the yard, a row of immense larch trees cast swaying shadows
over a yellow playhouse.

"How'd she sound on the phone?" Fowles asked as they
rolled up the gravel driveway.

"Mrs. Whitmore, you mean?"

Fowles nodded.

"Not thrilled. She made some comment about it being a
waste of time. But ultimately she agreed."

"And you think she can tell you something? Something
they missed twenty years ago?"

Darger shook her head.

"Maybe. My job is to get all the details and give an analysis.
To make intuitive leaps. If Christy Whitmore was killed by the
same person, she might have been his first victim. Finding out
more about who Christy was might tell me something new
about him."

She glanced over at Fowles. His mouth was quirked to one
side, and he had one of his pensive, but hard-to-read
expressions on his face.

"As a scientist, that probably makes profiling sound like a
bunch of woo-woo nonsense to you."

His eyes opened wider.

"Not at all. It was reminding me of being at the body farm during my study. In the lab, we can control most of the variables with such precision — lighting, temperature, humidity. In the field? Not so much. You think that as a scientist, I can't understand or appreciate the intuitive nature of your work, but that's not true. A good scientist has to have intuition to go along with our observation and analysis. Every new scientific discovery is born out of an intuitive leap."

She smiled when he was finished.

"I'm sorry for assuming."

"That's OK. I take it you've come across a few critics who doubted the credibility of criminal profiling as a science?"

Darger snorted. "A few."

"I know several colleagues who absolutely loathe being in the field. There are so many variables to consider outside the lab. A good field study endeavors to keep track of as many as possible, but so much is out of our hands. I had a colleague that was studying the foraging habits of bumblebees. On the third night of her study, a family of raccoons happened across the hive she was watching and decimated it."

"What does that mean?"

"They ate it. The little bandits dug up the hive and devoured it like candy."

Stifling a shocked chuckle, Darger asked, "What did she do? Your colleague, I mean?"

Fowles scratched the side of his head.

"She almost quit. In the end, she only swore off field studies. Said she preferred the lab, where there are rules and boundaries and nothing eats your study unless it's supposed to."

Darger glanced through the windshield at the Whitmore house. Paint faded and peeling in a few places. A rectangle two shades darker than the rest, where a missing shutter had once clung. Bushes on either side of the front step, so overgrown that their scraggly branches reached across the cracked sidewalk like arms trying to trip unwary visitors.

"Well, it's time we headed into the field, so to speak," Darger said. "Let's just hope there aren't any hungry raccoons waiting for us on the other side of that door."

Darger exited the vehicle and strode to the front door with Fowles close behind. She knocked three times and waited, spinning around to get a view of the place from the entrance. Nothing struck her as out of the ordinary. Another quiet, suburban neighborhood. There were thousands more like it across the country. But a young girl had died here. Murdered. Darger's scalp prickled at the thought.

Behind her, the sound of a rusty door hinge squealed like a pig. She turned back, found the pinched face of a woman staring back.

"Carole Whitmore?"

Mrs. Whitmore squinted at her through the warped screen of the door.

"You're the consultants or whatever?"

"That's us," Darger said, trying on a friendly smile. "My name is Violet Darger. This is Ted Fowles."

Mrs. Whitmore's already furrowed brow scrunched up even further.

"You a local?"

"No," Darger said, wondering if Mrs. Whitmore would

change her mind about talking to them if she knew they were working with Sandy PD.

Instead, Darger thought she saw a flicker of disappointment flash across the woman's face.

"Huh. Thought you looked familiar. Guess not, though."

With an impatient wave of her hand, she beckoned them inside and pulled the door closed. She shuffled into a living room and slumped into a saggy leather recliner. The upholstery had probably once been a rich cognac brown but was worn down to a drab beige. The yellow-tinged lighting was dim and gave the place a sad, used up feel.

Darger studied the row of photographs over the mantel and noted that even Mrs. Whitmore seemed like a faded version of her former self.

"Not sure what all you're hoping to learn," Mrs. Whitmore said in a hollow voice, picking absently at one of the buttons on the bulky sweater she wore. "I saw the news. About the girls they found in the river. Figure you must be thinking it might be related to what happened to Christy. Maybe it is. Maybe it isn't. I don't know why you need to talk to me."

She had a look Darger had seen before. The look of a woman whose life had ceased the moment she found her daughter's lifeless body. All her hopes and dreams had stopped there like a broken clock, never to tick again.

It wasn't coldness in her eyes but emptiness.

"Well, I'm hoping to get a more complete picture of what happened to your daughter. To Christy."

The woman's expression didn't change.

"If you're expecting me to tell you something new, you're apt to be disappointed. What I've got to say is the same shit I told the cops all them years ago. Or tried to tell. They weren't too much interested in hearing me out."

"I know it probably seems like too little, too late, but I want to hear it," Darger said, moving to a dusty-looking sofa where Fowles already sat.

"Too little, too late sounds about right," Mrs. Whitmore said and crossed her arms over her chest. "Maybe if that Chief Milton didn't have his head up his ass, he might have done something. Found who took my baby girl away from me."

"You know Milton isn't Chief anymore?"

"What's it matter? They're all the same." Mrs. Whitmore scoffed. "It was obvious from the get-go that they weren't going to find who did it. The cops around here, they give speeding tickets and collect money for the stupid fundraising raffle they hold every year. There's no real police work being done. And it's an Old Boys' Club, from the top all the way to the bottom. They never wanted to listen what I had to say, because it was ugly business, and I wasn't one of them. They're only interested in taking care of their own."

"Well, I'm interested. And I'm here to listen," Darger said, wondering how she was going to break through this woman's defenses. Maybe it would be better to be blunt.

Darger took a breath.

"Can you tell me about the day your daughter died?" she asked.

Mrs. Whitmore's mouth pinched tighter for a beat. A little twitch of pain at remembering.

"Sure. I came home from work. Found my baby girl stark naked and all bruised up. Dead," the woman said, Darger's own bluntness thrown right back in her face. "It had always been

166

just me and her. She was all I had."

Darger glanced over at Fowles, hoping he'd have another one of his moments where he seemed to say exactly the right thing at the right time. But he was staring into his hands, clearly uncomfortable with the contentious atmosphere.

Darger's eyes swept over the photographs above the mantel again, and she was struck by an idea. If she steered the conversation away from the investigation, perhaps then Mrs. Whitmore would open up.

"Maybe you could give me a sense of what kind of person Christy was. The things she liked to do," Darger said.

There was only silence for a moment, and Darger was beginning to think Mrs. Whitmore wasn't going to respond. Then she spoke.

"Some days I still think I'll walk into her room and find her there, painting her nails on her bed, like I told her not to do a hundred times."

She closed her eyes, shaking her head slowly.

"All those little fights. Little squabbles. Such a waste of the time we had together. You only realize it when you lose them. That you wasted it all. Pissed it away like you had forever. But you didn't. You don't. No one has forever."

Darger stared at a photo of Christy and her mother in matching sequined dresses, fully made up with their hair teased out. It had the look of the glamour portraits girls used to have done when Darger was a teenager. Mrs. Whitmore was like a broken record of despair, and Darger needed a way to jump the needle past this looping section of self-pity. But how?

Beside the glamour portrait was a trophy and a snapshot of Christy in a softball uniform. Another photograph showed

Mrs. Whitmore and a group of young girls grinning at the camera, all wearing matching t-shirts printed with the team logo.

"How long did Christy play softball?" Darger asked.

"Oh, I started her in tee-ball when she was four. Coached her all the way through elementary and middle school."

Darger thought she sensed something new in Mrs. Whitmore's voice. A tiny spark of life. Of the love she'd felt for her daughter.

And just as quickly, it vanished, the woman's shoulders slumping like an ice cream cone melting in the July heat.

"She quit her Freshman year. Another one of our big blow-ups. I was thinking scholarships."

There was a hitch in Mrs. Whitmore's voice.

"Of course she never even graduated, so what was the point? What did any of it matter?"

Darger felt herself being sucked into the despair. Why shouldn't Mrs. Whitmore be angry? Her daughter was killed. And to make matters worse, the person who did it was never punished.

"It isn't fair," Darger said. "For someone so young to be taken in such a cruel way. It's not right or fair. That's why I want to help."

The woman's eyes met Darger's.

"Are you going to bring her back?" she asked. There was a bitter note in her voice.

"No, Mrs. Whitmore. But I might be able to find who did it."

Tears welled in the woman's eyes now. Darger was out of ideas.

"I know it's not enough. Nothing ever is."

Her eyes strayed back to the line of photographs of the happy family that once was.

"I've seen so many lives ruined by this kind of brutality. And some days I feel like it's all a hopeless fight. Because even if I solve a case, the victims are still gone forever. There are some wrongs that can never be put right. Not really."

Mrs. Whitmore was staring at her wordlessly, moistness clinging to her eyelashes but not yet spilling. Darger lowered her gaze, ready to give in. She'd come here expecting too much.

The woman's voice stopped her.

"Where did you say you were from?"

"I'm a consultant—"

Mrs. Whitmore waved an impatient hand.

"No, I mean, where are you *from*?"

"Oh," Darger said, blinking and caught off guard. "I'm originally from Colorado. But I live in Virginia now. Outside of Quantico."

Mrs. Whitmore's eyes went wide, and before Darger could say any more, she'd leapt from her chair and bustled out of the room.

Darger turned to Fowles, who only shrugged.

Mrs. Whitmore returned, flapping a catalogue in her hands.

"I knew it! I knew I'd seen you before."

Darger realized then it wasn't a catalogue at all, but a magazine. *Vanity Fair*.

"This was Christy's favorite, actually. Loved her magazines."

"Oh," Darger said, trying to swallow away her discomfort. That interview just kept coming back to bite her in the ass.

"You didn't say FBI."

"Pardon?"

"You keep calling yourself a consultant, not FBI."

"Right. I'm… taking some time off."

"Let me guess. Another Old Boys' Club?" Mrs. Whitmore said, shaking her head. "It's all the same, isn't it?"

Her eyes drifted over to Fowles for a moment, a glint of suspicion in her eye, like perhaps the mere fact that he was male made him one of the so-called *old boys*.

But then she fixed her focus back on Darger. There was cold fury in her eyes now, and it wasn't until Mrs. Whitmore spoke that Darger realized it wasn't for her.

"You'll get him, won't you?"

"Who?"

"Whoever did this to my baby girl. You'll see that he pays for taking her from me."

Darger met her unblinking gaze.

"Yes. I will."

The woman's head nodded once, and she pushed herself to her feet.

"There's something I want you to see."

CHAPTER 26

Christy's room was painted sky blue, though only thin slivers of the color showed through the wall-to-wall display of posters, magazine collages, and India ink drawings that looked like projects from art class. And photographs. Actual printed snapshots tacked to the wall with push pins. Hundreds of them.

Darger couldn't remember the last time she'd seen actual printed photographs on a bedroom wall. Not since college. It was a throwback. A room perfectly preserved since the day Mrs. Whitmore came home to find her daughter's ruined body.

The woman stood aside while Darger studied the room, arms crossed, one hand fidgeting with a hole in the sleeve of her sweater. Fowles hung back, just inside the threshold, like he was uncomfortable with the idea of disturbing this place. Or maybe he was still thinking about the dubious look Mrs. Whitmore had given him earlier.

There was a thin layer of dust on the four-poster canopy bed, evidence of just how much the room had been left alone. A hook near the window held looped strands of purple and green Mardi Gras beads. On the opposite side, a selection of silk scarves, their colorful prints bleached to pastels by years spent in harsh sunlight.

It was a girl's room not unlike dozens Darger had seen growing up.

And yet something was off.

The disused feeling Darger got from the place was incomplete, she realized.

It was the smell, she realized, sniffing the air lightly. There were fresh notes of incense — sandalwood and something floral. Her eyes wandered the space, found the ash catcher with a half-burned stick on a shelf. Darger moved closer, inhaling.

The voice of Christy's mother came from behind her.

"She loved incense. Nag Champa was her favorite scent. I burn a stick every year on her birthday, and then I sit on her bed and cry my eyes out. The memories just come flooding back with the smell."

Mrs. Whitmore's emotions seemed more raw in here. Like she couldn't fit the walls she'd built around her grief through the door frame of her daughter's room. She had to leave them outside when she came in here, stripped of her defenses.

Darger turned to the woman and spoke softly.

"Was there something specific you wanted to show me?"

Mrs. Whitmore gestured to a dresser littered with makeup and nail polish and the kind of cheap jewelry that comes from shops at the mall.

Darger took a step closer, eyes on the cluster of photos tucked into the dresser's mirror. There was a theme to the photographs. They all featured the same dark-haired boy. A good-looking kid with a lazy smile. In most of the photos, he wore baggy skater jeans, often with a cigarette tucked behind one ear.

Christy was in several of the pictures, as well. Sitting on the boy's lap in one. Locked in a kiss with him in several others.

"Christy had a boyfriend?" Darger asked.

Of course she knew this already. She'd read the file. But Darger wanted the topic to come up naturally. Wanted to let Christy's mother lead the way.

When Mrs. Whitmore answered, her mouth puckered like the name left a bitter taste on her tongue.

"Dustin Reynolds. He's the one you should be looking at."

"You think he did it?"

Mrs. Whitmore scoffed.

"I *know* he did. Everyone knew. Everyone but the goddamn Sandy Police Department, anyway."

"Why do you think it was Dustin?"

"It's always the boyfriend, isn't it?" Mrs. Whitmore said, the acidic tone still there. "Besides that, he was a manipulative little bastard. I knew that from the start. He was a bad influence on my Christy. She never drank or smoked or anything like that before he came around. She was a good girl. But soon enough, she was stealing my cigarettes and pilfering booze from the cabinet. They'd deny it, but I marked the bottles. Caught 'em red-handed when there was an inch of vodka missing."

"Was he ever violent?" Darger asked.

Mrs. Whitmore gripped her crossed arms tight to her chest.

"Not to Christy. If he'd ever touched her, and I found out about it?" The woman paused to let out a short bitter chuckle. "I would have cut his balls off. No. But he had a temper."

She pointed to a hole in the particle board of Christy's bedroom door. Darger hadn't noticed it before, and now she crouched down to get a better look.

"He kicked this hole in the door?"

Mrs. Whitmore nodded.

"It's on the inside of the door, so he wasn't trying to get in. Why'd he do it?"

"If I recall correctly, Christy told me it happened when he was talking on the phone with his parents. There was a concert in Portland he wanted to go to. One of those alternative rock bands that was big back then. But the concert was in the middle of the week — on a school night — and they said no. I don't think he was used to hearing that. They pretty much let him run wild."

Darger raised an eyebrow, eyes still on the jagged hole in the door.

"Yeah, I'd say that's a kid with a temper."

"They were always fighting," Mrs. Whitmore explained. "He'd do some real lowdown thing, and my Christy'd break up with him, and then he'd be calling day and night, showing up at my door, begging to talk to her. And eventually he'd weasel his way back in. They'd just had one of their big blow-ups right before she died. She told him they were done for good."

Mrs. Whitmore's head swayed slowly from side to side.

"Three days later they were back together again. A week later, she was dead."

Darger peered back at the photos of the handsome, dark-haired boy. Could this really be who they were looking for? Had he possibly killed Christy during an argument, a crime of passion that eventually sparked in him a taste for murder?

"Did the original investigation look into Dustin?"

"What's your definition of looking? Because you can be sure I told the Keystone Cops all about Dustin and his little temper problem, but a fat lot of good it did. Buncha incompetent idiots. Besides that, Dustin's family goes way back in this town."

Making a mental note to double-check all of the information on Dustin in the original file, Darger's eyes flitted to a collection of photos on the wall next to the dresser. A scrawny-limbed, gap-toothed Christy at about age eight, smiling proudly over a pair of mud pies with another little girl about the same age. Above that was another shot of Christy from a few years later. She and a girl with lank brown hair posed in front of an old wooden rollercoaster, hooking their fingers together in a "Pinky Promise." A third picture in the grouping was Christy and a schoolmate, dressed up for what Darger figured was a school formal. Both girls wore long red satin dresses — not quite matching, but close.

It was a few moments before Darger pieced together the fact that it was the same girl with Christy in all three photos. And there were more. Darger glanced around and saw the girl in at least a dozen other pictures.

She tapped the nearest shot with a fingernail.

"Who's the girl with Christy in all these photos?"

"That's Cat. Christy's best friend," Mrs. Whitmore answered. "They met in third grade and were inseparable after that. She just worshiped Christy. They dressed alike, did their hair alike. I used to joke that if I didn't know better, I would've thought they were twins separated at birth. She even called me mom sometimes, as a little joke."

She pointed to the Pinky Promise photo.

"That was their secret handshake. There was a whole hand-clapping routine and a rhyme that went with it."

Her eyes slid up to the ceiling, squinting in concentration.

"*Cross my heart and hope to die. I'll never betray you, never lie. Best friends forever... you and I?* Something like that."

For the first time, Mrs. Whitmore smiled. It was small and sad, but a smile nonetheless.

"We called ourselves the Three C's — Carole, Christy, and

Cat. Had a movie night almost every Friday I didn't have to work, the three of us. We'd pig out on pizza and Pepsi and Red Vines and rent whatever new rom-com was out."

The woman's eyes seemed to glaze over as she went back over the memories in her mind.

"You probably saw their clubhouse out back as you drove up. The little yellow playhouse. That was what they called it. 'The Clubhouse.' Christy's birthday present when she was seven. My dad built it from his own design. She'd outgrown it in her middle school years, but then for a while, she and Cat sort of rediscovered it. They must have been fifteen, sixteen at the time. Used to take a boom box out there and listen to music, paint their nails, read their fashion magazines. They slept out there a few times, in summer. I'd go check on them, of course. Pretend I was just bringing out some snacks, but really I wanted to be sure they weren't up to anything… trying to sneak boys in or something. But they were always just hanging out like they said they would be. It's like I said. Christy was a good girl. It was that Dustin who messed everything up."

She shook her head. Then laughed a little.

"Sorry, I was just thinking of a time I went out there — oh, Christy must have been about ten. She had probably about eight neighbor kids crammed inside, and they were playing Spin the Bottle. Can you believe it?"

The smile slowly slid from her face with a sigh.

"I don't even know where they would have learned about something like that. I figured it was the kind of thing that went the way of go-go boots and polyester leisure suits."

Mrs. Whitmore's face tightened again, a fierceness coming into her eyes.

"My little girl was barely cold in her grave before Dustin took up with Cat. Can you believe that? His dead girlfriend's best friend? I mean… I tried to warn her that he was no good. That he was downright dangerous, but she was always such a mousy little thing."

Her gaze softened.

"Besides that, I think Cat loved Christy so much that it made her love anyone Christy loved. She just couldn't see Dustin as bad, because Christy had loved him."

"Do you know if Dustin is still in town?" Darger asked.

The woman shook her head.

"I never knew what happened with them. Christy died a couple months before graduation, and Dustin and Cat moved away after that. Together, I was told. I hope she got away from him. I honestly do. Because if he could do what he did to my Christy… well, then he's capable of just about anything, I figure. A monster is what he is."

She reached out a hand to one of the photos thumbtacked to the wall. Christy posed, tongue sticking out, in a comically tall stovepipe hat — the kind The Cat in the Hat wore — except this one was made of purple and green fur. Mrs. Whitmore stroked the likeness of her daughter, and Darger wondered if she imagined the soft warmth of her daughter's face under her fingers, instead of the cold glossy surface of the photograph.

"You know what I miss more than anything else? Being a mother. The most important job in the world, to me anyway, was being Christy's mom. Because it was more than that. She wasn't just my daughter. She was my best friend. And he took that away. He took it all away."

Tears fell from the woman's face now in earnest, and

177

Darger looked away. She suddenly felt like she needed to get out of the room. The cloying smell of the incense, the cluttered walls, the mother's grief — all of it had begun to close in on Darger, making her feel claustrophobic.

She turned toward the door, and as she did, her eyes caught a glimpse of the little yellow playhouse through the window.

"Mrs. Whitmore," Darger said, "would it be OK if I took a look at the playhouse?"

The woman sniffed, gathering herself.

"I doubt there's anything to see out there. Probably full of mice and who knows what other vermin. But go ahead. Knock yourself out."

CHAPTER 27

Painted pale yellow with white gingerbread trim, Christy's so-called Clubhouse stood at the far end of the Whitmore's yard.

There was a small heart-shaped window over the Dutch door, a sloped roof with a faux brick chimney. The whole thing was bordered by a white picket fence.

Darger pushed through the gate and held it aside so Fowles could pass through. Now that they were closer, she could see missing shingles and that the yellow paint was beginning to peel. Old window boxes on either side of the door held only bare dirt.

The door let out a whine of protest as Darger stooped to enter the playhouse. It smelled of mildew and mouse droppings, but she could still see that at one time, it would have been quite a charming space. It was pink and flowery, a girl-sized dollhouse.

And that was exactly what Darger thought Mrs. Whitmore had seen her daughter as. A doll. It wasn't fair, she knew, to judge this way. But she couldn't keep the thought from forming.

There was a loft at one end with a ladder leading up to it. The platform was just wide enough to fit a sleeping bag or maybe two. A small table and chair, painted pale blue, stood in front of a smudged chalkboard.

"I had a cousin who had a playhouse like this when we were kids," Darger said.

"What happened?"

She pivoted to face him, frowning.

"What do you mean?"

"You said 'had.' You *had* a cousin."

"Oh! She's still alive. I just haven't seen her in a while."

Darger pushed the chintz curtains covering the window aside and peeked out. Probably the curtains had once been bright and colorful — shades of pink and blue and green. But now they were a mottled and sun-bleached beige. Even the window glass was so grimy she could barely see through it.

"OK, so I *have* a cousin who *had* a playhouse like this. All I was really going to say was that I remember being very jealous of it. I wanted one so badly. My own little hideout."

There was a Barq's root beer can on the floor in one corner. Darger nudged it with her toe, sent it bumping and clanging over the warped floor tiles. Its progress stopped right in the center of the floor, between Fowles and herself, but it didn't exactly cease moving. The empty can hung there on an uneven corner of tile and sort of spun, slowly and lopsidedly, before coming to rest with the top facing Fowles.

Immediately, Darger thought of Mrs. Whitmore's story about Christy and the neighborhood kids playing Spin the Bottle. And it wasn't actually a bottle, of course, but…

She glanced up. Fowles was staring at her, a strange smile on his face, and she knew he was thinking the same thing.

Huddled together as they were, their knees and elbows crowding the small space, he only had to dip his head forward to kiss her. And he did.

Then he was pulling away, raising his arms into a shrug.

"Sorry, I just… could no longer resist the urge."

Darger was smiling, about to tease him, to ask what other

urges he'd been feeling. But the words froze on her tongue. She stared over Fowles' right shoulder, eyes not moving from the one dark spot on the trim of the heart-shaped window.

"What?" he asked. "You're not about to tell me there's a giant spider hanging over my head, are you? Because that trick doesn't work on entomologists."

"Look," she said, aiming a finger at it.

He turned, saw the small symbol scrawled on the wood. An upside-down heart with a cross. The same symbol that had been etched onto the fence outside of Shannon Mead's house.

☾

Mrs. Whitmore was no further help, not even after Darger dragged her out to the little playhouse and showed her the marking over the door.

"Does this mean anything to you? Is it something you ever saw Christy draw? Or maybe Dustin?"

Mrs. Whitmore shook her head, pulling her sweater tighter around herself.

"It's just kid stuff, you know? They start out scrawling on the walls and the furniture as toddlers. Once they get older, you think they've outgrown it, but it's just different. They doodle on their school notebooks and their backpacks. Christy and Cat, they used to draw all over one another with Sharpies, giving each other fake tattoos. One time, I came home and they each had a strip of hair colored in like rainbow zebra print. It looked cute for an evening, and then they washed their hair and all the colors bled together into a mess."

Her eyes seemed to blur then, like her mind was somewhere else, perhaps transported seventeen years earlier.

"They had a whole made-up language. Christy and Cat, I mean. So they could write secret notes back and forth no one else could read. They tried to teach it to me once, but I couldn't follow it. God, I'd almost forgotten about that."

She smiled sadly, glancing around at the abandoned playhouse.

"Kids," she said quietly, more to herself than anything, Darger thought.

Darger thanked her again for her time, and she and Fowles headed back to the car.

"What's next?"

"Tracking down this Dustin Reynolds guy, for one," Darger answered, sliding into the passenger seat and pulling the door shut behind her.

"You really think he did it? I mean, he would have been seventeen or eighteen at the time of Christy's murder, right? A kid."

The buckle of Darger's seatbelt clicked into place. She sighed.

"It's hard to imagine, but it happens. Ed Kemper killed his grandparents when he was fifteen. There's a theory, with some circumstantial evidence to back it up, that Ted Bundy abducted and murdered an eight-year-old girl when he was fourteen."

Darger sat back in her seat and watched the Whitmore house grow smaller in the side mirror of the car.

"Then again, right now all we have to go on is Carole Whitmore's gut, and I don't know if I should trust her instincts all that much."

"You think she was lying?"

"Not lying. Just… biased. You heard what she said, right?

She described her relationship with Christy as 'best friends.' Everything I saw in that house screamed Smother City."

"Just because they had a close relationship?"

Darger's eyes slid sideways to look at Fowles.

"There's such a thing as too close. A healthy relationship has boundaries, and the way Mrs. Whitmore talked, I don't think she had many with Christy. It sounded to me like the line between mother and daughter was totally blurred."

Darger rubbed her eyes.

"My point is, she's not exactly a reliable source. She probably would have resented any boyfriend Christy brought home, because it was something in Christy's life she couldn't take part in. Anyway, I'm sure it's hard to be objective about your daughter's murder," she said, then sighed. "That being said, Dustin Reynolds is still the best lead we have to go on. If he's been in town recently, I'd like to know what he was up to."

CHAPTER 28

Butterflies twirled in Darger's belly as they drove away from the Whitmore house. With the symbol in the playhouse matching the one on the fence outside of Shannon Mead's house, they were finally getting somewhere, and the stimulation seemed to shift and stir things in both her mind and her abdomen, little flutters of excitement flushing cold tingles through her core, making her twitchy.

She had to remind herself to not get too excited, though. They had something that felt tangible — a piece of evidence they could photograph and puzzle over — but at best it was a baby-step in the overall case.

The killer was still out there, whoever he was. As dangerous as ever. Lying in wait.

As Fowles pulled to the curb near the front door of the police station, he shifted into park but didn't turn off the ignition.

Darger had one foot out of the door when she stopped and turned back.

"Aren't you coming?"

"No, I have a few errands to run."

Darger raised an eyebrow.

"More pig leg experiments?"

"How'd you guess?"

"You've got a one-track mind, Fowles. Bugs on the brain. A little pork on the side, I guess."

He shrugged, smiling.

184

"I'll catch up with you later?"

"Sure thing," Darger said, pushing the door shut and waving briefly as he rode off.

Inside, Darger filled the Chief in on what they'd learned from Carole Whitmore, including a photo of the scrawled symbol in the playhouse, the one that matched the marking at Shannon Mead's house.

"Still don't know if it means anything," Furbush said.

"Yeah. But it's at least a small piece to connect Christy Whitmore's murder with the new ones."

They spent the rest of the afternoon searching for a lead on the whereabouts of Dustin Reynolds.

Furbush brought up Dustin's driver's license entry in the state database and immediately pointed at his listed height and weight.

"Over six-feet tall, 240 pounds. Not a small guy, is he?"

Darger nodded solemnly. She'd been thinking the same thing. It was at least one way that Dustin fit the profile.

"DMV's still got his driver's license and vehicle registration listed under a Sandy address."

Marcy came around to look at the computer screen, bending closer to get a better look.

"That's his parents' house. Or *was*. I don't think they live there anymore."

After confirming that neither Dustin nor his parents lived at the Peach Street address, Marcy called the post office and wheedled a forwarding address out of a friend that worked there. It was a Portland address — not too far — but when Darger finally got a call back from the management company for the property, it was another dead end. Dustin hadn't lived there in over seven years.

Darger tried Google, which only brought up the two addresses they already knew about. On a hunch, she typed his name into Facebook, hoping it would have a current location listed, but that was a bust as well. Dustin Reynolds didn't appear to be on the site.

"So he just disappeared off the face of the planet seven years ago?" Furbush said. "I mean, he's gotta live somewhere. Have bills. If he's still driving the same truck, it's getting to be pretty old."

"Christy Whitmore's mother mentioned a girl Dustin supposedly hooked up with after Christy's murder," Darger said, reaching back into her memories for the name. "Cat. She said they moved away together after graduating."

Marcy frowned.

"I don't remember a Cat. She was from here?"

"I think so. She was a friend of Christy's," Darger said, flustered at Marcy's fixation on this detail. "The reason I brought it up was to point out that if Dustin is living with someone, even if it's just a roommate, the bills could be in someone else's name."

"It's still a little suspicious. Him not having any current records," Furbush said.

"A little. But I wouldn't draw any conclusions from it."

Marcy let out an excited little yelp.

"Now I remember!"

"Remember what?" Darger asked, thinking maybe Marcy had recalled some rumor or whisper of Dustin's plans after high school.

"Cat! She was friends with Christy. Actually, she was

practically Christy's shadow. Copied everything she did. I always thought it was a little sad. Like, be your own person, you know?"

"Sure," Darger said.

Furbush hooked his thumbs into his belt.

"Do you remember her last name?"

"Well, no. Totally blanking on it. I mean, she had like no personality. I'm not surprised I didn't remember her at first. Anything remarkable about her was stolen from Christy. I can't believe she and Dustin had a thing. Mrs. Whitmore really said that? I never heard that."

"Marcy," the Chief interrupted. "Could you think on that last name again? If the two of them did go off together, we might be able to find a lead on Dustin through her."

Darger got out her phone and dialed Carole Whitmore's number. *She'd* remember the girl's name. But there was no answer. The phone rang and rang. No voicemail either, apparently. She clenched her molars together and jabbed at the End Call button.

Marcy was still considering the question, eyes squinted shut. In real or mock concentration, Darger wasn't sure.

Finally, Marcy shook her head.

"Sorry, I really don't remember it. But I bet I can call around and find someone that remembers. Oh! Or maybe my yearbook! I'm not sure where it is, but I can have a look when I go home tonight."

Furbush sighed.

"Thank you, Marcy."

After another round of fruitless internet searches, Chief Furbush suggested they check out the Reynolds family compound.

"His aunt Mamie is the reigning matriarch. A real ball-buster and just about as old school as you can get. The type that prefers the personal touch of a face-to-face visit over a phone call," Furbush explained. "What do you say we ride out and see if she'll talk to us?"

For the second time that day, Darger followed Furbush out to his vehicle and climbed in.

"Carole Whitmore said the Reynolds family goes way back in Sandy."

Furbush nodded.

"It's not exactly the same as going way back out east where you're from, you understand. There was a small community here at the turn of the last century. Pioneer types, come to live off the land. There are still two or three families in town that can say their great-granddaddy built the first post office or hotel or used to own half the township. The Reynolds clan came from one of those early settlers."

"She seemed to suggest that Dustin Reynolds wasn't treated as a real suspect because of that."

Furbush shrugged.

"I wasn't here, of course. And I can see how some folks might see it that way. Most of the township board is made up of old-timers who make no bones about the fact that they like a certain status quo. But you were there when we talked to Chief Milton. He didn't strike me as the type that would bow to that kind of pressure. Not with something like this. If he had any reticence about Dustin Reynolds being the guy, I would think it had more to do with the lack of evidence."

The Reynolds compound was a short drive outside of town.

The main house was a big Victorian farmhouse that overlooked a clearing with a pond. According to Furbush, there were two smaller homes — a cabin and a trailer — elsewhere on the sprawling property.

Porch boards creaked and popped under their feet as they climbed the front steps of the main house. A wind chime hanging near the door tinkled in the breeze.

Chief Furbush jabbed a callused thumb at the doorbell. A dog woofed somewhere inside, and then a tough-looking lady with steel grey hair was pushing aside the curtains near the door, peering out at them with a frown. A moment later she opened the door, stiff-backed and upright. Darger figured this to be Mamie Reynolds.

"Sorry to bother, ma'am. I'm Chief Furbush with the Sandy Police Department."

The woman's hard eyes didn't blink.

"I know who you are."

"Right. OK. Uh, we're looking for your nephew," Chief Furbush said.

Darger thought she detected a note of unease in his voice. Old Lady Reynolds was making him nervous, and she could see why. She was a tough old bird. Not intimidated by Furbush's uniform or position in the slightest. Darger noted with amusement that she was relieved she wasn't the one asking the questions.

The woman crossed her arms and stared at the Chief of Police like he was half-stupid.

"I have six nephews. You'll have to be more specific."

Furbush's Adam's apple bobbed like a buoy in rough seas.

"Of course. The nephew we'd like to speak to in particular

is Dustin. Your brother Frank's boy."

"And what do you want with him?" Mamie asked, lifting her chin ever so slightly.

"Oh. Well. We need to ask him a few questions is all. Just a… routine inquiry."

The corners of Mamie Reynolds' mouth twitched into a smirk, and a short, hard breath puffed out of her nose. Not quite a snort, Darger thought. She was too severe for a snort. But *almost* a snort.

"A routine inquiry," the woman repeated, the hard little smile never touching her eyes.

The iron gaze shifted to Darger then.

"Who are you?"

Darger cleared her throat, caught off-guard by the woman's attention suddenly pivoting to her.

"My name is Violet Darger. I'm a consultant."

The woman was an easy six inches shorter than Darger, and yet Mamie Reynolds somehow had a way of making her feel small. Like she was some orphan waif staring up at the towering form of her strict headmistress.

The icy eyes flicked back to Furbush.

"The last time I saw my nephew was probably eight months back. He wanted money. I told him he should get a job then. He said he had a job, but his boss hated him, so he got fired." The almost-snort came again, this time accompanied with an almost-eyeroll. "There was a laundry list of other excuses, each more feeble and unconvincing than the last."

"And he didn't say where he was staying?"

"Oh, he wanted to stay here. I told him that there are rules in my house, the first being that boarders pay rent. And if he was asking me for money, I didn't really see how that would be possible."

"Do you know where he might have gone after you turned him away?"

The woman's face pinched into a scowl.

"I wasn't *turning away* the desperate parents of Jesus H. Christ. This isn't Bethlehem. My nephew is a spoiled brat. If my brother Frank and his airhead of a wife still lived in town, I'm sure Dustin would be in their house right now, loafing around, eating their food, contributing nothing. Probably watching jerk-off movies in the basement or some godforsaken thing. They don't know how to say no. Most of my siblings don't, and as such, most of my nieces and nephews are entitled little narcissists."

Darger raised a hand, like she was a student in class.

"Where are his parents, if you don't mind my asking?"

"Frank and Lucy moved down to Ft. Lauderdale five years ago."

Darger exchanged a glance with Furbush.

"Any chance your nephew might have made his way down there?" the Chief asked.

Mamie Reynolds crossed her arms and blinked a few times.

"If he found someone to con money out of for a bus ticket, sure. For all I know, he's down there right now, mooching off them as we speak. It'd be just like him."

"Could we get your brother's phone number?"

The woman held up a hand and disappeared deeper inside the house. A moment later, she returned with a phone clutched in one hand. She read the number out loud while Chief Furbush copied it down.

"Thank you, ma'am. We appreciate it. And if you happen to hear from Dustin, or if he shows up again, could you give me a call?"

"I suppose so. But I doubt he'd come back here. I made it quite clear that I have certain expectations when it comes to adult behavior. I don't expect he liked what he heard."

In the car, Chief Furbush put his phone on speaker and dialed the number Mamie Reynolds had given them.

CHAPTER 29

Frustration bred frustration, Darger thought. It seemed to be the way of things out here in Oregon.

Dustin Reynolds' parents had provided another dead end in a case that seemed full of them. Darger listened on speaker-phone as Furbush made the call on the ride back to the Sandy PD, gritting her teeth while the two men spoke. Reynolds' father, Frank, told them in a deep voice that Dustin hadn't visited them in Florida in almost three years.

He also said he had no current address for his son, and that it'd been two weeks or more since he'd heard from him, though such breaks in contact weren't abnormal. Apparently Dustin wasn't big on phones or email or anything like that.

"Always been a bit of a nomad," or so Frank repeated a couple times.

Perfect. So for the moment, the Christy Whitmore lead had come to nothing. They needed to find Dustin to get anywhere in terms of checking him against the current cases, and at the moment, Dustin was a ghost. But on the ride back to town, Darger realized that she had new resources that might help.

She put in a call of her own after Furbush got off the line with Frank Reynolds, getting in touch with one Lawrence Snead, a private investigator employed by Prescott Consulting. Snead had asked her a few questions and would now go about the task of locating Reynolds, his supposed specialty. Snead seemed very confident about it all. Almost cocky.

With that in motion, Darger could relax for a bit. Eat. Sleep.

Let her mind think about something — anything — aside from this damned case for a few hours. She'd get back to the grind in the morning.

Upon arriving at the station, she offered a quick goodbye to Furbush and headed out to the parking lot. Visions of pizza and a bubble bath danced in her head.

She took the last three paces to her rental when a dark form approached from behind a different vehicle in the lot.

Instinct reached a hand for her weapon without her even thinking. Her fingers flexed. Found the grip. Securing it. Finally almost used to the little Smith & Wesson, she realized. Not frazzled to find it instead of the familiar form of her Glock.

"So did you find anything?" the man said.

Shadows still concealed his face, but she recognized the voice. It was Fowles.

Darger let out the breath she was holding in, took her hand away from her holster.

"You shouldn't sneak up on women in dark parking lots, Bug Guy. Especially not when they're armed."

"Sorry. Did I frighten you?"

"Only a little," she said, still feeling the rapid thump-thump of her heart beating against her sternum.

Darger cocked her head to one side, thinking she wouldn't mind some company.

"I owe you one for the Korean tacos yesterday. Want to grab dinner?"

"With you? Absolutely."

So maybe that scratched the bubble bath, but there were other ways to relax.

☾

They settled on a seafood restaurant that came highly recommended by internet foodies. The tall seat-backs of their booth provided a lot of privacy, and the dark walls and low light seemed to help ease the atmosphere into something relaxed. Just what Darger was looking for.

One of the specialty cocktails on the menu was a Tom Collins, with gin made at a local distillery. Darger ordered one along with her crab and goat cheese ravioli. Fowles opted for the grilled local-caught sturgeon.

Darger couldn't help grinning at the drink set in front of her a few minutes later.

"You look happy," Fowles commented.

"I've always loved a good, old-fashioned cocktail. They're so… not of this century. I mean, look how goddamned precious this is."

She picked up the skewer that pierced a maraschino cherry and lemon slice.

"It's like my drink comes with accessories," she said, taking a sip.

Fowles laughed.

It had been a while since Darger had consumed alcohol. First there was the head injury, and then the rehab, and then the pain pills that didn't mix so well with booze.

The gin hit her fast. The drink didn't taste strong, more like lemonade than anything hard, but she felt it after her second sip. It started in the pit of her belly, a tightness that felt like claws squeezing her insides. She wondered for the first few minutes if she might end up throwing up, which seemed absurd. She probably hadn't even had a half an ounce of gin so far. Had she developed some sort of sensitivity to it?

And then the uncomfortable feeling loosened. Warmed. Spread outward from her gut to her chest and then up to her head and eventually, as they ate and drank, out to the very tips of her fingers and toes.

Fowles was charming, which didn't surprise her at this point. A never-ending well of lightness and positivity. Easy to talk to. Not exactly hilarious but a dry enough wit to stay amusing.

They talked about their families — Fowles had an older sister in entertainment law. Where they grew up — Fowles was born in Arizona, and his family moved to the Portland area when he was 9. And where they went to school — Pepperdine and then Oregon State for the Bug Guy.

Anytime the topic seemed to be skirting near the case, they both nudged it gently back into casual territory. It was like they both wanted — or needed — a reprieve from the dreariness of dead girls in bathtubs and streams. Of bloated corpses and fly larvae.

"OK," Fowles said, pretending to crack his knuckles. "Tough question time."

"Uh-oh."

"Why did you leave the FBI?"

Darger finished off her drink before responding.

"I haven't officially left yet. I'm 'on hiatus.'"

Raising one eyebrow, Fowles said, "Let it be noted that the witness did not answer the question."

Darger snorted.

"I'm tired of the politics and red tape. The injustice. Of always having some asshole above me making stupid decisions."

"Sounds like academia."

Now it was Darger's turn to look dubious.

"I didn't think the academic world got very political."

"Oh, it absolutely does. The various disciplines are always competing for grant money and tenured positions, so there's constant infighting and sniping. Besides that, everyone wants their theories to be correct, and unfortunately, many people think the way to do that is to discredit any other approach. Instead of seeing how all of the branches intersect, they end up slicing everything into pieces and arguing about how their piece is best."

"Doesn't that drive you crazy?"

"Well, yeah."

"But you keep doing it?"

"Of course. The work is important. I can't let the fact that we are a stupid, selfish, argumentative species stand in the way of scientific exploration. Of seeking out the truths of the universe. That would be… like giving up."

"Now you sound like my partner."

"Well, he sounds like a man of considerable intellect and prowess," Fowles said, letting his crooked half-smile linger.

The second and third drinks went to Darger's head quickly, kind of swirled the evening into a blur of pleasant talk and delicious seafood.

The next thing she knew, he was dropping her off, walking her to her room, and she was standing in the open door, convincing him to come inside. The words weren't working, not coming out just how she wanted them, so she tried a different tactic.

She kissed him. He kissed back.

Moved down her neck. Brushed his lips against her collarbone.

She reached for his jacket, started to slide it off his shoulders, and then his mouth stopped. He pulled away.

"What's wrong?" Darger asked.

He shrugged back into the jacket, wiped a hand across his brow.

"I can't do this. I'm sorry."

Darger put a hand to her mouth. She'd just assumed he wasn't attached, but why would she assume that? He was neat, polite, charming, handsome. Why wouldn't he have a girlfriend?

"You have a girlfriend."

He shook his head, and Darger pressed her eyelids closed, fearing the worst now.

"Please don't tell me you're married."

"No. It's not that. It's… it would be better for us to keep things professional is all."

But it wasn't that, and she knew it. Besides the fact that she'd yet to meet a man that actually gave a rat's ass about keeping things 'professional' when it came to sex, there was something in his eyes. Pain. Sadness. If Darger wasn't mistaken, Fowles was on the verge of tears.

She ran back through the last fifteen minutes, searching for something she might have said or done. Something that would have offended him. Hurt him. There was nothing.

"Did I do something?"

"No. Please don't take it personally."

He turned away then, heading for the door.

"I'm sorry, Violet. I should go."

Darger watched him leave, the door falling shut behind him with a snick that sounded like the period at the end of a sentence. Game over.

She let herself fall into a sitting position on the bed and sat looking at the door for a long time, wondering what had gone wrong.

CHAPTER 30

You wake to the sensation of the blankets shifting around you in bed. A strange lifting of that weight resting on you. Disorienting. Cool air whooshing to fill the place where your sleep warmth had percolated for so long.

You open your eyes, and she's there in the half-light of the morning. Callie.

She climbs into bed with you. Her smile a devilish tilting of her mouth.

"I called in sick," she says just above a whisper. "Wanted to rush over so I could sleep in with you."

She giggles as she speaks these words. Nestles her cold body against the sweltering furnace of your chest.

And the images of last night flash in your head. The body slumped in the bathtub. The maggoty face. The blanket-wrapped corpse washing out into the river.

Panic surges in your blood. Cold current in your veins.

The two worlds spin out of orbit. Flailing. Threatening to touch each other. A prospect that makes you nauseous. Makes your heart thud faster in your ribcage.

And you tilt your eyes to look down at the top of Callie's head tucked beneath your chin. Loops of dark hair poking up to brush your bottom lip.

Could there be a smell she'd detect this close? Some trace of a dead body odor? Even a swampy river smell could be bad.

But no. You know there's no such stench. Know it for a fact.

You remember to breathe, and your heart's gallop seems to stop accelerating at last. The tension in your chest falls back.

Good thing you showered this morning after all. Tired as you were, you didn't want to.

Or was that yesterday morning? How long have you slept?

Time. Fucking with your head again. A whole day must have passed. Must have.

You only half remember standing under the shower head. Rivulets of hot water cascading down your back.

The heat felt so good after the chill of the woods had wormed its way under your skin. An incredible tingling warmth that saturated the meat of you, rubbed its heat in deep like some full body massage.

You're pretty sure that you were in and out the whole time you bathed. Falling asleep for a second and shaking yourself awake over and over. Blinking out of slumber to find steam clouding the bathroom, seeming to billow fog inside your head as well as out.

You have no memory at all of actually toweling off or climbing into bed. Nothing.

But she lays here now. With you. And the past does not matter. The rest of the world doesn't matter.

You may as well be trapped under a dome of glass together. Encased away from all else in the universe.

This room is all that's real, all that exists.

Her body slowly goes warm against you. Passes through several stages of cool that you almost experience as color changes in this moment. The initial blue retreating to purple before swelling to red to match your color.

Her breathing changes. Slows. Evens out. She's asleep.

And you're so warm together. So safe and so warm.

You squeeze her just a little. A careful touch that will not wake her.

You love her so much. So, so much. Sometimes you almost can't take it. The intensity of the love you feel. It makes your body tremble, makes your eyelids flutter. So stimulating. Overwhelming. Like maybe it could make you sick. Make you projectile vomit. Love sprayed all over the walls.

But other times, you can ride the waves of giddiness like a rollercoaster. Hold onto them. Survive the rounds of shimmies that crawl up your abs into your chest. Excited little puffs of breath chittering out of you now and then. Sometimes it doesn't make you feel sick, and it's the most striking and strange thing you've ever experienced. The most beautiful thing in the world.

The opposite of the violent feelings. The antidote to them.

And now your breathing slows to match Callie's.

Together.

Safe and warm.

As you drift somewhere between waking and slumber, you ponder how your life can work this way. How can you be both the one who loves Callie so and the one who kills those girls and dumps their bodies in the water? How can that wide of a gap in identities exist in the same skull? So much love and so much hate roiling out of one soul.

But these thoughts go nowhere. Spiral. Circle endlessly like a dog chasing its tail. And in the end, that's all they are. A meaningless flutter in your head. More words to be forgotten like all the rest in this endless stream.

What's real is the warmth between you and Callie. Your

bodies are real. Your heartbeats are real. What's between you right here and now is real.

And your love is real.

In those other moments — when you bludgeon and stab these women, hold their unconscious bodies under the bathwater until their breathing stills, carry them off to dump them — in those moments your hatred is real.

But not here. Not now.

Here only love exists, only Callie exists. No one else would believe it if they knew the things you've done, but it's true.

And you wonder how anyone can know a person. Even themselves, to a certain degree. How can you know all of someone? Too many pieces, you think.

All of those compartments locked away from each other. Because a person is made up of all of their parts. They are the good things. They are the bad things. Both. Everything. All of it.

When you're here with Callie, it's like you fall into a sit-com world. Everything makes sense. Everything works out in the end. The laugh track punctuates the never-ending amusement.

There are happy endings to every episode. Sappy endings to every episode.

The conflicts seem small. Entertaining. They all get resolved, ultimately harmless.

The emotional music swells in just the right places. Strings, mostly. Mournful cellos to jerk the tears off.

And it's all easy in the sit-com world. Everything comes easy. Maybe too easy.

But when she's gone, when you're left on your own, the sit-com goes away.

The world turns dark. Turns violent. Foreign. Creepy. Unknowable. A black hole you stare into that also stares into you.

A nothing that gets inside of you.

And you can't sit still. So you go out walking, go out stalking, go out ripping through the city. Go out shopping for… for something you don't have yet. Maybe something you can't have.

But you go out looking for something. Something you'll know when you see it. The kind of thing you can only know when it's in your grip.

You don't set out to kill. You don't plan it.

It's just a thing that happens to these girls. A thing that happens. That's all.

Isn't that all life is? A bunch of things that happen. This happens and then this happens and then this happens. There's no reason for any of it. No explanation that's quite sufficient.

The dark impulses come from nowhere. Set your teeth on edge.

It's a wave in the air. A frequency beamed into your skull from parts unknown. Sets you on a path of destruction.

And someone — some girl out there right now — is going to get it. She doesn't know it, but she's going to get it.

It happens to you as much as it happens to them, when you think of it that way. Comes without warning.

You don't choose to want something like this. No one does. It's just there. Part of you. You don't choose the parts of you.

The furnace clicks somewhere in the distance, and your mind ascends to the surface again. Consciousness swells. Real life comes back, and Callie is there, and the darkness recedes again.

For a while, anyway.

Wishing now that time would stop. That you might stay in this version of the world forever. The sit-com version. Under glass.

CHAPTER 31

Someone was screaming. A high-pitched, ear-splitting shriek of distress.

Darger sat up straight in bed.

Her first thought: *Where am I?*

Then she remembered.

A hotel. In Sandy, Oregon. On a case.

Heart still racing, she shut off her squawking phone alarm, only then realizing that what she'd thought was a woman screaming was just the electronic jingle of her phone trying to wake her up.

She rubbed her eyes, not wanting to get out of bed. The failed date with Fowles had left her anxious. Her sleep had been fitful. She supposed it didn't help that the case had seemed to hit a dead end, as well.

When she recalled that one of Prescott's private investigators was trying to track down Dustin Reynolds, she felt a little better. Maybe he'd been able to find something.

That hope gave her the little burst of energy that finally roused her for good.

Darger showered, dressed, and brushed her teeth. She spit a mouthful of foam into the sink and considered again how she was going to get to the police station. She'd realized in the middle of the night, in between two restless snatches of sleep, that her car was still in the Sandy PD parking lot. Fowles had driven to dinner and then dropped her off.

So that was just great.

She'd have to call for a car. Or she could walk, depending on the weather. It was probably less than a mile to the police station.

While she continued her morning routine, she drank a cup of crappy coffee from the little one-cup machine in her room. It tasted stale. She never understood these single-serve brewers. Who only drank one cup of coffee? It was a ridiculous notion.

Along with the pods of coffee and tea, there were packets of instant oatmeal and instructions for using the coffee machine to make it.

To her surprise, it actually worked. What wasn't a surprise was that the oatmeal sucked. Like most of the instant varieties she'd had, it was gluey and overly sweet.

She stood at the window and ate her sugary gruel while staring out at the milky sky. There was an angry graphite scribble of dark clouds off to the northwest. Did that mean rain? If she decided to walk, she should ask the front desk if they had an umbrella to borrow.

A knock at her door drew her to the peephole. Closing one eye and squinting the other, Darger peered out. It was Fowles, his tall frame distorted by the fisheye lens.

She stepped away from the door reflexively. Felt a flush hit her cheeks. Half of her was happy to see him again, the unmistakable feeling of butterflies in her stomach. The other half was still embarrassed about last night. And still unsure of what she'd done wrong.

She had a juvenile impulse to not answer the door. To pretend she wasn't there. But that was ridiculous. He could probably hear her inside. Besides that, what was she, a coward?

She glanced at her reflection in the mirror and steeled

herself.

Suck it up, buttercup.

She tugged at the sleeve of her jacket and smoothed a stray strand of hair before grasping the door's handle and pulling it wide.

It took some effort, but she conjured a calm, unbothered smile. She was determined not to show any sign of her damaged ego.

"Good morning," Fowles said. "A little birdie told me you might need a ride into the station."

Darger couldn't help but analyze the conversation. Was he consciously avoiding any mention of last night?

Well, if he didn't want to broach what went down last night any further, then neither did she. It was probably better that way.

"Ah, well that little birdie just saved me the cost of an Uber. So be sure to thank him for me."

She grabbed her bag from the bed, double-checked that she had everything she needed, and went back to the door.

"I'm ready, if you are."

Fowles led the way down the hallway and into the elevator.

As the doors closed and sealed them into the confined space, Darger couldn't help but feel a surge of agitation.

She inspected Fowles for signs that things were off between them. A clue to their botched evening. But he didn't even seem a little bothered or nervous. Or maybe he was just good at pretending.

The polished doors parted, depositing them into the lobby of the hotel. Outside, Fowles gestured at the dark smudge on the horizon, the same stormy front Darger had noticed earlier.

"Looks like rain."

Commenting on the weather, Darger thought. Classic small talk.

Had they discussed the weather before? Darger didn't think so. So maybe Fowles did feel some awkwardness under that cool veneer. Avoiding the heavy subjects. Back to the basics. Acquaintances rather than friends.

Then they were in the car, and the silence seemed to press in on all sides. Why had she accepted a ride from him? She should have lied and said she'd already called a car, and it would cost her a fee to cancel. Now she was stuck in chitchat Hell. Doomed to comment on the weather, bitch about potholes, and say things like, "Any big plans for the weekend?" It was like going to the dentist without all the fun of having a stranger put their hands in your mouth.

But even that inane blather was preferable to this oppressive silence.

Her eyes cast about the car, looking for something, anything that might spark a topic for conversation.

The car was full of Fowles memorabilia. It shouldn't be hard. She noted the stack of books at her feet and nudged them with her toe so she could read the spines. Starting at the bottom of the stack, she scanned the titles.

The Insects: Structure and Function

The Tao of Watercolor

The Blowflies of North America

Principles & Practice of Neuro-oncology

Bugs, art, more bugs, and brain cancer. She stared at the top book, trying to figure how it fit among the rest.

Finally, she gave up and lifted the uppermost book into her

lap.

"OK, you've got bugs, and you've got art. That makes sense. But how does cancer relate?"

He shrugged.

"It doesn't really. Other than that I study the first two and have the other."

Darger lost her grip on the heavy medical textbook, and the thud it made when it hit the floor seemed deafening in the silence.

She looked him in the eye, sure he was joking. Not much of a joke, really, since it wasn't funny at all. But when she stared into those cornflower blue irises, she knew he'd been speaking the truth.

"You have cancer?"

"Grade four glioblastoma."

"Grade four… that's…"

"About as bad as it gets. Terminal, actually. I was supposed to be over a year ago. So technically I'm a ghost."

He said all of it with an air of nonchalance that Darger couldn't quite comprehend. He wasn't exactly smiling, but he seemed… almost chipper about it all.

Sensing that she was having a difficult time processing the information, he patted her arm.

"Sorry if I seem a bit blasé about it. My sister says I'm not allowing myself to grieve, but the reality is that there's nothing I can do about it, and I've never been the type to fixate on the things I can't change in the world. She's a lawyer, so that concept is entirely foreign to her. In her opinion, everything is negotiable, even terminal cancer."

"Is it painful?" Darger asked, not thinking. Her mouth was

running on auto-pilot while her brain wrestled with the idea of Fowles being at death's door.

"Not really. I've been remarkably asymptomatic since surgery, despite the fact that the tumor has spread."

Another stretch of quiet settled over the car. Darger watched the restaurants and shops of downtown Sandy flick by without really seeing them.

Eventually, Fowles interrupted the lull.

"I'm surprised Dr. Prescott didn't mention it."

"I'm not," Darger muttered.

Fowles laughed.

"She is a curious creature."

"That's one way of saying it," Darger said.

((

Darger was still reeling when they reached the station. The apprehension and awkwardness that had overwhelmed her earlier were gone. She felt strangely empty now. Dazed and numb. Like she couldn't quite process it.

Chief Furbush bustled out of his office to greet them as they came through the front door.

Darger glanced over at Fowles, who was commenting on the wet-looking weather forecast again. She was struck by how healthy he seemed. He didn't look like a dying man. Thin, yes, but not emaciated. His physique looked more fit than frail, some masculine bulk to him. How could it be real? And how could he act so normal, knowing that tomorrow he might be dead?

Did Furbush know? She watched the two men interact. She thought not. It probably wasn't the kind of thing you went around telling people you'd just met. Fowles had only told her because she'd asked about the book in his car.

Swallowing, Darger summoned enough focus to ask if the private investigator had called yet.

"Not yet," Furbush said. "But I'm hoping to hear from him any minute now."

The Chief turned and headed for the conference room.

"Come on in and grab yourself a coffee and a donut. Take a moment before the day truly begins."

He gestured to a plastic clamshell case of assorted donuts — sprinkles, chocolate-covered, powdered sugar.

"Usually I'd grab a dozen from Moe's, but they're redoing the place. Had to settle for Fred Meyer."

As Furbush turned away to pour a styrofoam cup of coffee, Fowles nudged Darger with a bony elbow. She turned to look at him, and he winked.

The confusion on her face must have been clear, because he leaned in and muttered, "No comments or special opinions about donuts from Fred Meyer?"

It was a moment before she realized he was referencing the comment she'd made about grocery store donuts the day before.

"Oh. Yeah," she said and mustered a weak smile in return, not fully able to enjoy the inside joke.

The phone at the front desk rang, and they heard Marcy answer.

"Sandy Police Department. How can I help you?" After a brief pause, she said, "Just one moment, please."

Her shoes clacked over the tile floor.

"Chief? A Mr. Lawrence Snead is on the line."

"That'd be our PI," Furbush said, dusting powdered sugar from his fingertips.

He took a final slug from his cup to wash the remainder of his donut down and reached for the phone on the conference room wall.

"This is Chief Furbush."

What followed was a lot of *mmhm's* and *uh-huh's*. Darger tried to analyze his tone and body language in hopes of determining whether it was good or bad news, but she was still too distracted by the Fowles revelation to glean much.

Furbush finished the conversation with a, "Well, I certainly appreciate it."

He hung up the phone and hooked his thumbs into his belt.

"He found two more addresses, but they were even more out of date than the one we had for Portland."

"Shit," Darger said.

"He said he'd keep on it. Has a few tricks of the trade he can use, but seeing as we just talked to Dustin's parents yesterday and asked about him, he wants to let things settle for a few days before he tries anything. If Dustin's hiding out, he doesn't want to arouse any suspicion."

Now she felt a strange tightness in her chest. An almost panicked feeling.

Darger excused herself and found the bathroom. She locked the door behind her just as the first tears sprang to her eyes.

Jesus Christ.

What the hell was wrong with her? It was just a little roadblock in the case. Nothing to have a meltdown over.

But she knew she wasn't crying about hitting another dead end. She was crying about Fowles.

It felt like a bit of an overreaction. She'd only known him for two days. But something about it had rattled her, got its claws in good and deep.

What kind of fucking universe was she living in? A kind, giving woman like Shannon Mead has her life stolen by a psycho. A brilliant scientist like Fowles given mere months to live. It wasn't fair.

It wasn't fucking fair.

She was crying hard now, tears and snot flowing from her face.

What a crock of shit life was.

And maybe it didn't matter how long you knew someone. It wasn't like she'd never teared up at tragic stories about strangers in the newspapers. Felt a certain stab to the heart after reading a particularly grim police file. Been overwhelmed with grief for the victims and families in her own cases.

Darger took a long, deep breath, gathering her frayed nerves into something resembling calmness. And then she spent some time putting herself back together. Wiping the moisture from her cheeks, dabbing any mascara smears from under her eyes with a wad of toilet paper. Checking to make sure her face wasn't red and splotchy.

How was she going to get through the day when she felt like this?

She didn't know, but she had to try.

Thankfully, the others were back on the internet, hunting for any possible connection to Dustin Reynolds when she finally came out. They barely noticed her return.

But then Fowles swiveled in his chair, took one look at her, and frowned.

"Are you feeling OK?"

"What?" Darger swallowed guiltily and tried to appear perky. "Yeah. I'm fine."

Furbush was studying her now, too. She squirmed under their scrutiny, certain they could tell she'd been crying.

"Fowles is right. You look a little peakèd."

"I'm just frustrated, is all," she said, brushing them off. "Dustin Reynolds didn't just disappear into thin air. There has to be someone who knows where he is."

Furbush was still studying her.

"Did you eat breakfast this morning?"

"I had some instant oatmeal."

"Well that's your problem. Instant oatmeal and donuts? That's not the right way to start the day. You need protein."

"I feel fine. Really."

Ignoring her, Furbush called out through the open door.

"Marcy? Hold down the fort, will you? We're going over to The Early Bird for breakfast."

"I don't think—" Darger started to say, but Furbush cut her off.

"Can't run on an empty tank. You never know what kind of inspiration a hearty breakfast might stir up."

Sensing it was pointless to continue arguing, Darger got to her feet and trailed Fowles and Furbush to the door.

CHAPTER 32

You make Callie breakfast in bed. Hash browns and a fried egg on a bed of sautéed spinach and mushrooms. The shredded potatoes take up about two-thirds of the plate. Just the way she likes it.

There is something strange about cooking while she sleeps. Something hushed and reverent.

You stand over the hot stove. Frying pans spitting at you a little.

The warmth shimmers over the cooktop. Reaches out to touch the flesh of your cheeks. It feels good on a cold morning like this.

You like cooking for Callie. A lot of couples don't enjoy nurturing each other this way. Not these days. But you think expressing affection by taking care of your partner is among the purest forms of love.

It makes you happy to serve her, to work for her, to present her something you made with your own two hands.

There is meaning in it. Significance.

So many people take themselves too seriously for that, maybe. Too intellectual or hip to want to play the caretaker role.

Or maybe they merely want to consume their partner, reduce them to an image that exists for their convenience. An object to bring them entertainment and gratification.

Some people can get stuck so far up in their own heads that they kind of forget other people are real all the way, especially the people closest to them.

Whatever the reason, modern people seem to feel resentment when they have to do something for someone else. Maybe we're that addicted to feeling powerful, imagining ourselves as the heroes of our own story. Even the slightest sacrifice makes us feel small, makes us feel powerless, makes us want to lash out.

But for you, it's the opposite. You have all of these feelings for Callie. Intense, uncontrollable, passionate emotions that swirl about deep inside of you.

You look for any way you can to get them out, to articulate them. The urge to convey them is not even purely to communicate the information to her so much as a need to reveal this part of your soul to the world, to expel it, to assert this aspect of yourself out loud.

You're not great with words. Not an artist or anything. Cooking is one of the tiny pinholes you can try to squeeze those feelings through, try to express all of your soul through.

You hand her the plate on a tray that nestles over her lap, and she scoots to a sitting up position in bed to accept it.

A little smile curls at the corners of her mouth, and her eyelids flutter in a way you see as bashful, like maybe she thinks she doesn't deserve this.

This offering. This effort. She feels it might be too much for her, too good for her.

But she's wrong. You'd give her the world if you could.

Thankfully she doesn't want that. She wants food. Likes it. Really, really likes it. Hash browns, especially.

She appreciates your gift as fully as you meant it, as one plate of love from you to her.

And you eat. And life makes sense.

For a little while, anyway.

CHAPTER 33

The Early Bird was a dingy small-town diner like a hundred others Darger had been in, right down to the wood plank walls featuring historical photographs of the town.

They paused at the sign that told them to *Please Wait To Be Seated* until an older waitress with cherry-red hair led them to a booth near the back.

"I know the Chief here would rather die than drink decaf," she said, winking at Furbush, "but what about you two youngsters?"

Darger didn't hesitate.

"Regular is great."

"I'll actually take some hot water for tea," Fowles said, which elicited a suspicious look from the waitress.

She dealt the trio menus like she was a blackjack dealer at the Bellagio, and when it came time to recite the specials, she rattled them off so fast, Darger might have mistaken her for an auctioneer.

"I'll be back with the coffee." She narrowed her eyes at Fowles. "And the *hot water.*"

As she headed for the kitchen, Fowles lowered his voice and leaned in, like he was about to share a secret with them.

"I think our waitress might suspect me of being a communist."

Furbush smirked.

"Well, that's what you get for ordering something fancy in a town like this."

"See, I don't understand that. In England, tea has no class significance. It's consumed universally, rich or poor."

"Ah, but you said it right there. In *England,*" Furbush said. "One of the most prominent and symbolic acts of rebellion in our country's history was the Boston Tea Party. After that, it was considered downright unpatriotic to drink tea."

"OK, but that was over two centuries ago."

"Doesn't matter. Once tea was out, it was out for life. Done with tea. No debate. No looking back. That's where coffee came in. In fact, it was in a coffee house that the Declaration of Independence was first read aloud to the public. No lie."

"A historian, eh?"

If Darger wasn't mistaken, Furbush blushed a little at that. "I dabble."

Fowles let his eyes drift across the table to meet hers.

"What do you think?"

"About what?"

"Do you find drinking tea to be an un-American trait?"

He smiled, and it registered dully that he was trying to draw her into the conversation.

She could have played along with the joke and accused Fowles of being a traitorous Pinko bastard. Or she could have pointed out that it was unlikely to be a historical or cultural thing at all, and merely the fact that waitstaff hated when people ordered tea because they have to wait for the hot water — and servers hate waiting for anything. On top of the waiting, the tea also comes with all of these little accessories: the teapot, the lemon, the milk, a selection of tea bags. It was fussy and three times more complicated than fetching a cup of coffee.

But his effort was a hopeless one. Darger could barely

manage more than a two-word response. Couldn't seem to get her brain into conversation mode.

So she said none of these things, and instead muttered only, "No."

To avoid further attempts at luring her into the discussion, Darger buried her face in the menu. She didn't have much of an appetite, but she doubted Furbush would find that an acceptable excuse considering he dragged them all here because she looked a little "peakèd." She'd have to order something.

She scoured the menu for something she'd be able to choke down. Something soft maybe. Her eyes stopped on the blueberry pancakes, but then she remembered the overly-sweetened glue masquerading as oatmeal she'd already eaten. Anything sweet and doughy was out.

She moved onto the section focused on eggs, but realized that neither runny yolks nor a rubbery scramble sounded appetizing. She was quickly running out of options.

Finally, she landed on a heading for breakfast sandwiches. The only one that didn't have eggs on it was the BLT, so it won out by simple process of elimination.

Armed with a pot of fresh coffee and a small metal teapot for Fowles, the waitress bustled back to the table. She filled their cups with a steaming black brew and then set the pot on a nearby empty table so she could take down their orders. With her pad at the ready, she aimed her pen at each of them in turn.

When Darger was up, she asked for the BLT and an orange juice.

The waitress stalked off toward the kitchen, and Fowles and Furbush shifted topics. It sounded like sports to Darger. Maybe football.

"Offensive line is coming along. I didn't have much hope a month ago, but they're coming along."

"Good enough to beat the Rams?"

Furbush guffawed.

"Hey, I didn't say that. I may be an optimist, Mr. Fowles, but I'm not legally blind. That Rams front seven is ferocious. Pack of damn wolves. They'll eat the poor Seattle offensive line's lunch, I'm sure."

Darger wondered if Fowles actually liked football, or if he was only asking questions to humor Furbush. He didn't strike her as the type to be into sports all that much. Then again, he hadn't seemed like the type to be dying of brain cancer, so you never really knew, did you?

This dark thought brought the threatening prickle of tears to her eyes again. She held her breath.

Get it together, Violet.

She needed to think about something else. Find something to focus on.

Her eyes ran up the wall, landing on a stuffed fish mounted there. Its scales glittered under the fluorescent lights. The mouth was stretched wide, giving it the appearance of being permanently startled.

There was a place just like this where she'd grown up. The Moosehead Diner, it had been called, named for the trophy displayed over the front door. She glanced at the door. No moose head here.

Her gaze fell lower. They did have the exact same candy machines by the door. Put in a quarter and get a handful of Chiclets or some cheap trinket, like a faux gemstone ring that left a green mark on your finger if you wore it for too long.

Darger's father had abandoned the family when she was six, and one of her only clear memories of him was when he showed her how to work the gum machine. How you set the quarter into the slot with one hand and held the little metal door shut with the other. Then you turned the crank so the quarter disappeared and watched the colorful bits of candy shift in the glass case. She remembered the tinkle of the gum hitting the chute. And then carefully — so carefully — how her dad helped her cup her hand under the door. And finally the last step: lifting the hatch and catching the sugar-coated rectangles in her sweaty little palm.

Absently, Darger wondered if her dad was dead. She thought not. She'd have heard, right? It wasn't like he'd disappeared off the face of the planet. He'd only disappeared from their lives.

For a while, when she was in middle school, he'd been really good about calling on her birthday, on Christmas. And he made plans and promises. Said that he was going to come visit, come pick her up. But he never did.

Why was she thinking about this, of all things?

She pried her eyes away from the candy machine and noted something else this place had in common with The Moosehead. There was a counter at one end of the restaurant, each stool taken by an old man in flannel. There'd always been a similar group of old guys in the diner when she was a kid. Guys that knew every waitress by name.

Darger wondered if these were some of the so-called "Old Boys" Carole Whitmore had complained about. If so, they'd probably been coming to this place their whole lives. Having breakfast with the same group of men every morning, trading town gossip, complaining about the crops and the weather and the government.

The food arrived. Darger was surprised to find herself salivating at the sight of her sandwich. Maybe she was a little hungry after all.

Eating grounded her a little, brought her out of her head and back into the realm of basic animal urges and concrete sensations. The fatty, salty bacon on her tongue. The crispy toast crunching between her teeth. The tartness of the orange juice hitting the back of her throat.

From time to time, Fowles glanced over at her, like maybe he was worried.

She smiled, for real this time. Maybe Furbush had been right. She'd just needed some real food in her stomach.

Darger thought then of something her dad used to say when they were on one of their Sunday morning diner outings: *Breakfast like a king!*

She didn't think she'd ever heard him utter the rest of the phrase. He always stopped after the first line, as if that said it all.

Darger had looked him up when she'd first joined the FBI and gained access to their database. It wasn't exactly kosher, but according to her coworkers "everyone does it." And even though she knew that wasn't a valid excuse, she'd done it anyway, unable to stave off her biological curiosity. She'd had that same thought then, had used it to justify peeking into something she really had no right to: What if he was dead? That was something she should know, wasn't it?

Not everyone had an entry in the Triple-I system — only individuals with a criminal history — but it wasn't too wild a guess to assume her father might have a record. And, surprise, surprise, she'd been right. Two drunk driving citations and a more recent conviction for check fraud. Daddy, as it turned out, was on probation in Fort Pierce, Florida.

Father of the Year, William Darger was not.

More recently, Darger's aunt sent her a link to the family tree she'd been working on. Her Aunt Tess had been quite thorough — aside from Darger, there were entries for her mother and stepfather, her stepfather's children, and of course, her own father. After clicking her father's profile, she noted a marriage certificate issued in Ohio. Her father had moved to Ohio and remarried?

Then she noticed another document on the page. It was a birth notice for someone named Mary Alice Darger. According to the birth date listed, she was five years old.

Darger had a half-sister? A half-sister her father hadn't bothered to tell her about?

It shouldn't have been a shock. This was what he did. And yet her eyes had stung with angry, frustrated tears as she sat there staring at the computer screen.

That had been about a year ago, and now Darger wondered bitterly if dear old dad had abandoned little Mary Alice yet. Was six the magic number? The time most ripe for abandoning your family?

Why was she even thinking about her father right now? She glanced up at the fish with its mouth agape. Then at the old men lined up at the counter. It was this place. The memories it had loosened from the back of her mind. That was what nostalgia did for you. Dredged up all the old happy thoughts.

Right.

But there was something else. Something tugging at her conscious mind from deeper in her psyche.

Something relating to the case? It didn't seem likely.

And then it hit her. What everyone kept saying about Dustin's family.

The Reynolds clan goes way back.

Far enough back that someone might have taken an interest in entering the family history into a site like Ancestry.com? Where someone might have entered personal information about Dustin, like maybe that he'd gotten married recently or had a child. And often this information was accompanied by the city and state such an event had occurred.

A prickle of excitement ran through Darger's body.

It was a long shot. But it was something.

Darger tried to wait for a lull in the conversation, but it was taking too long.

"I have an idea," she said, interrupting.

Both men stopped talking and looked at her.

"I was beginning to think you'd lost the ability to speak."

Darger ignored Furbush's quip.

"Genealogy sites," Darger said, too antsy to properly explain herself.

Furbush's brow wrinkled.

"What?"

"We should check genealogy sites. They often have major life events listed — like marriages and births — and they usually say where the events took place."

"Wouldn't that have come up in our internet searches?" Furbush asked.

Darger shook her head.

"You have to be a member of the site."

"And if you are a member, you can see anyone's family tree?"

"Some are private. But most people keep them public, because that's one of the easiest ways to complete your tree. You end up finding distant relatives who can fill in the blanks with the parts of the tree they've already done."

The waitress had brought them a check, and the three of them were heading for the register now.

"It's a crapshoot," Darger said. "I know that. But it's worth a try."

"Better than sitting around twiddling our thumbs," Furbush said.

On their trek to the register, they passed the group of men seated at the counter, and one of them spun around on his stool and hailed Furbush.

"Hey there, Chief. Working hard or hardly working?"

"Tell you what, Sam. Working so hard we ran out of gas… needed to refuel."

"Heard ya went out for a chat with ol' Chief Milton," the old man said.

"That's right. Now we're trying to track down a local kid. Well, actually I guess he isn't a kid anymore."

Darger cringed at this and tried to catch Furbush's eye.

"Who's that now?"

Before she could stop him, the Chief had blurted, "Dustin Reynolds."

Jesus Christ, Darger thought. He should know to be a little more discreet. The last thing they needed was the rumor that they were looking for Dustin to get around town. From the sound of it, gossip traveled fast here.

"That wouldn't be Dirk Reynolds' boy, would it?"

"No, I believe this would be Dirk's grandson."

Darger bit the inside of her cheek to keep from muttering a string of annoyed curses. It was too late now.

"Good old Dirk. I was just thinking about him, it being Cascade bull elk season and all. We used to go hunting every year, back in the day. They had some family property out near Marmot. Real nice piece of land that was. Untouched by man, except for a little cabin just off the road there. They owned a big chunk of land, 100 acres or more. And we'd camp out under the stars unless it rained. If Mother Nature didn't cooperate, we'd hole up in the cabin there for a whole weekend, drinking and carousing. Used to get up to all sorts of mischief. One time Dirk switched Little Bart's and Big George's boots after a night of drinking. Snuck out of his tent in the middle of the night and swapped 'em without anyone knowing it. Then he woke everyone up saying there was a bear in camp. Bart and George came stumbling out of their tents still half-drunk, and it was the funniest thing I ever seen, watchin' them two struggle to get on boots that didn't fit right."

The old man let out a wheeze of laughter. Furbush and Fowles were chuckling along with him. But Darger was interested in something different altogether.

"This cabin… it was on land the Reynolds family owned?" she asked, giving Furbush a loaded look.

The Chief's eyebrows shot up when he got the implication. He hoisted his belt and stepped forward.

"Say, Sam… you wouldn't happen to know if the family still owns that cabin?"

"Not for certain. But I can't imagine Mamie selling it off, to be honest. Tighter than a duck's ass, that one," the old man said, then winked at Darger. "If you'll excuse my language, miss."

As they hurried back over to the station, Furbush grumbled and swore under his breath.

"All those records we sifted through. All those calls we made. And here the answer was right under my nose the whole time," Furbush said, tugging at his belt in irritation.

"We don't know that yet," Darger said.

"But it's something."

"Yeah," she agreed. "And it's a hell of a lot more than my stupid genealogy idea."

CHAPTER 34

Back at the station, Marcy worked her magic again with the local property tax records, bringing up a page that showed all property owned by the Reynolds family trust. She typed in the address and brought up a satellite map of the Marmot land.

Darger pointed at a small square outline on the map.

"I bet that's the cabin," she said.

Furbush nodded and reached for his jacket.

"I think I ought to pay another visit to Mamie Reynolds. See what she can tell us about this place. Maybe she'll even fess up to knowing he's camped out up there."

Before he turned to go, Darger thought of something else.

"Someone should drive out in an unmarked car and sit on the place. If he's there, we don't want his aunt or anyone else tipping him off."

"You volunteering?" Furbush asked.

"Sure," Darger said.

Fowles raised a hand. "I'm coming with you."

As they walked out to their respective vehicles, Furbush called over.

"You're not gonna do anything wild now, are you?"

Darger paused with her door half open.

"Like what?"

"I don't know. Storming in there on your own."

"Of course not," she said.

"It's just that you've got a bit of a reputation for being a hotspur is all."

"A what?"

Fowles, who was already ensconced in the driver's seat, leaned over to her side and said, "It means rash and impetuous."

"I am *not* rash and impetuous," Darger said.

Fowles only shrugged.

To Furbush she said, "I promise to stay in the car until given further orders."

"Good. You got your phone turned on?"

"Yes," Darger said, double-checking just to be sure.

"I'll give you a call after I talk to Mamie Reynolds. We can go from there."

"Great," Darger said. "Talk to you then."

She climbed into the passenger seat and pulled the seatbelt over her chest.

"Rash and impetuous," Darger scoffed.

Fowles chuckled, and she glared at him as he turned the key in the ignition.

☾

The road that led to the cabin was remote and pocked with poorly filled potholes. When the rustic log structure appeared on the left, Darger told Fowles to slow down a little. As they rolled by, Darger took a hard look at the place, trying to catalogue as many details as possible in the short amount of time she had.

The driveway was a bare dirt two-track, overgrown with weeds and vegetation creeping in from the surrounding forest. Set back from the road, a few hundred feet behind the cabin, was a small shed. A large fir tree had fallen across the far end of the property, missing the cabin by only a few feet. It didn't look like the tree falling had been a recent event, and no one had taken steps to move it. Darger didn't think anyone had been out here for some time. A perfect off-grid hideout.

The cabin itself was small, probably a one or two room affair. There was a single chimney, but Darger saw no trace of smoke. That wasn't too surprising. The weather was fairly mild at the moment.

Besides, she didn't need smoke to confirm that someone was home. There was something better.

A beat-up Dodge Ram parked in the driveway, maybe 15 years old. It matched the color and era of the truck registered in Dustin Reynolds' name.

They continued on past the cabin for several hundred yards before Darger had Fowles turn around and park on the side of the road.

He killed the engine, and the sounds of the forest surrounded them. Squawking birds and chittering bugs. The thought of insect-life brought her focus back to Fowles and his illness.

But she checked her sadness, forced it down, not wanting it to spill over again. She seemed to be able to stay above it at the moment. To hover over the darkest feelings without letting them touch her. It was like she'd gained the ability to separate her emotional side and observe the situation with an analyst's mind.

Still, studying Fowles from the corner of her eye, he looked… healthy. Happy.

She found it hard to believe that someone with so much vitality and enthusiasm for their work and life in general was so close to death, and it occurred to her suddenly that he very likely wouldn't finish his doctorate.

Before she could stop herself, she'd blurted, "What about your thesis?"

"What about it?"

"Well, with your illness…"

He raised an eyebrow but didn't say anything.

Darger fidgeted.

"If you won't get to finish… I mean, doesn't that make all your effort a little… pointless?"

"But why should it? I'm not doing the work for the diploma to hang on the wall. I'm doing it for science. For the pursuit of information. To improve forensic entomology. How could anything render that pointless?"

"OK, *pointless* was the wrong word to use. Of course I see how it's valuable work. Important work. But don't you want to… I don't know… do something fun?"

"You think I should be backpacking around Asia? Learning to fly an airplane? Following my bliss and/or heart? Standing windswept on the bow of a grand oceanic liner and yelling about how I'm the king of the world?"

"Maybe not those *exact* things…"

They were silent a moment. Then he looked at her, eyes squinted down to slits against the bright sun.

"Of all people, I would have thought you would understand. All that curiosity. All that drive to do something with purpose in your life. If you thought you only had a few years or a few months to live, would you really walk away from your work?"

Darger stared at him, then back out the window.

"I don't know."

And before she could gain any further clarity, her phone rang. It was Chief Furbush.

"Mamie Reynolds confirmed the existence of the cabin but denied any knowledge of her nephew staying there. Said that if Dustin is there, it's news to her."

"Do you believe her?" Darger asked.

"Under normal circumstances, I wouldn't. But she seemed pretty ticked off at the idea that he might be crashing there without her permission. She gave us the go-ahead to take a look around. Even gave me a spare key."

"That saves us having to get a warrant. I'm sure you're probably already thinking the same, but I think we ought to call in SWAT on this. Maybe you have a connection with the State Police, but the FBI SWAT teams are very good, and I'm sure the Portland team could be here in under an hour if I put in a call."

"That's not necessary. We have our own regional tactical team."

Darger knew what that meant. Part-timers. And it wasn't that part-time SWAT teams couldn't do the job. But this wasn't an ordinary suspect.

"Under the circumstances, given the seriousness of this investigation, I think it might be a more prudent call to bring in a dedicated team."

"I appreciate the offer, Miss Darger," he said, and again, she realized how much she missed being called *Agent* instead of *Miss*.

Darger gripped the phone a little harder, knuckles turning white. She had to tread carefully here.

"I'm sure your team is excellent. But we don't know Dustin Reynolds' state of mind. Or if he's armed."

"And our team is trained to deal with any scenario."

"I have no doubt. But there's a real chance that Dustin Reynolds is a very disturbed, very dangerous man. And I think it would be best if—"

"I'm sorry, but I have to cut you off right there. As I said before, I appreciate your input, but I really need to put the call in to our guys if we're going to make this happen."

The phone clicked. He'd hung up on her.

Darger's fist slammed into the dashboard.

"Goddamn it!"

So *that* was why he'd made her promise to sit on the house. He was worried she'd run in, guns a-blazing, and steal his thunder.

She'd been giving Furbush the benefit of the doubt, because they'd been working so well together. But it was always only a matter of time before the truth came out. Before the departments started jockeying for position, readying themselves for the big moment when they got to claim credit for catching the bad guy.

"Everything OK?" Fowles asked.

"Peachy," Darger said, then had a thought.

Margaret Prescott.

She snatched her phone up from where she'd dropped it in her lap and dialed the number.

"Violet," Dr. Prescott said. "How are things going?"

"Well, there's good and bad news. The good news is we think we finally tracked our primary suspect down. The bad news is that Chief Furbush is insisting on using his local tactical team to storm the house."

"And?"

"And I tried to impress upon him the importance of using a full-time team. State Police or even the FBI's team from Portland. This isn't a job for weekenders."

"I'm not sure what you think I can do about it."

"You could try talking some sense into him."

"I thought I already made this quite clear, Miss Darger. You are a consultant on this case. Nothing more. You have absolutely no jurisdictional authority. You are a civilian. You are *not* law enforcement. As such, it is your job to *consult* and then get the hell out of the way."

"This isn't about me. I'm trying to prevent a bunch of small-town cops from charging in and getting their heads blown off by a potential psycho holed up in a hunting cabin."

"And my response is this: You are to keep your head down and to stay out of the line of fire. I did not hire you to be a top gun." Dr. Prescott's voice was hard. "Now, was there anything else? I'm going to be late for an appointment with my acupuncturist."

Darger hung up.

CHAPTER 35

After breakfast, you clear the plates and crawl back into bed. Ready to sleep that little bit more, as is Callie.

With the shades pulled tight, shadows dominate the room. Swirling darkness smothers everything, growing thicker and blacker as you move deeper into the space like a cave.

Here, in this room, the night never needs to end. It can be extended indefinitely. You like that.

The cold sheets slowly go warm against your skin. Heat that builds in stages. Cold to cool to warm to toasty. A slow swelling in temperature like someone bringing up a dimmer switch in slow motion.

You cuddle again. Hugging and squeezing.

The lack of light purples her face, her smile beaming a brighter shade — more lavender than plum. And the dark makes the edges of her features indistinct in a way that becomes sort of maddening if you stare at it too intently. A twisting gloom over her face like smoke that won't keep still. The shapes just keep shifting.

Still, she is here. With you. In your arms.

And touching her, that incredible warmth comes over your body. That sense of security that seems the only thing that can still all the bad thoughts in your head, that seems to erase any notion or care about a reality outside of this room.

She brings you back to a simpler version of yourself and keeps you there. A childlike version without worries. Without dark impulses.

This moment surrounds you, envelops you, the beautiful and vexing experience of life and love, the immediate joy of living that can sometimes drown everything else out.

Again you are struck by the overwhelming desire to stop time. Freeze it. Pause all things and live in this moment forever. An endless night you can spend together.

She rolls so she's facing away from you and you loop an arm around her, settle against her once more. The big spoon and the little spoon.

And she is all you really need. She is everything.

You swallow and realize there's a lump in your throat. Your eyelids flutter, lashes flicking at the edges of your vision like moth wings.

Sometimes, in moments like these, your love of Callie grows so heavy in your chest that you could burst into tears. It's too much. Too big to bear.

You can feel them there, the tears, little itchy things in the corner of your eyes. Wet and heavy. Right on the cusp. The beads of water aching to spill down your cheeks.

And you worry that if and when that ever happens — the spontaneous waterworks bursting forth from your eyes — you won't be able to stop it. You'll just cry and cry for eternity. Reduced somehow to something less than before, less than a child even. Something else. No longer human. A weeping lump that lies in bed all day, pulls the blankets up over its head and trembles there. A blubbering mess. Lost in a way that can never be found.

But you hold it in. You hold all of it in somehow.

You take a breath. Hold it for a beat. Let it out. Little tremors rattling your chest all the while.

And the moment gets bigger. Swells up like a marshmallow in the microwave.

Something is happening here. Something sacred. You can feel it in the heat in your cheeks, in the shaking abdominals in your core, in the wetness clinging to your lips.

She feels so good in your arms. So good, you never want to let her go. So good, you almost wish you could meld with her. Fuse your bodies together so you'd never be apart.

You sit up a little. Grip Callie's shoulder. Turn her to face you. Going to kiss her, you think.

And the blade just appears there between you.

A butcher knife in your hand.

Its tip presses into the middle of Callie's torso. Moving. Fluttering there like a bird for a moment just beneath her ribcage, its shape shifting in the dark.

The point pierces her. Drives right into her like she's made of soft cheese. A long slow inward stroke, and you can feel how sharp it is in the ease of its progress. Can feel it entering her unobstructed. Unperturbed.

Electricity shoots all through you. A flash so bright it blinds you for a second. Fills your eyes with dark.

Confusion.

In that moment when your vision cuts out, all of reality whittles to the feel of the knife sliding into her. So slow. It keeps going long after what seems possible. Feels like it's about 3 feet long, but it just keeps fucking going into her.

And you hear it. The sound of the knife. The tiniest rasp that reminds you of a paper cutter.

Did you bring it from the kitchen after cooking? Have it here with you, stowed under your pillow this whole time?

Did you know you were going to do this all along? For days? Weeks? Months?

The knife seems to move on its own. Do what it wants to do. Still sliding in on that first cut. Going deeper, deeper, deeper.

Penetrating.

Impaling.

And there's wet and hot and red gushing over the metal, over your hand, onto the sheets. It rushes out thinner than what seems right. Flows like water, like wine, like red Faygo brought up to body temperature in a sauté pan.

And her mouth opens in slow motion. Wider. Wider.

Lips wet. A big capital letter O occupying most of her face.

And her eyes blink. So big. So big. Magnified by the water pooling along the bottom eyelids.

Your own eyes flick over hers. Making eye contact but somehow not. She's not there now. Not all the way.

There is no connection there. Nothing between you.

Just a small scared animal and a big strong one. Maybe there's something natural in that. A gap between you too big to comprehend let alone bridge.

Her mind cannot process this, cannot fathom what is happening. Somehow you know this when you look into the vacancy in her eyes. The emptiness.

Already her skin feels so cold. Wet and shiny with an even sheen of sweat.

Shock, you know. She is in shock.

And maybe you feel it, too.

Your heart hammers in your chest, its rhythm pounding in your temples, in your neck. And you can feel your breath thrusting in and out between clenched teeth. Ragged as hell.

This is happening to both of you, isn't it?

A thing that is happening.

She gags a little now. Choked sounds from deep in her throat. Retching sounds.

And now a bloody bubble pops on her lips.

Wet mouth moving.

Teeth red.

Little whispered syllables seeping out of her at the end, but you can't understand, you can't understand at all.

CHAPTER 36

Furbush and the others arrived about forty minutes later. When Darger saw the other vehicles approaching, she took out her sidearm and double-checked the mag.

"Didn't Dr. Prescott give you explicit instructions to let the law enforcement officers do the shooting and breaking down doors?" Fowles asked.

Darger stared at him.

"Sorry, but your phone is really loud. I kind of heard everything."

She kept staring.

"Seriously, how can you stand having it that loud? It has to be doing serious damage. Painful to even witness."

Removing her jacket and tossing it in the backseat, Darger tucked the Shield back into its holster.

"I know she thinks that it's better for her — better for Prescott Consulting — if one of her consultants isn't involved in a potential shootout. I can appreciate that. What I can't appreciate is letting a bunch of greenhorn cops walk into a death trap because their idiot Chief wants to play commando."

"Maybe we should both just stay in the car, and let them handle it."

Darger shook her head.

"OK, then I think I should go with you," he said.

"Fowles, you're not even armed."

"I have a gun."

"Where?"

242

He lifted the lid of the console between them, pointed to a lockbox.

"Everyone goes through firearm training and is certified for concealed carry at Prescott Consulting. It's policy."

"Well it's not doing you much good in that box."

Fowles pulled the case out.

"I never could get used to it. Made me nervous to have it around all the time. I kept imagining that I'd set it down somewhere and forget about it, and then some kid would walk up and start playing with it and blow his own head off."

"This is your argument for letting you come along?"

"You asked why I wasn't carrying it."

"And your answer is that guns make you nervous. So yeah, I'm going to have to insist that you stay in the car."

Just before she closed the door, she leaned back in and said, "You're not allowed to die yet."

To Furbush's credit, he didn't try to keep Darger from tagging along. In fact, she didn't even have to ask to borrow a vest. He just handed one to her without a word when she approached the back of the black SUV.

"Now before one of you young guys gets a little too enthusiastic and goes lobbing a stun grenade through a window, this is not a dynamic entry," Furbush said to the men clustered around him. "We will surround and call out. The property owner has given us a key with permission to enter. Is that clear?"

There was a round of rigorous nodding and *yes, sirs*, and then they were moving out.

It all seemed to happen fast from there.

They approached the cabin as one group. As they closed in

on the squat little building, half of the men split off to secure the back of the place.

Darger followed Furbush onto the front porch. The boards were old and weathered, some half-rotted through. She did her best to avoid the spots that looked the most likely to crumble under her weight.

Over the radio, the leader of the rear group signaled that all was quiet on their end of the cabin.

Chief Furbush pulled the front screen door ajar and banged his fist against the rustic wood storm door.

"Sandy Police. Anybody home?"

They waited. Nothing happened.

Darger was positioned near one of the grimy windows. She could see through a crack in the drapes, but it was dim inside. She could make out what looked like a dingy metal sink. Must be the kitchen area. She detected no movement.

A tingle started in her scalp and traveled down her spine. She shook it off, trying to convince herself that it was only nerves and not a premonition that things were about to go very badly.

Furbush knocked again.

Still there was no answer.

"Key?" Furbush said.

One of the men handed Furbush the key. She had a hard time telling everyone apart with the helmets and matching tactical gear, but she could read the patch on his chest. Mantelbaum. He'd been one of the uniforms asking questions when she'd presented her profile.

"Sandy Police," Furbush announced again. "We have permission from the homeowner to enter and are doing so now."

Furbush blinked and sweated as he inserted the key into the lock. The deadbolt clunked as it slid out of the way.

Just before he turned the knob, he glanced over at his men and gave a nod. His gaze paused when it met Darger's. He smiled nervously, but she saw a flicker of fear in his eyes. She wondered if he was now regretting not letting another SWAT team handle this.

Furbush nudged the door open with his foot and stepped aside to let the first two men through. Darger slipped inside behind Furbush, hugging the wall on the right side of the door as she entered, sweeping the corner and far wall with her weapon drawn.

She didn't breathe or blink. Watching for movement, listening for any sound.

The first two men held the door while she and Furbush proceeded further into the place. It was mostly one large common room, with walls of rough pine decorated with an impressive collection of antlers and pelts. A battered old velour couch faced a woodstove on one end, and the kitchen/dining area occupied the other. Passing the sink she'd spotted through the window, Darger noted an open box of half-eaten pizza. It was moldy and covered in flies.

It was starting to look like no one was home, but there were two doors toward the back. Probably a sleeping area and a bathroom, Darger figured. They'd need to clear them to be sure.

A strangled cough shattered the silence. Darger flinched before she realized it had come from behind her.

Just one of the other guys. She almost laughed, and while

she didn't allow herself to fully relax yet, she did finally take a breath.

She turned, wondering why the others weren't moving forward to clear the other two rooms.

Chief Furbush held a hand to his nose and mouth, face wrinkled in disgust. A beat later, the fresh-faced kid, Mantelbaum, was running for the door. He doubled over the railing and retched.

And then the smell hit her.

The rancid stench of rotting meat.

Her eyes met the Chief's. They didn't need to say anything.

They crept to the far end of the cabin, still taking precautions because that was protocol.

But Darger knew that neither one of them had any illusions now. They would not find any living occupants here.

They cleared the bedroom. It wasn't large, but with bunks stacked three-high on each side, could sleep six.

Furbush halted in front of the bathroom. His eyes swiveled sideways to look at her. She nodded and covered him.

He reached out a hand and gave the door a shove.

Hinges groaned. And then another sound. The hum of flies, buzzing in the air and knocking against the window with faint tapping sounds.

In the bathtub, a bloated corpse in an advanced state of decay oozed and stank, lying face down from the looks of it.

There were so many flies and maggots on the body, it almost appeared to writhe and squirm on its own.

Darger's eyes watered from the odor, even though she wasn't breathing through her nose. The stench of putrefaction felt oily and unctuous in her mouth.

Five Days Post Mortem

Flies circled everywhere now, released from their bathroom prison. Darger waved one away from her face.

"I think we just found Dustin Reynolds."

CHAPTER 37

The sun looked like a sphere of liquid fire as it melted below the tree line, leaving behind clouds streaked with orange and yellow.

Darger sat on the trunk of the downed tree in the driveway of the Reynolds property. The crime scene processing team had kicked all unnecessary personnel out of the small, stinking cabin some time ago, and Darger couldn't really say she was all that disappointed. The nose has a way of getting used to most smells, but she had yet to experience her senses reaching the point where she really, truly didn't notice the stench of decay.

Furbush tromped out onto the front porch with his hands hooked into his belt. She watched him take a few deep lungfuls of clean air before surveying the yard and spotting her. He strode over.

"Coroner just confirmed the body is male. If you pair that with the belongings we found in the house — the wallet, ID, and whatnot — I think we can say it's more likely than not that the deceased is Dustin Reynolds. We'll have to run dental records to be absolutely certain, but I'll be a son of a gun if we're wrong."

"Fowles still taking samples?"

The Chief blew a puff of air through his lips.

"Yeah. I don't know how he can stand it. I hate even being in a room with a DB like that. Makes my skin crawl. But he's in there, close enough to give it a kiss on the lips. Taking temperatures, scooping up maggots. And chattering away like he's giving a lecture the whole time. Got this real amused tone to his voice, too. Kind of creepy, if I'm being honest with ya. Sounds like a little kid playing in a sandbox, 'cept there's less sand and more corpse juice or whatever the fuck."

Darger did her best to push the images of Fowles elbow-deep in squirming larvae and putrefying flesh from her mind. Instead, she focused on the scientist's unbridled enthusiasm for his work and smiled.

"He should be able to pinpoint Dustin Reynolds' time of death with unbelievable accuracy. That might turn out to be invaluable to the investigation. We're lucky he's here."

Furbush crossed his arms and shook his head.

"God bless him."

The Chief stepped closer to the downed tree trunk and sat down beside Darger.

"Well, shoot," he said, gazing up at the setting sun. "In all the excitement, we skipped lunch."

Darger raised an eyebrow. After witnessing the scene in the cabin, the last thing she was thinking about was her next meal.

Furbush patted his belly and asked, "So what do you think?"

"Call me crazy, but something about a putrefying corpse gets me hankering for ham salad."

Furbush chuckled at her sardonic tone.

"I mean about Dustin Reynolds... I know this isn't the most politically correct thing to say, but I'm kind of hoping he offed himself. Sickened with his crimes, feeling remorse and whatnot. Or maybe just scared he was going to get caught."

Darger rubbed her knuckles along her jaw. She'd considered it.

249

"It's possible. Killing himself in the bathtub could have been his version of a confession. He'd have to be relying on us to have put the rest of it together, though. And I didn't see any obvious signs of suicide. No gun, and he obviously didn't hang himself. Most male suicide victims choose one or the other."

"What about an overdose?"

"That's possible," she agreed. "Self-poisoning is a more common method for women than men, but it's not unheard of. Could have even been an accident, but the bathtub angle seems like a pretty big coincidence."

Fowles appeared on the threshold of the cabin entrance, toting one of his specialized toolboxes and having an animated conversation with the coroner, Dr. Kole. Furbush pushed himself to his feet and crossed the overgrown lawn to meet them. Darger followed.

"My guys are just about finished inside. Should have him packed up and in the van in less than thirty minutes, I'd guess," Dr. Kole said.

A seemingly involuntary shudder of revulsion overtook the police chief.

"I don't envy you, having to make that ride with our stinky friend in the back of your van," he said.

Dr. Kole grinned.

"That's why I insist on bringing my personal vehicle to crime scenes. I have my assistant drive the van."

"Not to rush you, but how long before the autopsy's completed? More specifically, what's the timeline on the toxicology report?" Furbush asked.

The amusement drained from Dr. Kole's face, and his mouth drew into a hard line.

"Oh, I wouldn't hold out any hope on toxicology. Based on the level of decomp I saw, I'd say he's been dead for at least a week. I don't think we'll find any viable organ or tissue samples."

"Damn it all," Furbush cursed under his breath.

Fowles stepped forward then, toolkit in hand.

"I might be able to help with that. With the assistance of gas chromatography and thin-layer chromatography, I can detect toxins in the Diptera larvae, as well as in the shed pupal cases and feces. I've made sure to collect samples of all of those."

"Feces," Furbush repeated, looking a little green again. "You're talking about insect feces?"

"That's right."

The Chief sighed as a gurney bumped out through the front door, handled by two men garbed in crime scene bunny suits.

"I have to tell you, when I first decided to become a police officer, I did not envision that I would someday be standing in the Oregon wilderness, praying to the Good Lord Almighty that bug shit would be the nail in the coffin of a serial murder case," he said. "More than one way to skin a cat, I guess."

Darger watched the coroner's assistants struggle through the tangle of weeds with their load, eyes never leaving the black vinyl body bag strapped to the stretcher.

If this was the end of the road for the investigation, she couldn't help but feel like it was a bit of an anti-climax.

Then again, maybe she'd had enough of chasing down bad guys and taking bullets in the process.

CHAPTER 38

A mist falls over the night. Wets the asphalt and concrete. Turns both dark and shiny.

The faintest rain. Little droplets that seem to hover in the air more than fall. You can see them in the glow of the street lamps, floating everywhere in the yellow light.

But it's not enough to wash the city clean. Not even close. It would take a torrential rain for that, you think. Something biblical.

You walk over the wet terrain, the busted sidewalks, the streets pocked with potholes like acne scars.

You walk the night. Not even sure where you are just now. Lost among avenues and alleyways that all look alien and evil at this hour.

With your hood up, you mostly stay dry. You can only hope that lasts. You've got a feeling you'll be out walking a long time tonight. All night.

It's been over twelve hours since that thing happened to you. The thing with Callie. You're still not quite sure how you feel about it.

Repulsed. Scared. A little excited.

Confused. Maybe that above all else.

The images flare in your head. All of that blood spilling onto your hands, onto the sheets. Her mouth and eyes opened so wide they seemed to occupy all of her face.

It gets your heart thudding to remember. And your hand flutters to the inside pocket of your jacket. Props a cigarette between your lips. Orange flame flickers just beyond your nose to light it.

You quit smoking long ago, but you bought a pack after you took care of Callie's body. You didn't choose this action so far as you can remember. Your body lurched along on autopilot — feet carrying you to the gas station counter, mouth asking for a pack of Marlboro Lights, hands scooting the little white and gold box across the counter, tearing off the cellophane as you stepped away from the building.

You wanted to breathe smoke in and out. Feel it billow in your lungs. Taste it in your head and neck and chest.

Vaguely you recall peeling Callie out from under the tarp in the bed of your truck. Plopping her into a drainage pond off the lake. Can still see the body swallowed up by dark water, the ripples moving outward in circles, disturbing the surface, jostling some lily pads. Out in the woods somewhere. A dark patch of firs that blocked out much of the light. The sky going gray as dusk moved in.

But these fevered memories jumble in your thoughts, occur to you out of order. Already they feel more like a movie you watched than something you did. Already they seem to be fading, tangling, mixing the truth up with fantasies. Pictures in your head. That's all.

And you're thankful, for once, that Callie wanted to keep you a secret, keep your relationship a secret. This could have been bad, could have ruined everything, but you think not. You think now that nothing will happen to you, just like all the other times.

Little rivulets of water snake along the gutter, rushing alongside you as you walk. Draining down the grates every block or so. The chiming sound of the water echoes funny from the sewer, throaty and filtered.

All the scum creeps out at night in this part of town. Prostitutes. Drug dealers. Trashy types filing in and out of the liquor stores with bottles of fuel. Whiskey, gin, beer, and vodka to feed their dark dreams, plant themselves firmly between here and another world, destroy their souls a little at a time.

It makes you sick to walk among them, to know that you're one of them. Filth. The dregs of humanity. A person should aspire to something better, shouldn't they? Something more than this.

You watch a hooker lean over into the open window of a sedan, a scrawny girl with sticks for arms and legs, the tiny blouse more draped over her than worn. Looks maybe eighteen, if that. She smiles. Nods her head. You can see the little girl she must have been not so long ago in these mannerisms. She climbs into the passenger's seat, and the bile climbs your throat like an elevator car going up. Leaves a sour taste in your mouth.

And you picture again that knife penetrating Callie. The tip shoved into her gut, disappearing somewhere inside of her. And blood spurting out in watery sheets. Pulsing. Pulsing. Hot. Your hand thrusting it in, moving slow but so powerful, so strong.

You pitch your cigarette into that flowing stream along the curb. It sizzles when the cherry hits the wet, and you watch the butt surf along a ways before a storm drain swallows it up.

You walk a while, move out away from the ghetto bustle to a quiet residential neighborhood.

The dark seems to swell, beating back the light with cloudy

tufts of shadow stretched over everything like black cotton. Less streetlights here.

And the sound dies out. No more mob swarming around the liquor store like wasps. No more traffic to create that endless hiss of wet tires on asphalt and engine noises rising and falling as they passed. It is dead, this part of the city. Lifeless and still.

That pounding pressure in your head starts to wane as you walk into this emptiness. The acidic feeling in your throat fades away. And a calm settles over you. Something like that.

Good. It's always good to be away from people. Always brings peace to your state of mind.

The night's chill grips you now. Wraps itself around your torso. Makes your skin pull a little bit taut. Two sizes smaller, or so it seems.

And maybe the world will be colder without Callie. Maybe so. You lick your lips when you think about it, a gesture that reminds you of a nervous dog somehow.

But it had to go this way, didn't it? What happened, it wasn't anyone's choice.

In that flash when the image of Callie's body appears in your memory, you think you should kill yourself. Know you should. Hurl yourself out a window or swallow a shotgun.

You've stood there on the edge and looked down so many times. But you can't do it. Too scared.

Sometimes you think you'll live forever. Like a gift and a curse. Like you were chosen. Some strange power was bestowed upon you at birth. And these kills are the price you have to pay for that, maybe. The ritual you carry out. The blood sacrifice. It gives you power.

That would make sense, wouldn't it? Otherwise, why would you do all these things?

You act under orders from above, maybe. You like the idea of that. You like it a lot.

CHAPTER 39

While Furbush stayed behind to make sure the scene was properly secured, Darger and Fowles headed back down to where they'd left the car.

Night had fallen around them. Painted everything black. And it was even darker under the towering trees.

Fowles went to the trunk to secure his case full of samples and tools, and Darger climbed inside.

"I have to take these specimens to FedEx so they can be rushed to the lab. I hope it's OK if I stop there before dropping you off?"

"That's fine," Darger said.

She was in no hurry to return to her depressingly beige hotel room.

Because it was lonely, or because she wanted to spend more time with Fowles? Fresh crime scenes — especially those with dead bodies — always seemed to bring out unexpected emotions.

"Actually, what would you say to grabbing a drink?"

Fowles reached up and adjusted the frames of his glasses.

"Sure. If you're hungry, I know a Thai place that's supposed to be very good."

"I don't think I can eat after that." She gestured over her shoulder, figuring Fowles would guess that meant the grisly scene at the cabin. "I learned a while ago that I'm better off sticking to an all-liquid diet on a day like today."

She studied Fowles, realizing that he'd been the least rattled of anyone at the crime scene.

"I guess you've spent enough time around bodies in the advanced stages of decomposition that it just doesn't bother you anymore, huh?"

His hair brushed against the headliner of the car roof as his head shook from side to side.

"It took some getting used to. I had an incredibly visceral reaction to the first few corpses at the body farm."

"Like what?"

"I'd just freeze on the spot. Like a deer catching sight of a cougar. My legs would just cease to function, completely involuntarily. It felt almost like a spinal reflex," he said, rubbing at the back of his neck. "They look especially wrong laid out in the open like that. Even knowing what to expect, it was hard to wrap my head around walking into a picturesque clearing and spotting what were clearly human remains. And they tend to situate them spread-eagled, for some reason. It's quite unnatural."

When they reached town, Fowles pulled into the lot of the 24-hour FedEx/Kinkos.

"I'll be right back," he said.

Darger watched him jog across the concrete and through the glass doors with his box of samples. She wondered if he told the clerk what was inside the box.

Just a handful or two of maggots I found feeding on a human corpse.

She must have been smirking to herself when he returned, because he peered over at her with a curious expression on his face.

"What?"

"Nothing," she said.

They nearly stopped at a place in Sandy billing itself as a saloon, until Darger noticed the marquee announcing the "Live Music - Classic Rock Night." Not in the mood to shout over a mediocre rendition of "Free Bird," Darger suggested they keep driving.

After another fifteen minutes on the road, they found themselves in a random sports bar in the outskirts of Portland.

It was early, but since it was the weekend, there was still a decent crowd inside. The smell of Pine-Sol, stale beer, and fryer grease wafted through the air as she followed Fowles over to a booth. Moments after she settled into the red vinyl, a barmaid appeared to take their order.

"I'm sorry for what I said earlier," Darger said. "When I questioned why you would still be working on your thesis. You're right. I probably would do the same. Honestly, I think I was projecting a little."

"Projecting what?"

But the waitress returned then, and their conversation was interrupted. She set down the Sam Adams Fowles ordered and Darger's Moscow Mule. She'd wanted something clean and refreshing and the gingery drink definitely scratched that itch.

When the waitress had gone again, Fowles raised a quizzical eyebrow at Darger.

"You were saying?"

"I don't know. I guess it makes me angry that you're..."

"Going to die?"

She sighed and rubbed at her eyelids.

"Yes."

Fowles shrugged and took a long pull from his beer.

"I've been meaning to thank you, actually," Fowles said, adjusting the cocktail napkin under his bottle.

"For what?"

"For not trying to solve my imminent death."

Darger cocked her head to one side, not fully understanding.

"When most people learn about my diagnosis, it's only a matter of time before they start bringing up some new miracle cure they've heard about. Cuban drug trials. A mystical berry from the Amazon rainforest that brought back their cousin's mother-in-law's sister from the brink of death. An Amish faith healer. Marijuana tinctures," he said. "I've heard it all."

"Does that mean this would be a bad time to bring up the profound healing properties of certain crystals and gemstones?" Darger asked.

Fowles stared at her a moment, and though she tried to maintain a straight face, something must have given her away. He broke into a chuckle.

"You almost had me there for a minute."

She grinned and took a drink.

"I couldn't resist."

"I know they mean well. But sometimes when someone's going through something like this, advice isn't what they need or want. I want empathy. Understanding. Someone to just listen."

Darger propped an elbow on the table.

"That's harder than you think for most people. Just listening, I mean. Especially if the person they're supposed to be listening to is in pain. Their instinct is to try to fix it."

"But pain is a part of life," Fowles said, leaning forward.

"Denying that isn't healthy for anyone. I'm not saying we should all wallow in it, but not every unfortunate situation can be solved."

Darger poked at the lime wedge in her drink with a straw. Chunks of ice clinked against the side of the copper mug.

"That makes most people very uncomfortable. We like to think we have some semblance of control over how things turn out."

"Well, that's a lie. I'm going to die. I know that's hard for people to accept. But sometimes they act like the fact that I've accepted my diagnosis means I've given up. That I could have saved myself if I'd only raced around the world seeking out every kook claiming to have found the cure to cancer. In a twisted way, it ends up feeling like I'm blamed for being sick. Like I could have solved it by now, because no disease is insurmountable. But we all die. And it's not always when we're 85. Some people get dealt an unlucky hand. And I'm luckier than many."

She couldn't help but admire his attitude. Darger tried to imagine living that close to death on a day-to-day basis and didn't think she'd manage to be very stoic about it at all. For some people, that kind of knowledge would send them spiraling into the darkness.

She held her drink in the air and toasted his courage.

"I don't know if I'd call it courage, exactly," he said.

"Pugnacity?" she offered.

Fowles clinked his bottle against her cup.

"That'll do."

Darger was feeling a little drunk by the time the barmaid returned with a second round.

Something had occurred to her over the course of the day, and she'd been working up the nerve to bring it up. The second dose of vodka was helping.

"So is the cancer why…?"

"Why what?"

"Why you left last night."

"Yes," he said, sighing with what seemed like relief. "I'm sorry I didn't tell you then. The last thing I wanted was for you to spend the night worrying that you'd done something wrong."

Darger thought she'd feel relieved herself, but found herself confused instead.

"But I still don't understand why."

"Why I don't want to—" He stopped himself, shook his head. "No. Why I *can't* be involved with someone? I'm dying, Violet. It wouldn't be fair to you."

"Fuck fairness," she said.

He laughed at her abruptness before continuing with his explanation.

"I can't burden you with that. Or anyone else, for that matter."

"No," Darger said. She couldn't accept that as an answer. "That doesn't make sense. You just explained to me that you refuse to stop living before your time is up. But only when it comes to work? That's stupid."

"But my work won't get hurt when I die."

"You think it won't hurt me when you die, as long as you don't sleep with me?" Darger said, the words sounding more bitter than she'd intended.

They were quiet for a moment, and the noise from the

crowded bar seemed to swell to fill in the empty space. Fowles reached across the table and placed a hand on her arm.

"Maybe you're right," he said, and his hand slid from her wrist to her fingers.

Her eyes slid up to meet his.

"Maybe it's stupid to think I can protect other people from it. It's just a different way of trying to control things that are beyond my control."

☾

After that, it came as no surprise that he invited her back to his place.

Fowles lived in the first-floor apartment of an old Victorian-era house. It was painted blue and had a row of rosebushes planted out front.

He unlocked the door and pulled Darger across the threshold, bending to kiss her once they were inside.

She heard the door fall shut behind her but barely noticed.

Still kissing her, Fowles reached for the light switch. Illumination. And then Darger gasped, stepping back as she caught sight of the bookcase near the door.

"Is that a stuffed squirrel riding on the back of a tortoise?"

Fowles followed her gaze and then nodded absently.

"Oh. Yes. I guess so."

For some reason, probably the vodka, this made Darger giggle uncontrollably.

"It's not mine!" Fowles explained. "This place, I mean. I'm subletting from a friend-of-a-friend."

Standing on her tiptoes, she pressed her lips to his, but this time it was Fowles that pulled away.

"I should reiterate that I still don't think this is a good idea."

"Shush."

She kissed him again and reached for the top button of his shirt.

☾

Later, Darger watched his chest rise and fall with breath. He looked so healthy. So vital and alive. It didn't fit that he could be dying.

Was dying.

"You're really not afraid?" she asked.

"Of dying?"

She nodded.

He sighed. "Not really. Maybe it's my work. Seeing the life cycle of the insects. The never-ending spiral of reproduction, birth, and death. We're no different. It just happens slower for us."

They were silent for a time, with only the sound of crickets chirping outside the window.

"The fact that I have some control over when and where and how helps, too."

Darger didn't understand. It seemed to her that the one thing he didn't have was control.

"What are you talking about?"

"Oregon is a Death with Dignity state. When the illness becomes too painful or debilitating, I can choose to end my life."

The thought gave Darger a chill, but as Fowles continued to talk, she thought she understood why he felt that way.

"When I first got my diagnosis, one of the things I worried about most was wasting away. Mentally and physically. And putting my family through that slow downhill decline. Knowing I can prevent that gives me power, if only a little."

A car with a broken muffler rumbled down the street.

"I have regrets, of course," Fowles said. "Not many, but a few."

"Like what?"

"Oh, nothing dramatic. Just a few things I figured I'd experience in my lifetime, and now I don't suppose I'll have that chance."

"Skydiving? Climbing Mt. Everest?"

He laughed.

"I've been skydiving. Twice, actually. And mountain climbing has never appealed much to me. It's more the things in life you just sort of expect will happen for you… falling in love, getting married, having children."

Darger didn't know what to say to that, so she kissed his naked shoulder and then laid her head on his chest.

"What about you?" Fowles asked. "What things do you want out of life?"

Darger considered the question for a second before she answered.

"The same, I guess. A family. Kids. Though I sometimes have a hard time envisioning balancing that with my work. But when I imagine my future, I always picture kids."

Fowles ran a hand through her hair as she talked.

"I feel like a dork admitting this, but the older I get, the more I find myself daydreaming about various parenting scenarios and how I'd handle them."

"If that makes you a dork, then I'm King Dork," Fowles said. "I've thought a lot about what my approach would be as a father. I mean, I know a little about the popular parenting techniques and what have you, but I guess I mean it in a more personal way. Like if I were tasked with distilling my fatherly message down to a couple paragraphs, what would they be?"

"Let's hear those 'graphs," Darger said.

"Well, I'm going off the cuff here, so bear with me. It's a two-parter."

He swallowed before he launched into it, that oversized Adam's apple bobbing in his neck.

"In this world, you are largely defined by your dreams, by what you want. What you want sort of shapes everything about your time, your effort, your sense of yourself. It is arguably the most important choice you make."

His hands moved in the dark, gesturing like a professor giving a lecture.

"And if you look at it that way, the truth is, no one can really stop you from pursuing your dreams except for you. Sometimes maybe it won't work out exactly the way you originally pictured it, but if you really try, you can probably find a way to be part of the realm you've chosen — if you're 5'2", you're probably not going to play professional basketball, for example, but you could get into coaching or be a sportswriter. You could still be part of that world. See, so many people feel powerless and kind of accept that. They just give up on their dreams without a fight, simply flow into the path of least resistance. But you have just as much right as anyone else to the things you want. You are utterly free to embrace your passions, to chase your obsessions, to really go for it, and once you're armed with that knowledge, it kind of empowers you to tilt all things in life toward you, to advocate for yourself, to not take no for an answer."

He paused there a moment, a little puff of laughter coming from his nostrils.

"I know what you're thinking. 'Don't take no for an answer' sounds almost sociopathic, right?" he said.

"I was going to say 'rapey,' but yeah. A little."

"Well, I told you it was a two-parter. Because the second side of this fatherly message is that deep down, what really makes any of us happy is connecting to other people. The genuine connections we make are really the only thing that I think is sacred in this realm. And that means how you treat people is sort of sacrosanct by proxy. If you always remember that, the sort of spiritual weight of that, I think it kind of balances out the more hard-nosed aspects of fighting for what you want."

They were quiet for a beat. Darger smiled.

"I like that," she said. "So to sort of paraphrase it, I think what you're saying is that you've gotta fight for your right to party."

Fowles laughed.

"Exactly."

The chorus of crickets filled the next few seconds, and then Fowles spoke again.

"I usually try to avoid giving unsolicited advice, but this is a case where I can't help myself."

Darger adjusted her position so she could see his face. He was staring up at the ceiling, unblinking.

"What is it?"

"If you really want to start a family, take it from someone that won't get the chance: Don't wait too long."

CHAPTER 40

You sprawl in your apartment. Awake in bed. Eyes open and piercing the dark hung up all around.

You can't sleep. Can't even keep still. Shoulder blades fidgeting, working themselves up and down against the mattress in violent little strokes, two knives chopping and dicing and mincing away.

It's so weird that Callie is gone. So weird. So empty.

So impossible.

You thought it would hurt more than this. Sharp pain all over like your skin flayed from your body, all of your shell peeled off, all of you opened up, stringy red muscle tissue exposed, blood sluicing over the meat in sloppy pulses. You thought it would be torture, agony, torment. Unending and unendurable.

But no.

It's the dull ache of emptiness instead. Desolation. Blankness.

And it's everywhere. All around.

Vast expanses of nothingness trying to press themselves into your skull. A universe comprised of black seas, cold and vacant and meaningless. A kind of darkness that not even the stars can fight off all the way.

A black hole to stare into, to fall into forever.

It reminds you of walking at night, coming upon those shadowed places where it looks like the city has been ripped open, its innards laid bare before you. And you stare into those wounded spots as though they might offer you something, some explanation for any of this, some meaning.

Something. Anything.

You sit up, fumble a hand toward the nightstand, grab your glass of water and drink. The wet feels good on your tongue, in your throat. Makes you remember that you're still here, still real.

No matter who else has come and gone, you're still here.

CHAPTER 41

Darger's phone alarm blared from somewhere near her feet. She flailed a leg at it, hoping that a well-aimed kick would shut it up, but it continued its mechanical squawk.

With a groan, she sat up. The side of the bed where Fowles had slept was empty. A thin sliver of light glowed from under the bathroom door, and she could hear the patter of running water.

Darger slipped out from under the covers, the cold of the room gripping her right away.

She knelt. Fumbled with a pair of wadded up slacks, the legs somehow tangled in a way that made them seem nonsensical in the dark. More like a pretzel of fabric than a wearable garment. She wrestled with them a while before the phone dropped into her lap. At last, she swiped the screen to shut the stupid alarm off.

And then she was back in bed, her head falling back against the pillow, the warm blankets surrounding her again.

She let her eyes wander around Fowles' bedroom. Everything was monochromatic in the gray morning light. Self help books lined the shelves — a few by Dr. Phil, even. And posters for bad action movies adorned one of the walls. She wondered what the things in this room said about him, but then she remembered that he was subletting. Half of this stuff probably wasn't even his, maybe more.

He didn't belong to this place, and it didn't belong to him.

His stay here was temporary.

And so was hers, she supposed. They were both *in between*. The bigger events in their lives, the destinations, existed elsewhere in space and time.

Every time she remembered that Fowles was dying, it occurred to her that it was a strange thing to forget. And of course she hadn't really forgotten. But the brain had a way of pushing those painful, uncomfortable thoughts out of the way. It was a convenient defense mechanism.

A stubborn part of her brain — a superstitious part — wanted to believe that he wouldn't die. Maybe a smaller subset of that part even believed that she could assist in that somehow, like embarking on a relationship might save him.

If life were a movie, it could work that way. The power of love and all that crap.

But not here. No, these kinds of thoughts were the bargaining stage of grief, Darger knew. Her brain wanted to cut a deal. Offer up something to offset the disease, to pay the price hanging over Fowles' head. It had to work that way, didn't it? Had to be possible. Part of her would believe it until the end. A reality where we are powerless over such things would always be too big to process.

Fowles came out of the bathroom in a pair of bright orange boxer briefs and a white t-shirt.

Darger laughed.

"Wow. Do you have a pair of those in leopard print?" she asked.

Glancing down, Fowles continued toweling off his wet hair.

"Are you making fun of my underwear?"

Darger rolled over onto her side and propped her fist underneath her chin.

"They're kind of asking for it."

"You don't like orange?"

"It's a very loud orange. I'm afraid your penis might start directing traffic."

The half-crooked grin spread over his mouth, and he chuckled.

"You can shower here, if you want. But I figure you'll want to stop at your hotel to change before we head to the station."

"Right. Have to avoid that walk of shame," she said, waggling her eyebrows.

"Oh, are you ashamed now?"

"No," she said, leaning forward so she could smack him on the rump. "But *you* should be."

Darger got dressed while Fowles slipped into the kitchen to make coffee. A few minutes later, they were chugging the steaming brew in between bites of toasted bagel.

"You didn't tell me you could cook," Darger said, licking a smear of cream cheese from her finger.

"If you're that easily impressed, then I'll blow your mind with my vegetable lasagna."

It hit her again, his impending death, and she almost winced. He'd never have a wife to make lasagna for.

"What is it?"

She shook it off and smiled.

"Oh, I was just trying to decide if it's too soon to propose."

Fowles laughed. And she studied his wonky smile and his bony cheeks and his wiry hair, and he looked so happy, she thought, *Why not?*

"I'm serious. Marry me."

He stopped laughing after a moment. His brow drew into a

hard line.

"You're joking."

"I am not."

"But we only met three days ago."

"So? It'll be something you can check off your bucket list."

"Why would you do that?"

"Why shouldn't I? It'll be fun."

Instead of answering, he glanced at his watch.

"If you want to be able to shower and change, we need to leave."

Darger helped carry their meager breakfast dishes to the sink, worried she'd offended him.

It had been a stupid thing to say, she decided. A half-joke she'd tried to turn into something serious.

They'd been on the road for almost ten minutes when Fowles broke the silence.

"You'd really do that? Marry a stranger?"

"No, I only have sex with strangers," she teased. "But after that I consider them close friends, and *then* I'll marry them."

"I'm trying to be serious."

"So am I," Darger said.

She turned and regarded him with her head cocked to one side.

"You really consider me a stranger? Even after last night?"

"OK, not a stranger, per se. But we've known each other less than a week."

They were stopped at a red light, and Fowles was staring at her, scrutinizing her the way one might study a box of eggs at the supermarket to make sure none of them were cracked.

Darger threw her hands in the air.

"No, then."

"No?"

"The offer is withdrawn," she said.

"Why?"

"Because of the way you keep looking at me."

"I'm sorry," Fowles said. "I don't mean to. It's just... what would your parents think?"

"Oh, my mother would kill me."

He raised an eyebrow, as if she'd proved his point for him.

"Well, so what if she doesn't like it? It's my life." Darger plucked at her sleeve. "It's not like she asked my permission to marry *her* husband."

"Ah, now we're getting somewhere."

"Where?"

"To the heart of your willingness to marry someone you met a week ago."

"Let's not forget that there are extenuating circumstances. You're on a tight timeline. We really need to keep a brisk pace here, do we not?"

"OK, but if I needed a kidney, would you offer it up so willingly?"

Darger shrugged. "I probably would."

"You're just saying that."

"Maybe. But it's not the same thing. Not even remotely. If I agreed to marry you, we'd take a road trip to Vegas, go to one of those cheesy little chapels, and then boom, done."

"It's not actually that simple, you know. They show it that way in movies and on TV, but it's more complicated. First you have to apply at the license bureau, then you have the ceremony, and then you have to get the marriage certificate—"

Now it was Darger's turn to stare, looking amused as she did so.

"What?"

"You are such a scientist. So precise. So exact. Fine. It's not quite as simple as popping into McDonald's to order a Big Mac. It's also not as complicated as a kidney transplant."

They'd reached Darger's hotel then, and the conversation naturally paused as they crowded into the elevator with an elderly couple. Arguing about a shotgun marriage was a private sort of conversation.

In her room, Fowles took a seat on the edge of the bed, bouncing a little. Darger grabbed fresh clothes from her suitcase and hurried into the bathroom. She stripped, took a lightning round shower, and dried off. As she was buttoning her blouse, Fowles left his post on the bed and moved closer to the door.

"OK, what about the legalities? You would legally become my heir."

Darger puffed some dry shampoo into her hair and riffled her fingers through her roots a few times.

"Are you rich or something?"

"What if I am?"

"Then I'll sign a prenup. I don't care about money."

He laughed.

"You make absolutely no sense."

"Why do you say that?"

"You just don't strike me as the type that would jump into marriage with some random person."

"That's because I'm not. You're not random. You're special."

"Oh."

She stepped out of the bathroom.

"Ready?"

"To leave or to get married?" he asked.

Darger tried to suppress a smile. As dubious as he sounded, she knew he was thinking about it now. Considering it.

She also knew very well what her own motives were. She was a psychologist, after all.

It was bargaining, pure and simple. The third stage in the Kübler-Ross model of grief.

Part of her couldn't let go, was convinced that she could save him.

"Let's go, Bug Guy," she said, and they were off.

☾

Just as they pulled into the lot of the police station, Fowles' phone rang. He put the car in park and snatched his phone from the cup holder.

"It's the lab. You might as well go ahead inside. I'll catch up and fill you in."

A chime sounded as Darger pushed through the glass front door. Marcy glanced up from her post at the front desk and waved.

Hanging up her jacket, Darger caught a glimpse of Furbush stooped over the table in the conference room. He looked like hell. Bags under his eyes. A few spots of stubble he missed during his morning shave.

"Good morning," Darger said.

"Yeah?" Furbush said with a sigh. "What's good about it?"

"Rough night?"

"I just got off the phone with Dustin Reynolds' parents."

"How'd that go?"

"Oh, about as well as the Hindenburg."

"That bad?"

Furbush pawed at the back of his neck.

"It was surreal, really. You remember when I talked to his father the other day, and he got a little panicked? Assumed I'd called to deliver bad news?"

"Yeah."

"Well, since we'd already been through that, this time he interrupts right away and says he knows he doesn't have to talk to me, and that he talked with a lawyer friend of his that says if I keep calling, that's harassment."

The Chief's shoulders seemed to deflate as he let out a long sigh.

"When I told him why I was calling, I don't think he believed me when I said Dustin was dead. I think he sincerely believed I was jerking him around for the fun of it."

"Worst part of the job," Darger said.

She'd never been a cop herself, but she'd been around them long enough to know that none of them relished the task of informing someone that a loved one had died.

"Without a doubt. Finding the DBs is up there, as far as unpleasant tasks go. But a corpse don't cry." Furbush shook his head. "Anyway, I asked if Dustin had any troubles of late. Anything that might shed some light on things. He said Dustin was a Freegan."

"A vegan?"

"That's what I thought, too. But he repeated it for me. Freegan. Apparently they're all about rejecting consumerism.

They get all their food out of dumpsters. Clothes and stuff that like, too."

"Dumpsters?"

"That's what he said. This came up because I asked about Dustin's phone. Whether he had one, you know? We didn't find one at the cabin. Dad said no. He'd turned his back on the idea of 'buying stuff.' If it had to be paid for, Dustin wasn't interested. He'd barter and trade and was all about some website called Freecycle," Furbush said, pursing his lips in clear disapproval. "Sounds like a professional mooch, you ask me. But then I suppose I'm a little old-fashioned."

Darger snorted and sidled over to the coffee machine to pour herself a cup.

"I guess that explains why we've had a hard time finding anything in his name. Did Dustin's father mention if they were planning on coming to town?"

"He said they'd have the funeral here. The Reynolds family has a crypt in Greenbriar Cemetery. I told him to give me a call while they're here, set up a formal interview."

"Did you give any indication that Dustin is a person of interest in our other investigation?"

"Christ, no. No way Frank Reynolds would give us the time of day if he knew we liked Dustin for the murders, dead or not. We'd be conducting our interview through a lawyer."

Darger knew it was the right move, and yet she still felt a twinge of guilt. Not revealing that Dustin was suspected in the recent string of murders so they could wheedle more information out of a pair of grieving parents seemed opportunistic and manipulative. And yet so much of a serial murder case was about opportunity and manipulation.

"Where are we with everything else?"

"I've got Mantelbaum on the financials. Almost became an accountant before signing up for the force, apparently. Took a few classes at the local community college. He's working through Dustin's bank and credit files, hoping something shakes loose there. And I sent Kwan and Portnoy over to talk with the Auntie."

"But I thought you so enjoyed Mamie Reynolds' warm and pleasant disposition?"

Now it was the Chief's turn to snort.

"I thought we could spend the day going through everything we bagged and tagged from the cabin and from Dustin's truck. Maybe try to find something that ties Dustin to one of our more recent victims."

"Sounds like a plan," Darger said.

Furbush rubbed at his eyes with one hairy-knuckled fist.

"Hell, I don't reckon I should be so glum. We might have just sewed up our murder case, nice and tidy. Can't imagine most of your cases turn out this way, do they?"

"No," Darger said. "They don't."

"Not the most dramatic way to close a case, eh?"

"Maybe not. But my life could probably use a little less excitement, to be honest."

When Darger really thought about what she was saying, she felt torn. Confused. It was a shock to find Dustin rotting in that cabin bathroom like that. She'd gone in expecting a gunfight and come out with the suspect already long dead. Possibly by his own hand.

Suicide didn't fit with most serial killer profiles. But this one was different. She'd said so herself, noted that there was a dissociative factor. A killer fighting with two sides of himself. Had the more sane side, the side that still had a moral compass, finally become aware of his crimes? Had he been fighting it all along?

If so, she supposed she should be relieved. He'd stopped himself from committing any more atrocities. Most of these types of offenders kept going until they were caught. How many women had been spared when Dustin Reynolds took his own life?

"Now we just need to prove Dustin was our killer," Darger said.

"That's always the hard part, isn't it?"

CHAPTER 42

She and Furbush were sifting through the evidence photos when Fowles breezed in. He didn't bother keeping them in suspense for long.

"The specimens taken from Dustin Reynolds' body were negative for illicit substances."

Darger sat back in her chair and crossed her arms.

"So we can rule out overdose, whether it was accidental or otherwise."

"Damn," Furbush said, slapping his hand against the table. "I know this sounds callous, but Dustin Reynolds dying of an overdose would have wrapped this whole investigation up with a nice, pretty bow."

Darger's gaze fell on a photo of Dustin Reynolds' putrefying corpse in the dingy little cabin bathroom, his skin a mottled black and brown. There was nothing nice or pretty about it.

"I know Dr. Kole said we shouldn't hold out hope for toxicology, but maybe he'll find something else we can use," Darger said. "In the meantime, we keep looking."

They went back to the photos, searching for a clue. Anything that might tie Dustin to the murders. Something that belonged to one of the women. Or even evidence to prove their hypothesis that he'd killed himself. But there was nothing. No pills, no drug paraphernalia at all. No gun. No knives unless you counted a mismatched and dull set of steak knives in the kitchen area, all of which had been tested for blood residue and had come back negative.

A photo of the bedroom area showed a high-quality sleeping bag rated for sub-zero temperatures on one of the beds. Evidence that Dustin had been planning to make a go of the winter out in the cabin? An old battered Swiss Army knife lay open on the bedside table, with the small pair of scissors at the ready.

Darger riffled through a cluster of photos until she found the shots of the kitchen with the two cast iron skillets hanging over the propane range and the burlap curtains framing the window. Her eyes locked on a close-up of the moldy pizza in the kitchen area. If Dustin had killed himself, he hadn't even left a note. Or finished his pizza.

Next she paused on a picture of Dustin's wallet as it was found and another with the contents laid out: his driver's license, a Fred Meyer rewards card, what looked like a very old, very expired bus pass for the Portland public transit system, a handwritten note on a scrap of paper that said "DRR Custom Paint," and seven dollars in cash.

Darger stared at the money for a long time.

"Where was he getting money?" she asked, more to herself than anyone else.

Furbush leaned closer.

"You mean that measly seven bucks?"

"Not just that," Darger said, shaking her head. "I mean, his aunt says he didn't have a job. His dad says he's a Freegan. But there's nowhere to dumpster dive near the cabin. And he had a pizza."

Furbush picked up the photograph of the wallet contents and flicked his finger against it.

"Good point. He was miles away from the nearest garbage

bin buffet, but he was getting supplies somehow. Food. Toilet paper. Money for gas if he's doing any driving into town," he said and set the photo back down. "I'll make a note to ask the Reynoldses when they come in for questioning. Maybe they were sending him cash."

Through the open doorway, they could hear the phone on Marcy's desk ring.

Furbush closed his eyes and tipped his head back.

"God, I hope that's Dr. Kole with good news. Let's wrap this up and be done with it."

"Chief Furbush?" Marcy called from the doorway

"Yeah?"

"Phone call, Line 1."

Furbush waggled his eyebrows optimistically. He swung around in his chair and lifted the receiver from the phone on the wall.

"This is Furbush."

The hopeful expression on his face immediately twisted into a frown.

"Where at?" he grumbled into the phone. "Yeah. Have 'em hold down the scene until we get there."

He hung up the phone, and when he swiveled back to face them, he wiped a hand down the side of his face.

"We've got another body."

CHAPTER 43

Darger stood in the shade of a stand of cottonwood trees on the shore and watched the men in the water as they worked.

It was a gorgeous day, clear and sunny with a cooling breeze coming from the west. The wind rustled through the leaves overhead and tugged at the loose strands of Darger's hair. The movement made her scalp tingle in a way that was mostly pleasant.

She walked up the hill a little ways to get a better vantage point, planting her feet on the sloped land and turning out toward the lake.

The crystal clear water sparkled in the late morning light, looking like a scene on a calendar showcasing picturesque landscapes. On a day without the breeze to cause ripples on the surface, it probably appeared like a pool of glass, reflecting the silhouettes of the pine trees and the clouds scuttling across the sky.

As they'd climbed down from the access road, the lake had shone like a precious stone, shifting from emerald green to sapphire blue. She saw hints of the same effect as she moved back down near the shore.

The beauty of the scene was incongruous with the task at hand. Bloated body removal.

A tip line call had led them here. An older local man had been walking his dog when he'd spotted the corpse surging along in the current. The body had flowed into the lake from a little outlet stream running off the Clackamas and swept along with the whims of Mother Nature.

The divers had only been in the water for fifteen minutes before locating the body near the trunk of an old fallen tree, and now Darger watched the neoprene-clad head of the diver bob up and down in the water.

Two men from the Clackamas County Sheriff's Search and Rescue Team drifted nearby in a small boat and lowered what looked like a small inflatable raft into the water. The diver grasped the floating stretcher and maneuvered it closer to the dead tree before wrestling the woman's body onto it. Darger shivered at the sight of the fish-belly-white skin.

The men in the boat tossed out a sheet the diver used to cover the corpse. Thus far, this case had managed to stay under the radar as far as the national media was concerned, which was fine with Darger. But someone must have started to put things together, because there were already half a dozen news vans lined up along the access road to the lake when they'd arrived.

The diver attached a tow line from the stretcher to the boat. Even after securing the stretcher, he kept a firm grip on it with one hand. With his other, he held tight to the boat and allowed himself and his gruesome cargo to be slowly hauled to shore.

Two men in hip waders stood in the knee-deep water at the shoreline. As the boat came to a stop, the diver passed off the stretcher to them, and they began the arduous task of climbing the rocky, muddy slope up to dry land.

Suddenly the man holding the rear of the stretcher stepped on a loose rock and slipped backward. The stretcher teetered between the two men, threatening to spill the ghastly load, but finally the rear man regained his footing and wiped his brow.

"Shit!" the man in front cursed. He turned back to face his partner. "You OK, Bobby?"

"I'm good for now. But my fucking back is going to have something to say about all this tomorrow."

When they reached the top of the incline, they headed for a nearby tent where Dr. Kole waited along with his assistants and Fowles. Darger watched one of the underlings whisk away the sheet, and then the group huddled together over the corpse, discussing, prodding, inspecting.

A few yards away, Furbush was shaking hands with the Sheriff. He was a slight man with thinning hair and bushy mustache, and he had to brace himself as Furbush vigorously patted him on the back.

Darger didn't need to hear the platitudes out loud. She had them memorized from a hundred other crime scenes.

Appreciate the assist.

Just doing our duty.

Well, it was good work your men did today.

I'll tell 'em you said so. They're a hell of a team.

Furbush parted ways with the Sheriff and paused to issue orders to his own men. Having finished what they'd come to do, the Sheriff's Search and Rescue Team would clear out. It was up to Furbush's officers to take things from here: securing the scene, interviewing witnesses, and so on.

The Chief's demeanor changed as soon as he stepped away from the Sheriff. His shoulders tensed, and the set of his jaw hardened. He'd put on a brave and appreciative face for the Sheriff, but now the weight of the investigation settled firmly on his shoulders once more.

As Furbush moved to approach the tent, Darger followed.

"What's the story, doc?" Furbush asked the diminutive coroner.

"Thus far, everything I'm seeing is consistent with the other three victims."

"So Dustin Reynolds had one last hurrah? Killed this girl and then took care of himself?"

Both the doctor and Fowles were shaking their heads before Furbush finished speaking.

"The blow fly larvae I've found are first instar," Fowles said. "Assuming she was drowned elsewhere and then moved here like the others, that would put time of death between five and six days."

The coroner's head bobbed up and down.

"I concur. I think Dustin Reynolds was dead long before this girl."

"Hold on now. The doc said before that Dustin Reynolds had been dead about a week. You're saying this girl's been dead up to six days. Now if Dustin's at seven days, give or take, and she's at six days, give or take, isn't that enough wiggle room to say that he maybe could have killed her?"

"Except that I found pupal cases on Dustin Reynolds," Fowles said.

"Pupal what now?"

"The life cycle of the blow fly goes through several stages," Fowles began. "The adults are attracted to the body, where they lay eggs. The eggs hatch into the larvae or maggots, which feed on the remains. As they feed, they pass through three larval stages and into the prepupal stage, at which point they begin to migrate away from the body to fully pupate. They spend several days as pupa before hatching into adult flies, and then the cycle begins anew. Each of these stages takes place for a specific length of time, which varies depending on the surrounding environment. In this case, the predominant factor is ambient temperature."

"OK," Furbush said. "I'm with you. For now."

"The fact that I found pupal cases on Dustin Reynolds means that at least one life cycle has been completed."

"And how long does that take?" Furbush asked.

"Given the weather in the last few weeks, my current estimation for Dustin Reynolds' time of death would be fourteen days."

"Fourteen! That's twice what we originally thought!"

Dr. Kole cleared his throat.

"Once a body is in the putrefaction stage, it can be very difficult to pinpoint a specific time. I gave you my best estimation after a very preliminary examination at the scene. But after completing the full postmortem exam, my findings align with what Mr. Fowles is saying. I estimate Dustin Reynolds' time of death at 10-14 days."

The muscles along Chief Furbush's jaw bunched and unbunched.

"This makes no sense. No damn sense at all," Furbush said.

"I found something else during the autopsy." Dr. Kole's voice was restrained. Calm. "And I apologize I don't have the written report for you yet. I was in the middle of finalizing it when I got this call."

"Might as well drop the bomb and get it over with, doc," Furbush said.

"Dustin Reynolds had a fractured skull."

Furbush's hat came off. It seemed for a second that it did

this on its own, but then Darger saw the shaky hand latched onto the brim. She thought the chief might toss it on the ground and stomp on it. Instead, he only wiped his brow before replacing it on his head.

"Are you telling me that Dustin Reynolds slipped and fell in the tub? Cracked his skull?"

"Normally, that would be my guess. But the blunt force trauma occurred on the parietal bone just behind the coronal suture."

"English?" Furbush asked.

Dr. Kole patted his tuft of white hair.

"The top of the head. Now, if the injury had been almost anywhere else, I might be inclined to argue an accidental fall," Dr. Kole explained. "But a fracture on the top of the head… well, that's hard to sell as accidental, unless he was doing a somersault into the bathtub."

Darger's heart began to beat a little faster at the implication. Had someone struck Dustin Reynolds on the head in order to incapacitate him before drowning him?

"Did you check his lungs?" she asked.

The doctor shook his head.

"The decomposition was too advanced to determine whether or not he drowned, unfortunately. But considering the skull fracture, and the way he fits into all of this, I'm not comfortable ruling it an accident."

He paused and held up his hands to stop their inevitable next question.

"On the other hand, there isn't enough evidence at this time to label it a homicide either. I think his death certificate will read 'Undetermined' for the time being."

Air rushed out of Furbush's lungs as he heaved a sigh.

"Another dead end."

"No," Darger said. "We know we're on the right track now."

"But if Dustin Reynolds is just another victim, we're back where we started, aren't we?"

"Not at all. It's obvious that Dustin Reynolds was connected to all of it somehow. Twenty years ago, his girlfriend dies the same way. And now we have four other bodies, plus him, meeting similar ends? This isn't a coincidence. All of this has to tie back to Christy Whitmore somehow. And we know for sure now that Dustin was tied up in that. Maybe not directly. Maybe he's just the link between Christy and the killer."

One of Furbush's fingers stroked a spot of stubble on his chin.

"OK. Yeah. That's something to work with."

"We should go back through the witnesses and interviews for the other victims," she suggested. "If we can find a connection between the new victims and either Christy Whitmore or Dustin Reynolds, we might just find our killer."

The metal table laden with the grisly remains of the woman pulled from the lake was only a few feet from where they were standing. Even without looking directly at it, Darger caught glimpses of the pale bloated flesh in her peripheral vision.

"Any idea on the identity?" she asked.

Furbush glanced at the table and covered his hand with his mouth.

"Our other victims were relatively easy to ID since the women were all reported missing beforehand. But we haven't had anyone reported missing since Shannon Mead. We'll check with the surrounding jurisdictions, and the state police have a Missing Persons clearinghouse online. But for now, this girl is a Jane Doe."

CHAPTER 44

Back at the station, Furbush brought everyone up to speed.

"We're up to four dead women, five if you count Christy Whitmore. Dustin Reynolds, our best suspect to date, is now crossed off our list, since he was dead long before our most recent victim."

Pacing the front of the conference room, Furbush cracked his knuckles.

"How he fits exactly with the rest of the victims, we're not sure yet. But according to the coroner, his death is looking less like a suicide and more like a homicide. Our current theory at the moment is that he's another victim in all this."

Detective Kwan raised a question Darger had been grappling with herself.

"Isn't it rare for a serial killer to kill both men and women?"

"Yes and no," she said. "I'll use Paul John Knowles, The Casanova Killer, as an example. He killed fourteen women and six men, but the men were always collateral damage or opportunistic killings — husbands and fathers of his intended victims or someone he killed so he could steal their credit cards. That's what we tend to see if there are both male and female victims. Of course there are examples like David Berkowitz and the Zodiac Killer, who killed couples, but it's my opinion that the women were always the intended targets in those cases as well."

"Is that why Dustin Reynolds wasn't moved?"

"It might be," Darger said. "Dustin is a break in the M.O. in many ways. He's male, he was left at what we believe was the scene of the murder instead of dumped in a body of water. If the motivation is different — maybe he got in the way somehow or the killer wanted something from him — then that could be why the killer felt no need to perpetuate the rest of the ritual."

Darger heard audible swallows, saw multiple Adam's apples bob up and down. This was a concerned group of men and women that were growing tired of more questions than answers, and she'd just given them a boatload of *maybe*s and *might*s and *could-be*s. She could practically see the uncertainty buzzing like flies in their skulls.

Furbush took over then, handing out orders to his crew.

"Turco and Baughn, I want you to go through the state Missing Persons registry. If you come up empty there, check Washington, California, Nevada, and Idaho. Someone reported this girl missing."

Pointing to his detectives and another group of uniforms, Furbush continued.

"Mantelbaum, Reese, Kwan, and Portnoy, I want you to take photographs of our four confirmed vics, plus Dustin Reynolds and Christy Whitmore, and show them to our original witness list. It's a big list, so divvy it up and get through it however you can. Myself and our consultants will do what we can to pick up an interview here and there. But it's imperative that we find a connection somewhere. It's there. We just haven't seen it yet."

Officer Mantelbaum raised a hand.

"Does this mean I should abandon Dustin Reynolds' finances? I only really scratched the surface of his records this morning."

"Actually, no. Stay on that for now. Dustin is wrapped up in all of this. He may even be the missing piece we've been looking for. As for the rest of you… Good luck and Godspeed."

Waiting until most of the men and women had filed out of the room, Furbush tugged at his collar and turned a worried face on Darger.

"I feel like I'm treading water. Is it always like this?"

Darger gave what she hoped was a reassuring smile.

"You're doing fine," she said. "And yes, it's always like this."

"I don't know if that makes me feel any better, to be honest," he said with a sigh. "Any suggestions on our next move?"

Someone had collected photographs of all of the victims and tacked them to a bulletin board at the far end of the conference room. Darger let her eyes drift over the faces.

"I'd like to try talking to Christy Whitmore's mother again. I want to see who else she remembers from back then. Friends of Dustin she might remember hanging around. Other people they could talk to that spent time with Christy and Dustin."

"I take it I should sit that one out?"

"Probably so."

There was a knock at the door. It was Mantelbaum again. His eyelids were stretched wide, like he'd just been doused with a bucket of ice water. He had something, Darger could tell.

"Chief?"

"What is it?"

"This is going to sound a little odd, but… Dustin Reynolds just checked into a hotel."

"Dustin Reynolds is dead."

"Well, I know that. I guess what I mean to say is that someone using Dustin Reynolds' credit card just checked into a hotel."

"Where at?"

"Right here in town. The Sentinel Inn."

Darger and Furbush exchanged a glance.

"Let's go."

CHAPTER 45

The Sentinel Inn sat in a neighborhood that had seen better days. Sun-bleached boards adorned the windows of the businesses on either side — a pawn shop and a smoothie place, respectively. American dreams that had been shuttered and forgotten years ago, based on the looks of things.

The hotel itself looked dated. Beat up. A place best suited for meth deals and prostitution and people trying to avoid notice for reasons legal and otherwise. A shithole, more or less, though only slightly more low end than the places Darger normally stayed in when the FBI was footing the bill.

The stucco on the outside of the building sported pockmarks, little crumbled places that made it look like a cheek with acne scars. It had probably once been tan, but it had yellowed through the years, taking on the same nicotine tint Darger had observed on the stained teeth and fingertips of the incarcerated.

Darger and Fowles accompanied Furbush's SWAT crew as they crossed a craggy parking lot, avoiding the menagerie of potholes and mud puddles, and entered the lobby through the glass doors out front.

The clerk at the front desk was an older woman with a fluffy cloud of gray-blonde hair surrounding a face wrinkled by too many hours under a tanning bed. Darger knew for a fact that it was a tanning bed and not the sun because of the telltale white circles around her eyes from the little protective goggles.

She didn't so much as glance up as they approached, just

kept sucking her vape pen with her eyes glued to her phone. Judging by the obnoxious jangling noises coming from it, she was playing some sort of slot machine game.

Furbush cleared his throat.

"You have a room registered under the name Dustin Reynolds?"

The woman removed the e-cigarette from her mouth, looking unimpressed.

"Got a warrant?"

The Chief slid a copy of the search warrant across the scuffed desk.

With a sigh, she set her phone aside, stuffed the vape pen back into her mouth and tapped at the keyboard.

"Sure do. Room 414."

"And can you tell us if anyone has checked in yet?"

"Checked in yesterday afternoon."

"Were you working yesterday?"

"Nope," she said and exhaled a huge plume of vape smoke.

"Is there anyone here who might have been working when the occupant checked in?"

"Nope."

"Do you take down driver's license information?"

"Not when they prepay with a credit card."

"And this room is prepaid?"

The puff of hair bobbed up and down, *yes.*

"OK. What about the reservation itself?"

"What about it?"

"When was it made? Was it made online or did they call? Who booked it? How many guests booked?"

Another haze of smoke swirled out of the woman's mouth

as she jabbed her fingers at the keyboard.

"Reservation was made two weeks ago. Booked online, and the only name on the booking is the one that matches the credit card. One guest."

She pressed the vape pen between her lips, and the tip bounced like a conductor's baton as she spoke.

"Look, it ain't really my job to go around pokin' in other peoples' business. 'Specially not when they prepay."

Furbush let out a resigned sigh.

"Fair enough. We're going to need a key to Room 414."

After retrieving the keycard and the warrant, Furbush and Darger moved away from the desk to converse privately.

"You think we should stick with the plan?" he asked.

She nodded, hoping it was the right move. With a wave of his arm, Furbush gathered his men into a huddle.

"OK, men. We've already gone over this back at the station, but I'll lay it out once more just so we know we're all on the same page. Squad A, you're with Darger and myself. We'll proceed up to the fourth floor via the elevator. Squad B, you'll take the side stairwell. When we reach the hallway that gives access to Room 414, both teams will wait for Miss Darger to give the signal. Are we clear?"

A chorus of voices agreed that they were.

"Let's go, then."

Darger tugged at the shoulder of her jacket as she boarded the elevator. The Kevlar vest she had on was chafing the hell out of her left armpit. Everyone else wore their vests over their clothes, but Darger didn't have that luxury. Dressed in street clothes, she would approach the door alone and knock. In her blue oxford shirt and navy jacket, they hoped she'd appear like a hotel employee to whomever was on the other side of the door. They'd open up, Darger would have them step out of the room, and the strike team would take things from there.

Easy.

She hoped.

Beside her, Fowles tapped the button for the fourth floor. He'd requested to come along, and while Darger's answer would have been a hard *no*, they were on Furbush's turf. The Chief allowed it with the condition that Fowles wear a helmet in addition to the vest and that he stay well behind the squad until the subject was in custody.

Fowles looked funny with the vest on under his suit jacket. Bulky and strange. It took Darger a second to figure out what was off about it. Intuitively or not, the getup made his head look massive. An orb rested on his neck the size of a planet. And once she saw it, she couldn't unsee it.

She heard Loshak's voice in her head, "Get a load of the watermelon this guy's trying to pass off as a human head," and a laugh spluttered out from between her lips, no matter the effort she made at stopping it. It was like trying not to laugh in church.

Fowles arched his eyebrow at her and then squinted.

"Something funny?"

Darger shrugged, trying to reel the giggles in a little and succeeding.

"No. Just nerves. Adrenaline, you know."

He nodded after a second, but his squint didn't let up.

Darger turned her attention away to avoid renewed laughter, watching the glowing number above shift from 2 to 3.

She took in the details of the confined metal box they rode

in. Smudged handprints and dark streaks from clumsily handled luggage dotted the stainless steel door, and the walls were lined with a hideous brown carpet-like material. It smelled inexplicably like canned spaghetti.

She wondered if they'd made the right choice. They could have agreed to bust the door down, and maybe they still would, but they were going to play it low key first. This could be something benign, after all. A friend or relative could have had permission to use the card. Hell, they might not even know Reynolds was dead. News of his demise had only been spreading for a few hours now.

But after the anticlimax of the cabin — storming in and finding Dustin Reynolds dead — the superstitious part of Darger's mind worried that this would end up being the chaotic encounter she'd been anticipating.

The glow reached 4, and the car eased to a stop. The elevator door slid open in slow motion.

Fowles waited just outside the elevator while the rest of their group moved down another hallway of worn carpet. Maybe it was off-white at some point, but time and dirt seemed to have darkened it to something like the shade of old bones.

Pausing at a fork in the hallway, Furbush gave a tick of his chin to gesture at the appropriate door, and the whole posse pulled up. This was it.

Darger twitched her shoulders, trying to get comfortable under the vest. She proceeded the rest of the way on her own. Stopping in front of the door to Room 414, her gaze locked on the thick wooden slab set in a rolled stainless steel frame.

Loud music played inside. Deep driving bass. Fast, cheesy guitar wailing over it. It was hard to pick out the melody through the heavy door, but Darger thought it sounded like hair metal.

She wiped the back of her hand at her lip, brought it down to rest on the butt of her gun. Her heartbeat had accelerated the whole way down the hall and now reached a dead sprint. Pulse battering away in her right eyelid. Her mouth gone as dry as hay.

She glanced left, making sure that Squad B was in place, then back to the right, at Furbush. He nodded, eyes closing for the duration of the gesture.

OK. Go time.

Her fist lunged out to rap at the door.

CHAPTER 46

The door peeled open, and the girl standing in the opening showed wild eyes, a little wetness pooling along the lower eyelids. She brought a shaking hand to her chest.

Her jaw worked up and down. At first Darger thought she was attempting to speak, but it became apparent that wasn't the case.

Gum. The girl was chewing gum.

"Can you turn the music down and step out into the hall?" Darger said, lifting her voice to compete with whatever 80's trash was playing.

"What?"

Darger got louder.

"Can you turn the music down?"

"Huh? Hang on. Let me turn the music down."

The girl disappeared into the room, and after a beat the screeching vocals and big guitars cut out.

Some of the tension eased out of Darger's back, and she removed her hand from the butt of her gun. This wasn't directly related to the killer — she could feel that in her gut — but it still might lead to something. Instead of giving the signal that told the two squads to converge on the door, she caught Furbush's eye and gestured him over alone.

The girl reappeared in the opening. That look of fear still occupied her face, but the jaw chewing the gum seemed unperturbed.

"Thank you," Darger said, and now she flashed the warrant

along with her ID. "My name is Violet Darger, and this is Chief Furbush of the Sandy Police. This room turned up a hit on a credit card linked to a case we're working. Do you happen to know Dustin Reynolds?"

The girl hesitated a second, almost flinching, and then she nodded.

"He's my boyfriend. Er, I mean… he *was* my boyfriend."

She blinked a few times upon saying this.

Darger and Furbush exchanged a glance.

"Can we come in and talk?"

☾

Darger sat on the edge of the bed, rumpled blankets curling around the small of her back. Furbush remained standing, but Darger wanted to give a sense of casualness to this exchange right off. She thought it might make Jennifer more likely to talk.

So far they'd learned that the girl's name was Jennifer Strickley and that she and Dustin Reynolds had been together for the last several months. They'd had a hard time getting her to sit still, though, so the interview had yet to fall into any kind of rhythm.

Now the girl squatted in front of the mini-fridge in the corner.

"Y'all want somethin' to drink?" she asked. "Maybe some Mountain Dew?"

She held up the two-liter over her head with both hands as if to show them the offer was for real.

"No thank you, ma'am," Furbush said.

"I'll have a glass," Darger said. "If it's not too much

trouble."

In no way did she want the Day-Glo yellow fluid to touch her lips, let alone actually enter her body. But accepting hospitality still carried weight with people, won them over. It was a calculated risk she was willing to take.

Jennifer wore a big smile as she handed over the Dixie cup with the bubbling neon corn syrup inside. Maybe the ploy was working.

Darger thanked her and took a drink. Very bright and even sweeter. The word cloying did not do the experience justice. It reminded her of being in middle school.

She forced herself to take another sip. It was a small sacrifice to make.

Jennifer took a seat on a ratty chair against the far wall. Her jaw still chewed at a piece of pale blue gum, worked in an endless loop that reminded Darger of cattle chewing cud.

"If this is about the credit card, I'll have you know I had every right to use that," she said. "Dustin and I had planned to meet here when he got back. It was our little ritual. Whenever he went on the road for a bit, we got a room here to celebrate the reunion. I'd booked the room ahead of time. Of course, that was before… you know."

She smacked her gum in the silence that followed. Something about it reminded Darger of some valley girl stereotype character from an 80's teen movie. *As if.* But Darger could see that the girl's face was flushed. She must think she was in some kind of trouble for using the credit card.

"The credit card is the least of our concerns, Jennifer," she said, her voice soft. "We're just trying to figure out who did this to Dustin, OK?"

Jennifer blew little bubbles with her gum and popped them as she considered this, then nodded.

"I still haven't cried over him, you know. Over Dustin, I mean. I guess it just doesn't feel real yet. Not all the way. It's like my mind understands that he's dead, but my heart can't accept it. My mama said maybe the funeral will help. I guess maybe that's why they have 'em, you know?"

Darger reached out a hand and touched the girl's knee, making sure to avoid eye contact as she did it. Touching a stranger made them have warm feelings for you, something like affection. But if you made eye contact during the contact, the perception changed. The touch was perceived as sexual.

"Can you think of anyone Dustin had problems with? Anyone who'd want to hurt him?"

She stretched the gum out on her tongue, a pale blue serpent flitting out of her mouth.

"Naw. He was a sweetheart, you know? The kind of guy who'd give you the shirt off his back, give you his last cigarette, split his last beer with you. I can't imagine anyone holding a grudge. Not enough for something like this."

"What about the fact that you hadn't heard from him in a while? It must have been at least a couple weeks."

Darger almost referring to the decayed state they'd found the body in, but caught herself.

"The last time I saw him was three weeks ago. That wasn't uncommon. He has a cousin in Boise that he visited a lot. Did work for him. Odd jobs and whatever on his property. He'd told me he'd be down there for a few weeks. Told me he'd be back by today, in fact. Hence me booking the room."

"And you didn't talk to him while he was out of town?"

She sighed before she answered.

"Dustin wasn't big on phones. Face to face he'd talk your ear off, but he always got real quiet on the phone. I don't think he saw much point in having one, really. Plus, money got a little tight and everything. His unemployment ran out two or three months back. Had to tighten his belt and what have you. That's why he was heading up to Idaho for work. Or planning to, I guess. Seems like he never made it."

She went back to snapping her gum but just for a second.

"Makes him sound like a loser when I say all of this out loud, but it wasn't like that. This crap wasn't all of who he was. We had problems, but we had dreams, too. Like Dustin, he was a real talented artist. Painted custom artwork on the side of motorcycles. Little murals I guess you could call 'em. Unbelievable what he could do with an airbrush."

The girl's mouth scrunched up as she continued to talk.

"But Oregon isn't the right place for that kind of thing. In the cities, like in Portland, you got all the hipsters and whatever. More into mustaches than motorcycles. And out in the sticks, you've got your lumberjack types. More of that rural, conservative lifestyle. Hard-working, salt of the Earth or whatever. Dustin used to call them 'the hill people.'"

She sniffed out a chuckle at that before she went on.

"We were trying to save up to move down to San Bernardino so he could start a real business. In California, you know? It's a big biker town. Hell's Angels have their headquarters there and everything. I was going to do all the website stuff. I'm pretty good at customizing Wordpress blogs, and I was taking a photography class so he could get some of his work up on Instagram and everything, but...."

Again, they fell quiet. Darger decided to just wait, to let the girl talk.

"I was looking forward to coming here, I have to say. To this room, I mean. We'd been staying out in the cabin more lately, on account of how we were saving up for the move. It's rent free, but it's an isolated existence. Gets lonely. I couldn't stay there whenever Dustin would leave. With no car, I'd be stranded out in the boonies without him. I'd probably go crazy after a single night of that. It's too dang quiet."

"Where do you stay when Dustin's out of town?"

"With friends."

"Can we get the names of these friends?" Darger tried to keep her tone casual. She didn't want the girl to feel like this was an interrogation.

"Oh. Well, I kinda couch surf my way around town. Moving on when I feel like I've worn out my welcome, you know. But I can write out a list, if you want."

"I'd appreciate that," Darger said and handed the girl a pen and pad of paper from her pocket.

As Jennifer scribbled down the names, she sighed and shook her head.

"I kind of ran out of places to crash this time around, so I was happy to get a night here. Get cleaned up. Sleep in a real bed. I guess saving money doesn't matter now. Not with Dustin gone and all."

Darger let the silence linger a moment longer before she redirected with a fresh version of an old question.

"Can you think of anybody that got under Dustin's skin? Someone who irked him? Maybe a coworker or someone from his past?"

She was more or less rephrasing the same question from earlier, she knew, but this time the girl sat up. Her jaw finally stopped chewing.

"Only person I ever heard him talk bad about was his ex, but...."

"And who was that?"

"Kathryn."

"Last name?" Darger asked.

Jennifer shrugged, sniffing and looking away.

"I didn't have much interest in Dustin's cast-offs. But she wouldn't go away."

"What do you mean by that?"

"He was always asking her for stuff. Borrowing money and whatnot. It was, like, the only thing we ever fought about. I wanted him to make a clean break. I just didn't see why he would be going to her for favors if they were really through, you know?"

Darger nodded. A last name would be helpful, but pressing probably wouldn't help. Her instincts told her that she needed to keep the girl talking.

"I wondered if you might take a look at this. Tell us what you think."

Darger handed over a small photo album loaded with before pictures of the victims, all of them still alive and smiling and full of hopes and dreams.

Jennifer looked at the snapshots one by one and shook her head. When they reached the photo of Shannon Mead, her eyes opened a little wider.

"You know her?"

"Only from the news. That's the girl. The one they found in

the river. And the others? They're the same?"

Darger nodded.

"Do you recognize any of these names?"

She squinted.

"No. Wait. How is Dustin related to all of this?"

"That's what we're trying to figure out."

"Oh my word."

Jennifer brought a hand to her chest, the same gesture she'd made in the doorway.

"I'm sorry. I just never made that connection, that his death could be… related to all that."

Darger gave Furbush a look, wondering if he had any further questions.

He caught Darger's meaning and shrugged, getting to his feet.

He shook Jennifer Strickley's hand and thanked her, told her they'd appreciate it if she let them know if she planned on leaving town, that they might have more questions.

"Of course. Yeah, sure," Jennifer said. "Um… do I have to leave?"

"Leave?"

"The room? I mean, it's paid for through the next two days, and it just seems like a waste to let it sit empty."

Furbush grunted a little.

"Guess that's up to you, really."

They turned, Darger following the chief's lead, and just as they ducked through the doorway, the girl appeared behind them.

"Hey wait! I just remembered. It's Porter. Kathryn Porter. That's Dustin's ex."

Darger flinched, and the hair on the back of her neck stood up.

"Kathryn Porter," Darger said to Furbush. "Wasn't she one of the witnesses you interviewed relating to Shannon Mead?"

CHAPTER 47

Confusion rippled through Darger's head. Almost dazed her. The Kathryn Porter revelation was another huge stone thrown into the lake to get the water choppy and murky again.

After the excitement they'd felt upon getting the credit card hit, Darger couldn't help but be disappointed. It felt like starting over, somehow. Everything had seemed to circle back to what happened to Christy Whitmore twenty years ago, and their only suspect in that case was dead.

A pit opened in Darger's gut when she tried to fit the puzzle pieces together.

Kathryn Porter could be linked to two of the victims now, but what did it mean? She was Dustin Reynolds' ex-wife, and she had offered Shannon Mead a ride the night she disappeared, witnessed her getting into a dark sedan of unknown make or model.

In a town as small as Sandy, could those two events be coincidental? Possibly, but Darger thought not.

The key to the case must lie in Kathryn Porter's head, whether she knew it or not. She was too close, too wrapped up in it. Darger doubted Kathryn knew the identity of the killer, but some bit of idle information lay tucked in the folds of this woman's brain that could point them in the right direction. A clue or a suspect would come spilling from her lips if only they asked the magic question to pull it free. And now it would become a game of teasing it out.

Darger rode in the passenger seat of the rental, Fowles

driving. They'd talked a little upon first entering the car — idle chat about Strickley and Reynolds and Kathryn Porter — but the conversation died a rapid death. Darger fell quiet and tried to sort through everything they now knew.

Furbush's people had already tracked Kathryn down, and she'd agreed to come down to the station for another interview first thing in the morning. Darger pictured herself sitting across the interview table from the weird quiet woman who rarely blinked.

Would a talk with Dustin Reynolds' ex-wife give any clarity to the investigation? There appeared to be a missing piece to this puzzle, and every time they found a new piece, it only revealed that there was yet another one absent, only seemed to complicate things.

She gazed out the window, and the day inched toward dusk around them. Overcast skies going further toward grayscale, rain threatening from dark wispy clouds as it always seemed to here.

When Darger glanced at a slice of her reflection in the rearview mirror, she saw creases lining her forehead, wrinkled flesh that somehow matched her emotional state. Muddled. Confused. Tense.

She took a breath, slow in and slower out. She'd been here before, of course. Face to face with a pile of clues, interviews, evidence that didn't quite seem to jell into any kind of story that made sense. But she knew better than to give up. The process would get her there if she trusted it.

That sounded like something Loshak would advise: "Worrying accomplishes nothing. Trust the process, Darger. Do your job, and the rest will take care of itself."

Hearing his voice in her head seemed to calm her. Another deep breath eased a touch of the tension in her upper back, the muscles there releasing a little.

The killer was still out there, perhaps closer than ever now. She needed to stay focused on that notion. Because whining internally wasn't going to bring him to justice. Doing the work was.

So it was decided. She would push the worry down, elbow the confusion away from her thoughts the best she could, and she would press on. She'd interview Kathryn Porter with an open mind, with fresh eyes. Maybe the second go-round would shake something loose.

She would do her job. It was all she could do, really.

She would trust the process.

CHAPTER 48

Darger awoke the next morning to a sky so dark it felt like the sun had never risen. She knew it was somewhere behind that thick wall of threatening clouds, but she wouldn't know it from looking at the perpetual twilight outside her hotel window.

A scattering of half-hearted raindrops speckled Darger's rental as she climbed in, but by the time she'd steered onto the road, she had to put the wipers on full blast. At the station, she got a good soaking on the brief jog from the car to the front doors.

Darger brushed the wet from her jacket and her hair and found the interview room. The observation area was packed with Sandy PD staff watching like voyeurs through the two-way glass. On the other side, Kathryn Porter fidgeted in the interview room by herself. Darger had to elbow her way to the front to get a peek.

Kathryn seemed a frail thing sitting alone at the interview table. Somehow smaller than how she'd looked in the video. Still tall, but waify.

Darger drifted back, letting the locals have the front row, though her eyes never left the girl behind the glass.

Kathryn took little drinks out of a water bottle every few seconds, delicate little sips that reminded Darger of a bird, then set the bottle back down on the table, her hand trembling just slightly.

"We ready?" Furbush asked, eyes locking on Darger's.

She nodded.

315

He led the way into the room with Kathryn, and Darger took one of the seats opposite the girl.

The girl made fractured eye contact, clearly a little nervous. She didn't smile.

"Thanks for coming down here, Kathryn. I think you're really going to be able to help us out."

"I hope so," Kathryn said. "I can't imagine that I know anything important, but I'll do my best."

"Let's start at the beginning. Tell us a little about your relationship with Dustin Reynolds. How long have you known him?"

"We were just kids when we met, really. In high school. I think I was probably sixteen when we met."

Darger knew she needed to keep the tone as light as possible, to encourage, to behave as though this creature across from her was something fragile that might crumple up like a moth wing at the slightest touch.

"Is that when you two started dating?" Furbush asked. "High school sweethearts?"

Furbush must have sensed the same thing, as he proceeded in a very ginger manner with her, too. Almost talked to her the way a school nurse talks to a frightened kindergartner.

Kathryn's eyes went far away as she spoke, rotating off to the right.

"No, I knew him a long time before we ever dated. And we were always off and on, so I wouldn't call us sweethearts. Right away it was like that, and it stayed that way for a couple decades, I guess."

Just like the first interview, Darger was struck by how cold and distant this person was, her way of speaking somehow robotic and childlike at the same time. Hushed and small.

"You were off and on even during the time you were married?" Darger clarified.

Kathryn nodded.

"We got married around — I guess I would have been 22. Got divorced around 31. At some point you look around and you realize this person you're with... they aren't who you thought they were."

Darger resisted an urge to lean in and seize on this. She had to treat this one gently. Too much pressure, too much excitement, and she might frighten Kathryn into silence.

"That's how you felt about Dustin? Was there a reason? Did he change somehow?"

Kathryn's brow furrowed.

"No, it wasn't like that. I said it wrong, I think. Because maybe it's me that's not who I thought I was. Maybe I was the one who changed," she said. "I'm 37 now. And the last few years..."

She trailed off for a moment, and then her gaze locked on Darger.

"Do you ever feel like you're stuck in between places? Like you started somewhere in life, and you're supposed to get, I don't know, to someplace better, but it just seems like you end up going 'round in circles?"

Darger felt a chill run through her, because she knew exactly that feeling and had been sensing it often of late. She shook off the unease and found her voice.

"I do, actually. Is that how you felt? Leading up to the divorce?"

Nodding again, Kathryn brought her hands together in

front of her and knit her fingers together.

"Even after splitting up, we went another few rounds of on again off again." She paused and chuckled nervously. "It really was like one of those carousel rides sometimes. Up and down and around and around."

"Had you two been involved recently at all?"

"No, ma'am. We haven't seen much of each other these last few years. For a while there we tried to be just friends, but we always seemed to end up fighting. Too much baggage, I guess."

"You've had no contact at all, then?" Darger asked, wondering how Jennifer Strickley would even know about Kathryn if they hadn't been in touch for several years.

"Oh, I thought you meant *involved*. Because I did run into him at Freddy's a few weeks ago. I didn't even know he was back in town, so it was a bit of a shock."

"Did you talk?"

"A little."

"Do you remember what about?"

"Just basic how've-you-been type stuff. Nothing memorable."

"How did he seem to you?"

"The same. He ended up asking to borrow money, which was pretty typical. Almost the whole time we were together, I worked, and he didn't."

Furbush caught her eye, and Darger was certain he was thinking that this revelation plus the whole Freegan thing pretty much rounded out how Dustin Reynolds had remained so off-grid all these years.

"And did you lend him the money?" Darger asked.

Looking sheepish, Kathryn bobbed her head up and down.

"I always had a hard time saying no to Dustin."

"How much?"

"Eighty dollars, I think?"

"Did he say what it was for?"

"He said it was for gas to get to a job he had lined up, and that he'd pay me back as soon as he got his first check."

Kathryn's face morphed into a deep frown.

"Geez. I guess that would have been right before... right before he died, huh?"

Her hand went to her mouth and fluttered there like an injured sparrow.

"Gosh, I feel awful now. I don't mean to make him out to be a bad guy. He didn't have the easiest life, you know. There were things in his past... he went through some real rough times."

"Like Christy Whitmore?" Darger asked.

Kathryn's hand froze over her mouth.

"You know about that?"

Darger nodded. "Did he ever talk about it?"

"Not really. But it was always there. Under the surface. The anger and the guilt, just eating away at him."

"Why was he angry?"

"Well... I mean, people said he did it, you know? That he killed her. Which is a load of baloney. Dustin wasn't a saint, but he wasn't a killer, either. Still, I think he felt responsible."

"If he didn't kill Christy, why would he feel responsible?"

"Because he loved her. And when you love someone, you're supposed to protect them, right?"

Shaking her head slightly, as if trying to clear an Etch-a-Sketch, Kathryn continued.

"What I'm trying to say is that we had good times, too. Dustin… he could be sweet. But in the end, I kind of realized that we'd wasted the best part of each other's lives. And I could see it happening again. We ended up drawn to each other it seemed like. Better to leave it be, you know?"

Kathryn shrugged upon finishing her answer, a gesture Darger took as doubt as to how helpful any of what she'd said could be.

"I know it probably doesn't seem like it, but filling in Dustin's background is a big help to us," Darger said. "Can you think of anybody Dustin had trouble with? Anyone who'd want to hurt him?"

Again her eyes flicked up and to the right.

"No. I mean, we had our squabbles, but he was a pretty agreeable guy. A talker. A charmer. I can't see him getting that far afoul of anyone to lead to something like this. Even back in school, he wasn't one to get in any fights or anything. I mean, I'm his ex-wife, right? And I can't imagine him having any real enemies. That must say something."

Again she followed this with a shrug that seemed to question the worth of any of this.

Darger thought about what all had been said so far. Most of Kathryn's dealings with the victim had been years before. She decided to try to dredge up some memories about the scene of the crime.

"What about the cabin?" Darger said.

"What about it?"

"You lived out there for a time?"

"Yeah, quite a few years back. I think we stayed out there for close to a year."

"How were things between you and Dustin at that point?"

She tilted her head back and forth as she mulled this.

"About the same, I guess. We got along a lot of the time, but we peppered the peace with some pretty major fights. I remember him getting so mad he stormed out into the woods one night, not coming back for a few hours. He was too proud to admit it, but I think he'd gotten lost out there."

"And do you remember anything odd from around that time? Any conflicts or trouble Dustin had gotten into?"

For the first time, Kathryn jolted forward in her seat. Deep wrinkles creased her forehead.

"Wait. There was something. It's been so long, I didn't think about it at first, didn't relate it to Dustin's… to what happened to Dustin or anything."

Darger held her breath, didn't dare move, somehow worried she'd spook the girl out of elaborating.

"There was a man at the cabin."

"Staying there with you?"

"No. He was more like… a stalker or something. I mean, the first few times, Dustin seemed to have some kind of business with him, but then I saw him creeping around after that."

"Creeping around? Like, watching you?"

"Yeah."

"What did Dustin say about it?"

"Dustin always said it was nothing, this guy lurking around, but it was creepy, you know, seeing something moving out the window at night, something solid in the darkness."

Darger's heart beat a little faster.

"And you don't know his name? Or what kind of business

Dustin would have been doing with him?"

Kathryn frowned at the table top, head shaking side to side.

"No, ma'am. It must have been ten years ago, at least. He was someone Dustin knew, but he wouldn't talk about it beyond calling this guy Chicken. Like a nickname, I mean, not like he was calling him a chicken."

"Did you ever get a good look at him?"

"He mostly came at night, but I saw him once in the daylight. I was cooking breakfast. Bacon and eggs. So early it was still gray and dewy out, and he was there outside the kitchen window. Maybe ten feet off leaned up against a tree, smirking at me like he'd been watching a while. Amused that he'd scared me."

Darger swallowed, and her throat felt dry and sticky.

"I turned to yell for Dustin, and when I turned back he was gone. Still gives me goose bumps thinking about it, closing my eyes and seeing that face."

"Do you think maybe you could talk to a sketch artist, try to give us something to work with?"

"I only saw him for a second, and I was pretty shook up to see this figure standing there, but I could try. He had dark hair. Black or close to it. Real messy. Dark stubble crawling almost up to his cheekbones. Average height, probably. And a pointy nose, I think. You could tell he was a creep just looking at him, though. One of those, you know, weirdo types."

They fell quiet for a moment, Kathryn's eyes now darting everywhere as she remembered.

"I still have dreams about that cabin. Dreams that I'm back there. Isn't that funny? Only lived there a year, if that, but it embedded itself in my memories real deep, I guess. I kind of think I'll always dream of that place."

A knock at the interview room door interrupted, and Fowles poked his head in. He waved that Darger and Furbush should come into the hall.

"Excuse us for just a second," Darger said to Kathryn, though the girl barely seemed to notice.

"A call just came in from dispatch. Someone spotted something floating in a pond out by Bonnie Lure Park."

"Please, don't," Furbush said, wiping a hand across his brow. "Don't tell me we've got another body."

Fowles nodded.

"Dispatch sent a patrol car out. Mantelbaum and Parks just radioed in after taking a look. Said it looks like the body of a young woman. Nude."

CHAPTER 49

The downpour that morning had given way to an overcast afternoon with periodic misty drizzles. Everyone at the scene was wearing plastic ponchos over their gear.

Darger rubbed her hands together. Her fingers were freezing. That was the problem with the ponchos. They kept the wet off, but they couldn't keep the chill out.

It was the same thing with the strobing lights on the police cars. They could flash and glimmer all they wanted, but they added no real brightness to this dim reality.

The way the red flashers sliced through the gray day reminded Darger of the bright red gashes on the belly and chest of the woman they'd pulled from the pond. Sharp strokes of angry color where everything else was dull and ashen.

Fowles and Dr. Kole hovered over the body. Darger stood just outside the tent with an umbrella shielding her from the wet spray. They'd invited her to stand inside the tent while they worked, but Darger knew she'd only be in the way. She wasn't much value to this part of the investigation. So she stayed outside and gave them space.

Her mind drifted back to when they'd first arrived on the scene.

She'd watched the divers secure the body to the floating stretcher and felt an incredible sense of déjà vu. It was eerily similar to what she'd witnessed yesterday, though there were two marked differences. The first was that there was no boat. It was determined that the pond was so small and so shallow —

not to mention lacking a current like the river-fed lake — to require the use of the Sheriff's boat. And so the divers had handled the recovery on their own, swimming the small raft out to the naked corpse and then dragging it back to shore by hand.

The second thing setting this scene apart from yesterday was the body itself. While she'd have to wait for Dr. Kole's official word, if Darger wasn't mistaken, this body looked fresher than the others. And as she'd watched them load the remains onto a proper stretcher and move her into the nearby tent, she'd decided it only made things slightly less horrifying. It was still bloated and too pale and wrinkled from the time in the water.

Anyway, she supposed it made sense for this body to be found sooner. A pond like this didn't conceal things as well as a rushing river with twists and bends and rapids, not to mention the miles and miles of territory.

Her thoughts were punctuated by the flashes of a camera as one of Furbush's men photographed the scene.

They'd found footprints in the muddy ground near the edge of the pond and what looked like drag marks. The problem was, with the deluge of rain that morning, any definition that might have existed had been eroded away. Washed out. As a result, there was no discernible tread imprint. Even the shoe size was hard to determine because of the way the wet earth had collapsed in on itself. All they really knew for certain was that this was the place the killer had stood when he'd dragged the body into the pond.

It was yet another infuriating addition to the day. A detail like a specific boot design or even a shoe size could have given them something to go on. It felt like a definitive clue had been dangled before their noses only to be snatched away at the last moment.

And that feeling kept resurfacing in this case. Again and again they thought they'd found a lead. First with Dustin and then with his credit card suddenly and mysteriously being used. But instead of answers, what they seemed to end up with over and over were more questions. More complications.

And more bodies.

How many more would die before Darger put a stop to it?

Frustration and fatigue threatened to overwhelm her, and as she glanced around at the men and women at work, she knew many of them had to be feeling that same sense of defeat. She'd only gone through it twice. These people had been forced to re-enact this five times now.

She could see the exhaustion on their faces. In their movements. Processing crime scenes like this took an emotional toll on top of the physical work required. These people would be on their feet for the next several hours. Furbush would want the autopsy results as soon as possible, and she suspected that Dr. Kole would feel pressured to conduct the postmortem immediately.

Darger got out her phone and looked up the cafe she'd been to the other morning with Fowles. A woman's voice answered, perky and cheerful, and said delivery was no problem, so Darger ordered enough coffee and baked goods for a small army.

When the delivery arrived forty minutes later, Darger made the rounds with the boxes of pastry. The men and women working the scene thanked her, happy for the small, pleasant interruption. Because that's all it was. A brief pause to scarf a cheese danish and chug a small cup of coffee. Then it was back to the grind. Bagging, logging, photographing.

Darger dug her fingernails into her styrofoam cup, leaving behind a row of tiny crescent moons pressed into the white surface. Three bodies in six days. She knew the actual murders had been spaced apart, despite finding the bodies one after another. But it still suggested the killer was growing more frantic. More desperate.

What had she missed? Something, surely. She could feel it in her gut, along with the jitters from the caffeine and a sense of guilt for failing this woman.

The hours passed, and the sun sunk lower in the sky. And as the light of day dimmed, so did the color of things.

Darger glanced around the scene and found only bleakness. Like the woman's corpse laid out a few feet away, everything was gray and sad and sodden. Colorless and dull.

CHAPTER 50

Darger rode to the county medical examiner's office with Fowles. The windshield wipers beat out a plodding rhythm and left behind smears of moisture on the glass where the blades were worn.

"Find anything noteworthy?"

"Actually, yes," Fowles said.

"What was it?"

"Nothing."

"Say again?"

"No insect activity."

"But the others…"

"They all had substantial larval activity, because they weren't put into the water until approximately 1-2 days after death."

"So that means this one was dumped immediately?"

"Or close to it."

Darger shook her head, feeling any clarity she'd had about the case slipping away again. She closed her eyes and let out a noisy breath.

"Sorry to be the bearer of bad news," Fowles said.

"This case is just… it's like stepping into a mountain lake, the kind with water so clear you can look down and see your feet on the sandy bottom. Except with each footstep, more and more of the silt at the bottom gets stirred up until the water is as opaque and murky as pea soup."

He reached out and took her hand in his.

"Would some of my world famous lasagna cheer you up?"

She narrowed her eyes, smiling.

"You never mentioned it was 'world famous' lasagna."

"I don't like to brag."

((

Dr. Kole had already made the Y incision and was prodding the dead woman's intestines when they arrived in the autopsy suite. All thoughts of lasagna, world-famous or otherwise, immediately fled Darger's mind.

She didn't consider herself particularly squeamish, but there was something unsettling about watching the dissection of a human being.

It was rougher than one might expect, for starters. Cutting through ribs and sawing open skulls were not delicate tasks.

It reminded her a little of the first time she'd seen someone administer CPR in real life. She'd witnessed a car accident her first year in college, and she still remembered how violent it seemed when the paramedic began chest compressions on a man pulled from the wreckage. The woman threw her whole upper body into the effort, and the unconscious man convulsed with each thrust. It hadn't been a shock when she'd learned that recipients of CPR often sustained fractured ribs or a broken sternum.

She glanced over at her two male associates. Ever the scientist, Fowles appeared both completely at ease and rapt with the examination. Furbush, on the other hand, had a decidedly green tint.

"That's what I thought," the doctor said, talking to himself it seemed, but then he pointed out various landmarks in the abdominal cavity.

"See the lacerations here, on the left lobe of the liver?" he asked, gesturing at a large dark blob.

He moved a gloved finger to a paler organ Darger recognized as the stomach.

"And another here near the pyloric ring."

Glancing up at them through the thick lenses of his glasses, he frowned.

"It's always difficult to tell at the on-scene examination whether these types of wounds are ante or postmortem. Anytime they're in the water for any period of time, there's the potential for animal activity or dragging on rough surfaces. You'd be surprised the amount of damage a corpse can sustain just being pulled out by the divers. The skin is so delicate after being in the water for a few hours. It tears quite easily."

Dr. Kole pressed his lips together and gazed down at the body.

"However, looking at them now, the lacerations are very clean."

He drew their attention to a monitor nearby displaying close-up photographs his assistant had been busy taking all the while.

"You can see here, under magnification, there's almost no tearing of the tissue. These are neat cuts. And the depth of each wound, too, is quite consistent."

"Meaning?" Furbush asked.

"I believe she was stabbed to death."

"Not drowned?"

"That is correct."

"Could she have been stabbed as a means for the killer to

subdue her before drowning?" Darger asked. "We theorized that might have been the case with some of the other victims, based on their wounds."

Dr. Kole made something like a grunt.

"The key word there is 'theorized.' All of the previous victims were in such an advanced state of decomposition that I couldn't say definitively whether the wounds had occurred before or after death. But the point is moot, when it comes to this particular victim. I've checked for other signs of drowning. There is no water in the lungs. No hemolysis."

Darger was still trying to make sense of this as he continued.

"There's more," he said and now he and his assistant removed the stomach and liver.

He pointed to a thick pink tube toward the back of the cavity.

"The abdominal aorta was severed. She would have bled out in a matter of minutes," he said, crossing his arms. "I'm certain this girl was dead before she hit the water."

As the doctor continued his examination, Furbush and Fowles fell into conversation, but Darger was too deep in her own thoughts to follow it.

Was the killer changing his M.O.? Or could it have been an accident? Maybe he'd stabbed her to incapacitate her, hit the aorta, and she died too quickly to do the bathtub ritual. That could explain why he'd skipped it. He'd messed it up. Given up when things went wrong.

Something about the whole case still felt wrong to Darger. Off. Right in the middle of everything they knew, there was a big gaping hole in the shape of a question mark.

A hand on her shoulder sent these thoughts scattering. She blinked at Fowles questioningly.

"Are you OK?" he asked.

"I'm fine," she said. "Just thinking."

Furbush cleared his throat.

"So she wasn't drowned. And Fowles says the insect evidence suggests she was put in the water almost immediately right after death… are we sure this is even the same killer? I thought the drowning was integral to his little ceremony of whatever."

"It's him," Darger said. "It's too coincidental. Someone else stabs this girl and decides to dump her in a pond? There are a thousand places you could hide a body around here. Places where the body would stay hidden."

She rubbed her eyes.

"Regardless of whether he stabbed any of the previous victims, there was something different about this girl. It was more personal. He lost control here for some reason. Took things too far. It's like… this was more of a crime of passion than his usual meticulous ritual."

Furbush remained unconvinced.

"What if it was staged to make us think it was our killer?"

Weighing this in her mind, Darger wrapped her arms around herself. She had the sense that Furbush was growing just as impatient with the case as she was.

"Maybe," she said finally, studying the woman laid out on the cold metal table just a few feet away. "But she feels like one of ours. I don't know why, but she does."

CHAPTER 51

Sweat smears your palms. No matter how many times you swipe them at the knees of your pants, the moisture remains. Fresh blooms of it seeping out to slick your skin as fast as you can dry it.

You walk through the dark. Through a gutted section of town where tall grass grows to shroud the empty factories.

The buildings watch you passing by. Busted out windows peer out at you like swollen pupils.

Otherwise you are alone. As alone as you've ever been. Cold and empty and useless.

When you close your eyes, you can still see the black and white of the newsprint. They've found Reynolds.

Callie, too.

It's close now. The end looms closer than ever.

They will know what you've done, will know who you are. Everyone will know.

And then what? Then what happens?

You wrinkle your brow. Ponder it a moment.

Shame. That's what will happen. Shame without end, without any chance of release, relief, redemption.

And maybe that makes sense. Maybe.

That's what happens to the monster people, right? They cease to exist. Once we know the darkness inside of them, we erase them somehow. Render them less than human. Cast them out. Forget them.

We lock them up in the dark somewhere where our eyes

don't have to go. It makes us feel safe.

But it's not real, is it? The safety we feel isn't real.

Because the darkness is always there, always part of humanity, always part of us. It cannot be defeated. More and more and more of it. No matter what we do.

You walk past the last of the buildings, past a few park benches and rotting picnic tables set off in the strip of grass along the roadside, some half-assed park where the factory workers could go for lunch, probably.

And that's it. You've arrived at the end of this industrial neighborhood. The end of the city.

You reach the place where the streetlights end, that strange point where the city's glow shears off into black nothing. Feels like moving toward the mouth of a cave. An enclosed blackness you must enter.

You press forward into the gloom. Let the shadows swallow you whole. Let the darkness have you. And the strangest thrum vibrates in your chest.

Your hand balls into a fist. Presses itself to that fleshy spot just left of your sternum. You remember reading somewhere that a kid's heart is the size of a fist and an adult's is the size of two fists.

You can feel it in there now. That crooked ball of muscle squishing along, beating against your ribcage.

And now the dark closes around you. Total. Complete.

Everything and nothing spiral in your head, your brain intent on holding onto both at once, trying to wrap its wrinkles around them, use either/or to explain the universe, to explain existence. Some paradox. A loop that repeats and repeats and repeats, feeds back into itself eternally like those layers of self-consciousness that plague you. Watching yourself watch yourself watch yourself and on and on.

You push each foot forward into the black, and the soles of your shoes scuffing on the blacktop seem to be the only evidence left that you are real, that you exist at all in a physical sense. The dark somehow seems more real than you now, bigger than you.

And you love it and hate it at the same time. Tingling. Overwhelmed with the strange power of the night touching you like this. It's too much. Too much to hold in one heart, in one skull.

Sickness creeps over you in waves. A wriggling nag in the abdomen. Squishing liquid in your gut that wants to loose itself up, up, and away.

The darkness in your head seems to seep out into physical reality. Your internal world coming out to play in the dark.

And images flare there in the emptiness. The figments in your head projected outward, made real.

You see the Channel 7 news report about Reynolds again as though the reporter and B-roll footage of the cabin lay before you, the pictures somehow blossoming from the asphalt in 3-D.

Interviewed faces congeal and shift and morph. People connected to the case.

What did that bitch tell the police? How bad is it? You wish you could go to her. Show her your side of the story with the tip of your blade. But you can't. You can't.

The anger swells, a seething fever that tints the dark with the slightest red hue, but you push it down. Move deeper into the dark, into the black.

Snippets of the report play again and again, broadcast into

the night out of order, the pictures perpetually in front of you, bobbing a little along with the rise and fall of your gait.

The cabin. The director seems to dwell on the cabin. Those shots of the ramshackle building holding longer and longer as the loop plays on. Sunlight glinting on the worn shingles of the roof.

Yes. The cabin. It makes sense.

The cabin has become something of a beacon now, you think. A place of great energy after being still for so long. A wound that people will be drawn to. Everyone wants to go to that torn open place and gaze down into the hole, try to make sense of it. The dark energy will pull them to it like a magnet. Will draw them right to you.

You can wait out at the cabin like a spider. Ready. Lying in wait for them to move into the sticky strings of your web.

You smile in the dark.

CHAPTER 52

Night was falling by the time they left the medical examiner's office. It wasn't raining anymore, though everything still glistened with moisture and the air felt thick and cool.

The floodlights that lit the parking lot buzzed overhead as the three investigators trudged out to their vehicles.

Furbush paused next to his Explorer and rested a hand on the roof. He looked dog-tired, with heavy bags under his bloodshot eyes.

"I'll call everyone in for a meeting tomorrow morning so we can try to… I don't know…. Figure something out. You know the State Police offered to take this all off our hands after we found the Mead girl. But I was a stubborn old boar and said no. I thought we could handle it. Thought *I* could handle it. Maybe that was a mistake."

"I wouldn't have joined the investigation if I thought that was the case," Darger said, not wanting him to give up.

She reached out and patted his arm.

"Go home, and get some rest. You're exhausted. We all are. Tomorrow we can take a look at everything with fresh eyes."

He nodded, only seeming half-convinced, and climbed into his car.

Darger's stomach grumbled as she followed Fowles across the lot to where they'd parked earlier that evening. She went over the events since the morning interview with Kathryn Porter, somehow not believing it had all occurred in a single day. It felt like a week had passed since yesterday.

She glanced over at Fowles as he started the car, knowing that if she was feeling exhausted, he was probably doubly so. He'd been on his feet for most of the hours spent at the crime scene. As much as she hungered for a home-cooked meal, she couldn't imagine allowing him to cook for her on a night like tonight.

The car glided out of the parking lot, headed for Portland. Darger spoke up over the sound of the tires humming on the asphalt, and suggested they order takeout.

"You're not holding me to my promise?"

"You're off the hook," she said. "For now. But you can't just throw around labels like 'world famous' and not expect to have to prove yourself, you understand. I will expect a make-up lasagna."

"Fair enough. There's a great Chinese place not far from my house."

Darger's nose wrinkled. Normally she was a big fan of Chinese, but she had rules about what she could and could not stomach after a crime scene.

"Nope. Can't do rice. Or noodles. Haven't you ever seen *The Lost Boys*? Nothing that looks like maggots or worms, thank you."

"But there weren't any maggots today."

"Doesn't matter. The mere possibility of maggots is enough to put me off all maggot-like foods for at least two days. Maybe that makes me particularly maggot-suggestible. So be it."

Fowles shook his head, amused.

"Pizza?" he suggested. "Or does that look too much like viscera?"

"Pizza is fine. As long as you don't say 'viscera' again."

When they got back to Fowles' apartment, she was surprised just how hungry she was. After devouring four slices, she sat back against the couch. She felt satiated and also totally drained. Her feet hurt, and the dampness from the weather seemed to have seeped into her bones, making them feel creaky and ancient. Her back and shoulders ached from the long hours of standing.

The corner of her phone dug into her hip, so she pulled it from her pocket and tossed it on the coffee table. She caught sight of Fowles, who was also leaning back against the cushions, eyes closed. Here she was cataloguing her list of bodily complaints when he'd actually been in work mode the whole time. Analyzing, collecting samples, brain no doubt working a mile a minute.

She scooted closer and reached out for his neck and shoulders. He let out a groan of satisfaction as she rubbed at the tired muscles.

While she massaged, her mind wandered over the details of the case. That sense that they were missing something big had become stronger and stronger over the last few days. And today, finding this new body, with the method of killing suddenly changing, seemed to solidify that concept in her mind.

Something was wrong. The profile was off. She'd known it all along somehow, but she still didn't know why.

It was like Fowles with his conflicting insect evidence. Larvae where there shouldn't be larvae.

The killer's basic shape writhed and shifted in her mind, never keeping still. She knew that if she could only pinpoint what felt so dissonant about all of it, the mixed up pieces of the puzzle would fall together, show her the big picture.

Fowles reached out and brushed her cheek lightly with the back of his fingers.

She realized she'd stopped massaging and was just sitting there with her hands resting on his shoulders.

"What's the matter?"

"Hm?" Darger said, the fog of her thoughts dissipating slowly. "Oh, it's nothing. I mean, it's not. Just… something isn't right."

"With us?"

He'd gone rigid then, his face all concern. He looked so serious, Darger couldn't help but chuckle.

"No." She watched him relax. "It's this case. More specifically, my profile. Something is off. I've felt it for a while now, but I can't put my finger on it. I constantly feel like I'm being pulled in two directions."

She shook her head.

"It's like the stuff you found with the insects. You knew something didn't add up. The bugs didn't match up with what the medical examiner was telling you."

"Which you solved, by the way," he reminded her. "You'll figure this out, too."

"Eventually. Maybe. But what if it's too late?" She rubbed at her eyes. "What am I saying? It's already too late. He's killed two more. If he does it again, and I haven't figured it out…"

Fowles pulled her closer and kissed her, and then his hands were in her hair and on her body, and Darger tried to let go of the worry, of the anxious thoughts scratching at the dark corners of her mind, but even as they made love, and after, when she started to drift off to sleep, there was a part of her mind still occupied with unease.

☾

Darger's phone was ringing. Her eyes snapped open, glanced at the clock on the bedside table. She'd only dozed off for about half an hour, dusk now hitting its full stride out the windows, but the brief nap left her feeling groggy and confused. By the time she kicked out from under the sheets and stumbled out into the living room to retrieve her phone, she'd missed the call. Her eyes squinted into slits as she read the number from the call log. She didn't recognize it.

She left it and went into the kitchen to chug a glass of water and snag a cold piece of pizza.

Halfway through the slice, Darger perched on the sofa and checked her voicemail. There was one new message. It was from Kathryn Porter.

The woman's tone of voice sounded even stranger than usual, and Darger thought her detached demeanor and flat way of speaking would make her the kind of person her mother referred to as a "space cadet."

"Hi. It's Kathryn Porter, and um…. I guess after we talked, I got to thinking about Dustin and the cabin. And I thought and thought until this urge to go out there overtook me. I don't know. I guess I just wanted to see it. For… closure, I guess. Something to make his death feel more real to me. Something like that. We were together for so many years, even if we didn't get along most of the time. It's hard… hard to wrap your head around something like that. So I'm driving out there now, just to peek in the windows, I guess, before it's all the way dark, anyway. I don't know. I guess I thought maybe I should let

341

someone know."

The message ended abruptly, with no goodbye, and Darger stared at the phone for some time after she'd disconnected. There was something about the woman and the cabin and Dustin Reynolds that felt important. She'd never lost the sense that Dustin Reynolds in particular was the key to finding the missing piece.

Darger had an urge to go up to the cabin while Kathryn was there. Who knew what she might remember visiting the scene in person? More than that, she might be more open, more willing to talk. Not that she'd seemed evasive before, but Kathryn Porter was not what Darger would call a particularly open or accessible personality. Being there at the cabin where she'd spent time with her ex-husband and where he'd ultimately met his demise might put the woman in a more expressive mood. Nostalgia had a way of getting people to talk, to open up. To make connections in their mind they maybe hadn't realized before.

But Darger's car was in Sandy, and she felt guilty asking Fowles to drive her all the way back. Maybe she could borrow his car. She was still staring down at the phone in her hand when Fowles walked out of the bedroom.

"You look like you're scheming."

"Kathryn Porter just called me. She's going up to the cabin to look around."

The space between his eyebrows crinkled up.

"The Reynolds cabin? It's almost full dark out. That's kind of odd, isn't it?"

"Well, *she's* kind of odd, so…" Darger waved her hand in the air. "Anyway, I think maybe I should go up there and try to talk to her again. I still think that Dustin Reynolds is important in all of this, somehow. And Kathryn Porter is probably the person who can tell us what we need to know. It's just a matter of getting her talking again."

"Let's go then."

"Really? You're not totally beat after today? I feel guilty asking you to get back in the car and drive me back out there."

"Of course I'm tired," Fowles said. "And I'll expect a full body massage when we get back. But this sounds important."

Darger smirked.

"A *full body* massage?"

"I expect certain parts will need more attention than others."

Darger snorted as she grabbed her jacket.

Then Fowles did a double take as he saw her laughing and pursed his lips.

"Oh, it'd be just like you to try to turn that into something dirty," he said. "I'll have you know that I was talking about my penis."

CHAPTER 53

For the hundredth time, Darger ran through what they knew, trying to line things up in a way that allowed her to see the big picture. Nineteen years ago Christy Whitmore died in a bathtub. Her mother was convinced Dustin Reynolds was the killer, though no evidence was found to that effect.

Now Dustin had joined Christy and five others in death. So he wasn't the killer, but he was tangled up in all of it somehow.

A dark thought flitted across Darger's mind. Something Kathryn had said about Dustin feeling guilty after Christy's death. And responsible. Could Dustin have known who killed Christy all those years ago?

It wasn't until they turned on the isolated road that led to the cabin that an even darker idea struck her.

"Holy shit," she said out loud, feeling a chill run over her skin as the full weight of it settled over her.

"What is it?"

"What if Dustin Reynolds knew the killer? Or even if he didn't know who, maybe he knew *something*. Something big enough that it scared the killer into thinking he needed to be permanently shut up."

There was just enough bluish light from the dashboard that Darger could see Fowles' eyebrows go up.

"That would be a pretty convincing motive."

"Well," Darger continued, "Kathryn Porter is his ex-wife. What if Dustin told her something? The killer only has to wonder or worry that she might know something to put her on his radar. To put her in danger."

"Wouldn't the same go for Jennifer Strickley, as well?"

Darger's stomach shrank in on itself at this thought, felt it quiver there in her abdomen like a trembling ball of muscle.

"Yes. Jesus. I need to call Furbush," she said.

She pulled her phone from her pocket.

"The service is shit out here," Darger complained.

"I think it gets better near the cabin."

Shoving the phone back into her pocket, she resisted the urge to nag at Fowles to drive faster. It was dark, and they'd already seen two deer near the shoulder. The last thing they needed was to swerve around an animal and go careening off one of the steep cliff edges.

She just had to hope that her new theory was wrong. Or that they weren't already too late.

"We might have made a very big mistake," Darger said.

They arrived at the cabin minutes later. Kathryn Porter's vehicle was parked next to the rotting fallen tree — one of those smaller model pickups, purple and downright dainty — but Kathryn herself was nowhere to be seen. The cabin lights were dark.

Darger's hands instinctively grasped for her gun.

"I don't like this."

Fowles opened the console between the seats and pulled out the lockbox where he kept his weapon.

"That's a bad idea," she said. "You should stay here and see if you can get Sandy PD on the phone."

"Forget it," Fowles said, removing the pistol from the case and checking the magazine. "I'm not letting you walk in there without someone watching your back."

Darger eased herself out of the car and closed the door as quietly as she could. Her pulse whooshed in her ears as she padded toward the cabin. She could hear Fowles a few feet behind her, legs swooshing through the overgrown grass.

She paused just before stepping onto the porch, remembering how creaky the old boards were.

Her eyes had mostly adjusted to the dark now. The cabin squatted there in the blackness, and Darger squinted at the hedges and the property beyond. No movement inside or out. Aside from the gentle rustle of the trees overhead and the chirping of the night insects, everything was still and quiet.

She wondered if Fowles could identify the bugs based solely on sound, but it was a question for a less tense moment.

Darger lifted her leg and stepped up onto the porch. The sole of her boot had barely touched down when a light inside snapped on. She flinched against the glow and crouched down reflexively, not wanting to be seen.

A rattling sound told her the front door was about to be opened. She snatched Fowles' sleeve and pulled him roughly to the side and out of the light.

As the door peeled open, Darger held her breath and stared into the cabin. In the backlit door frame, a silhouette took shape.

"Who's out there?"

Darger recognized the shape and the voice. She stood up, holding her gun to her side and pointed down.

"Kathryn?"

"Oh, thank God, it's you!" Her hand fluttered about her neck and chest nervously. "Hurry, come inside!"

Darger took a step closer to the door, and Kathryn

346

scrambled backward suddenly.

"Stop! Who is that with you?" Kathryn asked, holding something out in front of her like a shield.

Looking closer, Darger saw it was a cast iron skillet. She put a hand on Fowles' shoulder, a gesture that said, It's OK, he's one of us.

"This is Ted Fowles. He's working the case with me."

This eased the woman's fear enough that she lowered the protective frying pan.

"Kathryn, what's going on?"

"I wasn't sure you got my message. I guess I'm lucky you did."

As soon as they were inside, she hastily shut the door behind them and locked it.

"I thought I was being silly. Seeing things."

"Seeing what?"

"There were headlights behind me the whole drive up here. And it's such an isolated road, I started thinking I was being followed or something. Only, I knew that was crazy. So then I told myself, 'Kat, you are being a silly goose! There is no one following you. When you turn off into the driveway for the cabin, they are just going to keep on driving.'"

"And?" Darger asked.

"And that's exactly what happened!"

A funny smile quivered on her lips as she continued her story.

"So I got out of the car, and I started looking around, peeking in the windows, just like I said. I swear, I never planned on coming inside, Miss Darger. I know it's a crime scene, and that I shouldn't be messing with anything and all that. But then I saw him."

Darger felt a prickle spread over her scalp and down her neck.

"Who did you see?"

"A man! He was creeping around out by that old shed in back. He must have driven on down the road a ways and then snuck over here on foot. I panicked when I saw him, and then I remembered there used to be a spare key for the cabin hidden on the window frame to the right of the front door. And would you believe it? It was still there! I'll tell you, I've never unlocked a door so fast in my life. Once I was inside, I got down behind the couch, and I hid. I don't know for how long, but it felt like hours. When I heard your car pulling into the drive, I thought, I don't know who that is, but I hope they'll help me."

"Do you think he's still outside?"

Kathryn brought a trembling hand to her mouth and spoke through her fingers.

"I thought I heard something around the back end of the cabin just before you pulled up. A soft crack, like someone stepped on a twig."

Darger spotted a flashlight lying on a side table near the couch. She reached for it, tested that it worked, and held it in her non-shooting hand.

"I'm going to take a look around," she said, heading for the door. "Stay here."

Kathryn hugged her arms around herself.

"You're leaving me?" Her voice was like an over-tightened violin string, high and tense.

Darger glanced at Fowles, who had followed her to the front of the cabin. He gave a wordless nod.

"Fowles will stay with you until I get back," Darger said to the woman, then turned to address Fowles. "See if you can get ahold of Sandy PD from in here. If you can't get a signal, don't leave the cabin. We'll figure out what to do next when I get back."

"Be careful," he whispered as she slipped through the door and into the darkness beyond.

CHAPTER 54

Darger waited for her eyes to adjust to the darkness, and then she crept around the side of the cabin, keeping to the shadows. She moved slowly and quietly, eyes scanning the trees for movement.

She wasn't sure what to make of Kathryn's story. The woman was so skittish, so twitchy, it was hard not to wonder if maybe she'd gotten out here — in this isolated place, alone in the dark — and freaked herself out. Let her imagination get the better of her.

She didn't doubt that Kathryn had seen something in the forest. There were deer, cougars, bears, even wolves out here. Plenty of things that could snap a twig underfoot or rustle through some dry leaves. Darger felt a little spooked herself as she navigated the inky landscape, everything black, blacker, blackest. The sky, the ground, the foliage. Her eyes only made the barest distinction between the shades of darkness.

She felt vulnerable as she wove between the trees. Visible, even with the flashlight off. Like someone was watching. Because there was a serial killer out there somewhere. Maybe he was in these woods right now, maybe not. But the thought was a hard one to shake.

Tightening her grip on her gun, she brushed these feelings off and kept moving.

Finally, she reached the shed. It was a rickety-looking wooden structure with an old metal roof streaked with rust, so worn it looked like it would tumble down with one good huff-

and-puff by the Big Bad Wolf.

She flattened herself against the wood siding, careful not to put her weight on it, lest she knock the whole thing over.

Air whispered in and out of her lungs as she side-stepped around the perimeter.

Nobody outside.

She sidled back around to the front, felt around for the handle on the door. It felt cold and rough in her hand.

As smoothly and quickly as possible, she wrenched the door open, flicked on the flashlight, and swept the interior, gun drawn. The walls inside were lined with ancient-looking tools and equipment. Everything was covered in a generous layer of dust.

She hesitated to step through the door, not quite able to shake the idea of someone slamming it shut behind her as soon as she passed over the threshold. The beam of the flashlight highlighted a snarl of cobwebs in one corner.

She took one shaky step through the doors. It smelled like cedar and earth with a hint of motor oil.

Crack!

Darger whirled around, expecting to see nothing but the blackness of the closed door, but no. The door still stood open. No one was there.

Crack!

The sound came again.

And then her ears and her mind finally started communicating properly. She realized what she'd heard when the noise repeated itself.

Two gunshots.

And they had come from the cabin.

CHAPTER 55

Darger closed on the cabin in slow motion, legs numb beneath her but somehow propelling her forward anyway, gun raised at her side.

The skin on her scalp crawled, little pinpricks everywhere beneath her hair. She resisted the urge to scratch it.

Gravity seemed to flee her in this moment, release her from its grip, make her lighter and lighter. Her head fluttered inside, so tingly that she bordered on an out-of-body experience.

She crossed the dirt driveway now, a few loose stones underfoot wobbling her ankles but not slowing her.

And her eyes remained locked on the front door, fastened to the rectangular slab of wood in such a way that it seemed to be bobbing along with her steps, not ever really getting closer. Just a thing that hovered along with her like watching the moon out of a car window. Along for the ride.

It didn't seem like she'd ever get there, but she did.

She climbed the stairs, took them in two bounds, the wood of the porch sagging a little under her choppy steps.

And she hesitated for just a beat at the doorway, at the threshold. Swallowed hard. Whispering little nonsense syllables to try to psych herself up.

It occurred to her that part of her expected to find the cabin empty. The other half expected something worse. Much worse.

She called out, her voice wavering but somehow still assertive, still confident.

"Fowles?"

It took her a second for her panicked brain to cough up the girl's name.

"Kathryn?"

No answer to either of these.

Shit.

Her heart hammered so hard she could feel her ribs quaking with each beat, all those muscles stitching up the walls of her chest being stretched like rubber bands.

She adjusted the grip on her gun, wishing more than anything that someone would answer. Anyone. But no.

Still, better to announce herself, avoid the threat of friendly fire. She swallowed again before she spoke, felt a strange sticky feeling in her throat that made her worry a second that she wouldn't be able to get the words out.

"Alright. I'm coming in."

Her voice sounded smaller this time, some of that confidence having leaked out in the past few seconds.

And life snapped into slow motion as she peeled open the screen door and prepared to cross through.

Lifting her gun. Holding her breath. The screen door leaning against her right shoulder.

Hand moving to the knob. Throwing aside the storm door and easing through the opening.

The gun pointed the way, its muzzle scanning across the cabin's interior along with her field of vision. She took in the cabin's interior slowly, ready to shoot or duck or dive at the slightest movement.

Nothing there. No one.

At first she thought her panicked premonition had been right. They were gone, somehow. Just an empty cabin. But when she wheeled the full 90 degrees to her left she saw it.

A body lay on the floor — a man — sprawling just where the oak plank flooring of the living space gave way to the kitchen's linoleum, a faux tile the color of brick. Her eyes snapped to the shiver of movement along the trunk of the body. A wetness.

Bleeding. The abdomen opened up. A red puddle spreading outward from the wounded place. Gushing out like water from a spring.

The words thrust themselves into Darger's head as if from nowhere: *Bleeding out.*

Her eyes lingered on that tattered bit of exposed flesh, red sludge and pale belly skin poking out from the blood-stained splotch in the white dress shirt.

And for a second this body looked foreign. Alien. Some stranger who burst in and was now dying on the kitchen floor. Some unlucky fool in the wrong place at the wrong time.

But no. The figure was not foreign.

It was Fowles.

CHAPTER 56

A breath hiccupped in Darger's throat, a stuttering click of air stopping and starting and wheezing. The panic swelled, grabbed her by the scruff of the neck and squeezed, froze her every muscle, but just for a second.

Then she went to work.

She stormed down the hall pistol-first, clearing the bathroom and hall closet before moving to the bunks. She needed to make sure the cabin was secure before she tended to Fowles. Needed to be quick about it, too.

Peeking through the final doorway, she spotted something in the corner she'd have to deal with — the tiniest shivering thing. Making sure there were no lingering threats came first, though.

She plunged through the doorway, flicking the gun to the left and then the right. Nothing.

Lowered herself to peer under each set of bunk beds. Kicked at the clothes hanging in the closet. Swiveled her shoulders to check the entirety of the space. Empty, all of them.

Clear. Good.

Now she moved to that tremor which had caught her eye just beyond the bottom mattress to her left.

Kathryn Porter huddled in the far corner of the bedroom, tucked in the shadows, half obscured by the antique dresser there. She held her head in her arms and rocked herself from side to side, a catatonic look to the behavior.

Darger knelt, sensing once again that she needed to be

gentle with this one. Delicate. She spoke just louder than a whisper, placed a hand on the girl's forearm.

"Kathryn. Are you OK?"

The girl stopped rocking, removed her arms from her head, peeked out, slow blinking like a lemur. She said nothing. Nodded her head after a second.

Darger stood and reached her hands out, helped Kathryn up. The frantic urge to scramble back to Fowles roiled over her skin, but she needed to find out what happened here first.

"He was there," Kathryn said, whisper-yelling, a weird rising pitch in her tone. She sounded terrified. "He was out there. Right out there."

She gestured out the window, not pointing with a finger so much as a floppy hand at the end of her wrist.

Darger's mind tried to process this in fast speed. *He was there.* Outside. Did that make sense? Had he fired through a window? Darger hadn't heard breaking glass. Only the gunshots.

She clenched her teeth. Needed to keep it simple. Of the many questions percolating in her head, she asked one.

"Who?"

Kathryn didn't answer. She slow-blinked a couple more times and then shuffled off toward the door to the hallway, her arms once more hugging at her torso, her face going a little blank.

Darger grabbed her by the shoulders and spun the girl to face her again. There was no point in trying to get answers out of her just now, but she could still help.

"I need to see to Fowles. Do you have a phone?"

After another slow-blink, Kathryn nodded again.

"I want you to try to find a signal. Call 911. Tell them there's an officer down."

It was a lie — Fowles wasn't actually law enforcement — but Darger didn't care about that. She wanted the whole damned cavalry to descend on this place with urgency.

Darger rushed back to the sprawled figure at the edge of the kitchen. Tried not to note the stillness of his ribcage, the absence of any obvious signs that he was still breathing.

She knelt next to him. Held her breath as she checked his pulse. Still there, but faint. The beat felt thin against her fingers. Hollow. *Thready* was what they always called it in the first aid classes she'd taken. He didn't have long.

She ripped off her jacket. Wadded it up. Pressed it to that ragged opening in his middle and applied pressure.

If Kathryn couldn't get someone on the phone, they'd have to move him. Darger tried to go through the steps in her head. She should have Kathryn move the car closer to the door so they wouldn't have to carry him across the whole yard. Kathryn could sit in back and apply pressure while Darger drove. Or maybe Darger should sit in back so she could perform CPR if that became necessary. She didn't exactly trust the woman to drive in the state she was in, but her options were limited.

Fowles' skin was so cold it felt like something pulled out of the back of the refrigerator, but the sheets of blood pulsing up to saturate her jacket seemed feverish. Too hot. Wrong.

She pressed harder, closed her eyes and tried to will the bleeding to slow, to stop. The jacket was already sopping in her fingers.

She thought maybe she should grab a towel. Were there towels in the bathroom? She couldn't remember. The mattresses sported no blankets from what she could recall, all stripped bare.

She opened her eyes again and movement drew her gaze upward.

Kathryn stumbled out of the bedroom doorway, arms hugged around herself, a listless look in her eye. Mindless, Darger thought. Like a zombie.

"Did you call 911?"

No answer. Kathryn just kept shambling forward, feet sliding over the floor more than taking steps.

Darger hardened her voice. Tried not to sound too aggressive, tried not to let her fear and frustration seep through even though what she really wanted was to grab the girl by the shoulders and give her a good shake.

"Kathryn. Are you OK?"

"He was out there," the girl mumbled just above her breath. She arrived at the kitchen counter and stopped, gazing out the window above the sink.

And again Darger sensed that something wasn't right. Kathryn wasn't making sense. She must be in shock.

Fowles moaned a little then, a sleepy sound emitting from his parted lips. Far away perhaps. Still there, though. Still alive, but they were losing time. He wouldn't make it much longer.

Darger pulled out her phone, streaking blood all over the touchscreen with her red fingers. She couldn't rely on Kathryn for any help in this. She'd have to do it all herself.

Her hands shook as she picked out the numbers on the dial pad, but before she could dial the second 1, a dark figure lurched for her.

She looked up, flinched, dropped the phone as she tried to

shield herself with her hand, confused to see Kathryn Porter swinging something, something black and mean and arcing toward her head, something that looked like a cast iron skillet.

She sensed the first crack of the impact, a deep musical tone like a struck bell inside her skull, and then everything went black.

CHAPTER 57

You stop. Hover over the limp figure. Make sure she's out. Little wheezes snuffle in and out of her, but otherwise she keeps still. Good.

You cup your hands under her armpits and lift. Lean her torso against yours. And now you move. Drag her inch by inch. Her legs dangling along behind you all loose like rag doll parts.

Her frame feels small in your arms, against your abdomen. Delicate. Like a bird or a baby turtle, you think. So small that the shell is still soft.

She is weak and you are strong, and this is how you fit together, how you've always fit together. Always and forever.

But the weight is dead. Limp. A floppy heap that strains against you. Makes your muscles quiver.

It's not far, though. Not far to where she's going, where you'll make her clean.

Her pant leg gets caught on the metal threshold strip in the bathroom doorway. The fabric rips a little when you jerk her free.

And now you're there. Her destination.

You slump the body into the tub, and the skull cracks into the polymer all loud. Sounds like you dropped a bowling ball or an anvil. Makes you think of cartoon characters trying to kill each other in elaborate ways.

You step back, and again you're struck by how small she looks. And how perfect. She is something tiny and precious. Something totally at the mercy of your every whim.

Your hands move to twist the knobs, and the water rushes forth. Cascading out of the spout and slapping the floor of the tub. Little specks of spray flick up onto the rim just next to you. Spatter.

As soon as the faucet turns on, you feel better. The sound of the water soothes you. Sloshing and babbling. Makes life simple again. Makes everything small and clean.

You've always belonged together, haven't you? Always.

Way back, all those years ago, you couldn't be. Things were different in so many ways. And maybe she never wanted you the way you wanted her. Sometimes you can remember it being that way. This sucking emptiness in your chest, a world that brought you here to humiliate you, a universe full only of meaninglessness and pain.

Other times, though, she loved you. She really loved you and things just went wrong.

The bad thing just happened to her like all the rest. An accident, almost.

Cross your heart and hope to die.

It's all happened so many times now. Like an endless loop. It gets hard to keep all the stories straight.

But you are together now. Together again. And she is yours. She is all the way yours.

Your possession.

You blink, and the real world comes into focus again.

She is there in the water. Floating face down.

But some sense creeps over you, an impulse like an itch crawling up your spine that something is missing, some element of the ritual forgotten in the rush of events.

You need a blade.

CHAPTER 58

Darger drifted in the dark, somewhere between awake and sleeping. Apart from reality. Alone in her skull.

Part of her knew this was so, knew that she lay prone now in a strange place far from any road. At the mercy of something or someone to be feared. Something cold. Dark. Savage. And this conscious part of her held tight to some fractured awareness of the terrors waiting beyond that thin barrier of her eyelids.

This panicked portion of her mind struggled to alert the rest of her, to shake her from her sleep, but it did not know how. Most of her just floated in the emptiness, knew only the dark inside, only the peacefulness of the here and now. The abyss.

And she marveled at this sense that she was floating. Weightless. Unchained from the ground at last. Like a child free of any and all concerns.

Wherever she was, all sounds had been muffled. Dampened. But the quiet was strange. Wavering and wet and not right somehow. Not normal. The high end sucked out so everything lacked clarity, lacked a sense of space. A quiet that seemed right on top of her, pressing itself into her.

And then it hit her. Made her body jerk, that spinal reaction jolting her limbs before she really knew what was happening, like when she used to dream she was falling as a child and would startle herself away.

Cold.

Shocking cold.

Not just the cold. The cold and the wet.

It throttled her.

She opened her eyes. Ripped her head back from the water's surface and felt the cold fluid all around her. Sucked in a big breath.

Water. Water and light so bright it stung through her eyelids. She couldn't open her eyes.

Her mind struggled with this information. Made sense of it in stages.

Cold water all around her. Cupping her. Submerging her.

And the light wasn't sunlight, she thought. Something artificial about it.

What the hell?

Her heart raced. Eyelids struggled to open. Her limbs flailed and crashed into something hard beneath the water. Thumping out a hollow sound.

Fear. Even if none of this made sense just yet, she knew she should be scared. That was something.

She blinked a few times, her wet lashes smearing in and out of her field of vision before staying open at last.

Bright white everywhere. Blinding, searing light. Pastel colors. A light blue paint adorning the top half of the walls. Some kind of soft green tiles covering the walls from the midpoint down.

Again, her groggy brain took a second to process the world around her.

The bathroom. The bathtub.

And the sound came to her as if from far away. The faucet gushing water into the tub even still, roaring on the way out and tinkling when it hit the standing water like a wind chime.

The water jostled around her. Disturbed. Miniature waves rolling away toward the tub's rim before lapping back at her. She could see her hands moving about in it, jockeying for position, distorted by the water so they looked like strange flippers.

The room was empty apart from her. And she could see nothing stirring in the thin rectangle of the hall visible through the open doorway.

She tried to push herself up, to get out of the water, but her arms wouldn't oblige her. Her muscles were shaky and weak. Offering only jerky little movements that reminded her of a hermit crab dragging itself along the shoreline in slow motion, leaving a strange trail in the sand.

The memory came free then. Played in her head: Kathryn Porter swinging that hunk of cast iron at her, everything going black. And the crime scene photos flashed in her mind's eye one after another, of all those drowned bodies found in rivers and ponds in the outlying area, all of them found with bathwater in their lungs.

The final puzzle piece snapped into place, much later than it should have.

Porter was the killer. A woman connected to multiple victims. A woman whose behavior seemed strange and erratic, whose grasp on reality seemed shaky at best.

A woman.

A woman who had killed Fowles.

No, she shouldn't think that. She could still feel the memory of his pulse pattering along in the tips of her fingers, galloping and jerky and sort of hollow somehow, his skin going cold from shock.

He was alive then. Could still be alive even now. Maybe.

And hot tears flooded Darger's eyes. The acidic kind that stung as soon as they hit. Like public pool water with too much chlorine.

She gritted her teeth, blinked to fight back the wet from flooding her eyes. And some bitter flavor arose in her throat, earthy and disgusting like licorice without the sweet.

Kathryn Porter.

They'd interviewed the killer twice. Darger should have seen it sooner, should have pieced it together, should have known. This was the wrongness she'd felt all along. Why hadn't she seen it?

She'd let her routine blind her to the truth. Let a sense of the way things ought to be disrupt her view of the way things really were. The accepted probability of a male perpetrator pointed her in a different direction, led her astray.

She pushed these thoughts down, though. Buried them.

Her fuck-up didn't matter at the moment. She needed to focus, needed to get out of here. Now.

Her head darted around again, taking in the tiny bathroom, the open door leading out into the hallway. Porter wasn't here now.

This was her chance, it seemed.

Again she tried to push herself up, but her motor skills remained inarticulate. Still woozy and weak from being knocked out. The little hermit crab scrabbling at the sand, not really getting anywhere.

She stopped. Waited. Breath heaving in and out.

She couldn't panic. Couldn't break herself here, expend all

of her energy in hermit crab mode like a fool. No. Better to catch her breath, gather her strength, wait for her muscles to come around.

When footsteps sounded out in the hallway, Darger didn't think. She plopped her head back in the water to play dead.

CHAPTER 59

The water still roars out of the faucet, patters at the pool below. And the girl still lies there face down.

You flex your fingers around the handle of the steak knife in your grip. If she moves at all, your blade will take care of it. Calm her back down. Poke holes to let the tension out, the fight out, the blood out.

And you can picture it now, the pink swirls spilling out of her wounds and dancing in the water. Little clouds of it shifting around with the waves.

You can tell by the pitch that the stuff coming out of the faucet is cold, much colder than a bath should be. The tone sounds wrong. Feels wrong. And you vaguely remember encountering this with Dustin long ago.

The hot water heater out here poses problems. Unreliable. It annoys you for a second, but then you remember that it doesn't matter so much this time, does it? Not to her and not to you. The cold will do just fine. Just fine.

It's not until the bathwater lifts strands of the light brown hair that you see it. Realize it's not her. Not the one you were thinking of all this time, the one you're always thinking of.

And your chest shudders in a big breath, and an emptiness seems to enter you.

You long to go back to her. Back into the past. More than anything, you wish you could go back to her. To live out your ritual over and over. The real thing. Strong and weak.

The small body in the tub is the cop lady, of course. The

one who keeps meddling in things.

Just as well to off her, right? Just as well.

You turn her a little to look upon the face. Attractive. Not like the one, but attractive enough. An object of great beauty.

And Dustin's face flashes into your head as well, all those angular man features swathed in stubble. You see him both as he was all those years ago and how he ended in this very tub. The dead face superimposed upon the living one.

He was attractive, too, Dustin. A rugged kind of handsome like the Marlboro man or something. You've always liked both. Masculine and feminine. Soft and hard. Never really distinguished between the genders. Maybe you would make more boys clean if they weren't so difficult.

And heavy. You couldn't even move Dustin after his ritual, and it had almost ruined everything.

Almost.

You turn the pretty face back into the water. Watch the water lap at her hairline and temples. It won't be long now.

CHAPTER 60

The bulk of Darger's torso kept her half afloat like a buoy. Reminded her of swimming lessons when she was small. Doing the dead man's float to get used to being in the water and sort of on top of it at the same time.

She kept her mind blank. Didn't let herself think about the building tension in her chest, her lungs aching, her brain sending stronger and stronger impulses to breathe.

She needed to wait. To be calm. To be patient.

The water lapped at her ears, her hearing bobbing in and out. She knew from the approach of the footsteps that Porter had entered the room, had felt the woman's hands on the back of her neck for just a moment, but the choppiness in the following sounds made the rest unclear. Was she standing over her now? Had she just checked quickly and moved on, busying herself with God knows what as the tub filled and Darger slowly drowned?

Busying herself with Fowles perhaps. That would make sense.

And Darger wondered if Porter would move to her eventually. Grip her by the back of the neck. Shove her head all the way under and hold it there.

She suspected she would. Obsessive killers like her typically made the ritual as intimate as possible. Personal. An aggressive tactile experience rather than a passive one. She would want to feel the power in her skin, in her muscles, in her grip.

Darger would wait then, if she could. Wait until the

moment Porter reached for her. She'd lurch at that moment of contact and hopefully surprise her, catch her off balance.

Something in the sound changed then. First there was a pair of squeaks, some metallic squawking, sort of shrill. This same sound repeated itself. Familiar.

Then the roar of the faucet cut out all at once, and the silence grew to fill the emptiness, swelled into something huge and striking and strange, something that made Darger's skin pull taut into goose bumps.

She knew now that the first sound had been the knobs twisting, that the woman hovered over her just now. This was it, then.

Darger wrenched free of the water, pushing herself up onto her knees, relieved to find at least some strength returned to her limbs, arms reaching out to grab for something that wasn't there.

The emptiness around her seemed wrong. It had to be wrong. The water sluicing down from her hair made it hard to see.

Movement caught the corner of her eye, and she weaved out of the way of Kathryn Porter's punch, a right hook intended for her jaw. The miss carried Porter a step to her left, off balance, and Darger got a good look at her.

Porter had morphed into something new, something awful. Eyes opened wide and psychotic. Lips curled up to expose the teeth. She looked like something rabid, something possessed.

Darger's hands moved to her holster as Porter tottered and moved to regain her balance, but the leather flap at her side was empty. Her gun was gone. Of course.

Her eyes snapped to Porter's hands, to the dark solidness

gripped in the one that hadn't struck out at her. But no. Not her gun. It was a knife.

Darger plunged forward, a diving thrust that launched her out of the tub and delivered a shoulder-first blow into Porter's ribcage. She drove her left forearm into Porter's throat while her right hand looped around the wrist to keep the knife at a distance.

The momentum of the hit seemed to arrive a beat later than the initial impact, and whatever hold gravity had on them tipped out of control then.

Toppling. Floating.

Darger felt a weightlessness. Reality tilting.

And then they crashed down, teeth and bones rattling. Porter's back took the brunt of the collision with the linoleum, her legs somehow folded up beneath them.

Darger's wind left her. Knocked out as soon as they hit the ground. A screaming void seeming to implode her chest, leaving it empty and useless and paralyzed, but she didn't panic.

She scrambled to get her weight onto the arm holding the knife, pinning it to the floor with her knee, feeling the flesh and bones of the forearm pinched and sinewy under her bulk.

They grappled. Ripping and flexing and twisting.

Porter clawed with her free hand, fingernails gashing at Darger's cheek, wrenching away wads of flesh with each stroke, leaving grooves of blistering pain everywhere they touched.

Darger fought to get the other knee around Porter's torso to fully trap her. She brought her hands to Porter's ears, fingers wrapping around them, tangling in her hair, grasping her by the back of the head.

And she rocked up and down a few times. Lifting that cranium and slamming it down. Bashing the back of the woman's skull into the linoleum floor like she might break it open here and now and be done with this.

Each hit shook the cabin floor, the pounding echoing everywhere around them, the sound itself somehow violent.

The crazed look in the girl's eyes seemed to soften, seemed to dim. A glazed quality now occupying them.

Her lights were going out.

But then Porter bucked her hips. She came alive again. A wild thrashing thing between Darger's legs. The second big thrust dislodged Darger from her perch, loosened her grip, and the follow-through flung her up and off entirely.

Reality tilted again. Floating. Toppling.

Darger crunched down on her shoulder in the bathroom doorway. Confused.

She flopped a moment like a fish before she disentangled her limbs and got her feet underneath her. Then she stood and shuffled toward the living room.

She needed to find the gun.

CHAPTER 61

Darger scrabbled over the wood plank floor, head swiveling to scan every surface. Her mind suggested places to look, flashed pictures of her 9mm in every possible location. The coffee table. The kitchen counter. On top of the TV. But they were all empty. Blank.

Can't find it. Can't find it.

Her hand dug in her pocket as she searched, feeling for her phone, but that was gone, too.

And then Darger moved fully into the living space and the legs came clear, jutting out from behind the small dining table. Fowles. He sprawled in the same position — belly up, his motionless body stretching over the line where the living room and kitchen met, his torso still tucked out of her view.

Darger held her breath as she rounded the corner, the entomologist's upper body slowly coming clear to her. She didn't know why she did this. Maybe she hoped to hear the tiny rasp of his breathing, hoped to notice the tiny patter of his pulse in his neck or the rise and fall of his chest. Some tiny detail that would prove he was still here, still alive — something so minuscule it would surely require total silence to observe. Even the little moans of the wood floor under her feet seemed possible hindrances to knowing the truth.

The body lay utterly still, though. A stationary thing, stagnant to a dramatic degree. And the words that popped into Darger's head didn't seem to offer promise, either.

Lifeless.

Inert.

The face looked a little off. Waxy and puffy and limp looking. Closed eyelids more gray than normal, a shade that reminded her of the blue-gray Crayola she had as a kid. She tried to stop herself from thinking it, but he looked like a body laid out in a casket, maybe one who could use a touch-up from the makeup artist.

She knelt alongside the fallen figure. And a dissociative tingle started at the back of her neck and spread over all of her flesh. Pulled her outside of herself, almost outside of her body. Detached. Apart. She would watch this moment rather than live in it.

Her hand reached out for Fowles, an act that seemed to be happening more than something she was doing, the orders coming from elsewhere. Her fingers and thumb rubbed themselves together in little circular motions as they approached the entomologist, and then the digits splayed to touch the neck.

Cold. His flesh was cold. Cold and soft.

And no stirring persisted within this skin, no beating or thrumming or pulsating in the great blood vessels strung along the length of his throat. Nothing at all.

Fowles was dead.

The world fell as quiet as it had ever been. Hushed and hollow.

She drew her hand away from the corpse's chill, brought it to her own neck all warm and palpitating.

She blinked. Twice. Three times.

And then she remembered herself and went for his holster, throwing back the flap of sports jacket in the way.

Empty.

No holster.

Shit.

She remembered the stupid little gun case in his car. His hands were likewise empty.

No gun. Of course Porter would have taken that too. Now what? Think.

Keys. Fowles drove. She needed his keys.

She dug in his pockets, realizing only then that her own keys were gone. She could feel their absence in her pocket like a missing tooth. That probably meant....

No keys in Fowles' pants pockets. Just a wallet and a wadded-up Kleenex. Porter had taken their keys. The notion made her stomach feel swollen and empty at the same time.

She moved to his jacket. Nothing in the side pockets, but a bulk protruded from the inside pocket.

His phone.

No keys, but it was something. She could call for help.

Where the fuck was the gun?

She pawed at Fowles' phone, part of her sure that it too would fail to work, the screen forever remaining blank, but after a beat, the little display glowed back at her, bright white.

Before she could check for a signal, the gun made itself known at last.

The crack split everything in the small cabin open. A piercing, impossible sound, a metallic click accompanied by the explosive noise of the muzzle blast and the little snort of the flash.

And glass burst somewhere just over Darger's head. The window over the kitchen sink. Shards of it spilling down around her and shattering on the floor.

She wheeled.

Kathryn Porter stood in the bathroom doorway, the 9mm leveled, arms flexing, finger squeezing again.

The microwave door shattered now. Clear plastic splintering away from the entry wound. The light inside clicking on in confusion.

Darger scrabbled over the plank floor once more, shuffling from kneeling to standing in stuttering stages like some beast trying to master running upright.

More glass exploded. A front window this time.

It wasn't until she hit a sprint that the pain in Darger's head made itself known. The hurt wobbled her. Made her remember that cast iron skillet coming for her skull. Turning everything black.

But she fought through the wooziness, found a rhythm with her steps. Crashed through the screen door, picking up speed.

And she was out, out of the cabin, down the front steps, into the night.

She loped out into the woods, out into the dark.

CHAPTER 62

You lick your lips. Shock still settling over you.

And that final image plays over and over in your skull:

The girl stumbling down the front steps and the woods just swallowing her up. Gone. As soon as she's out the door, the dark takes her whole. A wall of black that consumes her.

You blink in the face of it. Eyelids cinching closed hard and popping back open even harder. Electricity buzzes in the sockets around them. Little tendrils of current that splotch the edges of your vision.

She escaped. Disappeared into the gloom. This is the thing that could not happen. Could not. The unthinkable. And you just watched her vanish like some magician's trick.

You can taste the defeat in the stomach acid creeping up the back of your throat. Astringent and sour.

They've tried to get away before. Scraped and clawed and struggled. But you were stronger. Smarter. You handled them.

You need to handle this one.

If not, the world will know you. Know who you really are. And all will be lost.

You don't think now. You step forward and squeeze off another shot and then another. Firing bullets through the doorway into the void, out into emptiness, your arm bucking at the gun's force, flailing like a limp thing, a small thing. You don't like it.

And you stagger on a few more paces. The fever of all of this so hot in your head that you can't think straight, can't move right. Legs feel heavy, numbed out like that novocaine feeling you get just before the dentist takes the drill to you. Dead numb.

You stop at the threshold, standing in the place where inside gives way to outside, where the dark snuffs out the light.

Can't see shit. Can't feel shit. Not from the waist down, anyway.

You just breathe in that dark like smoke. Feel its chill enter through your mouth, through your nostrils, saturating your chest with each wet flutter of respiration. Thick twirls of vapor filling you and emptying you, rushing in and out.

Hot liquid flushes through your skull. Hatred lurching and sloshing around in there. Frothing up into a lather.

And your finger trembles on the trigger guard. The gun twitching in your hand, intricate little movements like a dancing marionette. An object that wants to thrash and buck and come alive.

You want to destroy. Anything. Everything. You want to fire again and again. Empty your magazine out into the dark. Empty your magazine into your skull. Spend it all and be done.

But no. No. You need to save the ammo.

You let the gun fall to your side. A bulk at the end of your dangling arm.

It's not over yet. She's out there somewhere. You still have reason to hope.

You pat the lump in your left hip pocket with your wrist, and it jangles. Still there. The car keys. So she won't be getting far, will she?

And you lick your lips. Stand up a little straighter. Steel yourself to give chase.

Yes. Chase. That's all it is. The cat and the mouse carrying out their roles. They were born to it.

And part of you thinks it's all just a game now, isn't it? She wants it this way. Wants to play hide-and-go-seek. That's all.

When you take that next step, the dark devours you, and you're not worried anymore. You just have to win, that's all.

You adjust your grip on the gun at your side, press forward into the blackness.

Ready or not, here I come.

CHAPTER 63

Darger darted through the forest, not really thinking about avoiding the trees in the dark so much as letting her instincts guide her away from the blackest shapes. The phrase "run to daylight" popped into her head, though it wasn't entirely accurate here. Anywhere emitting moonlight, however, she raced toward, constantly redirecting her shoulders to the faintly glowing places.

Branches clawed at the opened up places on her cheeks, where Porter had scratched her. She barely noticed the stinging pain. She kept running, much more conscious of the rasping of her lungs and the burning in her thighs.

And the cold. She'd been cold in the cabin, but out here, the night air clung to all of the wet places. Sunk into her skin. Leeched the last remaining warmth from her blood.

Her steps went choppy now and then, the grade underfoot slanting up and down at random, throwing off her equilibrium. She hit a low spot and jammed her left knee. It broke the rhythm of her steps, and then she was falling forward more than she was running, arms spinning wildly at her sides to try to balance things out. She stumbled along for several yards before she was able to catch herself and hit the accelerator again.

Distance. She just needed to put some distance between her and the psycho with the gun and then she could call for help. The phone waited in her left pocket, rattling against her hip with each step, just itching to be used.

She ran until the foliage tangled up around her ankles and

pulled her down, the sense of falling somehow more terrifying in the dark. The landing jolted her arms and legs, slammed her teeth together, flashed bright white in her head. Pain crawled upward from her wrists and knees, but she was OK. Roughed but uninjured. She picked herself up and kept on.

After bursting through a cluster of firs, the boughs taking turns whacking at her face and chest, she sensed the woods thinning some around her. An opening ahead. And beyond that, something sparkling like silver in the moonlight.

The river.

Soon she hit the water's edge where she veered left to run along beside it. The river babbled next to her, and the way here was clear. No trees. Little growth. Just smooth rock and patches of moss.

She ran along the riverbank for a long time, let herself get fully winded, and then she pulled up. Leaned over and rested her hands just above her knees, mouth wide open, sucking in great lungfuls of air.

This was far enough. This would work.

It had to.

She fished the phone out of her pocket.

CHAPTER 64

You pick your way through the trees and foliage, moving with care. Soundless for the most part. Gun clenched in your sweaty palm.

A creeping shadow in the night.

Waves of panic wash over you as you press deeper into the darkness. Fevered notions that she has gotten away, sprinting through the forest like some Olympic runner. You picture her hurdling deadfall without slowing down, pole vaulting ravines. If so, it's already over. You've already lost.

But deep down, you think not. She took a good wallop to the head, a cast iron skillet to the skull. More likely hiding than running, she is. You hope so anyway.

The woods seem malevolent at night. All those crooked shadows bending down from the tree branches.

You sense a dark force present here. Something that was around before any of us and will be around long after we're gone. A wild, thrashing, violent thing. Something that got inside you, maybe. Wormed its way beneath your skin when you were small. Took root there and pushed you to be who you are, how you are, what you are. Something that put all those bad thoughts in your head.

You stop. Listen. Thought you heard something move. A snapping branch. The crunch of dead leaves.

But the silence rises up around you. Vanquishes everything. Keeps the whole world still.

You duck under some pine boughs to get through a tight

cluster of them and keep going.

And finally the river wobbles ahead. A fluttering in the blackness. Little ripples catching the moonlight.

Your gut tells you that you will find her near the water. Screams it in your ears without words. Just feelings and pictures that gush into you from nowhere, project themselves on the black screen hung up all around.

You walk along the bank now, on top of the great rocky crags that line the water. Treading carefully. You know from experience that the slate-like surface of the stone can get slippery in places, especially where the moss grows.

The air feels colder along the river's edge. Wet and heavy and chilling.

But the cool of the night makes no match for the heat rolling off of you in waves. Every cold breath comes back out of your chest all hot and sticky. Your hatred makes a furnace out of you. Cranks the knob to burn it all, inside and out.

And you think that hatred alone can sustain a person like this, keep them warm with fever, keep them agitated, keep them pressing ever onward into the dark night of existence. Food. Sleep. None of these matter when hatred gets hold of a person's heart. No. Only hate can drive a being this way. The restless ones who walk the night, who find no satisfaction here.

It almost seems like you should be able to smell her. A predator like you should be able to pick out her fear from a few hundred yards out, track the stench right to her.

And then you see it. Some glow up ahead, a hundred yards or so from where you stand. A beacon. A sign.

No. You recognize the shape.

It's the screen of a phone.

CHAPTER 65

Come on.

Darger spun in a circle, checking the signal. The bars flickered. One, then two.

Yes.

She dialed the three digits and lifted the glowing phone to her head, cupping her fingers around the edges to try to block the light out. The ringing gurgled in her ear.

Her heart thundered in her chest, and her breathing seemed fluttery and panicked. It was hard to stand still, but she had to. So close now. So close to finding a way out of this. Please, just let the call go through.

The line clicked, and Darger was certain the call had been dropped.

"911, what is your emergency?"

She was so startled by the voice, she nearly lost her grip on the phone.

"My name is Violet Darger," she choked out in a whisper. "I'm with the Sandy Police Department. My colleague has been shot. We're at a cabin on the old logging road north of Marmot. I need an ambulance and—"

She experienced the gunfire in slow motion.

The thwack of the bullet hitting the bark of a tree to her right seemed to happen first. A violent sound, little flecks of tree spilling down from the point of impact.

And then a tiny orange burst flared in the distance, something she saw out of the corner of her eye. A momentary burst like a sparkler on the Fourth of July, there and gone within a blink. The muzzle flash.

The booming crack seemed to arrive last, at least in her consciousness. It reverberated wholly unlike the gunshot in the cabin. Loud, yes, but it somehow sounded smaller in such a big space, as if out here, the sky could swallow much of the volume up.

She ran.

Veered away from the bank to brave the rough stuff again for the added cover, stumbling through varieties of plant life, large and small.

She tripped on a tree root at top speed, launching forward as if shot from a catapult. Colliding. Skidding over dusty earth.

She came up with a sore ankle. Twisted but still functional. She'd knocked her head against something back there, too. A branch, maybe? Too dark to know.

But she didn't worry about these things. She ran.

Weaving and dodging and keeping upright.

A sharp ache slowly sharpened under the right side of her ribcage. The side stitch swelled until it killed. And her breathing had gone ragged some time ago, she realized, her mouth and throat dry and raw.

She needed to rest, needed to hide. She had one idea.

She veered to the right, coiled back toward the river, slowing a little. Prioritizing quiet over speed now.

The dark blobs around seemed unchanging, seemed unkind. She started to think the river would never emerge, that she would run in the woods forever, some endless terrifying loop.

But that flutter of black and silver came to her then,

appearing there through the crisscrossing net of branches in her way. The moonlight glittered atop the water's surface, little shards of white light reflecting everywhere.

When she got to the river's edge, she studied the rocky shore until she found what she was looking for. A place where one of the huge rock formations jutted out over the water like a cliff.

Would it work? She hoped so.

She ducked low and braved shining the phone's light down into the jagged stuff for a split second.

An open space yawned back from beneath the overhang, mostly concealed by a tangle of vines. The water had carved an indentation in the rock here, chiseled it out, eaten away at it while the water was high and then retreated.

It was at least a twelve-foot drop down to the tiny cave, maybe more, but she thought she could manage it.

Darger gripped the rocky edge with her hands, lowering her legs down into the dark and letting them dangle there in the nothingness for a moment. Her arms quivered from the strain. She took a deep breath, held it a beat, let it out in a long even heave.

Then she swung herself toward the face of the cliff and let go.

CHAPTER 66

Sounds crashed through the woods for what felt like a long time, menacing and hard to place from her hiding spot. Everything echoed funny from the water and the walls of rock around her, somehow giving the impression of being right on top of her and far away at the same time.

Sticks snapped. Leaves swished and rattled and popped. Tiny little percussive sounds like someone pinching a bunch of bubble wrap.

All the running had kept the chill mostly at bay, but now Darger was shivering so hard she had to clench her teeth to keep them from chattering.

At one point heavy footsteps seemed to patter just at the edge of the cliff above. Frantic. Restless. Darger held her breath until the sound receded, falling back into the woods.

Now she listened hard and heard nothing but the babble of the water, turning her head to the left and then the right to try to be certain of the quiet.

The peaceful sound of the river seemed out of place here, poorly cast for this moment. No thundering rapids. No ripple of white water juddering over rocks with violent purpose. Darger heard only laziness in this little bend of the stream, calm and quiet.

She took big breaths to try to keep calm herself, in through her nose and out through her mouth. For the moment she would stay put. This rocky semi-enclosure made for good cover, a good hiding place, and the throbbing in her head seemed to be receding some now.

The fog of shock had begun to clear.

God, she was cold. Colder than she'd ever been in her life. The slab of stone she was sitting on felt like ice where it pressed into her flesh. Her fingers were almost numb. Still quivering uncontrollably, she clenched and unclenched her hands, trying to get the blood flowing again.

What if the 911 operator hadn't understood her? Or wrote her off as a crank call? She might be stranded out here all night. Cold and wet. Her hair and clothes were still soaked from the bathtub.

She closed her eyes and focused on her breathing. Slow and even. The clean smell of the woods enveloped her.

She just had to stay calm. Patient.

And then the picture of the legs jutting out from behind the table in the cabin interrupted her moment of clarity.

The camera in her mind slid up to that funereal looking face, the eyelids already gone blue-gray, the lips looking puffy, pursed a little like the sucker of some bottom-feeding fish.

That's when it hit her with full force.

Fowles was dead.

It was like a shard of broken glass lodged somewhere in the back of her mind had suddenly come loose, and now it cut and wounded from the inside.

This wasn't how it was supposed to go.

When Fowles had talked of his death as an inevitability, it somehow took on a noble sort of feel. Something he bore down on. Something he faced with bravery, without fear.

But up close to the real thing, those ideas seemed hollow, Darger thought. Empty gestures. Sound and fury signifying nothing. Tomorrow and tomorrow and tomorrow.

Meaningless.

It didn't seem fair. Even if he didn't have long to go, it didn't seem fair, didn't seem right. His time had become so precious, so scarce as to be made sacred, and now the last little bit had been ripped away from him. Stolen.

And for what?

For no good reason Darger could see.

And something about the gravity of Fowles' death in this moment made the weight of the loss of all the victims hit as well. Holly Green. Maribeth Holtz. Shannon Mead. Dustin Reynolds. Christy Whitmore. And the two most recent bodies, the ones they hadn't even identified yet.

But Darger knew it wasn't only these local victims. It was all of them. All the loss out there. Every day. Everywhere.

She hugged her knees against her torso and squeezed herself into a ball, tucked her face into the tiny space between her legs. The tears gushed out now as she rocked herself back and forth. Silent spasms jolted outward from her core. Water poured from her eyes.

Heat flushed her face, and she couldn't imagine that this weeping would ever end, that this wound would ever close. Because this was it, wasn't it? The big wound. The fatal one. The one that could never heal, not for any of us.

The big sleep waiting for each and every being. The ticking clock that counts down for one and all, the clock in every chest that unwinds and one day stops.

And she wondered where Loshak was at that moment. Probably out there working a case, fighting the good fight for as long as he could. How did he keep going, day after day, knowing that any justice they brought was a mere pinprick of light in the darkness?

She thought of her mother. Of Luck. Of Owen. Of all the people who meant something to her, their faces painted there in the blackness.

The people she loved. The people she seemed hell-bent on running away from. Focusing everything on work instead. Like maybe that would keep her safe from all the pain life seemed to have in store, for her and everyone else. Like maybe she could defeat death if she assigned herself a seek-and-destroy mission to find these killers and make them stop. Maybe if she gave everything, it could be bigger than the sum of its parts. Maybe she could sacrifice the time from her own ticking clock and somehow keep everyone else safe.

It had a warped logic to it, but the world didn't work that way.

And now she was alone, and Fowles was dead, and it hurt worse than anything she could remember.

CHAPTER 67

It's over. Unraveling the rest of the way.

You crash through ferns and vines and prickers now, but you no longer know why. Don't know what you expect to accomplish.

She called for backup. Maybe called 911. Something. Anything. They will be here soon.

It's already over. Already past. The end of your story already etched in stone. You cannot change it.

You had your chance. One final shot to end her, to end it. To put a bullet in her before she spoke into that glowing phone in the distance, but you failed. Missed again. A fatal mistake. You heard her voice rise above the river's whispering, if only faintly. Heard her speaking. Telling your secrets.

The panic seems to settle over your body before you really sense it. Finality.

Sweat engulfs your torso. Puddles in your armpits. Dampens your hairline. Weeps down from the corners of your brow.

And your stomach gurgles out strange sounds. Strangled and squished noises that remind you of those recordings of whales singing in the depths of the ocean.

You feel cold and hot all at once. Sweating and shivering. The hatred still churns heat out of your middle, but your arms and legs have gone icy and half-numb.

The core reality driving this panic hits you after the fact.

She is gone. Escaped. Far from here.

You've lost the game.

And the people will know now. They will all know who you are, what you are.

They will know everything. They will know the truth.

Yes. The truth remains your enemy here. That's the one thing that could always hurt you, isn't it? The one threat you could never fully eliminate.

You believe way down deep that you could live with the lie indefinitely. Comfortable to hide behind a mask for always, to never really know anyone and never really be known. Just kind of here, kind of quiet, kind of alive during the days, the real you only creeping out at night when no one would see.

The dark hid you for so long, but not tonight. It turned on you at some point. Seems to close in on you now. All those gnarled shadows stretching, bending, arching toward you, reaching out their crooked fingers.

And sirens moan somewhere far away. Mournful wails bending out of key, distorted by wind and distance.

The last part of you still looking for her seems to lose faith all at once. A crumpling of willpower. A sagging of posture.

If she were near, you would sense her, wouldn't you? You would feel her there, sense her presence.

But it's over. You know that. You knew it as soon as you heard her voice ring out over the night.

So let it be done.

You veer for the river. Splash out into the water. Pick your knees up high to push through. Feet slapping into the wet. Kicking up all kinds of watery noise.

The current swells around you, tugs at your thighs, at your hips, a living thing that lurches and spits.

And the cold touches you everywhere. A sharp cold that reminds you of metal. Biting. Penetrating.

As if on cue, you see the police lights rise up over a hill to twirl in the distance. Red and blue spiraling in the dark. Disconnected from everything else, at least from your vantage point. Just the strange glow casting light over all that darkness. Spinning and spinning and spinning.

This is the end.

It's over now.

In a way it doesn't seem so bad, you think. In a way, it's a relief.

An easing of all of that tension. A way, at last, to disconnect your head.

A way to keep all of those bad thoughts still. Forever.

CHAPTER 68

Sound shook Darger from the dark place where her thoughts still drifted.

Footsteps clattered past on the cliff above. Heavy footfalls like a galloping Clydesdale, somehow desperate. Wild. Reckless.

Darger peeled her face out from between her legs, snapping to attention. Listening.

She realized that she'd stopped crying some time ago. She didn't know when. Had lost all sense of time, all sense of reality until these fresh sounds brought her back.

And splashes rang out from the river somewhere just upstream. Weighty explosions of wetness that sounded like a series of bowling balls being plunged into the muck and somehow ripped straight back out, little sucking sounds accompanying the plops and slaps.

Footsteps.

Darger leaned forward, edging out of her small rock enclosure to try to get a look.

Hunching her shoulders. Squinting her eyes.

At first, she couldn't see much.

Light shone on the ripples in the water. Yellowed curls and quivering lines reflected back the glow from the moon and stars.

But the disturbances in those crooked bars of light led her eyes to what they sought.

Movement. Shadows.

A dark figure wading out into the river. It seemed to move in slower and slower motion as it progressed. The figure looked tall and stick-like in the half-light. Stretched out.

It must be Kathryn Porter. Must be. But why? Was she trying to cross the water? Still seeking after Darger?

The figure stopped toward the middle of the stream, the water rushing around her nearly chest high now. The jerky rise and fall of her shoulders marked big uneven breaths.

Darger got to her feet now without thought. Started walking a straight line toward the place where the woman stood in the water.

And then she saw the gun in Porter's grip, the silhouette of the weapon and the hand and the little stick arm protruding from the rippling water. Lifted just above shoulder high and pointed at the sky.

And now that she'd stepped out of the little semi-circle cliff enclosure, Darger could hear the sirens warbling out there, getting closer, could see the police lights spinning through the black of the woods.

She picked up speed, moving toward the figure in the water, waving her arms to try to catch the woman's eye, lips puckering, mouth poised to speak with no words actually coming out.

What could she say? She didn't know.

The sound of the sirens kicked way up in volume all at once. Probably cresting the last hill on the road, at the cabin, pulling into the driveway.

She waded out into the river, running against the current now. Icy cold water gripped her feet and ankles and calves and knees, slowing her down more and more with every step. She could barely move once it reached waist high, legs kicking at the frigid water as hard as they could but barely getting anywhere.

She wasn't going to get there in time, so she jumped up and down.

Screaming.

No words. Just a furious sound tearing out of her throat. Ragged and raw and alive.

And the scream seemed to swirl out over the water and come echoing back from the pines on the other side. A harsh and dry and ugly noise coming out of her, her own voice one she couldn't recognize by the time it bounced back to her.

If Kathryn Porter heard the awful sound, she showed no sign of it. She brought the gun to her head, the barrel coming to rest under her chin.

And Darger's scream went up half an octave, more shrill, more disturbed, but it did not falter.

The figure in the water squeezed the trigger. The little muzzle flash looked like a bottle rocket going off from this far out, the tiniest orange burst in the dark, glinting off the water.

Darger recoiled from the sight, arms drawn into her chest as though to hug herself away from this horror, hands crawling up onto her cheeks to cover herself, shield herself.

Darger's scream cut out, and the sirens wailed no more. The whole world quiet but for the sound of the rushing river.

The figure hovered for just a second before the head jerked forward. One final nod. Flung hard on the limp neck.

And then the silhouette slumped down into the black water and disappeared.

EPILOGUE

Kathryn Porter's body was spotted by a kayaker three days later, tangled in branches some 26 miles downstream.

Darger watched the divers bring in the corpse and wondered if Kathryn had any sense that she'd end up looking like one of her own victims. Pale and bloated and waterlogged.

The only real difference was the clothes. They swaddled her body more like rags than garments, tattered and torn, and the waistband of the pants constricted the bloated torso like a string of butcher's twine around a pork loin. But they were there. The other victims had traversed these rivers, lakes, and streams naked. Stripped of that final dignity.

A brief journal found at Porter's apartment had filled in most of the lingering gaps about her personal life and crimes. Extensive references were made to Christy Whitmore and Shannon Mead in particular. A manifesto of obsession. Darger thought it sounded more like she wanted to *be* them than be *with* them. Her secret relationship with the final victim, Callie Snodgrass, was laid out pretty well, too.

All written in the second person, the few dozen pages of writing were eerie. Unsettling. Distant but still vivid. Aloof yet insightful.

A heavy hand fell on Darger's shoulder, and she turned to see Furbush standing beside her, using his fingers to shield his eyes from the sun.

"I should have figured it out," she said, half talking to herself. "We talked to her twice, and I just… didn't see it.

Because she was a woman."

"I imagine it's a pretty rare deal. Female serial killers, I mean."

"Female killers account for 17% of all serial homicides. So it happens. I've never seen it up close, but that's not an excuse."

Furbush didn't respond, and they watched the divers work to get the body secured. Darger couldn't help but shiver a little at the thought of how cold the river would be, how cold it had been the other night. Even more, she couldn't imagine being within an arm's length of that bloated mass that used to be Kathryn Porter.

"Kind of an ironic ending to her story, though, isn't it?" Furbush said, as if sensing Darger's earlier thoughts about Kathryn's end matching those of her victims.

"Yeah," she said.

She thought she should perhaps say more. Give some profiler's insight into all of it, but she was just too damn tired. She hadn't slept well since the incident at the cabin. Every time she closed her eyes, she saw Fowles sprawled on the floor, his body opened up, blood spreading over his shirt.

A heavy silence fell over them, as thick as a velvet curtain.

For several minutes, they watched the divers splash about in the river, kicking their flippered feet against the current.

"You know, there's something I've been meaning to ask you," Furbush said, and Darger worried he was going to make her go over that night again.

Each time she relived it, she came up with another mistake she'd made. Another way she'd failed Fowles.

His gun, for example. It turned out that Kathryn Porter had shot Fowles with his own weapon. If Darger had only insisted he leave it in the car....

She closed her eyes, pushing these thoughts away.

"What is it?" she asked Furbush.

"When we arrived on the scene — at the cabin, I mean — when Mantelbaum and Parks got down to the river and pulled you out...."

He trailed off, seeming uncertain.

"Yeah?"

"Well, they said it looked like you were running toward Kathryn Porter. Yelling something."

The wind blew a strand of Darger's hair loose, sent it fluttering over her forehead. She swept the hairs back and tucked them behind her ear.

"I was trying to... I don't know. Stop her."

"From killing herself?"

"I guess so."

"But she was armed. And you weren't. You didn't worry she'd turn on you and shoot?"

Shaking her head, Darger said, "I wasn't really thinking about it. I guess it just seemed like the right thing to do."

"Even after she murdered Fowles? I mean, not to mention all the others."

Darger flinched. Every time she heard Fowles' name uttered out loud, she felt like someone had walked up behind her and jabbed her with a thumbtack.

How could she could explain it when she didn't even understood it herself? Her gaze fell on the puffy white body being loaded onto a gurney at the riverside.

"It's just such a waste."

A moment later, Dr. Kole stepped out from beneath a white

tent and signaled to Furbush. He was ready to get started on the preliminary exam.

Furbush spun toward her and patted her shoulder again with one of his giant bear paws.

"I'll see you at the service? For Fowles?"

Darger clenched her teeth together and nodded.

☾

The service for Fowles was held outside, in a park overlooking the Willamette River near where he grew up. They weren't calling it a funeral or even a memorial service, but a "Life Celebration," which Darger thought sounded cheesy as hell, but overall, it turned out to be very touching.

His family stood beneath an arched arbor draped with honeysuckle and wisteria, greeting the mourners as they arrived.

His mother had exactly the same eyes — dragonfly blue and sharp with intelligence. He'd obviously gotten the wiry hair from his father, though the elder Fowles tried to tame it with some sort of pomade. And when she smiled, his sister had a similar one-sided quirk to her mouth.

Darger wondered how long they'd been planning this service. What would that be like, to plan someone's death in advance? Or had Fowles planned it all himself?

There was no casket, just a large, poster-sized photograph of Fowles and a memorial plaque surrounded by a wreath of white roses and blue hydrangeas. In a way that truly suited his scientist's heart, Fowles had donated his body to the same body farm where he'd done his study.

Had that been part of what made him feel more at peace

with dying? Knowing that his death would benefit science?

When they invited people to speak, Darger took a turn, reading from something she'd copied down in her notebook that morning.

"I'd only recently met Ted. But he was inspiring and dedicated and—" She felt a swell of emotion and paused to let it pass. "He knew so many things. And not just bug stuff."

There was a murmur of laughter from the crowd.

"He could draw and paint. His lasagna was world famous, or so he claimed. And he could also rattle off these lovely little quotes. He told me his grandmother used to give him a dollar if he could recite a poem or quotation."

His sister was seated just a few feet away, and she began to nod. She caught Darger's eye and gave the patented crooked Fowles smile.

"This is one of those quotations: 'Truly the universe is full of ghosts, not sheeted churchyard specters, but the inextinguishable elements of individual life, which having once been, can never die, though they blend and change, and change again forever.'"

At the end of the service, Darger stood looking over a table laden with photographs of Fowles throughout his life: an eight-year-old Fowles fishing in a rowboat, a 23-year-old Fowles in cap and gown, graduating from college. Someone approached the display and stood close enough that their arm brushed hers. She assumed it was Furbush, but when she turned, it wasn't the big bear of a Chief, but a woman. Cat-like eyes flashed as she held out her hand.

Margaret Prescott. In the flesh.

"So nice to finally meet you in person, though what a

shame it's under such unfortunate circumstances."

Darger took her hand, not surprised at all to find that Prescott's grip was almost forceful.

"I wonder if we could find somewhere to talk? I'd love to buy you a cup of coffee."

"Of course," Darger said.

"There's a Starbucks about five minutes from here," Prescott suggested. "Meet you there?"

Darger agreed, and as she walked to her car, she hoped Prescott wasn't going to make her rehash everything that had happened. The service for Fowles had been less gut-wrenching than she'd expected, but her emotions were still raw.

☾

The cafe was filled with twenty-somethings with laptops, busy typing away while they sipped caramel macchiatos and listened to earbuds. Prescott gave their order to the barista and then led Darger to a quiet corner near a ficus tree. Loshak was always pinching and prodding indoor plants to determine whether they were fake or the real McCoy, and Darger had to resist the urge to fondle one of the waxy leaves.

They made small talk about the service and the weather and Prescott's flight into town until their order was called, but with her double shot dirty chai in her hand, Margaret Prescott turned all business.

"I want you to know that no one blames you. I understand you did everything you could." She paused to sip her drink. "Still, it's such a shame things turned out the way they did."

Darger assumed she was talking about Fowles, but then Prescott leaned across the table and said, "Wouldn't you have just loved to pick her brain?"

"Excuse me?"

"Kathryn Porter. I mean, just to be in a room with her… I bet there was some energy. You talked to her. What was she like?"

"What does it matter?" Darger asked. She had no interest in magnifying Kathryn Porter's mystique.

"Are you kidding? You must know how unusual it is to find a female serial killer. She would have made an amazing subject for a case study. An absolute treasure trove of information."

Darger listened to her go on about it, staring out at nothing, only half hearing the spiel.

Prescott talked about Kathryn Porter's psychological profile, the likelihood of sociopathy mixed with, perhaps, schizotypal personality disorder, though they may never truly know. She referred to Porter at one point as a "priceless specimen," which instantly brought to mind an insect preserved in alcohol. That, of course, made Darger think of Fowles, and suddenly she felt the sting of fresh tears in her eyes. She excused herself abruptly and rushed to the bathroom.

Darger chose a stall and locked the dusty pink door behind her. The cheap toilet paper was rough against her cheeks as she angrily dabbed away the tears. It smelled like cinnamon potpourri and disinfectant.

What the fuck was Prescott going on about Kathryn Porter for? Even though she'd tried to stop Kathryn from shooting herself, part of her was so filled with rage over the heinous acts she'd committed that she was glad. Glad Kathryn was dead. Glad she wouldn't ever hurt anyone again. Glad she'd been punished by the universe for her crimes even if she'd never be punished by the law.

An ever darker part of her thought it wasn't enough. Thought that Kathryn Porter should have suffered for her crimes. Tit for tat.

But the noble side of her, the side that accepted humanity as a flawed creation, knew that none of this was for her to decide. She was not judge, jury, and executioner.

Maybe that was the real reason why she'd tried to stop Kathryn from taking her own life.

When she came out of the stall, Prescott was standing near the line of sinks, arms crossed.

"What has you so upset?"

Darger stepped past her and ran some warm water from one of the taps.

"In case you've forgotten," she said, pumping some soap from a wall dispenser, "we just came from a funeral."

Prescott glanced down at her fitted black pant suit.

"I sure as hell hope so. Otherwise I don't know why I'm wearing so much black," she said, capping it off with one of her demonic laughs.

Darger scowled.

"Do you even care that Fowles is dead?"

Prescott's smile vanished. She fixed Darger with that leopard stare.

"Don't project your grief onto me, honey. Fowles knew what was coming. He'd made peace with it."

"He had time left."

"Not very much, as I understood it."

"That doesn't make it any less of a loss."

Prescott was rifling through her purse, and she paused to

scoff.

"Life is never easy, dearie. I thought you'd have figured that out by now."

Lipstick in hand, the woman turned to the mirror and began touching up the coral red on her lips.

"Look, Violet — and I'm saying this as a friend, not your employer — just because you've decided to be all broken up about it doesn't mean you get to judge when the rest of us don't fall to pieces."

Darger swallowed, tasting a bitterness at the back of her throat. She watched Prescott press her lips together to even out the application of color.

"But as I was saying before, I'm thinking I have enough to do a whole series on female serial killers for the *American Journal of Forensic Psychology*."

She ticked the names off on her perfectly groomed fingernails.

"Elizabeth Bathory, Aileen Wuornos, Marjorie Diehl-Armstrong, Kathryn Porter. I've already got a prospective title. Femme Fatale: Women Who Kill." Studying Darger from the corner of her eye, she added, "I'd love to get an exposition of the investigation from your perspective."

When Darger didn't answer, Prescott went on.

"I'd be willing to give you byline credit."

Trying to sweeten the pot. As if Darger gave a fuck.

"I'll have to get back to you on that," Darger said and walked out of the bathroom.

She strode past their table, leaving her unfinished coffee behind as she pushed through the glass doors and out into the golden afternoon.

COME PARTY WITH US

We're loners. Rebels. But much to our surprise, the most kickass part of writing has been connecting with our readers. From time to time, we send out newsletters with giveaways, special offers, and juicy details on new releases.

Sign up for our mailing list at:
http://ltvargus.com/mailing-list

SPREAD THE WORD

Thank you for reading! We'd be very grateful if you could take a few minutes to review it on Amazon.com.

How grateful? Eternally. Even when we are old and dead and have turned into ghosts, we will be thinking fondly of you and your kind words. The most powerful way to bring our books to the attention of other people is through the honest reviews from readers like you.

ABOUT THE AUTHORS

Tim McBain writes because life is short, and he wants to make something awesome before he dies. Additionally, he likes to move it, move it.

You can connect with Tim via email at tim@timmcbain.com.

L.T. Vargus grew up in Hell, Michigan, which is a lot smaller, quieter, and less fiery than one might imagine. When not click-clacking away at the keyboard, she can be found sewing, fantasizing about food, and rotting her brain in front of the TV.

If you want to wax poetic about pizza or cats, you can contact L.T. (the L is for Lex) at ltvargus9@gmail.com or on Twitter @ltvargus.

LTVargus.com

Made in the USA
Monee, IL
21 August 2021

76233409R00246